THORNBROUGH BENT OVER AND KISSED HER . . .

She kissed him back. Then she stood up with a small laugh. Out came the hairpins, and down came her wavy mass of hair. Her stockings and shoes followed. She watched his strong figure stretched out on the river bank and an excitement rushed through her.

"It is so beautiful here," she said. "One could become immortal here. Like the gods."

Calmly she began to unbutton the row of pearl buttons which fastened her dress, pausing to let him watch the picture she was creating standing half-naked, her hair down her back, one foot in the water, the other on the bank. He had made love to many women, but never had a young girl seduced him in a violet wood.

He reached out with shaking fingers to touch her. . . .

SWEET SEDUCTION

Travis Forsyth

A DELL BOOK

This book is dedicated to my mother, Bethia Caffery, the best mother in the world.

SWEET SEDUCTION

Chapter 1

Mr. George F. Pendleton's yacht, the *Ultima*, was nearing its destination, the British Isles. Despite the fact that its fittings were lavishly splendid, featuring fine wood paneling, Persian carpets of unknown value, a small but choice library of leather-bound volumes, and several cooks who toiled throughout the day to feed the passengers innumerable delicacies, all of the passengers had begun to grow a little weary of the routine of ship life.

There were only four passengers: Mr. Pendleton and his wife, their daughter, Isolde, and Mr. Pendleton's business partner's daughter, Elizabeth Wilcox.

The pleasures of idleness had bored Mr. Pendleton long before the ten-day journey was completed. It had never been his idea to leave New York and dash off to England. Wilcox had wanted him to go, and his wife had begged him to agree. Wilcox might claim that there would be plenty to do in London: drop into the Exchange, pick up some English real estate, and view the competition. But spending almost two weeks on a blasted yacht watching his wife do needlepoint was too gruesome a price to pay, no matter how fine the cigars or smooth the brandy. He read Shakespeare and Fielding continually, but even Shakespeare palled on him after a time; and the modern poets that his daughter read, Swinburne and Morris and this Wilde—with their absurd adjectives strewn like garbage all over their prose—he could not enjoy.

Mrs. Pendleton wished that she had had the foresight to invite a few of her friends to make the trip with them. It was deplorable the way Isolde behaved. The child spent most of her time sneaking off to her stateroom to read or to daydream, or she mooned over the side of the ship at nothing. It was impossible to gossip with her; she seemed to have forgotten the names of every one of their acquaintances in New York, and she took no interest in the scandals that made them memorable.

Elizabeth Wilcox was also ready to disembark. She had composed several speeches she was ready to deliver to her fellow suffragists in London. And although she had no scandalous reputation, she enjoyed a taste for flirtation impossible to gratify on a journey unaccompanied by any male save Mr. Pendleton. "Dear Uncle George," as she called Mr. Pendleton, working together with her father, had discovered a method of extracting copper from low-grade sources in Colorado and then set up the foundry. Pendleton had discovered the technique; her father had supplied the money to build and buy machinery, to furnish railway lines cheaply. Together their partnership was a fruitful one. But Elizabeth's father, on a ten-day journey to England with nothing better to do, would have gotten remarkably drunk, gambled a great deal, eaten enormously, and slept the rest of the time. Mr. Pendleton never seemed to sleep; and she had even seen him more than once with a book of verse in his hand. And after this voyage Elizabeth could understand why his daughter Isolde was so unsuited for society, why her nature made her a strange creature indeed.

Only Isolde Pendleton thought nothing of the voyage's length or the pleasures that lay before them. She was satisfied to spend her time doing nothing and seeing no one. To her mother she was annoyingly absentminded about society affairs. To Elizabeth, who was more knowledgeable, she was actually peculiar. For Elizabeth knew what her reputation was in New York. It approached scandal. Whispered scandal about Isolde filled drawing rooms in New York.

Elizabeth was aware of the shock with which her own occupations were considered by Mrs. Pendleton. Imagine an unmarried young lady marching in a parade! She was amused and curious to consider how the good woman would receive the tidings that her daughter's behavior was far more appalling than marching in a crowd in daylight could ever be.

"They should marry that girl off and soon before there is trouble," her father had said to her one morning at breakfast in their newly finished mansion on the lower West Side.

"But I don't think she wants to be married," Elizabeth replied cheerfully.

"Then why does she keep getting herself engaged? This is her third one, isn't it?"

"I think so. You know, I asked her that once."

"And?"

"Oh, Isolde never answers questions."

"I know. I once tried to have a conversation with her at one of your damned parties. I think I ended up telling her how steel was made."

"Did you? I'm sure she was interested. I think the reason why she is constantly getting engaged is that none of her young men know how steel was made. Her mother is strictly interested in the Diamond Horseshoe type, or perhaps a nice, worthless European title for a son-in-law. But none of them seems to suit Isolde."

"And what about you, miss? What are you waiting for? When am I going to be a grandfather?"

"Surely not before you see me safely bestowed on some worthy man, Papa?"

"Oh, I'm in no hurry. But tell me, missy, you are every bit as pretty as Isolde and have just as much money coming to you. Don't the gentlemen flock around you, too?"

"Oh, yes," said Elizabeth serenely. "But I don't mind. I think Mrs. Pendleton drags poor Isolde out. If she were left alone, she would be much better off. Or perhaps if they simply arranged a marriage for her, the way Juliet's mama and papa did for her. It would be much simpler."

But Mr. and Mrs. Pendleton lacked the moral fortitude to impose their arbitrary choice on their daughter. In fact, neither had ever yet found a way of dealing with her.

"She should be beaten," said Mr. Pendleton unconvincingly.

"My father would have beaten me when I was a girl had I acted as she does," said his wife. "But her punishment is for you to decide, George."

The Pendletons sighed once more and looked at each other. Isolde had developed some tricks her mother considered very reprehensible, but she had no way of dealing with them.

She had only been presented two seasons ago. During these two years, she had already been crowded with friends, attentions from gentlemen, and invitations to innumerable parties. At first she had enjoyed these functions and attentions, but as the seasons dragged on, she became more and more bored and obstinate about attending parties which most girls would have lived for.

Mrs. Pendleton was at a great disadvantage with her daughter. She had a secret, but unfortunately, Isolde had discovered it when she was a precocious little girl rummaging innocently about in old books, lockets, and drawers.

Mrs. Pendleton had met her husband when they were both very young. His family had been rather wealthy and had educated him at Yale; hers was not quite so well off, but they were established. He was a stubborn youth, and over the strong protests of his parents, marched off to fight in the War of the Rebellion of the Southern States. They thought his actions were folly; he could have easily bought out and spent the time making a fortune by selling goods to the Union Army at exorbitant prices.

He had met young Anne Wells, a beautiful, quiet girl living at home with her father and two younger sisters. She had then possessed the same melting looks Isolde had now and had thought the young, slender soldier to be wonderfully noble. They had had a brief love affair, and he had come back from the war to marry her—but not quite in time. Isolde was born out of wedlock.

Naturally his own family refused to have anything to do with his new wife and daughter, and with a furious certainty of his own strengths, he left the city to migrate to Colorado.

Their days of poverty were so short that Isolde could not even remember them. Possibly because her father was one of the few men in Colorado to be usually sober, or because he possessed an unusually ingenious mind, he was able to come up with a method for extracting copper from low-grade sources. His was the method, the invention, the dream. Richard Rolfston Wilcox, a crony of his, thought he could lay his hands on sufficient capital to get a mill going. Pendleton never did discover how Wilcox came up with their first investment; he simply took the funds and built one of the best little copper mills in the country. Soon he was pumping out enough money to enable

Wilcox and himself to take their families back East to live in splendor in New York. Pendleton's parents welcomed him back quite willingly, happy that their prodigal son could supply his own fatted calf and feed them all. No further mention was made of Isolde's premature entry into their world.

Wilcox, on the other hand, was at first dazzled to find himself in such high strata, but he soon discovered that all was the same in the mansions as it had been back in the shacks of Colorado; the men spent their time drinking and trying to find excuses to leave their wives to smoke cigarettes and get into trouble. The women had an inordinate taste for plastering themselves with jewels. After he had bought his own wife a diamond stomacher, an emerald necklace, various brooches, rings, and more, he began to find the whole thing very boring and went off to look at other mills. Like Carnegie in Pittsburgh, he was fond of acquiring a new one, preferring them greatly to collecting Aubusson carpets, for example, or Louis Quinze furniture.

Pendleton, too, enjoyed this hobby. Together they rode about the country on their private Pullman and inspected their string of mills. Wilcox harassed the bookkeepers and made the deals; Pendleton liked to look over the places and see if something new could be added here or there, something that would bring the place up a little bit in production.

Mr. Pendleton, leaving his daughter in the care of her mother, her governess, and her nurse, assumed that all would be well with her. But Isolde, ill with a cold and playing in her mother's room one day, found the dates on the documents of their marriage and her christening. She asked some straightforward questions, having first pumped the Irish housemaid for exact details regarding the biological process of birth, and her mother could not find a way to smooth over her questions. The date of Isolde's christening told the story itself; Isolde had been born two months before her parents were legally married.

Anne Wells's love affair with the young soldier was the first and last time in her life that she disregarded the canons of society. All had turned out very well for her. She was now Mrs. Pendleton, and the passion she and her husband had felt for each other in their youth had grown more solid with the passing of time. Mrs. Pendleton was an upright matron, spending her husband's newly made money generously on the opera, building a number of mansions with suitably lavish grounds, purchasing carriages made in England and dresses made in Paris. Her secret was well kept by a discreet family.

She entertained an unspoken wish that her daughter would someday be moved by a love as powerful as she had found, by a man who suited Isolde as George did her, even if Isolde broke the laws of society to do so. Thus, it was with a very unrepentant tone that she explained to Isolde the circumstances of her birth. No mention was made that she had erred and repented. She did not think she had erred, for all had turned out well, and she had certainly never repented. Even if George had died in the war, she would have preferred to live alone for the rest of her life with his child to love, bearing the isolation from society, than to have married any other man.

But she communicated the events of Isolde's birth to her in as few, carefully chosen words as she could, and only by tone did she imply that she was actually proud of what she had done all those years ago. The Irish housemaid had expressed in far more certain terms her own feelings of the moral worth of girls who let their men take liberties before the walk to the altar was safely made. The young Isolde was left alone to sort out the two modes of thought. Her mother offered no explicit advice or blueprint of behavior. She patted her daughter's hand and said that she hoped in her time she would marry someone with whom she too was very, very much in love. The discussion ended, never to be resumed. Isolde was left with her thoughts.

Was not King Arthur himself illegitimate, Isolde considered, sired by Uther Pendragon on the beautiful Igraine in a night of stolen passion? But even in those idealistic medieval times, a knight born out of wedlock, even to the most noble parents, might wear his father's coat of arms in battle only if he added to its design the bar sinister, symbol of bastardy, admission of his birth from the "left side," tainted with immorality and illegality.

How could her mother help but be ashamed of her? How much pride did she feel in her daughter when she kept matters so secret? When Isolde imagined her mother, dressed in a Paris gown and diamonds, sitting with her friends in her box at the opera, exchanging confidences about the birth of their children, she knew all of the ladies of her mother's acquaintance would feel, or pretend to feel, complete horror at the tale of Isolde's birth.

Despite the frustration her mother felt about her at times, Isolde did know what century she was living in. Medieval times were gone. Bastardy could no longer be acknowledged even on a coat of arms. "Bastard" was a word her father used when he was angry, making her mother scold and look shocked. It was an ugly word, a word not to be spoken before other people. And yet she was a bastard.

The Pendleton fortune amounted to $50 million. She was the daughter of astounding wealth. But if her mother died, and her father remarried, she might legally inherit nothing at all; she was not a legitimate heir. She could end up sewing buttons on ladies' undergarments for a penny a dozen or painting china or teaching schoolchildren French. Perhaps her mother feared that for her, too. Perhaps that was why she was so anxious for her to marry, to establish herself.

Only when she was alone did these thoughts assail her. When she was with her comfortable, worldly mother, or her loving, impractical father, no daydream seemed more absurd. But she was left alone too often.

Both Isolde and Elizabeth could be described without exaggeration as beauties. Both had blue eyes, but the shade of blue and the shape of their eyes were very different. Elizabeth's eyes were her greatest asset, being very large and of a lovely sky blue, almost dreamlike in character. Her coloring was very fair, showing some Dutch ancestry; her hair was brushed into short blond curls over her forehead, and long ringlets fell down her neck.

Isolde was a dark beauty, straight and slim. Her eyes, too, were blue, but a deep dark blue. Her hair was thick and luxuriant like a coiled snake, as one ingenuous young man had described. Her skin had received its portion of likenings to lilies, peaches, and new milk. But it was Isolde's eyes that her suitors remembered most and could never describe. Although her suitors mistakenly thought her eyes were flirtatious, in reality no part of Isolde was ever flirtatious in the silly way of ordinary young ladies. But her suitors never actually noticed Isolde herself; they were too caught up in the aura she projected.

After Isolde had been out for several months, long enough to cause a furor whenever she entered a ballroom, her mother began to notice that the attention paid to her had died down somewhat, and that one young man, rather noticeably handsome, was becoming omnipresent. But Isolde was not a confiding child, although she had a knack for getting others to talk. Her mother, although she waited and hinted hopefully, never received her daughter's confidences, and one day, without explanation, the young man disappeared. Mrs. Pendleton made inquiries of her friends; she was informed that he had left for Africa with a broken heart. She heard no more about that young man, but in a few months another took his place, also pleasant and good-looking. Mrs. Pendleton began to entertain new hopes.

After two seasons and four young men, if one counted the off-season ones, Mr. Pendleton demanded to know what Isolde did with all these boys.

"If your mother won't speak to you, I will," he said sternly to her one evening after supper. "Are you secretly engaged?"

"In a way, Papa."

"In what way?" he roared. Mr. Pendleton was a large man, over six feet tall, possessing an impressive set of whiskers and a large bay window acquired through a fondness for late night suppers at Delmonico's. He looked as if he could not be frightened by a polar bear; but in fact his wife and daughter possessed most of the family courage.

Isolde sighed her delicate, water nymph sigh, and said, "Dear Papa, you don't realize how many difficulties one has being a woman."

Mr. Pendleton could not disagree. Mrs. Pendleton, who could not recall ever besting Isolde in an argument since Isolde had celebrated her twelfth birthday, remained silent.

"You see, Papa, when one is female, one must wait. One must sit and be courteous until one is asked to dance, to go for a walk, to take some refreshment— and to become engaged. It is the man who decides when he wants to begin. It is for the woman to wait."

"Go on," said her father, feeling as if he were being

dragged off on a long journey he had not wanted to start.

"Well, you see, Papa, for some reason more than one man has decided to ask me to do these things. They jostle each other. I sometimes feel like a horse at a race that everyone wants to bet on. It can become quite tedious. I had to decide to say yes or no to all kinds of things, whether to wear whose flowers today, whom to go to which play with, why I wouldn't marry whom almost every hour of the day." She paused, and sighed again.

"Well?" Mr. Pendleton asked. "And what did you decide?"

"It seems so unfair," Isolde pleaded. "Doesn't it seem unfair to you? I was so tired of being begged to do things all the time. So I said yes—perhaps—to one young man. That got rid of the others. Then when the young man and I tired of each other, we parted friends. You see? All quite harmless."

Mr. Pendleton stared first at his daughter, and then at his wife, who sat by helplessly. " 'Tired of each other' indeed!" he thundered. "Connell told me to my face that you secretly engaged yourself to his son and then jilted him for no reason he could understand. He had to pack the boy off to another continent. This has got to stop, Isolde!"

"But Papa!" pleaded Isolde. "It is so difficult being a woman!"

"What do your friends do? Can't you just be decently civil?"

"Papa, it is very difficult to be civil when someone is trying to make love to you."

"Did Connell's boy try to make love to you? Is that what you're saying?"

"Now, Papa, dearest," said Isolde, gently devastating her father, "doesn't every young man try to make love with every pretty woman he sees? And if he does love her, and she loves him, won't he do anything for her? Didn't you and Mama?"

A short and complete silence ended the conference. A few days later Mr. Pendleton listened to the pleas of his wife and the urgings of his business partner, R. R. Wilcox, and made arrangements to take his new yacht to England.

It was to be hoped that a change of scenery might alter Isolde's deplorable habits. At least they might leave town until her scandalous reputation was partly forgotten. Mr. Pendleton did not relish hearing his daughter called a jilt.

He would have relished even less hearing her called a seductress, but this appellation no one had yet had the courage to call her in his presence.

Although Isolde knew her parents' secret, they had never discovered any of hers. Isolde had practices that would have horrified her mama and upset even her eccentric father.

Isolde's first young man had been handsome and reassuringly in love with her. To love him in return had seemed so right, so romantic, so exciting. Isolde had spent most of her childhood between the covers of Tennyson's *Idylls of the King*; medieval romance seemed infinitely preferable to the decorous styles of modern courtship, with its commercial overtones and dull certainty of outcome. So she had met her lover secretly, awkwardly in hotels, and once at her parents' vacation home. For a few weeks an accidental encounter at a tea, exchanging glances over slices of bread and butter and china cups, had lent glory and excitement to Isolde's world, bringing life to her dreams.

But the young man had been very young. In addition to being quite good-looking, he was rather selfish and began to plume himself on having made a conquest of her. His love for her was only a little less

great than his ignorance of female anatomy. Having
only enjoyed a chance meeting once or twice with a
prostitute, he was unaware that his technique had
shortcomings. Isolde expected such knowledge to be
inborn and was left feeling unsatisfied and angry, but
unable to explain why. Her passion had bound her
lover tight to her, but he had never succeeded in giving her the pleasure that would have bound her to
him. She felt free, untouched. After a few months, she
refused to see him again.

When she met a new young man, even better-look-
ing and more amusing, she thought she was ready to
try again for a new love, a true love. But when the
hurt came, as it must, the frustration, the boredom, the
certain knowledge that she had once again made the
wrong choice, the parting full of pain and anger, she
still felt untouched. Each encounter increased her in-
ward certainty that she was looking for someone who
did not exist, that she herself was unnatural in some
way, all wrong from birth, that it was all hopeless.
Then a depression would descend on her that bewildered her parents. She spent weeks in her room, claim-
ing some illness. She read, she painted, she practiced
doleful songs.

Her mother should not have been surprised that
Isolde had so little interest in making calls, having
teas, or going for socially polite rides or drives in the
park. It was no pleasure for her to chance to meet
one of her unsuccessful young men. All Isolde wanted
was a little peace and quiet, and a burning, flaming
passion that would not flicker and die in the first
breeze that blew.

Chapter 2

"Afternoon, Tuttle, afternoon," said Albert, earl of Toye, pleasantly to his butler, as Tuttle helped him stagger across the threshold of his lodgings. Only a faint aura of brandy clung to his handsome, youthful visage, but his manner, always somewhat fuzzy, was more vague than usual. His lordship did not adapt well to life in London, Tuttle reflected. He was much better off in his castle in Warwickshire, messing about with his inventions. Here in London, a city gray with fogs, dim, and damp, his lordship, always very susceptible to atmosphere, seemed to wander about somewhat in a daze a good deal of the time. However, Tuttle was relieved to discover, as he helped his lordship out of his overcoat, that he was quite presentable.

"Good afternoon, your lordship. Mr. Thornbrough has been waiting for some time for an interview."

Bertie had turned to straighten his mashed tie in the hall mirror, but even as his hand reached up, it paused and began to quiver in midair. Bertie's eyes met the sympathetic orbs of Tuttle in the mirror.

"Here? Long?" Bertie asked in an appalled tone. "Has he been here long? I haven't forgotten anything recently, have I, Tuttle? Did anyone die? What day is it?"

"He arrived here shortly after you left and seemed

to think some arrangement had been made between
you."

"Oh, lord! What do you think of this waistcoat,
Tuttle? Do you think he'll like it? He's so fussy about
these things. Is he in a mood? Does he like stripes? I
can't think I've ever asked him. Do you like this
waistcoat? You can have it. I'll take yours. I like yours
much better."

"No, my lord," said Tuttle firmly. "I do not believe
your cousin is here for an inspection of your garments. He appears to be in an abstracted but not
overly unpleasant mood. I have served him coffee."

"Pleasant, hmm. Well, after all, my affairs are none
of his affair."

"Exactly, my lord," Tuttle replied. "Except, of
course, that Mr. Thornbrough does pay your allowance."

"There is that," Bertie admitted.

Finishing the onerous task of readjusting his tie,
smoothing his locks, and applying just a touch of
Colonel Carter's Compound to his small but very
dashing mustache—acts which took a surprising length
of time—he turned toward the entryway and said
in valiant accents, "Lead on, Tuttle! Are you sure
about this waistcoat business?"

"Absolutely," Tuttle replied.

"Ah, well."

Tuttle opened the sliding doors that led to the parlor, and Bertie stepped across the room, smiling
brightly.

"It's not like you to be sitting about in the afternoon over coffee, coz!" Bertie said with an attempt at
cheery chat.

"Exactly so," his cousin replied, as he sat ensconced
in a wing chair by the fireplace. "Had you opened
the note I sent you three days ago, or the letter re-

minding you about the note I posted to you two days ago, you would have been here with me."

Mr. Thornbrough raised his eyebrow. He was considerably taller than his noble cousin, and of a more muscular build. His most distinguished characteristics were his excellent tailoring, his strong features, and a quirk he had of lifting his dark eyebrows one at a time or in conjunction almost to his hairline, usually throwing his friends into confusion and ending any argument. He lifted one eyebrow now, but Bertie was not troubled; he was staring off into space, his own eyebrows knit together in puzzlement.

Thornie, always amused by his cousin's remarkable reserve, said, "What are you thinking of, coz?"

"Bicycling."

"Good God!"

"I've been out bicycling, you know. In the countryside. Nice time of year. But, you know, something has to be done about these roads. We're not beginning to make the progress of having them macadamized that you see in other countries."

"Shocking!" said Thornbrough, in mock serious tones. Thornbrough considered the bicycle a faddish toy to be used only by the middle classes for exercise and recreational travel, and found his cousin's fascination with the machine to be another example of his impractical nature.

"I know you don't care. I don't mind. But one of these days there won't be any more horses on the roads. Just bicycles. Gliding like birds over beautiful long stretches of smooth roads. And then everyone will be healthy and much better off, you see. Bicycling is the finest exercise man can enjoy."

"Why don't you toddle on over to the House of Lords someday and make a speech? One so rarely sees you there."

"Me?" said Bertie, horrified. "I can't make

speeches. And they're like you, they'd all laugh at me."

"It does seem likely. But you know, cousin, I am curious. I hardly ever see you at Parliament. You would think that we might just bump into each other by accident occasionally. I always look for you at the opera, but I can't seem to find where you are seated."

"Now you know I never go to the opera. Went to a music hall last night. Good bill. Lots of music. Dancing. Can't remember any of the songs, but they were very jolly."

"Ah, well, that accounts for the opera. But then one might think we would at some time during the season go to the same parties. I was at the Double Duchess's last night. Weren't you invited?"

"Never go to those bashes. Too much noise. Too many people. Have to dress."

"And then there was a house party at Blenheim last weekend," pursued Thornie.

"Told you I was bicycling."

"Ah, yes. But the clubs? Surely we should meet at the clubs occasionally. I believe you are a member of the Pelican Club?"

"I go there," said Bertie indignantly. "Go and get drunk there all the time."

"Ah, perhaps that explains it. You see, I never go anymore. The tone of the place has become so raffish of late."

"Yes," said Bertie, grinning with unconcern. "That's why I like it. You're so snobbish, Thornie, I wonder you ever have fun."

"In my way, dear Bert, I assure you I do have fun."

Thornbrough was in possession of one of the oldest names in England and was related to half the families of London's Upper Ten Thousand. Even more fortunately, coal had been discovered on the Thornbrough estates in his father's time, so that Thornie enjoyed a fortune larger than many possessed by those of far higher rank, his cousin in particular. He was able to choose his entertainments as few of his generation could, but his ideas were somewhat stiffer than those of his contemporaries. He went on house parties with the Prince of Wales set, but he had been known to raise a somber, disapproving brow over some of his prince's less brilliant practical jokes, and even refused to let him win at cards upon occasion. His dark good looks made him attractive to the ladies, despite the fact that he never engaged in seltzer bottle battles or slid down the stairs on a tea tray.

He was accounted for as a jolly good fellow. He rode to hounds with a stable of the best hunters, had had the felicity of seeing two of his horses win at Ascot, and played for any stakes. The ladies courted him anew each season in fresh clouds of gauze, but in vain. He was one and thirty and planned on working a bride into his schedule sometime in the future, perhaps when he was nearer to fifty. He was in no hurry to subject himself to the bore of courting a young girl; his favors were reserved for the wives of men who had fathered three or four children and gone off to discreetly enjoy their own affairs elsewhere. Thornie had also established a succession of mistresses in cozy houses in St. John's Wood; he had only recently broken off just such an affair with a beautiful but surprisingly bad-tempered woman.

His cousin Albert's most distinguished feature was his singular lack of distinguishing features. Born Albert Taunton, earl of Toye, owner of Toye Castle, he enjoyed none of the prestige or debts that usually attended such a position. A deplorably carefree attitude toward his own social importance was deemed by Thornie to be his worst quality. Besides this social easiness, he was seldom sober after teatime, and had regrettable taste in all matters pertaining to dress and women. He, too, had a knack of lifting his eyebrows up to his hairline, but since his were a sandy color and rose in pairs, they resembled monarch butterflies searching for shelter rather than storm clouds of disapproval. His eyes were blue; Mr. Thornbrough's were brown. His hair was a dark blond; Mr. Thornbrough's was almost black.

"Something afoot, dear old boy?" asked Bertie.

"Your acumen continues to amaze," replied his cousin. "I am greatly relieved to discover that you are not dead. Perhaps that should be reason enough for this visit. I did not look forward to arranging your last rites."

Bertie gestured ineffectively. "Well, there you are," he said. "Not dead at all! What's more, don't know why I should be. I'm only four and twenty. Old cousin Allerby is eighty if he's a day, and he's not dead. So I don't really see why I ought to be dead."

"No reason that I know of," said his cousin mildly. "It did seem odd, of course, that after a few weeks of leaving messages at your club and notes at your lodgings, you should find yourself unable to spare a few minutes of your time in conference to me. But I see that you were merely overcome by social obligations—or was it these voyages of discovery you take on these revolutionary machines of yours? Or perhaps even some feelings of the self-worth natural to the head of a noble family of ancient lineage overcame you. You were right, of course. It was very rude of me to ask you to visit me. I abase myself before you."

"No, no!" Bertie exclaimed, alarmed. "It's all Tuttle's fault. I had no notion!"

"Does Tuttle also act as your secretary?" inquired Mr. Thornbrough, brow upraised.

"Acts as my secretary, acts as my butler, acts as my valet, acts as anything you like. Acts a really lovely recitation of *Charge of the Light Brigade*—you know,

'Half a league, half a league, half a league onward'—but only after we've had a few."

"Had a few?" asked Mr. Thornbrough. "Do you
mean you drink with your servants? Oh, really now,
Bertie."

"Lord, yes," Bertie said cheerily. "Although I can
never get Tuttle to sit down while he does it. Very
unnerving! But I do recommend it, coz! It puts them
all into the sunniest humor. Except Mrs. Eastman, of
course. She's a Methodist."

"And so does not indulge."

"Oh, she indulges all right, but she can't hold her
liquor. Gets weepy and starts to tell awfully dull stories about husbands and children. Starts to talk about
the Lord, and not meaning me either."

"Albert," began his cousin in a patient voice, "the
style of your life, even the manner in which you have
been reared, has been a trifle informal."

"Oh, don't start in on my mother again. Mrs.
Pankhurst would have thought up women's rights by
herself if Mama hadn't. And Mama couldn't help
being thrown into jail—why, it was your mother who
thought of chaining themselves to the doors of Parliament."

Mr. Thornbrough lifted a hand to silence him.

"One might almost say *unusual*. Yours is an anoma-
lous position. You possess an ancient title and one of
the foremost country places in England—yet, unfortunately, none of the wealth necessary to uphold these
traditions."

"Yes, well," hemmed Bertie.

"Perhaps—if I may be very outspoken—it would be-
hoove you to consider some means of gaining the fortune your father was unable to leave you. And since
you seem to have no turn for business, I wonder if
you have ever considered the possibilities of making
an advantageous marriage?"

"Considered it, certainly," Bertie replied firmly. "But if you're talking about the Vassily girl, the answer is no! With all due respect, of course, I mean. Well, dash it, the girl's cross-eyed! There you are, talking to her at some damned ball or another—and she's not pretty, y'know—and one eye starts wandering away! And you don't know where it's going or when it's coming back! Now someone like Charlie Masterton can go right on chattering away happily, but everything goes out of my head. And then she just sits and stares at me, with her eyeballs rolling around in her head! I feel like a fool! I can't think of a thing!"

"Poor Bertie," murmured his cousin with a slight smile. "You do have a handicap, don't you?"

"Well, you can laugh," Bertie said indignantly. "But I promise you, it's a hardship, it truly is!"

"Happily then, what I have to suggest may please you more. It involves a fortune which, as near as I can estimate, approaches ten million pounds."

"Good lord!" gasped Bertie. "American?"

"Astute, my dear Albert. You are perhaps aware that I have had some dealings with the inventor and manufacturer, R.R. Wilcox."

"Good lord!" Bertie repeated.

"As you say. His daughter, Elizabeth Wilcox, will be arriving here in England in a few days. She might have already landed in Liverpool, I believe, in the yacht of her traveling companions, the Pendletons. A private yacht. Ostensibly, her purpose is to transact some business with me, but I make no doubt that, like all American heiresses, she is interested in acquiring a husband with a title and an estate. Her father's money is very new; I'm not certain just how he made his start in the business world. Some American fortunes, of course, are founded on slave trading or selling whiskey to the American Indian. I know he now possesses two very fine railroads, in addition to several foundries which pour metal using processes he has invented. A rather assertive gentleman; it is to be hoped that his daughter is a little more gently behaved. But despite the fact that his money is very new and very American, you will find that it can mend your roof, scythe your lawns, and furnish you with all the luxuries that more aristocratic money could buy. To you, dear Albert, do I offer first shot at this exceedingly plump pigeon."

"Well, you can't!" Bertie exclaimed. "She'll take a suite in the Clarendon or some such place and in four and twenty hours she'll have been invited to every party of the season. I shall never get near her!"

"No doubt. For this reason, we will invite Miss Wilcox to Toye Castle, where you, Albert, will attempt to engage her lasting affection."

"Oh, lord!" Bertie exclaimed once again, somewhat dejectedly. "When was the last time you saw the place? Practically a ruin, I promise you. All the rooms shut up, nothing at all in the cellar. Cook quit, all the servants are octogenarians or Irish, the roof leaks—really, it's a terrible place to try to entertain in. Couldn't be more than six servants on the place. I know m' father kept at least fifty."

"I am aware of your staffing problems, Albert," said Mr. Thornbrough sweetly. "I pay their wages. But tomorrow my secretary shall spend the day at an agency and engage a sufficient number to run the place in style, at least for the present. You may join him in this task if you wish."

"Nothing I would dislike more, dear boy. Not a judge of character. The last man I engaged stole all the spoons and hopped it overnight. But this much I do want to know. How are we to lure this unsuspecting American into our lair, hmm? You think she'll just walk in, as easy as that? And also, I thought you loathed Americans. At least, you always told me that."

"I never said I loathed Americans," Mr. Thornbrough said indolently. "I said I regarded them as barbarians, unfit for association in civilized circles; and that is certainly still true. But alas, dear Bertie, it is you who will lay himself down before mammon. I shall remain in London while you become the fodder for American social ambitions. Poor Bert! How we are made to suffer for the sins of our fathers! Mine was such a respectable, provident fellow."

"She could have a mustache," Bertie said, growing nervous at the thought. "Jenny Churchill's sister-in-law has one, so they tell me."

"And a beard, too," Mr. Thornbrough inserted.

"No!" Bertie exclaimed.

"Not a full beard. Just a goatee. Jenny made her remove it. Perhaps she was unaware that mustaches are not commonly seen on ladies in the best circles of England society. Who knows, they may be all the fashion in the United States."

Bertie glanced around his abode. The furnishings were quite nondescript, even shabby. On the walls hung a few faded prints of hunting scenes. In a little while he would be getting out of his comfortable chair and perhaps toddling over to his club, where he would find another comfortable chair and some cronies. He would dine simply on ham and eggs, come home very late at night, let himself in with his own key, and wake up in the morning to the pleasant sound of Tuttle's voice. Nothing fancy. Nothing like Thornie's place, crawling as it was with obsequious servants. Just a dark little hole on a dark little street in a not particularly fashionable neighborhood. But it was a comfortable hole. Bertie was not at all certain he wished to exchange it for a mansion filled with mustachioed ladies.

"I have heard from Cousin Mattie that she is quite pretty, in an American kind of way," said Mr. Thornbrough sympathetically. "Mattie would have mentioned any outstanding peculiarities."

"She won't want to go to Toye, not at this season," Bertie said with a vestige of hopefulness.

"Well, I don't like to break it to you, dear Bert, but she has already accepted."

Bertie's eyes widened, his eyebrows fluttering. "How could she! I haven't invited her!"

"It's all very complicated, Bert. Cousin Mattie met her when she went to the United States."

"This is a conspiracy then!" shouted Bert. "She is *my* Cousin Mattie, not yours. You don't even like her."

"I like her, Bert," Mr. Thornbrough said soothingly. "It may be true that you have heard me express the opinion that it is a pity a woman of Mattie's connections and quality must choose throwing bricks through store windows as a hobby, inciting the populace to riot, and leave her family—"

"What family?" asked Bertie indignantly. "The old lady croaked three years ago."

"—And travel to uncivilized parts of the world, there to stir up discontent among women even more poorly educated than herself."

"My, my, you will hit it off with this young lady, especially since she is such a good friend of Mattie's."

"It is not important whether or not *I* hit it off. I am not in the market for an American wife. Now, if I may continue, Cousin Mattie has promised the American young lady—Miss Wilcox—a real look at an English castle, and this refers to Toye."

"It's not a very big castle."

"Oh, but it crumbles so nicely, Bert. Let us not forget the American love of the picturesque. Not only has she been promised a castle, but more importantly, a treat that is traditionally given by the lord of the manor for his villagers every year. It is to honor this treat that Miss Wilcox will especially make the trip down."

"Now really, Thornie, you are laying all this on much too thick. First you tell me that Cousin Mattie had such an idea at all and decided to tell you, of all people. Why, she despises you. You are all she considers most reprehensible in England today. Then you would have me believe that she would talk such a lot of nonsense about Toye to some American. She knows there hasn't been a treat at Toye for the last twenty-five years."

"Fifty."

"Exactly," replied Bertie. "Well, there you have it. What a notion! Why, Cousin Mattie practically grew up at Toye! She and I once barricaded ourselves into the old castle and no one found us for three days."

"Or missed you for two and a half, I know, I know. And because of this great fondness Matilda cherishes for Toye, and for your mama, and apparently you as well, as soon as she reached the great continent, so well noted for its tinned lobster and heiresses, she began casting around for some fish to attach to the Taunton line. Tomorrow you will call upon Aunt Honora and arrange the guest list with her."

"But think, dear boy, think!" Bertie urged.

"I believe I have," Mr. Thornbrough replied.

"Aunt Honora at Toye Castle! It might rain! I might never get rid of her again!"

"I myself will hasten to Warwickshire and oust the lady if our schemes fail to come to fruition."

"But what did Mattie say about this American? She could be forty! Or engaged! Or unpresentable!"

"The first is unlikely, since she made her debut in New York recently. The second is also unlikely. Why seek new pasture if the old is verdant? The third, I

am afraid, is inevitable. But roofs must be mended,
Bert."

"She won't hit it off with Aunt Honora," Bertie
said glumly.

"My dear Albert," his cousin replied with a glimmer of humor, "*your* presence must alleviate any disgust Aunt Honora will suffer by being forced into
intimacy with the vulgar."

"What makes you think Aunt Honora will come?"
asked Bertie, aggrieved.

"I pay her servant's wages too," replied his cousin
gently.

Chapter 3

London was all Isolde could have hoped for. Although they arrived in the city at about three in the afternoon, the lamps were already lit. Nothing so gaudy as a sun could be seen in the sky. Indeed, one could hardly see the sky. It seemed to hang about their shoulders in the shape of a thick fog greedily lapping at the streetlights. Her parents might consider such weather to be rather grim for spring; Isolde loved it. The city was just as dark and gloomy as she could wish.

The streets were narrow and twisted; the stones of the buildings, which seemed to have grown up haphazardly, were dirty with soot. In traveling from one part of the city to another, she seemed to be going from one world to another. Here the buildings were crowded and the streets filthy. As they neared their destination, fine town houses and beautiful parks sprang up. But all the buildings shared a peculiarity, as if they were wildflowers accidentally sprung up by seeds blown in the wind rather than neat rows of blossoms planted by a careful gardener.

All was strange; the past seemed to stand on every corner, never dispelled by the rushing changes of a new time. The present seemed to be of no particular importance at all, like a dull child.

Isolde longed to put up at one of the small dark hostelries they passed in their carriage. Figures ambled in and out of public houses that bore wonderful names like the Red Lion or the Elephant and Empire. She yearned to mingle with shabby Dickensian characters in search of gin and rum, but one of her father's friends had recommended a hotel named the Swanhome, which he described as a trifle expensive, but very cozy and with good food. The owner was something of a character too, he had said. Isolde's parents ignored her pleas and hints and drove to the more fashionable neighborhood where the Swanhome was situated.

They were greeted at the door by the proprietor herself, who was dressed, to their surprise, in a superbly cut riding habit. Rosa Hurst was very fond of Americans, at least so she said in her warm cockney accent. She ordered up a jeroboam of champagne to be served to them in her office. The champagne would, of course, be totted up on their bill later on, but to such a wealthy species as the American tycoon, such a minor item could hardly be noticed. Rosa Hurst's hotel was just as colorful as Isolde could have wished, although it was neither shabby nor dank. She ran her hotel on generous terms. It was her belief that everyone should eat and drink in plenty, and that those who could should pay. Americans never complained. Besides, she reflected privately, they had just come over; they probably hadn't even figured out English money yet.

She invited them into her study for a bottle of bubbly with a few other guests as if she had invited them all to stay at her house in the country. Mrs. Pendleton did not think champagne for Isolde at three in the afternoon would be a good influence on her behavior, and she shepherded her daughter and Elizabeth off to their bedrooms to rest. Mr. Pendleton was happy to be swept up by his hostess and found there were two other gentlemen already lounging about in her office.

"Lord Elmore, I want you to meet Mr. Pendleton 'ere, 'e's from America. And this is Mr. Cochran 'ere. Is this yer first visit, Mr. Pendleton? Glad to have you stay. 'Ope you find the place to yer liking. Just give us the word and you can 'ave anything you want."

Mr. Pendleton did not know what to make of Mrs. Hurst, a most remarkable woman, he reflected, as she poured champagne into tulip-shape glass. She certainly didn't behave like the obsequious hotel managers of New York. In fact, the whole hotel looked like someone's home. The furniture was good, but old and comfortable. There were none of those spindly gold French chairs and marble floors the elegant hotels in New York went in for. The doorman was an odd character, too, that Fred, with his dog Scottie trotting at his heels, and the butler looked as if he had returned from the grave to do the honors here. Maybe this was what all English hotels were like, though. Mrs. Hurst, with her cockney accent and good humor, certainly was pleasant enough. She was talking with that lord about an upcoming horserace, and he found himself drawn in. Very nice fellows, not stiff at all; he talked with them until Mrs. Hurst ordered him upstairs to dress for dinner. "And you go too, Wormy," she said to Lord Elmore. "If you're going to eat my food, you're going to have to deserve it."

He went upstairs reflecting that a man couldn't ask for a more pleasant place to rest. Mrs. Hurst watched him shut the door behind him and remarked to Lord Elmore, "Quite the looker his girls are too. Nice straight figures, both of them. A lively one and a quiet one. I wonder where they're headed."

Although the matter was not uppermost in Mr. Pendleton's mind, he also had some reflections

concerning the disposal of his young ladies. He would
not be at all chagrined if Isolde found herself an English husband, and if the fellow were to have a title,
well, they had come to the right country, and apparently the right hotel for that. It was time Isolde
settled down. As for Elizabeth, he never thought of
making a plan concerning her.

"You know, I'm rather afraid of that girl," said Mr.
Pendleton to his wife as he waited for her to finish
dressing for dinner.

"My dear, I know exactly what you mean," she responded sympathetically as she clasped a diamond
earring in one fleshy lobe. "I am terrified of her, and
if I weren't more terrified of her father, I never
would have consented to this arrangement."

"I hope her vivacity is not too wearing on poor
little Isolde's nerves. After all, it was for Isolde's
health that we made this crossing."

"No, no, I believe she exercises a beneficial influence upon Isolde." Mrs. Pendleton stood up and surveyed her reflection in one of the several full-length
mirrors in her room. "It is a pity that Isolde's health
has obliged her to be so shut up of late years. She
seems to be growing actually eccentric, and that cannot be a good thing for a girl her age. Lizzie cheers
her up greatly. I almost wish she were continuing to
Italy with us, but you insist she is not? What is this
business about seeing Mrs. Pankhurst while she is in
England? What does Wilcox think of having such a
firebrand for a daughter?"

"Oh, I know nothing about that," said Mr. Pendleton, shuddering inwardly. "Are you ready?" he
added, offering her his arm. "All I know is that she
has quite a head for business. She can talk Wall
Street as well as many men I know. Right through
here, is it? Our own dining room? Mrs. Hurst does
things in style, doesn't she?"

"I can hardly believe it, Mr. Pendleton," said his wife, holding back a moment. "How can a girl who attends the balls she does—remember that marvelous affair she gave this year?—be involved with such work? She would be overtaxed to the point of breakdown."

"So it would seem to us," said Mr. Pendleton mildly. "But perhaps Lizzie possesses faculties unknown to us. It is true that even if I were nineteen I could not attend a single ball each night, as you ladies do, without ever tiring. I could certainly never get up in the morning and go pay calls, organize charitable bazaars, or give afternoon teas. Perhaps Lizzie has discovered what we men have always known, how pleasant and soothing business is, and has the knack of balancing the furor of her social life with the tranquillity of running an industrial empire."

"You are ridiculous," his wife laughed. "Come, the children must surely be waiting."

Miss Wilcox and Miss Pendleton were indeed waiting. They were both dressed in white. Elizabeth perched gracefully on the edge of her seat, so as not to disturb the rows of gores in back of her highly trimmed gown, her hands folded demurely in her lap. Her dress was cut low and tightly laced, revealing an hourglass figure very much in vogue among the women who were accounted beauties. Isolde, despite any attempts of her mother, wore very simple dresses and seldom submitted herself to any corset at all. She said bows and frills irked her and were not truly artistic. Her mother produced fashion plates from Paris, but Isolde merely rolled her eyes at these, casting her gaze heavenward and saying, "Well, Mother dearest, if you allow a dressmaker in Paris to clothe you, perhaps you are right. But my soul is cramped in such clothes. I can't wear them." She had been known to actually sit down and cut furbishes off her dresses.

Mrs. Pendleton soon gave up and allowed her to have her way, admitting to herself that with her slender figure, she did look very elegant.

Although they were both members of the same set, Isolde and Elizabeth had not seen a great deal of each other in New York. Lizzie was always in a rush of activities very different from Isolde's. They had always known each other, however, since their fathers were so closely associated, and during the last week on ship a strong affection had grown between them. Lizzie, hearing a great deal of New York gossip about Isolde, had always wondered how such a quiet young woman could behave in such an eccentric way, and she was still very puzzled.

It was true, as Isolde's mother pointed out, that Lizzie's company enlivened her; but without Isolde, Lizzie would have been horribly bored. Lizzie was no great reader, had never mastered a musical instrument, and cared nothing for embroidery. In New York a task arose to fill every hour, but on ship she had been grateful for Isolde's conversation. Having spent so much of her youth among men much older than she—her father, her uncle, and their associates—she privately found most of the girls in New York her age to be very silly indeed. They worked for hours making glove cases and music covers, when such things could be purchased for a few dollars. They labored over the piano and the harp when Melba or Tosti could be hired for a musical evening, yielding up far more divine music than any young miss could ever hope to achieve. They never had any conversation and thought her the oddest creature because she read more than the society page of the newspaper.

But Isolde was quite different. When Isolde played the guitar and sang Scotch ballads in her soft voice, Lizzie felt mild stirrings of envy. It seemed such a pleasant thing to be able to do. Isolde read a great deal, and not just the ordinary rubbish young women read. She was never a bore, but conducted the business of her life in ruthless contrast to the conventions her mother would have preferred, eating odd foods, wearing strange dresses, even reading classics rarely seen in female hands.

Although the *Ultima* had been loaded with every delicacy and a chef knowledgeable enough to produce masterpieces at sea, Mrs. Hurst's menu seemed even more lavish. She had honored them with her famous quail pudding and one of her truffle dishes; the room was perfectly decorated and filled with flowers. There was nothing slipshod about the service, no matter how odd her staff was.

"Hardy put me onto the right thing," said Mr. Pendleton, contentedly helping himself to the *jambon de Prague aux feves*. "What a place this is! Seems to be a party going on above us too. Hope it won't keep you up all night, Isolde."

"Would you like to trade bedrooms?" her mother asked anxiously. "You know what a light sleeper you are, dear, and you need your rest."

"Yours faces the street and would probably be even noisier, poor Mama," said Isolde. "How long do we stay in London now that we are here?"

"I hate to bring this up, dear ones," said Elizabeth, "but I did promise Matilda Taunton that I would go visit her cousin in the country as soon as I got here. Some nonsense about village greens and rural festivities. In the morning I must send a wire to her cousin, the earl of Toye, and find out my dates, but I think the whole thing is supposed to start in a day or two. And if I'm not going to look utterly shabby, I shall have to do some very serious shopping in the next two days."

"You brought four trunks with you," Isolde scolded lightly.

"That's almost nothing at all," replied Lizzie. "You know how these dresses are. Thank goodness, we don't wear crinolines anymore! I don't see how you ever managed."

"Ah, crinolines," Mr. Pendleton said fondly. "The crinoline has passed away, thank God. Your mother was wearing one when I first met her. She looked like a balloon."

"George!"

"Well, so you did, with a very pretty head sticking out. You know, it's a very odd thing. They tell me that in these castles of England one can see old suits of armor decorating noble halls, a reminder of days past. I wonder if in a few years the younger generations will unearth the crinolines and set them up beside the armor, a reminder of the battles women fought in the nineteenth century over fashion and beauty."

"George! My heavens. *Crinolines*, of all things. Really. Elizabeth, I should think an invitation to an English country house would be very pleasant, particularly at this time of the year. They tell me England in the spring is a wonderful sight."

Miss Wilcox smiled and shook her head. She squinted up the left side of her face and winked, directing this odd motion at Isolde, who merely widened her blue eyes in answer. In a second her face had resumed the grace of a young goddess smiling.

Mr. Pendleton recalled the jam that had occurred at the dock when Miss Wilcox's suitors discovered that she was making a hastily planned journey to England. Jacqueminot roses had arrived by the dozen; orchids were sent, and since a rumor had lately sprung up in New York that white lilacs were Miss Wilcox's favorite flower, whole boughs of the rare and fragrant blossoms soon perfumed the Pendleton suites, flowing out onto the decks. Chocolates had been delivered by the pound, not only by young men, but by Mr. Wilcox's business associates, all of whom Miss Wilcox seemed to be on the best terms with. Miss Wilcox was such good copy for the Sunday papers, in fact, that one of them had even sent a young man to harass her at the dock for last minute gossip and details.

"I know you are interested in English shops," said Mrs. Pendleton. "Are you at all interested in English men?"

"I think I'm more interested in English women," said Elizabeth. "This is a wretched country for a female."

"Then you do not aim to form an English alliance?" Mr. Pendleton said dryly. "I have seen so many American girls fascinated with the prospect of becoming 'my ladies.' Bradshaw's girl did last season, if you remember." Mrs. Pendleton nodded.

"Marry an Englishman?" Lizzie hooted. "I'd as soon fly to the moon! They seem to be such a dull breed."

Though the young woman's suitors resembled the Khan's Golden Horde in number and ferocity, Mr. Pendleton admitted ungrudgingly that she quite deserved her admirers. He held his own daughter in great esteem, but it was easy to warm up before Lizzie's high spirits.

Chapter 4

The party above Isolde's room did not end at the same time as the Pendletons' supper. Nor, in fact, did it end after Isolde had undressed, brushed out her hair, read a little poetry by Swinburne, and laid in bed for about an hour.

Finally she rang her bell, and after an even longer wait a stiff, white-haired butler tapped at her door. She opened it slightly, dressed in her lawn nightgown with its puffing bishop's sleeves, and said, "Please give a message to the party above me. Ask them if the fellow singing 'She's Only a Bird in a Gilded Cage' could possibly find a quieter selection, and if they could clink their glasses and roar a little less, please. Tell them the lady below their rooms has just finished a very exhausting journey. Tell them anything, but please make them be a little more quiet."

The butler bowed but did not reply. After a few minutes, the noise did not abate.

She rang her bell again. After waiting for some time, she rang again, more vigorously.

There was a loud knock on the door, and it opened. Mrs. Hurst herself stood on the threshold and said, a trifle red in the face, "'Ere, what's all the bloomin' racket about. This is a 'otel, people are supposed to sleep 'ere."

"I know this is a hotel, Mrs. Hurst," replied Isolde patiently. "And I am trying to get some sleep, but I am a very light sleeper and there seems to be a very loud party going on above me."

"It is loud from in 'ere," Mrs. Hurst acknowledged. "It's a good one too. 'Ere, you lovey, you 'aven't been in England very long, 'ave yer?" and she surveyed Isolde critically. She seemed to approve of her, for she handed her her coat from the wardrobe and said, "Put this on, and I'll go introduce you around. The gentlemen have all 'ad one or two too many, p'raps, but they are gentlemen and you should meet some Englishmen. There's Lord Madwing and Bertie Taunton and a few others. Come along. It's too early for bed anyway."

And before Isolde could protest, Mrs. Hurst had bundled her into her coat and taken her up a flight of stairs. The room was filled with men and women who seemed decidedly more at ease than Isolde was used to seeing at parties in New York, and she could not help wondering if they were not all drunk.

"Here, Rosa," said one of them, "is this the nice clean tart you promised me?" And he took Isolde in his arms and kissed her. Everyone laughed.

"Now, now, George, this is a very nice girl. She's Stubblefield's niece, you know, the daughter of the one that went to America to find out about gold mines or pantomimes or some twaddle like that and married over there. 'Ere, you Bertie, pour the young lady a glass. You've been keeping her awake all night with your noise. You owe her one." And then Mrs. Hurst moved on to the other side of the room, leaving Isolde still standing in her coat over her nightgown, but near enough to the door to make an escape at the right moment.

A cheerful young man tottered toward her carrying a glass full of champagne. "Here you are, is it Miss Stubblefield?" he asked, handing her the glass.

"No, it isn't," she said frankly. "I never heard of the Stubblefields."

"Oh, that's very like Rosa. She never forgets a name but she often mixes them up."

"And I don't drink champagne. At least I don't think I do." She took a taste.

Bert eyed her suspiciously, and after a quick summing up look, he said, "I believe you are a young lady. A very young lady."

"Not horribly young."

"But not married, I mean."

"No."

"Then what are you doing at a party like this?"

Feeling as if she were swimming in troubled waters, she took another sip and said, "Mrs. Hurst brought me, remember? But she doesn't know who I am."

Bertie reflected on this information for some moments and then said, "But who are you?"

"Oh, just an American young lady."

"Are you really?" Bert asked eagerly. "Because if you are an American, you can tell me about other Americans, can't you? It would explain why you're here, wouldn't it? American women can do anything, can't they?"

Isolde, if not fond of actually lying, was never averse to leading people on. Such a chance encounter could be of no importance; she might as well enjoy herself to the fullest.

"Almost," she replied cheerfully. Champagne had an unpleasant taste, but one could ignore that.

"But I notice you don't have a mustache."

Somewhat taken aback, she agreed.

"Then American girls don't always have mustaches! I thought Thornie was wrong. It doesn't seem natural, does it?" Pondering this thought, he added, "But Thornie said it was the heiresses who had mustaches. Perhaps you are not an heiress?"

"Of course I am an heiress," she responded majestically. "My papa owns most of the state of New York."

"Ah, but what kind of state is New York in?"

Ignoring this, she went on, "Papa is one of the wealthiest men in the United States."

"Does he own a yacht?"

"Of course."

"A private railroad car?"

"Naturally."

"Does it have a marble bathtub?"

"Several."

"His own railroad?"

"Well, no. But his friends lend him theirs."

Bertie digested this thoughtfully. After a moment, he said, "You know, I am to marry an American heiress. At least, Thornie says so. Of course, I don't see how it could come off, but then, Thornie is never wrong."

"Indeed? Perhaps I know the young lady?"

"Perhaps you do. Her name is Miss Wilcox. Do you know if she has a mustache?"

"Miss Wilcox!" exclaimed Isolde, choking somewhat on the last sip of her wine. "No, I don't believe she does. May I know who you are?"

"Oh, I beg your pardon. Please forgive me. If I were sober, of course I would never have forgotten. When I'm sober, my mind is sharp as a razor. Like Thornie's. Never forget a lady's name. So sorry."

"And your name please?" Isolde gently nudged him.

"Oh, yes, my name. I am Albert Taunton, but everyone calls me Bert, you know. Or Bertie. Earl of Toye."

"You are the earl of Toye?"

"That's right. Born that way. Not actually born. M'father died young. Drank himself to death."

"Then you are incredibly rich? Do you have vast

estates and wealth? A private yacht? Your own railroad?"

"No," said Bertie, regretfully. "I have Toye, of course. It's a castle. A very nice castle. And I have my bicycles. But no money, you know. No money at all."

"I see," said Isolde. "How do you get along with no money at all?"

"Oh, Thornie takes care of me. Thornie wants me to marry a rich American girl. He even found one for me. But it won't work. Of course there is the earldom. Thornie says all American girls are interested in titles. Do I look picturesque?"

"Not at all. Who is this Thornie?"

"Thornie says if I would act more like an earl I could snabble up one—like this Miss Wilcox—in a minute. But I don't think that's true, do you?"

"I don't believe any girl would be willing to marry you," Isolde replied firmly.

"Oh, but you're wrong! After all, I have an earldom, and I have Thornie. There are plenty of English girls who are even poorer than I am. Of course, it's nothing like poor Thornie. They crawl over him like maggots on a dead bird."

Turning rather pale, Isolde said, "Who is this Thornie?"

"Maggots," said Bertie dreamily. "Just like maggots. All of them wearing different hats. And some of them are very pretty. Thornie? Haven't you ever heard of Thornie? He's in all the newspapers."

"Not the American ones."

"No," admitted Bert. "I can see that. He's English."

"And who is he?"

"You must feel sorry for Thornie," said Bert, his conversation becoming more and more inappropriate. "Thornie is so rich. He's so handsome. He always knows what to do. He can't help it. That's just the way he is. Women crawl over him like maggots."

"You said that before," Isolde complained indignantly.

"Did I? Well, let me tell you the sad part. He doesn't even like women! Not that there's anything wrong with him. He has plenty of mistresses, but he says they always bore him. Now how could he have mistresses that *always* bore him? One or two, maybe, but always? I can't understand it. I don't think he really likes the modern world. He doesn't believe in the bicycle, you know. The bicycle is going to revolutionize travel in another three years, mark my words. He loathes Americans, particularly American young ladies. Why, I'm giving a house party for this Miss Wilcox I told you about, and he won't even come! And he made all the arrangements, decided whom to invite, and paid for everything! He thinks Americans have no social tone. He thinks I don't have any either, but I'm an earl, of course. He thinks all this stir about bloomers and voting is a lot of pernicious revolutionary socialistic talk, and they should all be deported. Poor, dear Thornie. You can't help but love him."

"I think he sounds rather nasty."

"You wouldn't say that if you really knew him. Of course you never will. How he hates American women! It really is too funny."

Isolde was about to reply when she noticed that Bert's face, which looked toward the door of the ever louder party, had instantly become rigid with horror. Glancing in the direction of his gaze, she saw that a dark-haired gentleman of ordinary height but strong build had just entered. It was the sight of this personage that seemed to cast her earl into such frozen terror.

"Good God!" exclaimed Bert rather squeakily. "That's him! That's Thornie!"

"Ah, then perhaps you will introduce me to him.

Everything you have said has made me very curious," she said easily.

"No, no, you don't understand," Bertie gritted urgently through his teeth. "Just this morning he wondered why we never happened to meet in London. I put him off, of course. But the reason is that I hate to see him when I'm smashed. He has such a withering way about him." Bertie turned his back to his cousin and faced the wall, whispering, "Could you tell me when he is looking the other way? I wish Rosa would put more than one door in her rooms! It's damned annoying."

"I'll divert him for you," Isolde promised.

"Tell me one thing first," Bertie begged. "Do you like my waistcoat? It's been worrying me all day. No one likes my waistcoat. Tuttle positively despises it."

Already far too caught up in Bertie's Mad Tea Party mood, she replied sweetly, "I think your waistcoat is utterly charming. I don't believe I have ever seen one as appealing in America. It almost wins my heart."

"Ah, you are a darling," said Bertie warmly. "I shall remember you. But take my advice and stay away from Thornie. He is very hard on the ladies. Do you know, I knew a young lady, very pretty, rather broke, who thought Thornbrough would make a very good husband for her. Pounds and shillings walking around unattached. Well-bred girl, good parents. She flirted with him, and he flirted back. She was coy, and he went after her. We all thought we were going to lose the dear boy. But just when people were beginning to wonder when the day would be, he went to Paris and lived a happy bachelor life in the big city. A very happy bachelor life. She died, I think. Or married an Irish peer. I can't remember which. So you see, perhaps you had better let me escort you to your rooms. You shouldn't be here at all, you know."

"Nonsense," said Isolde. "I am an American girl, remember, and I often go to men's parties and smoke cigars and play poker. It is considered quite the thing for us heiresses."

"It makes sense," said Bert thoughtfully. "Good way to really know a man. Have one of my cigars? They're not very good."

"Yes, thank you, I will," said Isolde. And parting from the earl of Toye, she glided gently across the room in her long fur coat. It hung open in the warm room, her shapeless white nightgown puffing out in a cloud of fine lawn and lace, her long dark hair hanging down her back, and her pink feet quite barefoot. Such an entrance into London society might have laid her mother low on her bed; even her father would without hesitation have borne her off to still another part of the world and perhaps hired an extra maid to look after her.

Thornbrough was surveying the room from an elegant distance. He had just entered and had not yet made up his mind which group of friends he should join, or indeed, whether he wished to stay at all. Isolde kept her eye on him. It was a talent she had cultivated to a fine art long ago. She swished toward a lamp on a table near his gaze, which could not but be riveted to a young lady attired as she was. With a polished air, she lit her cigar at the flame of the lamp, and straightened up again, a thoughtful gaze in her eye, combined with perhaps a touch of lonely wistfulness. She caught his eye. He bowed reluctantly, and she smiled a sad smile.

"Good evening," he said punctiliously.

"*M'sieur?*" she queried.

"*Est-ce que vous êtes française?*" he asked.

"*Je ne suis pas anglaise.*"

A beautiful young Frenchwoman, seemingly unescorted, must probably be a lady of the night on a tour of duty. Perhaps she had been invited across the Channel with promises of protection by an Englishman who had then left her, or with whom she had battled. She did not look quarrelsome, but women who lived from one man to the next often became tigresses to acquire a little security, such as diamond necklaces. If a sponsor did not yield to these ever-increasing demands, a battle ensued, and the young women began to look for more quarry. Thornie had had plenty of such encounters, but tonight he was not at all averse to acquiring a French mistress for a short period of time. He had very recently broken ties with his current mistress, a music hall girl who had become increasingly jealous and demanding of his time and his purse, and who had begun to reveal a disgusting overfondness for champagne of low quality taken at all hours of the day. Thornbrough also was enjoying the favors of the wife of one of the Prince of Wales's cronies. They met at house parties in the country, where bedrooms were carefully arranged for midnight prowls by the amorous. But she could not always be available to him.

"*Est-ce que vous êtes seule dans cette grande ville?*" he asked with sympathy.

"*Mon Dieu, je suis très malheureuse,*" she replied sadly.

"*Peut-être je peux vous aider?*"

Isolde was trying to think of some way to prolong her joke. Of course she had no intention of going anywhere with this unknown hater of American womanhood, but it seemed a pity that she could not carry the lesson a little further. She was racking her brains, a dreamy expression of warmth on her perfect features, when a young lady charged into the room with Rosa Hurst on her heels.

"You get out right now," Rosa shrieked at the

woman in angry cockney. "This 'ere is a party for
gentlemen. I won't 'ave you in my 'otel."

The young woman was very blond and very fair,
with pink cheeks much rouged. Her eyebrows had
been colored with charcoal, giving them a dark effect
which she in her frenzy had somewhat smeared, giving her something of a look of an outraged owl. She
was dressed in remarkably poor taste and was carrying an enormous muff.

"There he is!" she screamed, pointing to Thornbrough, to Isolde's dismay. Isolde began to button her
coat. "Look, he's found himself a whore already! Oh,
this is a fine hotel you keep, indeed!"

"That's not a whore, that's Stubblefield's niece,"
said Rosa indignantly. "Now you just come downstairs right now, miss, and I'll give you a nice supper
to soothe your nerves. Either that or 'Arry throws you
out."

Thornbrough stood rigid with rage. "I have finished my dealings with you," he said coldly. "You
may go now."

This enraged her more. She pulled a firearm out of
her muff and began to wave it about, shouting, "So
you've taken up with another, have you? And why
not me? Ain't I enough of a lady for you?"

"That's enough," he said sternly. "Put that gun
away."

"I hate you! You're cruel and you're cold!" Thornbrough, enraged, stepped forward to take the gun
from her, but at that she backed against the wall and
leveled it at him. "You deserve to die! Wasn't I
enough of a lady for you?!"

"Be silent!" he shouted, startling her. Inadvertently
she squeezed her trembling fingers on the trigger, and
a loud report was heard. Bert had escaped to the lobby
by this time, but upon hearing gunshots, he thought
he would toddle back up and see what kind of uproar

he might be missing. Thornbrough, after checking himself quickly for a wound, glanced around the room to see where the damage had been done. Everyone stood frozen in place; just like a woman, he thought, to fire a gun off in a crowded room and not manage to hit anyone. All the ladies had screamed, of course, when the gun went off. That was to be expected of women. Then he noticed that the French girl he had just been speaking with was staring in dismay at a steady trickle of blood flowing from her arm to a small red spot growing larger on Rosa's Persian rug.

"Good God!" he exclaimed. Rosa hustled the weeping young woman out of the room, and he strode to Isolde's side. When he was conveniently within range she fainted, landing neatly in his arms. He caught her and easily picked her up, her coat open and her long glossy hair hanging to the floor.

"Room 7," she murmured in his ear. Mr. Thornbrough was not romantic. He was far more annoyed by his gentle burden than tender, but he knew where his obligations lay. After all, the gun had been aimed at him. So he carried the girl to her room, and deposited her in the bed there. It was rather curious that Rosa had let her stay. Rosa smiled brightly on all extramarital affairs between properly married gentlemen and ladies. She had been known to recommend to her friends where they might go to find beauties of the town who were not likely to be diseased. But she did not let rooms to *filles de joie*.

"Let me see how badly you are hurt," he said, removing her coat. She gazed up at him wordlessly, but he paid no heed to her as he searched for her thin, pale arm in its voluminous cloud of sleeve. It seemed odd that the lady was wearing a nightgown; surely, if she had gone to the party looking for an English escort, she would have worn a gown, something low cut, tightly molded, in some flashy color and material.

The white nightgown, edged in a delicate lace and demurely high in the neck, was just what a young girl would wear when her lady's maid put her to bed at night.

He had located the wound, which was just above her elbow, and began to try to stop the bleeding. It was not deep, a scratch several inches long, but it bled more than it should.

"Handkerchiefs?" he asked. *"Mouchoirs?"*

She shook her head and bit her lip, evidently in some pain. He went to a dressing table and began to go through the drawers, hurling objects about. He was busy at this task when the door resounded with a loud tap, and thinking it was Rosa come to lend him aid, he shouted, "Come in!"

Bertie, much sobered from fresh air but stimulated by the excitement, crossed the threshold saying, "You here! Now this is a night of miracles!"

"Are you drunk or sober?" demanded his cousin.

"Ten minutes ago I was drunk. At this moment I am sober."

"Then help me find something to stop the bleeding. She's got a gash on her arm from that damned woman."

"Why don't we ask her?" he said brightly. "Where do you keep your handkerchiefs?"

Isolde merely shook her head, moaning slightly.

There was another knock on the door, but this time the visitor pushed it open without hesitation and surveyed the scene, which was a rather gruesome one. Elizabeth took in the sight in a moment. Her friend Isolde was lying on the bed, apparently in some pain, and two gentlemen were rifling through her possessions. With the authority of a born manager, she demanded, "What has happened to you, Isolde? Who are these people? Have they injured you?"

Triumphantly Bertie found Isolde's four dozen handkerchiefs, neatly folded squares of fine-embroidered lawn tied with pale yellow and blue ribbons. He turned to hand them to Mr. Thornbrough when his gaze fell upon the newest member of the party. His hand remained outstretched, but he was too struck to speak. Thornbrough snatched it from him and began to continue his handiwork on Isolde's arm, swearing as he did so.

"You're lovely!" said Bertie chattily. "Tell me, who are you? Shall we introduce ourselves? My name is Bertie. Are you an American heiress too? If you are her maid, I'd like to further my acquaintance with you."

"You fool, you are drunk," said his cousin, highly annoyed. "This is no time for indecent proposals. Please excuse me, madame, but you may return to your bed. An accident has occurred. If you wish to be of help, you may summon Mrs. Hurst."

"Certainly," said Elizabeth, taking her candle and going down the hall. In her absence, Thornie said angrily, "Now go away, Bert. You are too drunk to be of help here."

"No, I'm not. Besides, I'm here to chaperone you. I can't leave you alone with this young lady."

Isolde, who was by no means highly tolerant of pain, had begun to dislike Mr. Thornbrough thoroughly. As he applied an unpleasant pressure to her arm and began to shred her handkerchiefs, swearing at their flimsiness, he did not bother to speak to her, or even reassure her as a good groom would an injured horse. Her small joke had had painful results. At least she could lie back and enjoy the confusion between the cousins and Mr. Thornbrough's dismay when Elizabeth returned and he was confronted with the failings of his machinations to dispose so easily of Elizabeth and her wealth.

"Oh, go away, Bertie. It's not likely that I'm going to ruin the reputation of a French whore by bandaging her arm."

Bertie widened his eyes. "French whore!" He turned to Isolde and said suspiciously, "I thought you told me you were an American heiress! Were you leading me on?"

"An American heiress!" snorted Thornbrough. "It's not likely. After all, my poor misled cousin, the Americans speak a dialect which closely resembles English. This poor girl only knows French."

"But you're wrong!" said Bert. "I don't speak French."

"I know."

Trying to pursue the mystery, Bert said, "But I talked to her." Mr. Thornbrough paid no attention.

"*Est-ce que vous êtes plus tranquille?*" he said to Isolde.

"*Un peu,*" she replied. Bert listened in amazement.

"I must have been more tipsy than I thought," he said, puzzled. "I had a long conversation with her."

"It must have been very one-sided," said Thornbrough, as the door opened and more ladies arrived.

"All right, Thornie, let's take a look," said Rosa. "Poor thing! And it was all my fault for bringing 'er. Are you much hurt, miss?"

Isolde remained silent, looking very limp and pale on her white pillow, her long wavy hair spread around her. It was an attitude which suited her.

"Just a moment," said Thornbrough. "Who is this young lady?"

"She's Stubblefield's niece," Rosa replied shortly.

"Excuse me, Mrs. Hurst," said Elizabeth firmly. "She is Miss Pendleton, and I am Miss Wilcox. She is traveling with her father, Mr. George Pendleton, and I believe he will be extremely disturbed to find his daughter has suffered an injury while she was a guest at your hotel."

"And right he should be," said Rosa stoutly. "Any dad would feel the same way. I'll make my apologies to him in the morning. And you," she said, turning on Mr. Thornbrough. "You, Thornie, are responsible for that woman charging in here. Lucky for me there wasn't a murder in my house."

"I will make him my apologies in the morning," said Mr. Thornbrough stiffly. "At the same time, I am curious to know why Miss Pendleton, smoking a cigar and wearing, I might add, a nightgown, was at a party being given in the rooms of an unmarried gentleman."

"Did you really smoke a cigar?" asked Elizabeth, amused. Isolde looked wan, but Elizabeth knew she was greatly enjoying the scene being enacted around her bedside. It was just the sort of turmoil she would enjoy creating.

"It tasted horrible," she admitted.

"They do, don't they?" agreed Bert. "I don't think I'll buy that kind again, but I got a lot of them very cheaply."

"You misled me into believing you were a French-woman," Thornbrough said angrily.

"I don't see how," Isolde replied sweetly. "I simply addressed you in French. I thought you were French."

"But your conversation was such that—" He broke off his sentence, trying to remember what she had said.

"I merely said I was unhappy. Mine is a very lonely life. I'm even unhappier now. I don't think I can move my arm." The others were silent, so Isolde heaved a great sigh and went on. "Mine is a search for a kindred soul. While others—like you, Elizabeth, Bertie—can chat happily, I seem to hover on the periphery of life, looking for some kind of inner knowledge of other people, seeking a companion whose dream world shares my visions."

The others were silent. Mr. Thornbrough was taken aback, and Rosa and Bertie fidgeted. It was for Elizabeth to speak up. "That's enough of your nonsense for tonight, Isolde. Should we summon a doctor, Mr. Thornbrough?"

"I don't believe it is necessary," he replied, staring at Isolde as she lay on her bed in a miasma of white nightgown, her dark hair around her and one arm lying on her breast.

Bertie was staring at Elizabeth. "Are you Miss Wilcox?"

"Yes," she replied calmly, ready to shepherd him out.

"Are you the American heiress?"

"Yes."

"I'm happy to make your acquaintance. Are you really coming to Toye, or was Thornie wrong? Or does this change everything?"

"Excuse me," said Elizabeth. "I don't believe we've met."

"How stupid of me! I am the earl of Toye, you know. You know my cousin Mattie!"

"Ah yes! Well, your lordship, you must call on me tomorrow and we will discuss this." Her gaze sweeping the room, she said, "Am I to know that this is Mr. Thornbrough? I believe you have corresponded with my papa."

"Yes, yes, but he isn't coming," said Bertie hurriedly. "To Toye, I mean." Glancing at Isolde and unsure of just how much he had told her about Thornie, he added, "Other business, haven't you, Thornie? Going abroad?"

Mr. Thornbrough could not but admit to himself that the events he had arranged to occur in neat succession—Miss Wilcox's visit to Toye, her acceptance of Bert's proposal, their marriage, and the successful new launching of the Taunton fortunes—had been greatly disarranged by this evening. For one, Miss Wilcox was very pretty, and pretty heiresses, he had found as a general rule, were far more immune to flattery and sudden proposals than ugly ones. Her friend Miss Pendleton, daughter of the George Pendleton who had launched the Poughkeepsie Steel Works, was in all probability just as wealthy. In his eyes her looks were even more striking. Poor Bert had no chance with either one of them.

Still, a week spent at Toye at this moment would not be so unpleasant—for Bert or for him. Miss Pendleton had tricked him tonight—and he was almost certain it was a trick—as few women had in the past. Mr. Thornbrough had been caught in other awkward and even more desperate situations before, however, and had managed to emerge unscathed through the utilization of his supreme tact and even more supremely high opinion of himself. A week of such an ingenious girl as Miss Pendleton would not be tiresome. And perhaps he could arrange, to some small degree, for the turning of tables.

"Not at all," he answered his cousin, as he took Isolde's hand and kissed it. "I must certainly come to Toye, if only to make my apologies to Miss Pendleton." Elizabeth cleared the room, administered laudanum to her friend, and went back to her bedroom. An interesting evening; everything one could have hoped for, considering it was their first night in England.

Chapter 5

Bertie remembered the events of the night before more vividly than was his wont. His friend Madwing had recounted to him the wonderful scene Thornie's music hall girl had made, screaming at him and pointing a gun at him and creating the kind of disturbance Thornie loathed.

Even more vividly, Bertie remembered the two Americans. Unlike Thornie to reverse his plans like that; very odd kind of a girl too, getting herself shot unchaperoned. But her friend! Mattie's comrade! Now there was a girl! He sighed sadly to himself. He must go and call formally at the Swanhome, and by teatime too; but before this was done, he must go and do his duty like a man at Charles Street.

Bertie dreaded visits to his Aunt Honora. She insisted on living in Charles Street, and if the address was good, the house was not. It was falling to bits; there wasn't a comfortable chair in the place except the one she sat in, and no matter how long he stayed he was never offered anything more than tea and thin bread and butter.

When he was a boy, his mother, almost a nonconformist in some of her views and always a woman of high ideals, had quarreled violently with Aunt Honora, and for years he had been spared the sight of her and her relentless prying into his poor schoolboy secrets. She had deplored his lack of stature, adjured him in deep tones to cultivate a more frank, open gaze, and had given him horrible stories to read about poor, starving children that made him have nightmares. If her fund of advice ran short during a visit, she settled back in her chair, her feet, in their thick, ugly boots, placed on an ottoman before her, and while he squirmed in a straight-backed chair, Auntie demanded answers to questions such as, "Have you done anything you can be proud of today, Albert?" or "What was the last act you performed for which you feel shame?"

When his mother died, Aunt Honora descended on him and collected him at once, carrying him away like a triumphant lepidopterist with a butterfly he is eager to put a pin in. She kept him at Charles Street for three dreadful days. She gave him a ring made of his father's and mother's hair intertwined and urged him to pray for his mother's soul, which she assured him was due for a long stay in hell. Children in her house were raised sensibly and simply, with no modern nonsense. They rose early, washed in cold water, enjoyed a breakfast of bread and milk, said prayers, and did lessons before their dinners, which were always very simple since too much food or pudding was bad for children. A nice long walk in the park, then more lessons, a supper of bread and milk, and bed. It was very bad to coddle children, especially little men. They certainly did not need fires, and washing in cold water strengthened their moral characters. Bertie's chilblains had begun to pain him all the time, but then his cousin Thornbrough swooped down on him and carried him off to Eton, where the sixth-form boys seemed like ministering angels.

Holidays were spent at Thorn Manor, so he saw Aunt Honora rarely. He had encountered her only once this season, when she had served him up at an afternoon tea to several of her friends and their daughters, every one of them a mug.

"Well," he comforted himself as he drew the knocker, "at all events I'm of age now. She may be bigger than I am, but I outrank her. And Cousin Thornbrough will be at Toye. He'll manage her. And there's always Tuttle."

The door was opened by an ancient, bird-limbed servant, and he was led through dark hallways crammed with dreary furnishings.

The servant announced him, and he entered Lady Honora's sitting room. Ladies' sitting rooms always made him feel uneasy, but Aunt's made him positively woozy. He mopped his brow and made the mistake of glancing around the room in an attempt to calm himself. Lace curtains, velvet drapes, potted plants, photographs in fretwork frames, silhouettes, handpainted screens, and a number of carved occasional tables topped with vases, bowls, dried flowers under glass, and natural curiosities such as shells met his eye. That part of the wall not concealed by fretwork knickknack shelves, framed sketches of ancient ruins, and a few stuffed birds his aunt had loved in her youth, was covered by a paper of most decorative design of scarlet lilies at least two feet wide. Bertie paused, dazed, and his aunt, enshrined in the midst of this abundance of grandeur, grasped the reins of the conversation.

"You may kiss my cheek, Albert," she said in her deep voice. Shuddering inwardly, he stepped forward and performed the task.

"Now what is the purpose of this visit? I know by now that you have not come out of love for me. I believe your clothing smells of tobacco; is it possible you contaminated yourself with the filthy plant on your way here?"

"I don't smoke," Bertie averred. "Just a cigar now

and then. I've come to ask a favor of you, Aunt.
Cousin Thornbrough and I are thinking of having a
little house party down at Toye Castle, and we would
be honored if you would consent to act as our
hostess."

"A house party!" exclaimed his aunt, staring closely
at him. "At Toye! And in this season! This is a new
start." Her pug began to bark, and Bertie winced.

"Cousin Thornbrough is having a guest from
America, and he thought Toye might be of interest.
Very historic spot, y'know, ghosts and what not."

"If Thornbrough is too ashamed of this guest to allow him to be seen in London during the season, or
even give him access to Thorn Manor, why does he
entertain him at all?"

"It's not him, it's her," said Bertie. "A Miss Wilcox.
The only child of R.R. Wilcox, big manufacturer
and inventor."

Lady Honora smiled an unpleasant smile. "Your
purpose is obvious, then. Or rather your cousin's purpose, because I cannot suppose that you possessed the
acumen to engineer this. I suppose he finally wearied
of paying your debts."

"Oh, I haven't any," said Bertie cheerfully. "Not a
gambling man."

"Your father was known to have dropped five thousand pounds in one night at White's," Lady Honora
said in accusing tones.

"May have. Wouldn't know. Died when I was in
short coats. Never saw five thousand pounds at one
time in my life, m'self."

"You become vulgar."

Bertie was silent. He felt a stiffness settling in over
his faculties, a numbness on his limbs, and wondered
vaguely if a visit to Aunt Honora's salon was akin to
the first stages of rigor mortis. He certainly felt death
creeping over him in stages. Perhaps his debility was

more like that of a small rat fascinated by the quiet, threatening motion of a cobra. Yes, that must be it; Auntie was very like a cobra. He must remember to tell Tuttle, and he settled himself back as best he could into his uncomfortable chair, leaning his head back on its crocheted antimacassar and waiting to be eaten.

"Am I to suppose, since your cousin is sponsoring this affair, that he will also provide the necessities and luxuries required for a party of this nature? Toye Castle, if you do not object to plain speaking, has been decaying for more years than I care to think. It may be picturesque; I am sure it must retain enough grandeur to impress Americans. But I am an old woman and must have my comforts."

Bertie, saddened by the thought of his aunt searching for her luxuries in his own private, drafty, unheated, castle, said, "Quite right. It's Thornie's picnic. He's sending over domestics now and whatever his housekeeper thinks is lacking. Taking care of everything. We just have to come up with the guests."

"When it is known that Thornbrough is sponsoring the party, guests will not be difficult to find, but we would do well to try to keep the party in the family, in case the Americans are overly underbred. My niece Cathleen and my nephew Edwin cannot object to an invitation."

A sickly, whining pair, Bertie thought, but no worse than he had expected. Cathleen was starting her fourth season this year; her parents would never get her off their hands and might as well spare the expense. Edwin was an obnoxious little brat, but it would be easy to avoid him on Toye's thousand acres of grounds. Maybe if he gave him a big enough gun, he would go out and shoot himself. Lord knows, all London would thank him. Letters and telegrams would pour in. Not a popular fellow. But the old lady must have someone to bully, and by all means let it be one of them.

"We can't make it strictly a family party," Bertie said airily. "Americans would be suspicious. Supposed to be a party."

Lady Honora paused.

"Perhaps Major Brooke and his wife?" Bertie suggested. "I don't believe you know them, but they are a rather fun couple. Friends of mine, friends of Martin's. Everyone knows them."

"*I* do not know them."

"True, true, not your set. Don't want to bore Thornie, though, I mean Martin, that is, and it is his party. They probably shouldn't mind too much coming down on short notice at such an odd time."

"Brooke?" his aunt said indignantly. "Who are these Brookes? Have I ever seen them?"

"Knew their mother—at least her mother—old Augusta Brackenridge, didn't you? Might be her grandmother. Might be her aunt. There somewhere, though."

"It is so hard to understand what you are talking about, Albert," said his aunt irritably. "Are they respectable?"

"Oh, they go everywhere. She rides in the park every day. Rides a nice little mare—dappled, too, quite the talk of the town. The mare, that is. Awfully good seat."

"What regiment?"

"Guards."

"Oh, well then," she said agreeably. "And a daughter of August Brackenridge. Not that Lady Brackenridge had any great moral tone, mind you, but her breeding was good. You must furnish me with their direction, and I will send them a note. That will make up a party of eight, four men and four women, quite a sufficient number for intimacy and amusement too. I am well satisfied with the plan."

Bertie could only nod his head. He thought briefly of mentioning the companion to his aunt, but when he considered the manner in which he had met her, he thought he had best take the sanest course and remain silent.

The thought of his aunt ensconced at Toye was very depressing. She would probably poke about and complain a great deal. Perhaps they all would. At least they couldn't complain about it being cold at this season—ah, May at Toye! The hawthorne would be in bloom. What a happy thought! He must remember to buy new tires for his bicycle.

"I hope you are aware, Albert," began his aunt, her tones deepening again to a threateningly low pitch, "of just how much you stand in Cousin Thornbrough's debt. He owes you nothing, nothing at all. You are merely related to him through your mother, his mother being your mother's sister. He has no family obligations to the Tauntons! Why, Edwin is as nearly related to him, and he scarcely takes any notice of him. He has done all for you, educated you, set you up; I have even heard that he gives you an allowance, and now this! It is a great benevolence indeed. You owe him the honor you would accord a father."

"He was very fond of my mother, you know," Bertie said, not without some wariness.

"Indeed! There was no cause for him, a Thornbrough, to feel any inordinate fondness for your mother. I cannot think of any great favors she could bestow on him to earn such gratitude."

Bertie bowed politely and ended his visit quickly, removing himself from the room with as much speed as was courteous. Thornie might be a little pompous, and he was certainly overbearingly old-fashioned, but at least he never pretended to be fashioned of anything but clay.

Chapter 6

Bertie's duties at Charles Street completed, he thought he really ought to run right over to Rosa's and invite the Americans. But it was still early in the day. They would probably be out, chasing about the way Americans always did when they first came to London, looking at St. Paul's Cathedral and places where famous writers had died and doing silly things like that. So there was plenty of time to pop over to his lodgings and see Tuttle and have something to settle his nerves a bit.

"Hello, Tuttle," he shouted cheerily, letting himself in with his own key and leaving his cane by the door. Tuttle appeared from the inner recesses in which he always stowed himself and said, "Good afternoon, your lordship."

"Looking forward to a visit in the country?"

"It does seem an ideal season for it, my lord, inasmuch as you are not an addict to sport."

"Sport! Heavens, no. And that reminds me, be sure to get the things I'll need to fix my bicycle. Maybe we should rent a few for our guests, too, some nice ladies' bicycles. Cheaper than horses. And," he gloated, "I have those six new safety bicycles for my collection. Who knows what I can make with those."

"Indeed, my lord."

Toye Castle was located in the glowing green countryside of Warwickshire. It had admirably withstood almost a century of neglect; even now, with this wretched party in mind, Bertie could not look forward to a visit to it with anything but gladness. As a boy, he had spent very little time in it. His father had preferred the house in Leicestershire, a smaller, more comfortable place built by a Georgian ancestor. And after his father had died, his mother had even more reason to keep household there, since it was located closely to her sister at Thorn Manor. Most of Bertie's time as a very young boy had been spent between the nursery at the big house in London and the nursery at the Leicestershire house; Martin, ten years older than he, had been an object of admiration, but never a companion.

They had made occasional visits to Toye Castle, when they were visiting friends in the neighborhood. He remembered one visit in particular, when he and his mother and a number of friends of hers from the Pre-Raphaelite set she happened to be running with at the time descended on the place. He remembered this visit in part because his father had complained so much about them. "A set of damned lunatics!" he had cried. "Artists! Fellow had the nerve to come into my study and tell me how I should decorate it! Take down a set of hounds and put up some kind of silly 'artistic decoration.' An artist. Deplorable!"

And in part Bertie remembered the visit because all the guests had looked so wonderful. The men all wore long beards and hair, even longer than the whiskers much affected by their less enlightened brethren. Their clothes were brightly colored silks and velvets, appealing much more to Bertie's eyes than the omnipresent pastels worn by fashionable virgins and the black worn by married women.

"Oh, it is a terrible, drafty old place," Bert's mother had warned her young friends on the train. "None of us will be comfortable and we'll all have to eat our soup cold, since the kitchens are miles from the dining room. And I'm afraid I can't begin to explain the plumbing to you."

But they had descended on the old place with enthusiasm. The new wing, which Bertie's great-grandfather had added on in the last century, was deplored by all, but since by great good luck he had been the last Taunton with a penny to call his own, no other harmful improvements had been made. The Pre-Raphaelites, their long medieval curls blowing behind them in the drafts, explained to Bertie the importance of the preservation of ancient buildings in a perfect, unmeddled-with state. They showed the young earl the simple beauties of the place, with its enormous, ancient hallway and grand staircase, unaltered by modern touches. If the bedroom arrangements were a little peculiar and the plumbing almost nonexistent, if the cooking was done over an open spit, if the floors were all stone and icy cold in winter and the snow drifted in through the ill-fitting windows, well, the wood was beautiful, the lines of stone were simple and perfect, and the whole thing, young Bertie was told, must be left just as it was. It was just as well, one of the young men said, that all the fine paintings that had been collected by Bert's ancestors had been taken down from their places on the dining room walls, the good ones to be sold, and the others placed in whatever rooms did not leak too badly. They were not in keeping with the *feel* of a medieval dining hall, he said. And so they went on, happily playing dress-up in silks and velvets, some members of the party sketching others draped in appropriately Arthurian attitudes, and after a weekend or so, they trouped away again, taking an impressed Bertie with them.

All the finer portraits and pieces had been sold, of course, by his father and grandfather, but Bertie never missed them. Martin might deplore their lack; he could remember when the last Rubens was taken down to be sold discreetly, financing some pressing debt and postponing bankruptcy by a degree. Bertie knew little about art; the love he secretly cherished for Toye was fierce and private, but had nothing to do with pride of possession. Bertie, whom his Aunt Honora had once described as appallingly furtive, found that he could always make good an escape from anyone at Toye. Comfort had never been his as a youth; not until he had encountered the admirable Tuttle had he experienced a well-poached egg.

Tuttle was a very practical individual. His father and mother had been respectively a valet and a lady's maid until they had been pensioned off. He abominated the idea of service and intended to stay with Albert, earl of Toye, for as much time as was required to save his passage to America or Australia, where a man might begin again. But each year Tuttle found himself postponing such a break; service with such an earl was not an unpleasant way of life.

He could remember his father describing to him the journeys made by train with his master. His noble master rode first class, of course, and he rode third. At each stop the elder Tuttle jumped from his seat, ran to the first-class car, offered to pour his lordship a cup of hot tea from a Thermos, a glass of wine, or procure for him a biscuit from one of the tins packed in the laden picnic basket. His lordship waved him away, with a "Not now, Tuttle. Later perhaps," and usually went back to sleep.

Things were very different with Lord Albert. They both traveled third class.

Lord Albert's fondness for Toye was beyond Tuttle's understanding. Indeed, Albert's fondness for the old place had been the first surprise which his character had afforded to his cousin Martin. After the tragic train wreck which had killed both their mothers, Martin Thornbrough had tried to go over the problem of his inheritance with the boy as best he could. Mr. Thornbrough, just twenty himself, had explained that there were a great many debts encumbering the Taunton estate. If he could find a means, Toye Castle could be sold and enough funds would be provided by the sale to settle the greater part of the debts that hung over the Leicestershire house. The London house, of course, must be sold, too.

But the boy had looked at him, his fair eyebrows fluttering, and murmured, "Don't want to sell Toye. I don't like Briardale House. I don't care about a house in London, either. But I like Toye."

"I know you must be overcome now, Bertie, but you must think practically."

"I am thinking practically. When I grow up, I shall want to have Toye Castle. It's more fun there. There are ever so many ducks about."

"That may be so," said the youthful Thornbrough with some understanding. "But you can't live in a house just because it has a lot of ducks. And the roof is falling in."

"Well, roofs can be fixed, can't they?" asked Bertie stubbornly. "I'm not like you, Thornie. My papa was not like your papa. It's the ducks that are important, I tell you; and besides, I can ride my bicycle in the halls at Toye. I've thought it all over, and that's what I want."

"Oh, Bertie, you are just a boy," his cousin had admonished him.

"Toye Castle is a perfect example of medieval art, extremely well preserved," said the young Albert pompously. "It will last forever."

Thornbrough had been very properly reared. He subscribed to the correct charities and maintained several estates, conducting his business affairs in a discreet and eminently successful manner, more like a man of thirty-five than a boy of twenty. His very careful father had taught him proper notions of rank and its due, and had left him a sufficient number of secretaries, vice-presidents, and stewards to insure that all would go smoothly until the boy attained his majority. The clockwork ticked admirably, and Martin made no objection to being the focal point of the endeavors of some several thousand people.

Bertie's father had left behind no such clockwork. In fact, the seventh earl had never recovered from the mountain of debts left him by the sixth earl, Bertie's grandfather. Bertie's mother had been very cheerful about living always on the brink of disaster; she and her sister, much more successfully married to a man of substance, went about London breaking windows and throwing pamphlets at visiting dignitaries, demanding their rights as women with the greatest calm and cheer, totally unrelated to their respective economic worth. Martin, carefully ensconced with tutors, governesses, and good schools all chosen by his father, envied his little cousin Bertie, who seemed to live from day to day in the most informal manner possible. He was taken to rallies, fed at odd times of the day, and treated quite like a little puppy. And so, on this day, several weeks after the train crash that deprived Martin and Albert both of mothers—their fathers having died several years earlier—Martin saw Albert as quite a different little beast than most boys his age, such as his wretched cousin Edwin. There were those, in future years, who were to say that Thornbrough was all business, that there was no heart to be won under his black brows, but Bertie was never among their number. But then, few people ever paid much attention to Bertie.

Chapter 7

As soon as the maid had brought Elizabeth her hot water and she had washed her face and hands, she went next door to visit her friend. She knew Isolde well enough by now to have come to the conclusion that she would reveal no secrets in her parents' presence. If Elizabeth wished to discover what had really transpired last night, and what tricks Isolde was up to, she had better surprise her early before she had the chance to manufacture a subterfuge.

"Well, did you like Mr. Thornbrough?" she demanded, as she applied question after question to Isolde, who simply lay lazily in bed, replying with various unsatisfactory and inappropriate comments. Elizabeth believed in dealing with forthright information.

"Mr. Thornbrough? Dearest Elizabeth," said Isolde, stretching, "Mr. Thornbrough is not a likable person. And I am not easily given to the state of liking. Liking is not an emotion that suits me. Certainly not the liking of virtual strangers. Now, of course, there are exceptions. I liked Bertie. A little lacking in grandeur, perhaps, but pleasant in a very fuzzy sort of way. Oh, and dear one, I fear I must warn you. Mr. Thornbrough has made arrangements for him to marry you. I believe the date has been chosen. Toye Castle requires some immediate repair."

Elizabeth took this news with equanimity. "I shall

murder Matilda Taunton when I get back to New York," she said. "She's arranged this whole thing, I know. Well, we won't make a fuss about it. Believe it or not, Isolde, but wherever I go, someone always has a brother or a son or a nephew or a favorite godson they think it would be very nice if I happened to fall in love with and marry. Don't you have this problem?"

"Dearest Elizabeth," cooed Isolde, "quite the contrary. People are getting to be actually reluctant about introducing me to their young men. Especially if the young men are remarkably handsome and have that innocent, wide-eyed charm I find so appealing in youths."

Elizabeth stared thoughtfully at her friend, whose features were warmed by a small, dreamy smile. "Isolde, I don't believe you are a proper young lady."

"Ah," replied Isolde. "And what is a proper young lady? I'm not like you, Elizabeth. I wish I were. What a jolly time you always seem to be having! Marching in noisy parades and giving speeches to crowds of angry women and grappling in masculine company with the mysteries of money and its strange and curious ways. You're such a modern woman, Elizabeth. I am in true awe of you."

"You're ridiculous," said Elizabeth. "You're not in awe of anyone, or anything either, are you? Just what are your intentions for the next few weeks? Are you going to remain in London with your parents or come to Toye with me?"

"I don't know why I should come to Toye," complained Isolde. "I'm rather tired this morning. It is very exhausting being shot by people's mistresses. I think it was too much excitement for me."

"I notice the roses. An apology from Mr. Thornbrough?"

"Yes. A blossom for each drop of blood I shed for him."

"I think you were cheated then. The ratio looks more like ten to one to me. Surely you shed more than two dozen drops of blood?"

"I was speaking metaphorically. I have a poetic soul."

"You *are* a difficult child. Now, once more, are you coming to Toye? If you have *ennui* this morning, think how dull you'll be when I am gone, and your mother will drag you to all the shops in London. Or to make calls. Or do you like shopping?"

Isolde shuddered.

"And if you come to Toye with me," said Elizabeth, "you will be able to pursue your acquaintance with Mr. Thornbrough."

"Or his with me."

"True. Was your papa annoyed that you had been shot while under his escort?"

"Yes, but not with Mr. Thornbrough. For some reason, everything that goes wrong in my life is blamed on me. How could I help it? I didn't even know the woman was armed. And yet, Papa insists that I should know better than to go to such parties where domestic—or postdomestic—quarrels will be featured as entertainment. I tried to explain that I had been dragged there unwillingly, but no! I should have known better! You might have thought he would at least have been a little angry with Rosa Hurst, but he is too fond of her cooking. Tell me, my dear, while we are both being so frank with each other, what did you think of the young and attractive earl?"

But Elizabeth had no estimations to share with Isolde; she had seen too little of him in the chaos of the previous evening. It was not until he made his afternoon call that day to invite her formally for a visit that she discovered Bertie brought a little chaos with him wherever he went.

Bertie did not feel at all strong that afternoon. When Miss Wilcox joined him in the lobby of the Swanhome, he was tempted to turn right around and go out of the room again, canceling all plans and disappearing to an out-of-the-way place, such as Bloomsbury or Afghanistan, until everything blew over. But Rosa made introductions, unnecessarily, and smoothed things over in her own rough way.

"And 'e's a very nice young man," Rosa reassured Miss Wilcox, who smiled and bowed politely. "That can't be said about every young man on the town. Now I won't 'ave 'is cousin in the 'ouse. No, not Thornie, Bertie, I didn't mean Thornie—although 'e *is* too thorny for my taste, never relaxes, always the great man—but the other one, that little Edwin. Edwin," she said, warming to her subject, "is about as welcome 'ere as a runny nose in January, even though I can squeeze his bill out of 'im, something that's very difficult to try on our Bertie."

Bert writhed. Mrs. Hurst went on and on. Miss Wilcox was absurdly lovely. The whole thing was ridiculous. Eyes that color of blue, a figure like that, and all that money too! It was absurd. And Thornie expected him, Bertie, to take this beauty up to a moldy castle in a wet part of England and win her love in three days' time.

"Your lordship," Miss Wilcox was saying, "excuse me, but I'm not at all sure what I should call you."

"Call me Bertie," Bertie begged. "Everyone does. I really hate being called your lordship. The boys used to do it at school to tease me; m'father died when I was young, you see."

"Well, Bertie, I should love to come to Toye this week, but I am traveling with the Pendletons—I believe you met Isolde last night—and I would hate to leave them."

"Have them too!" Bertie said desperately. "You really must come! And Thornie told me most particularly to include Miss Pendleton in the invitation just this morning. Sent a note to my lodgings. Rosa, tell her to come to Toye Castle. It is so nice there in spring. No one ever visits me, either. You may not like that, though. I'm afraid it's a very inconvenient kind of place. I know you Americans like your conveniences. So clever and all."

" 'Ere, Bertie, have a cup of tea," Rosa said sympathetically. "Listen, miss, Bertie's not used to women. Doesn't go to tea parties, not the sort. 'E's a nice boy, like I said. Give 'im a chance."

"The Brookes will be there," he urged. "You'll like them. There are two of them, husband and wife, you know, very good fellows. And Thornie. He'll be prime minister some day. And my cousins Edwin and Cathleen. No avoiding them, they are nasty." He added in gloomy tones, "Aunt Honora. I couldn't help it. Had to be someone, and all the others are dead."

"Your lordship," said Miss Wilcox in a cool tone that belied her inner desire to double over with private mirth, "I should be honored to come to Toye Castle. Shall we say the end of the week?"

"Ah, yes, let's," agreed Bertie. She rose, and he stood up. There was an awkward moment; he would have liked to have shaken hands with her, but she didn't offer hers.

"Hope Miss Pendleton is better," Bertie said forgetfully.

"Yes, there is quite nothing wrong with her today," said Miss Wilcox. And she passed out of the room, her train following regally behind her. "Isn't life interesting?" she thought to herself with some satisfaction.

Bertie sat down again, somewhat breathlessly. Rosa regarded him with a practiced eye and said, "I don't know where you found her, but you'll never keep her."

"I know," Bertie said glumly.

Chapter 8

Bertie and Tuttle were met at the station nearest Toye Castle by an ancient chaise, the remnant of one of his ancestor's days of glory. It rattled them over the seven miles to Toye through Toye Village. Bertie always tried to look the other way as they rode past cottages in disrepair, poverty showing in the broken windows covered with oil cloth, rags, and even newspapers to keep the cold and wet out. His cousin's generosity did not extend to maintaining the tenants too. When Bertie was younger, he had sometimes dreamed of going away somewhere, perhaps to South African gold mines or to the west of America and making a fortune, returning in triumph to Toye. He would then set up as a proper lord. He would refurbish all his people's cottages, give a great treat on the lawns of Toye, such as the ones Martin gave his tenants, and he would restore Toye to the grandeur it enjoyed in past centuries.

But it was a dream. Land was worth nothing, and farming was ruined in England forever by colonial imports—wheat from America and lamb from Australia. Martin's notion was a good one, but now that Bertie had actually seen Miss Wilcox, he knew that he was pitching his hat at the moon.

The coach turned up the avenue to Toye Castle. On some estates fine old oaks, yews, and hardwoods were felled for the high price their wood brought on the market. Owners of estates with incomes similar to his, but lacking providential cousins, after having sold the plate, the pictures, and the good furniture, were known to bargain for a little more time by reducing century-old trees to lumber. But not at Toye; Martin's allowance did not extend to providing succor for improvident cottagers, but Bertie did not actually cannibalize the place to pay the taxes.

The chaise stopped before the entrance of Toye. The drawbridge had long ago been removed, and the moat filled in, but Bertie always felt as if they were both still there. He could step out of his carriage, amble up the bridge, and raise the draw at any time to shut out his enemies. He hopped nimbly out and stood surveying his ancestral home.

Its gray stone was unchanged as always. It had been there for so long, it seemed almost to grow out of the earth, as if some glacier had come and left it in the course of the last ice age. The grounds were all a wilderness, of course, but Martin's men had scythed the tallest grass, leaving fields of green lawn surrounding the castle, which were now beginning to be speckled by the pastel shades of spring wildflowers. The air smelled clean, very different from London's lung-choking smokiness. Bertie was satisfied. He was home.

The door was flung open by a butler liveried in an exquisite black frock coat, both tasteful and regal at once, and he was flanked on both sides by footmen attired in the gorgeous Thornbrough blue-and-gold livery. Bertie winced.

"Good afternoon, my lord," said Windmore, the butler. "Tea will be prepared immediately and served in your library, if you desire."

"Quite all right, quite all right," Bertie mumbled. "Let Tuttle do it. He knows what kind of tea I like. And he must serve it to me."

Windmore and the footmen exchanged glances. Mr.

Thornbrough had informed his secretary that he must send down a few footmen and housemaids, as well as his own butler Windmore and his cook to look after things.

Windmore had heard rumors about the earl of Toye. He suspected that he was one of these modern mashers, a care for nobody. He had the look of it. His clothes lacked the formal certainty his more prosperous cousin achieved.

Everyone on the staff felt very curious about the earl. When Mr. Thornbrough's highly respectful secretary had asked whether a valet should be hired for the occasion, Mr. Thornbrough had shrugged and said, "Oh, my cousin has his Tuttle."

"A groom of the chambers?"

"Oh, Tuttle answers for everything to my cousin," Mr. Thornbrough said carelessly. "And don't choose young men too high in the instep. He may insist that they ride bicycles up and down the corridors with him."

Windmore deplored such an attitude and viewed Tuttle with contempt. If he were a valet, he should not permit himself to serve on the lower floors. If he were a groom of the chambers, or an under butler, he should under no circumstances attend to his lordship's gear or unpacking. And most importantly, whichever Tuttle thought himself to be, there could only be one butler, and that peak of profession Windmore naturally reserved for himself. Windmore should be the one to sit at the head of the table belowstairs, not an underbred and self-demeaning person named Tuttle. It was Windmore who would command; Tuttle was merely another servant fitting into Windmore's carefully disciplined staff.

When the three footmen and three housemaids, chosen carefully from a horde of applicants by Thornbrough's agent and approved reluctantly by the fastidious Windmore, made the journey by train from London to Toye Castle, they all rejoiced at their good fortune. As they compared their histories, it seemed odd that such an inexperienced group should have been engaged; after puzzling about the matter for some time, two of the housemaids, more diligent than the others in the perusal of the society sheets, began to remember just who the earl of Toye was. He was one of the Bledsoe sisters' sons. A nob, all right, but rather a peculiar one. A bachelor, he had no large establishments staffed by a sufficient number of servants to inform the world of service what manner of man he was.

Perhaps he was an eccentric like his mother. But then, perhaps he was more like his rigidly correct cousin Thornbrough, who seemed to have a hand in conducting his affairs. Perhaps he was quite an ordinary young man, a member of the crutch and toothpick brigade, one of those smart young nothings who strolled Piccadilly armed with smart walking sticks with crutch handles chewing gold-tipped toothpicks. It was likely enough.

So it was with no inordinate degree of awe that the young group arrived at Toye Castle, and when they actually beheld the kitchens, the pantries, and the original staff, they became very puffed up indeed. Even in their previous engagements as tweenies and houseboys, their labors had been undertaken in circumstances far more luxurious than those Toye could afford. A staff of twelve to put to rights a place as big as—well, as big as a castle! It was all very well for that Mrs. Eastman to say that everything would be done before his lordship's arrival, but how could it, work as they did from dawn until candlelight? And candlelight it was, because there were no gas lamps in a place like this.

Pierre, Mr. Thornbrough's French cook, arrived,

took a look at the kitchen, and threw up his hands in disgust. To cook on a veritable open spit! Mrs. Eastman calmed him. "Just wait till his lordship arrives," she said. "His lordship is very easy to please and don't like a lot of bother. This is the perfect time of year for the party. Here we are in the country, just at the tail end of the asparagus and strawberry season, and the new sprouts and veggies will be in any day. Bacon and eggs is what I always serve his lordship when he pops down here, and he likes it well enough."

"I could make a *cassoulet*," Pierre conceded. "As a boy, I used to eat pot-au-feu every night, and the flavor of that simple dish was magnificent."

"Now there you are," Mrs. Eastman agreed encouragingly. "I've heard a lot about French cookery, about how fancy and expensive it is, but I can't believe that everyone in France pays a lot of money to eat well."

"Ah, Mrs. Eastman," said Pierre, his eyes glistening, "you appear to be a woman of intelligence! If the English would only take a little more time!" And he proceeded to tell her some very interesting things one could do with the simplest of ingredients, a few truffles, five-week-old veal, and a few spices.

After Bertie arrived, he spent the evening in his ancestral home apparently in conference with Tuttle. The next day he came down to breakfast looking rather put out. It was a very odd household, but knees still quaked as the new servants, the footmen very proud in their powder and liveries, caught a glimpse of their noble employer. According to the locals, it was quite a comfortable berth. At least Mrs. Eastman and Fielding in the stables seemed to think so; no perks at all to speak of, but in a household with no mistress and no nursery, and not enough money for weekend parties and the hunts which involved vast amounts of labor, Toye did not sound to be a bad place at all. They were all engaged as temporary, but there were rumors that some or all of them might be considered for permanent situations. Already rumor of the American ladies had gotten round. It was said they owned millions of pounds. That was a ridiculous amount, but then, America was a preposterous place. People were said to actually dig gold out of the earth there! Imagine excavating shillings in Wales. Who put the money in the ground in the first place? And why?

The earl ate his soft-boiled eggs without a word behind closed doors with Tuttle. William and James, the footmen, watched with appreciation as Windmore's expression darkened. They knew what Windmore's opinion was of an earl who allowed himself to be served by his valet, but they couldn't blame him for preferring Tuttle's face to Windmore's. Not that Tuttle wasn't an odd sort, very closed-mouthed. But he was pleasant. Not the stiff old goat Windmore was.

At the end of the meal Tuttle threw open the sliding doors of the dining hall and gave orders that his lordship had asked to see all his new employees. They lined up, the footmen on one side, and the women servants, fetched from their tasks of washing and cleaning, wearing their print work gowns and feeling very awkward opposite the grand footmen. Mrs. Eastman headed one line, facing Windmore at the head of the manservants' line. Tuttle hovered about, as if he were not a servant at all, but a guest watching the proceedings from a distance.

Down the row marched Bertie. A tea table had been brought into the hallway, and he pushed it down the row, saying "Ale? Or do you prefer a glass of wine at this hour?" When each had been served, Bertie stood before them and, raising his glass in the air, he said, "I don't know what you've been instructed. I don't ask for much, but I do think that it would be a good idea while you are here at Toye to take a look about you and enjoy yourselves a little. I can't say how long I can keep you, and it would be so dreary if you had to return to London not properly rested. That's all. Drink up! To America!" And with no further explanation, he tossed off his ale. Mrs. Eastman followed his example, and then herded her girls back to the nether regions. Bertie lingered for a moment until they were gone, and then he said in low tones to William and James, "Must you really wear all those clothes? They look awfully hot for this season."

Windmore said icily, "It is customary in Mr. Thornbrough's household for footmen to wear full dress and powder."

"Ah," Bertie smiled, "but even my cousin Thornbrough would concede that this is not his house. He doesn't even particularly like it, you know. Perhaps you haven't thought about it, my dear Windmore, but this is a castle. At least most of it is a castle. It's not a palace or a manor house or a hunting lodge or anything modern, you know. And we don't have footmen in castles. Pages, perhaps, but not footmen. They came later."

Windmore, bewildered for once, could only stare at him. Bertie sighed.

"You see, footmen were invented later, after castles. Not that I don't like footmen," he added hastily. "I don't think there is anything *wrong* with being a footman. But you should be pages. Or churls, but I don't think you would like being churls." Bertie looked at Windmore and sighed again. "What I am getting at is that I don't want powder being worn here. Or wigs or whatever you're doing to make your hair white. I think it's silly. And no fancy dress. Just wear ordinary clothes, like Tuttle's."

James and William were silent. Windmore bowed

and said, "As your lordship wishes. I only hope the young men have something suitable in their wardrobes."

"Oh, well, I'm not fussy," said Bertie. "And don't keep lounging about waiting to open the door for me. It makes me awfully nervous. Why don't you all go for a walk on such a nice day as this? Explore the countryside. It's quite pretty around here. See if Mrs. Eastman can spare any of the girls and make a party of it. I'm really very proud of our spring flowers."

Windmore, feeling as if the ground shook beneath his feet, watched the earl stroll casually off.

"Go for a walk?" said Tuttle. "When the cobwebs in this room are so thick a man could swing from them?"

"Cleaning cobwebs is a maid's work, Mr. Tuttle," said Windmore frostily.

"If either of these young gallants wants to squire a maid about, he had better begin to do a little of her work first. His lordship is right; you might as well go upstairs and get out of these pretty clothes. I hope neither of you gentlemen is allergic to dust. Windmore, you and I must do something about the plate. It seems the oxidation process has taken place sometime in the last twenty years; all the silver is black with tarnish."

Major Frederick Brooke and his wife, Georgette, arrived later that afternoon, a day before Lady Honora was expected.

"Georgie!" Bertie exclaimed, kissing her cheek and taking her outstretched hands. "And Babylon! How kind of you this is. Do you know, Aunt Honora is not even on the grounds yet! Isn't that smashing! We can stay up late tonight and be naughty. I depend on you, dear Georgie, to draw her fire. You must be very modern. You must smoke cigarettes and talk of purple prose."

"Devastated to disoblige, Bertie dear, but I didn't bring any cigarettes with me and the only thing I read is yellow journalism. Dear me, how many shades of reading material may we have these days," said the major's lady, as she divested herself of her light traveling cape. "Hello, Tuttle. I hope you will see to it that there are no ghosts in my wing of the castle. And I do want at least one wing to myself."

"And where will poor Fweddie sleep?" asked Bert.

"Fweddie may come and get in bed with me if he gets frightened," said his wife. "Really, Bert, I had no idea Toye was so beautiful! What a showpiece it could be!"

"I'm awfully fond of it. Shall I give you a tour? Or tea? But no, tell me what's been up in London since I left."

"Oh, Bert," said the major, a tall, slender young man with a preposterous mustache and a lisp, "you know London is always the same. Ten thousand twagedies and ten thousand comedies. But the most wonderful thing has happened! Do you know that wild party that went on at the Swanhome last week sometime? When Thornie's mistress came in and shot Stubblefield's niece? She shouted, 'Ain't I enough of a lady for you?' as she pulled the twigger, or so I'm told. The Variety is now featuring the whole incident done up comically to music, with the chorus 'Ain't I enough of a lady for you' sung by a gwoup of partially clad young ladies. It is wonderful! Is this why Thornie is escaping to Toye? We came to this wetched countwyside—and I am afwaid of owls—to find out what little Bertie has in his bag."

"You might have *warned* us at least," Georgie added. "Think of our astonishment when an invitation—written in her own hand, too!—arrived for us from *Lady Honora Battersbottom*. All about some house party being given by our own Bert—you don't give house parties—and Mr. Martin Thornbrough! After framing the invitation and hanging it next to the picture of my mother over the bed, we began to ask ourselves, what's in the wind? What is Bertie up to? And then London suddenly became rife with rumors, simply rife. Staying with Rosa is better than advertising in the newspapers. I was at the Swanhome night before last, and Rosa told me you were engaged to marry Stubblefield's niece. I didn't know Stubblefield had a niece, so how did you get to meet her?"

"She's not Stubblefield's niece," said Bertie indignantly. "That's the other one, and she isn't either. I'm not up to anything. I have nothing to do with this whole business, and I expect you, Georgie, and you particularly, Fwed, to be very sympathetic and understanding to me. Georgie, you must hold my hand, and Fwed, you must stay up drinking with me all night."

"Is it true then?" asked Georgie. "Is there an heiress?"

"So rich," said Bertie mournfully. "So rich and so beautiful. I never realized before just how indecent the clothes you women wear are. Aunt Honora always told me they were but I didn't listen. And she was right." Georgie and Frederick waited, but Bertie struggled, at a loss for words.

"She wears indecent clothes?" asked Georgie, puzzled. "During the day?"

"No, no, I don't mean that. I mean, there a woman is, with one of those hats on and the hair up and all that, and she's wearing one of those very tightly cut dresses you women are going in for right now. Well, the eye becomes accustomed after a while, but now and then one meets a woman who seems to make it all come fresh again . . . And then you think, my

God, if she can look like that *in* clothes . . . oh, never mind," he ended hopelessly.

"Sounds like a wegular beauty to me," said Fweddie, impressed. "And this girl is coming here?"

"This girl! My god, there are two of them! The heiress has a friend."

"You seem distwessed," Fwed said. "Ought you not to wejoice? They are in your clutches."

As Bertie was about to protest, the door was opened, and Tuttle escorted Mr. Edwin Battersbottom into the room, planting him firmly by Bertie's side.

"I am conducting Lady Battersbottom and Miss Battersbottom to their chambers," said Tuttle.

The major groaned loudly; Georgie moved away from the pimply youth a bit; and Bertie appeared resigned.

"Beasts!" Mr. Battersbottom began by way of introduction. "But Auntie has told me what's afoot, and I mean to have a touch at the heiresses, too."

Cathleen and Edwin had not been overjoyed when their aunt informed them they were about to receive a holiday in the country. Cathleen almost wept when she discovered who was to be at the party. "But Aunt, Cousin Martin and Cousin Albert aren't even polite to me! Cousin Martin only bows to me if he chances to see me on the street, and once Cousin Albert cut me on Regent Street."

"He was probably in a stupor," her aunt replied regally.

"And the Brookes are friends of Cousin Albert's! Please let me invite Agatha Wythy, or Constance Murdock, just to keep me company!"

"Absolutely not! Company, indeed! You are very lucky, young woman, to be invited out anywhere. The party may be small, but a woman with *charm*," and here Lady Honora's tone deepened into scorn, "can find amusing companions in any circle."

"Bert is a bully," Edwin struck in. He was about to expand on his point when his aunt turned toward him and regarded him with piercing black eyes.

"*Albert Taunton a bully*," she repeated incredulously. "Did you say that *Albert Taunton was a bully?* Did you?"

"Yes," Edwin whimpered.

"You are a toad indeed," said Lady Honora. "A bully! A jack-straw promenader! A modernity! Next you will be telling me that your nurse gives you nasty warm milk with a skin on it. I am all out of patience with you."

Edwin and Cathleen both squirmed.

"At Toye Castle will be two of the wealthiest women in the world, I fancy. Young and unmarried. Naturally, Thornbrough hopes a satisfactory arrangement can be made between one of them and one of our family. I need not tell you he favors Taunton; he always has, for some absurd reason. But I act as chaperon to the family, and I will see to it that you, Edwin, shall act your part, if you can, like a man."

And so the young Battersbottoms were packed and bundled off to the countryside. Cathleen had two new gowns, the first she had been allowed in the season. Her mother was not at all pleased with her since she had allowed her last hope, Lord Skipshup, to slip through her fingers. He had been extremely eligible for her, being not more than sixty and still possessing most of his teeth and a large portion of his faculties. Cathleen was a great disappointment to her family. Some genteel occupation must be found for her. Perhaps she could become a companion, or even a secretary, to a well-born woman of wealth. Marriage seemed hopeless, and she would be penniless when her parents died.

The castle itself seemed to be a very odd place. Aunt Honora was greatly displeased with the rooms she was given. The bed was unspeakably poor, the windows small, and the hangings very shabby indeed. Mrs. Eastman smiled at all criticism.

"I need not tell my lady that the place hasn't been kept up as it should or for what reason. But Mr. Thornbrough will be here tomorrow; perhaps you would prefer to discuss the matter with him? I'm afraid his lordship doesn't quite understand these things."

"Indeed," said Aunt Honora. "I must try to take some rest after that exhausting journey, so you may run along, Cathleen, and find the others. Tell Albert his domestic arrangements are deplorable."

Mrs. Eastman smiled and bowed herself out. Cathleen followed her. "She is like that to everyone," she said awkwardly to Mrs. Eastman. "You mustn't mind her, but you'll have to get used to it. She is not very prone to, well, overindulge in praise."

"I see that," said Mrs. Eastman dryly. "And what about you, Miss Battersbottom? Would you care to rest before tea?"

"Oh, no!" said the young lady. "But can I watch tea being made? I mean grilling the muffins and that, you know. They never let me watch at home anymore."

Startled, Mrs. Eastman looked at the young lady from the corner of her eye. Miss Battersbottom had the same pale complexion as her brother. Too pale, almost washed out, with very light blue eyes. But her skin was clear and her eyes brighter. She was plain, but not unpleasant. Like her turnip of a brother.

"Indeed?" Mrs. Eastman said.

"Can I meet your cook?" Cathleen went on timidly. "I know how to make muffins and scones, if you'll let me try and not mind mistakes."

"I'm afraid our kitchen is a bit plain, miss," said Mrs. Eastman. "But I'll be glad to take you downstairs and introduce you to Pierre. And if you'll excuse me, he ain't prone to overindulging in praise either, as you call it. Pierre can be very sharp."

Windmore had promised William and James that when Mr. Thornbrough arrived they would be ordered to refurbish themselves in their cast-off grandeur. "I am not employed by the earl, and I cannot explain his fancies. Mr. Thornbrough, however, is not a modern," Windmore said, intoning the last word rather harshly. "Things are run according to rules in his establishment." Tuttle yielded the head of the table belowstairs to him without question, but Windmore wanted the whole pie. He knew that Tuttle's orders were obeyed, not his. None of it was right. None at all.

But Mr. Thornbrough disappointed him. "Hello, Windmore, hello, Tuttle," he said, as he entered the grand hall. Two days of cleaning had removed most of the surface dust, and the rest, Tuttle hoped privately, would be put down to aging.

Windmore had hoped that Mr. Thornbrough would immediately seize up the situation as it was. That the footmen had been ordered to strip off their noble regalia and take up degrading work; that he, Windmore, was ordered to work side by side with a valet; and that this was not a proper house for a gentleman to entertain in.

But Mr. Thornbrough merely said, "Ah, I can hear my cousin. Are the Brookes down yet?"

"They arrived several days ago," said Tuttle, taking Mr. Thornbrough's hat. "The party is out in the garden now. Chairs have been set out there; I believe tea will be served soon."

"How delightful," said Mr. Thornbrough

pleasantly. He strolled over the flagged stone floors of the hallway down a corridor that led to a door which opened out into the garden. Windmore escorted him, but he paid little heed to the aggrieved mien of that servitor.

"Ah, Bertie," he said, entering the garden. It was quite lovely. A plot of spring flowers, hastily purchased and planted by the gardener at Thornbrough's orders, furnished the background for a small group of people, their chairs drawn together. "And Georgie, my dear, how are you," he said, kissing her on the cheek. "Frederick. And what have you done with the rest of my relations? I know I sent them down to you."

"They arrived safely enough," said Georgie. "But dearest Martin, I'm afraid your Aunt Honora does not care for Toye at all. She says very rude things about it and hurts poor Bertie's feelings terribly."

"What we all want to know," said Frederick, "is that if you have an aunt such as this, why display her? You must know that I am a man of weally little pwejudice. Show me a cwipple, and I will say, 'Poor man, he just can't walk.' Show me a blind man, and I will say—well, something kind. But show me a man who has an aunt like Lady Battersbottom, and I will say, hmm, weally now, some things are not wefered to in public."

"Well, I have to admit, she is my aunt too," said Bertie. "Oh, Martin, you must see the younger Battersbottoms. Quite a change has come over them."

"Indeed?" said Martin.

"Yes," said Frederick. "We dwowned him and mawwied her to the cook."

"In just two days? My, you have been busy."

"Oh, and it's been fun too," said Georgie.

"I notice that my poor Windmore is now tottering on the brink of retirement."

"Give us a few more days," promised Bertie. "Right over the edge. You can settle a little pension on him, send him off to live with his niece, and start afresh with someone a little more fun. Tuttle has a brother."

"I also notice that the footmen are wearing very odd clothing."

"Aren't they, though?" said Bertie. "I've been noticing it myself. You should have seen what they put on first. Fancy dress. Powdered hair and all that. Isn't it amazing? To work in a country house in May. And they're both in love, one with Mrs. Eastman, of all people, and the other with one of the maids."

"How idyllic," said Martin. "Any news of the Americans?"

Bertie's face saddened. "Have you seen those girls?"

"You know I have," said Thornbrough, irritated.

"Yes, tell us a little more about them," urged Fweddie impishly. "We have been heawing so many intewesting stories in town. Bert seems to be in love with one of them alweady."

"Oh, hush," Bertie said indignantly.

"It turns out, dear boy, that either young lady is eminently suitable," said his cousin smoothly. "Miss Pendleton is the only daughter of Mr. Wilcox's partner, so she is a considerable heiress as well. However, she seems to have some reputation as a flirt. Miss Wilcox, on the other hand, appears to be a firebrand who would probably put your name on the front page of the papers with various socialistic causes she interferes with."

"How did you think Cousin Mattie met her if it hadn't been at some hired hall, giving speeches to shop girls? And my mother was a firebrand, Thornie, and so was yours, so don't be so unbearably righteous."

Mr. Thornbrough's eyebrow lifted in surprise, and

he glanced around the company. The silence which followed Bert's outbreak only upset him more and he added, "Oh, hang it all, Martin. You lure this poor girl down here on some trumped up story and then sit about and make unpleasant remarks about her reputation. What . . . what a philistine you are." And he stormed out into the park.

"Dear me," said Mr. Thornbrough. "Does Bertie know what a philistine is?"

"I don't think so," said Frederick. "He didn't learn it from me, at any wate. What is one? He's in love, you see."

"Oh, hang Bert," said Martin cheerfully.

Chapter 9

After much discussion and debate, Mr. and Mrs. Pendleton admitted that they would prefer to stay in London rather than go out into the countryside.

"This Lady Battersbottom will be there to chaperon the affair, so I know you won't need me, dear children," said Mrs. Pendleton. "And your father, I hate to admit, has become addicted to English music halls, a form of comedy to which I would prefer you, Isolde, not be exposed. So you children run off to the country and go on picnics and get lots of fresh air, and I hope in a week or so your father will have recovered himself."

So with a great deal of fussing Isolde and Elizabeth and their dozen or so trunks were packed up and sent on the train to Toye Castle, along with picnic hampers from Fortnum & Mason, newly purchased umbrellas, a number of periodicals and novels, Scottish lap robes in a popular tartan, and one French maid to share between them.

They enjoyed a long talk on the train down. The new city had enchanted them both, but in very different ways. They had done much ordinary sightseeing, seen the Tower, gone shopping, and watched the changing of the Guards.

But in the crowded hours, Elizabeth had found the time to take a hansom to the Young Women's Christian Association in the notorious East End, more noted for its squalor and filth than its appeal to American tourists. She had tried to communicate to Isolde some of her contempt for a nation that would allow such an enormous segment of its people to live in total degradation. Isolde had sympathized. She nodded and listened. She readily agreed that hungry children should be fed and the cold should be clothed. But when Elizabeth began to explain to her about the importance of modern sewerage, her mind began to wander.

As a serious joke Elizabeth's papa called her his conscience. She had the same forceful character as he, the same ability to see things as they are and know she could change them to become more as she wanted them to be. Isolde was more aware of this strength in her friend than Elizabeth was herself; Elizabeth thought it was merely callousness and cruelty that kept things in their present state, failing to understand that few people possessed her imagination and energy. Isolde noted this and admired it a great deal, especially because she had no such power herself or any desire to acquire it. She found her own life to be rather dull, a simple routine, a blank canvas. What Isolde wanted most was to enjoy other people's lives or a taste of them. Elizabeth explained to her the rigorous anguish of working long hours in a shop, standing on one's feet all day, waiting on customers, being underpaid, underfed, and having no hope that such a life would improve. Isolde sympathized, but secretly she wondered what such a life would really be like. She would like to try it. For a night, a week, or a year. Perhaps just one evening spent as a barmaid in one of those crowded, darkened East End pubs. Thornbrough had thought her a French whore. It would be an interesting experience.

Lady Battersbottom made a formal call on them to invite them to Toye Castle, managing, at the same time, to impress upon them just how much honor she was bestowing upon them. Elizabeth and Isolde were inured to such snobbery; Mrs. William Backhouse Astor had looked upon their entry into New York society with even more haughtiness. Mrs. Astor tried to make it clear to them and their parents that new money was not socially acceptable into her set, which was the only set of importance. But their papas considered their money to be just as good as Mr. Astor's, possibly even better; the Pendleton and Wilcox fortunes had their beginnings in innovations in the making of metals. The first Astor had sold whiskey illegally to the Indians and the family still based its fortunes on vast real estate holdings in New York City, buildings that could only be described as slum tenements. So the Pendletons and Wilcoxes had gone their own cheerful way, giving their own parties, and soon Mrs. Astor found that her own sons, nephews, and daughters were begging her to include them.

So Lady Battersbottom was free to scorn them; they didn't care. They found her to be an appallingly villainous old woman, complaining about servants and the ingratitude of the poor. Elizabeth found her viciously selfish and began to understand the strength of the socialistic movement in England.

Isolde disliked her, too, but for a different reason. She could find nothing in Lady Battersbottom of remote interest, no incident or element of her life she might wish to base a daydream on, no quirk to emulate. To her, Lady Battersbottom represented all that was undesirable, but her reasons were far different from the practical Elizabeth's. Lady Battersbottom was a stuffy old bore.

"There she is," said Elizabeth, "that awful woman, actually believing that she has her place and that some poor baby born today in the slums deserves his miserable lot. And should be kept there. No, I'm not sure I'm going to like the English."

"They are going to be determined to like you," said Isolde.

"I know. Ah, the joys of wealth! At least the earl is nothing like his aunt. Such a confused individual! Well, perhaps we won't have to stay more than a few days."

"You may very well like it," said Isolde. "Just think! A castle!"

"It's probably not a castle at all," said Elizabeth. "They probably just call it that. I wouldn't be a bit surprised if it were just a country house with perhaps a tiny little bit of castle left somewhere on the grounds."

Elizabeth was proven wrong. If Bertie spent his bumpy ride from the station to Toye in quiet contemplation of the disaster to come, if his aunt spent her time in annoyance at the unworthy vehicle placed at her disposal, the American girls admired everything from the beginning of their journey to the end. Neither was at all accustomed to the country; when Elizabeth vacationed in the summer, it was at Newport, the delicious summer resort exclusive to members of New York's four hundred.

Mrs. Pendleton often bemoaned the fact that she had not taken Isolde out of town that summer, but when all of her friends fled to the seashore and to Newport, she could not bring herself to follow them. Isolde had loathed bathing in icy salt water on rocky shores as a child and did not beg for a change, and Mr. Pendleton did not care for the long journey into town every week, so they spent a great deal of their year in the city, making only a few visits to the houses of friends during the hottest part of the year.

Here everything was green and beautiful. There seemed to be no wilderness, but rather a countryside

all planned out as if all Warwickshire were a formal
garden. Hawthorne bushes wearing white buds bor-
dered the roads and marked off farmland, instead of
the rows and rows of ugly, cheap wire and wooden
fences they were accustomed to seeing in America.
The road turned here and there like an old river in
its ancient riverbed, worn into a meandering shape.

As they passed through the village, it seemed as if
the cottages could not be airtight or watertight. Yet,
how pretty they were! By the time they reached Toye,
Isolde was almost spellbound. They passed under the
long avenue of trees, thick and gnarled, which ran
through flowing green park.

The gardens of Toye were in a sad state. A few
plants had hurriedly been put down, but the roses
were long neglected. The kitchen gardens, with so
few mouths to feed, were not as large as they had
been; the herb gardens were almost gone. But all
along the west wall of the gray stone castle bloomed
hundreds of daffodil bulbs, which Bertie's mother,
acting on a whim, had had planted. They had grown
and multiplied, coming up each year, and they were
out now, the last of them.

As the American girls drew up before Toye, they
saw the creeper-cloaked gray walls of a castle as Arthurian as legend could make it, set atop the green of
the park almost as if it had grown up out of the
earth, made by nature, not man. The journey had
been a long one and night was coming on, enshroud-
ing the castle in fog. Perhaps eyes older than Miss
Pendleton's and Miss Wilcox's would have shuddered
at the castle's prospective dampness; to them the
place seemed ethereal, as if they were suddenly entering a world of mists.

They were met at the door by Tuttle. He had not
yet met either one of them, although he had heard
his master's ravings, and he was rather impressed.

"The others have all gone up to dress for dinner," he lied easily, knowing that Bertie was fast asleep after a late evening the night before and that he never changed his clothes for supper. "I shall have some hot water brought up to your rooms. Dinner will be served in about an hour or when you are ready. Dress," he added, "is very informal."

There had been something of a row over this the previous evening. Lady Honora had said she was disgusted to see Bertie's belted hunting jacket at the dinner table.

"But now I'm a belted earl," Bertie had joked. Various members of the company had snorted into their soup, and even Martin, attired with propriety in a frock coat, had looked amused.

"You are disposed to be jocular," said his aunt heavily. "But I must inform you that you present a very peculiar appearance to a woman of taste. Your physique is not such that a woman could be immediately attracted to you, your mind seems to be full of nothing but brandy fumes, and yet you choose to wear clothing that reflects your impoverished income. I cannot think this is wise."

"Dear Aunt Honora," said Martin, "please don't insult Bertie at the dinner table. It quite upsets my digestion."

Cathleen and Edwin exchanged amazed glances. They had never heard their aunt spoken to in this manner, and keeping their eyes on their plates so as not to draw her fire, they finished eating as silently as they could.

Now all were eager to catch a glimpse of the American girls; the news soon spread throughout the house that they, with an inordinate number of trunks, had arrived.

"Really, Fwed," said Georgie, as she was changing her dress, "it does seem unfair that I should be put to shame by these American beauties. You know how Americans always dress; I'm sure they can buy anything they want, and we shall soon be so poor I will have to purchase my clothes ready-made. All the dressmakers have begun to realize that they are never going to be paid."

"Poor deawie," said her husband, kissing her cheek, "you always look nice in what you wear."

"Well, of course I look nice, Frederick. But I don't want to look nice. I want to look ravishing. Do hurry up. I want to watch them descend the grand staircase."

All the company was gathered about in the grand hallway for this event. Bertie, appropriately attired in a frock coat, was nervously waiting, while his cousin Martin, looking bored, lounged up against a wall. Lady Honora, unmoved by the advent of persons from America, sat in a wing chair, ordering Cathleen to fetch her a succession of lap robes and improving books, while she complained about the drafts, the food, and the service.

Isolde and Elizabeth made their entrance. Martin thought them rather overdressed for a country visit, especially Elizabeth, whose dress was certainly much flounced and covered with lace. There was no denying that her dress fit her to elegant perfection, and also no denying that Bertie's eyes were dazzled by the wearer. He seemed stunned.

Martin's eyes went with more curiosity than admiration to Isolde. When he had seen her last, she was lying in a much undressed state. If Martin felt any emotion toward her, it was annoyance that she had been the cause, however innocently, of creating an incident extremely embarrassing to him. The song being hummed in London about "Lord Prickly and the Gel Who Ain't Enough of a Lady" displeased him greatly. A hundred years ago, he might simply have shot the author; today he could not even sue, had he wished to.

But Isolde, as she moved gracefully across the room toward them, wearing a gown much simpler than her friend's, and to his eye, much more elegant, was indeed pretty. Perhaps even a beauty. On the whole, Martin was quite pleased with Cousin Mattie. If Albert did manage to capture the heart of one of the young ladies, he would be set for life.

Introductions were made, and then dinner was served by Windmore, who was beginning to look rather the worse for wear.

Lady Honora was not inclined to be amiable, and Bert seemed too nervous for speech, so Martin, who had been placed next to Miss Pendleton, engaged her in conversation and Major Brooke, on Miss Wilcox's right, inquired about their journey. The conversation soon became general.

"How did you come to know Mattie Taunton?" asked Georgie somewhat underhandedly, since she knew very well the likely answer.

"She is very much involved in women's emancipation, you know," answered Elizabeth casually. "I believe we discussed the subject at some party or another in New York and found our views to be similar."

"Really?" said Edwin. "When she's in London she goes about pitching bricks through windows and being incarcerated."

"I think she mentioned that," said Elizabeth. "In fact, jumping bail must explain why she is in America. The women here certainly need her works more than their sisters in America. Englishmen seem to have their way in everything—the home, the shop and Parliament."

"My dear Miss Wilcox," said Lady Honora, "you are new in this country, so perhaps you will not object to receiving a piece of advice. In this country it is not customary to embark on discussions at the dinner table which will solve nothing but merely create bad feeling among those involved. Such an atmosphere of dispute is not conducive to the simple living we enjoy, or even to good digestion. At your age, perhaps such a matter seems of no importance; to one who has observed the controversies of half a century, squabbling at the dinner table seems nothing less than ill-mannered and useless."

Miss Wilcox bowed politely and was silent.

"How beautiful the countryside is here!" Miss Pendleton exclaimed innocuously. "This castle seems like something quite out of a dream."

"The plumbing seems like something out of a dweam too," said Frederick. "It goes bump in the night."

"That does not prevent it all from seeming very romantic to me," said Isolde. "My mother was always addicted to the poems of Tennyson, and now I feel as if I have stepped into the *Idylls of the King*."

"Are you Isolde of the white hand or the other one?" asked Georgie.

"I'm afraid neither behaved quite as she should. I would have liked to be Guinevere, I think. She did seem to have the most fun."

"Ah, how too unmaidenly of you, darling," said Georgie. "I can't but agree with you, when all is said and done, even though Lancelot seems to have been a stuffy lot too."

"And then the treat to which we have been invited will be such a splendid spectacle," Elizabeth said sweetly. "I've heard so much of them, the tents of bright-striped colors, full of long tables of mugs filled with tea, and plates full of cakes and sliced bread and butter. The children running about playing games. It all sounds enchanting. Tell me, for how many years has the treat been a tradition here at Toye?"

The Brookes looked silently into their soup, pleased that none of this was their affair. The Battersbottom entourage twitched, flinched, and appeared not to notice that a question had been asked. Mr. Thornbrough looked irritated and was working an answer out in his head as swiftly as possible when his cousin, sitting at the head of the table, said pleasantly, "Ah, you have us there, don't you, Miss Wilcox? If you think I'm going to put my head in that noose, you're much mistaken. Of course I could say, 'Oh, the treat, the Toye treat, well, well, quite a tradition here goes back to old Gilbert de Taunton's celebration after the Roundheads were kicked out, and then I could go up and show you a picture of a man and say, there, you see, old hook-nosed Gilbert himself before he died of apoplexy. Ah, we Tauntons, we came over with Methuselah, or whatever the fellow's name was. Then, my dear Miss Wilcox, you would go back to London and mention to someone, 'Oh, I've just had the good fortune to be at Toye for the treat. So charming, all the little village brats running around punching each other on the heads.' Then your companion would quite happily explain with an air of horror, 'Aha! You poor thing! Didn't you know! Those Tauntons have not had tuppence to call their own for almost a century now. The whole thing was a put on.' "

There was silence for a moment. Bertie added, "And then, of course, you would never speak to me again. And that's a risk I can't take. Not that many people do speak to me," he continued in his vague manner. "I don't really have a lot to say to people. For example, I went to a party the other day and had to take a young lady in I had never met before. What did she want to talk about? The weather. How dull.

Shooting. I don't shoot. Horses. I ride bicycles. Do you ride bicycles, Miss Wilcox?"

"I should like to learn very much."

"I'll teach you tomorrow. We still have Mattie's boneshaker around somewhere. No, what this young lady really wanted to talk about was vegetarianism. 'Do you know, Lord Albert, that the meat you are eating is really a dead cow?' she said. 'Well, I'm afraid I did know,' I replied. 'Isn't it too tragic?' she'd say. 'A living creature, perhaps as intelligent as yourself, and now you're eating its dead body.' "

"Poor Bertie," laughed Georgie. "It could have been worse, you know. It could have been transmigration of souls."

"*I* believe in transmigration of souls," said Miss Pendleton stoutly. "It's a lot better than believing all those horrid little tales they tell you as a child about how wonderful it is to die and be at peace."

"A smile on his lips as he beheld the greater light beyond?" said Mr. Thornbrough. "Still, it's not a subject that can be settled by discussion, and I'm not willing to put it to the final test."

"If you allow Bertie to teach you how to wide his Bonecwusher, Miss Pendleton, I'm afwaid you will be doing vewy advanced wesearch in the field. Pe'haps more advanced than you care for."

"That's not fair!" Bertie exclaimed. "You don't mind falling off a great, mean brute of a horse! How can you object to a nice little machine weighing no more than fifty pounds?"

"I hope that none here entertain unorthodox religious beliefs," said Lady Honora, entering the field a trifle late, due to the excellence of the chef's *poularde flanquée de cailles.*

"In India they are not unorthodox," said Bertie.

"Levity in the face of eternal death is not a subject for the dinner table," said Lady Honora. "I hope that in America such things are treated seriously," she said, nodding to the American young ladies.

"Oh, very seriously," said Isolde.

"Nor can I think that a self-propelled machine is a suitable mount for any person laying claim to birth and good breeding, especially a young lady. I do not know that such experiments should be countenanced."

This set up a general protest, and when Mr. Thornbrough pointed out that the whole matter was merely a fad, and no doubt a passing fancy that would disappear the more thoroughly it was indulged, Lady Honora allowed herself to be persuaded to permit Bertie to give the young ladies lessons the next day.

"I need not, I am sure," she said with a thin smile, "state that bloomers should not be worn."

"Bloomers! Heaven forbid!" Miss Wilcox agreed. "So unflattering, with all that material billowing out around one's waist!" Inwardly she smiled. Tucked into one of the trunks upstairs, whose contents were being unpacked by several enthralled maids, was a newly purchased, very daring pair of knickerbockers that set off her luxurious figure to perfection.

The dinner finished, the young ladies felt the eyes of Lady Honora inexorably drawing them out of the room to leave the men to their wine and, probably, cigars. It had been an odd evening, Miss Pendleton reflected, as she followed the others down the long, stone-flagged corridor that led to a sitting room. There was so much formality practiced by some, such as Lady Honora and Mr. Thornbrough, and none at all by Georgie, Fwed, and Bertie. Mr. Thornbrough was an interesting study in character. The last time she had seen him, he had been bandaging her arm; today he hardly referred to the incident, or even indicated he had met her before.

The house, too, was very odd; the lines of the

rooms were magnificent, just what she had always imagined in a castle, but it was a very uncomfortable place for all that, and she could not help wondering what it would be like in the winter. There seemed to be no creature comforts: no books, no flowers, no beautiful hangings, not even a piano in any of the rooms. It was lucky she had brought her guitar; otherwise, she might have been bored indeed. Isolde was always amazed at the ready way in which Elizabeth could jump in with a new set of people, find points of interest in common, and in a few minutes be quite at ease with them, just the way she was talking and laughing with Mrs. Brooke right now.

"She is a little too much at ease." Mr. Thornbrough was summing up Miss Wilcox to the gentlemen at that moment. "This is her first visit with English people. One would expect her to be a trifle more reticent, more like her friend, Miss Pendleton."

"That's just because you think I stand a better chance with Miss Pendleton," said Bertie petulantly. "I think you're a blackguard, and in a few more minutes I shall get very drunk and run through the house shouting rude things about you and then everyone will be embarrassed and leave."

"Don't do that, Bertie," said Frederick. "All my cweditors are tailing me, and if I have to go back to London this early, I am a dead duck."

"I think that's very ill-bred of you," said Bertie crossly, "coming down to a party just to escape a lot of poor but honest tradesmen."

"Not as ill-bwed as getting dwunk in fwont of ladies and embawwassing your guests, hmm? Look at it that way."

"You are both ridiculous," said Mr. Thornbrough. "This is Friday. Tomorrow you and Tuttle and Eastman and whoever can begin to make preparations for a treat next Friday. Next Saturday, you can teach those girls how to bicycle. Then on Sunday we will all behave like proper Church of England and attend services. On Monday we can all go visit the nearest ruins."

"We shan't have to go far for that," said Frederick unkindly.

"Cease the babble," continued Thornbrough. "On Tuesday we will drive up to Chillingsworth and pick out the toys for the children. Then on Wednesday, Thursday, and Friday we will allow ourselves to be caught up in the gaiety of it all."

"Deah Thornie," said Frederick. "It is so utterhly nice to see you swept away like this in gay pwepawations. Suddenly you are so animated, so full of life. We have neveh seen you so happy, as you weflect for pe'haps the first time how much joy you can bestow on othe's. Is it not a wonde'ful thought?"

Edwin looked on, his mouth open in adenoidal vacuity.

"He who gives to the poor, lends to the Lord," reflected Bertie.

"Oh, I am vewy, vewy poor," said Fwed.

"Be silent, Babylon," said Thornie. "This is Friday, and next Friday it will all be over. So try to behave with a little dignity, just a small amount. Just enough so that there is no extraordinary amount of gossip when we return to London."

The gentlemen rejoined the ladies well before tea was brought in, and Georgie rejoiced secretly to see that her husband was in very good order. There was a bit of awkwardness when the men arrived; it was not quite understood exactly what topics of conversation were considered proper in America. In England one might talk of sports, politics, or, if one must, the weather. But what rules governed polite conversation in America?

In the temporary lull in conversation, it was left

for Edwin, anxious to show off his conversational prowess, to speak up first. Turning to Miss Pendleton, who had set aside her guitar, which she had been strumming softly, he said in a rather loud tone, "I say, have you ever seen an Indian?"

"No, I haven't," said Miss Pendleton gently. "I know that must seem to be a deplorable ignorance to you, but America is really much bigger than England, and it is more than a month's journey to the West. We were only ten days on the *Ultima* to England."

"I see," said Edwin in a somewhat disdainful tone. "I thought there were quite a few Indians in America."

"Oh, there are, but I am ashamed to say not very many in New York City. The Indian is not regarded as a very desirable neighbor, so in all cases he has been pushed to the outskirts of civilization."

Elizabeth, who was seated in a chair at the other side of the cavernous hall, made an amusing remark, and Bertie and the Brookes gathered around her to reply. They soon made a very comfortable little group and Mr. Thornbrough, determined not to subject Isolde to any more of his cousin Edwin's gaucherie, attempted to engage her in conversation. He was not successful. Perhaps this was from her shyness or possibly embarrassment over their last encounter. He wondered if she knew what the word "whore" meant. She had hardly looked conscious when he had said it, but she seemed very cool now.

Her guitar was lying beside her, and he begged her for a few songs. With very little show of modesty, she picked up the instrument and in a few moments was singing Negro spirituals. In London he had heard street bands in black-painted faces play some hideous imitation of Negro plantation songs—cockney accents attempting a slurred Southern United States accent. They were very popular in the East End, but of course, Thornbrough had paid them no attention. These songs were different. Isolde sang them in her own clear American accent, free from twang. The words of the songs were very simple, and Isolde's voice was not magnificent, but the tone held a yearning, sad, searching quality that silenced her listeners and drew Cathleen to her side.

Mr. Thornbrough revised his opinion of her; she seemed more quiet than shy. Even as she sang, she did not suddenly open up. Her manner was soothing, her songs sweet. She was really a very pretty girl and held herself quite well. He had thought at first that her dress was too showy, but he saw now that it was quite simple. His eye had been dazzled by the abundance of Elizabeth's riches and ruffles. Isolde wore a simply cut dress of pale pink, very becoming to her dark hair, with a small ornament tied around her neck on a piece of ribbon. She did not affect the flashing jewels Elizabeth wore, and her hair in its simple knot was quite becoming.

To everyone's surprise the evening passed quickly. Tea came in at ten and Lady Honora ordered them all off to bed at eleven. The American young ladies were both too tired and pensive for much talk; they spoke little about their first evening in the English countryside.

Only Major Brooke and his lady enjoyed a good gossip as they dressed for bed. "Pooh Beht," said the major. "It is such a gwief to see such a deah, deah fwiend so totally beside himself. I actually saw him dwink a cup of tea tonight."

"Did you now?" asked his spouse. "Well, let me tell you something. Do you realize Thornie was with that Pendleton girl for two whole hours?"

"He had to," said Fwed. "He was entehtaining heh, you know, being a host."

"It's all highly suspicious," said Georgie. "And quite exciting. I think I can sell a piece about this to the social editor of *The Chit Chat*."

"Geowgie!" exclaimed her husband, horrified. "And what about honoh! We've been invited here as guests."

"I know, but we could get rid of that wretched little man who keeps following you about with papers in his pocket."

"Oh, I've alweady bowowwed the money from Thownie for *that*," said Fwed.

"How provident of you! Good night, dearest."

Chapter 10

Isolde awoke early the next morning and lay in bed stretching her long, relaxed limbs between the sheets, trying to remember where she was. She certainly had never slept in a room like this one, with its high, narrow windows and enormous bed. Even her body felt different.

She was in a castle. Of course everyone was very practical and matter-of-fact about actually living in a castle, but she was drawn into its ancient aura, as if she, too, had become a part of it, like the ancient, dusty furnishings and the stories about Bert's long dead ancestors. She no longer felt herself to be simply a modern young lady, but a part of the castle itself.

In the big brownstone mansion her parents owned in New York, filled with dark mahogany furniture, potted plants, horsehair sofas, and extremely well-trained servants, everything was always dull; she was accustomed to a routine of unrelieved boredom. There were books, there was music, and there were parties when she was in good enough health to attend, but none of these things stimulated her. Everyone was so pleasant, so well fed. So much time was spent discussing genealogies, the health of their acquaintances' business, and keeping an inventory on the quantities of diamonds each tycoon's wife owned. Isolde was bored, always bored, hopelessly and completely bored. Only her interludes of intimacy with young men had stirred her. Then she could add the color of emotions to the blankness of her life. But when these same young men began to think of her as a potential wearer of their own oversize family diamond necklaces, her frustration multiplied and a sense of disenchantment descended upon her like a shroud.

In this enormous place she felt more solitary than she could ever have been in New York. Because the castle had been neglected for so many years, and no fashionable owners had periodically renovated it, each leaving his or her own taste imprinted on it in the form of hangings, furnishings, pictures, furniture, or new and inappropriate wings; because none of these things was present, the castle seemed more like a thing of nature than of art. It was like a gray stone that had been shaped by the sea, all its rough edges smoothed away. Isolde could pocket it and hoard it as a touchstone, using it as her imagination wished.

Lying in her big bed and looking out the window at the park below, she felt something stir within her, a feeling of solitary splendor, of independence, as if the countryside could be made hers just by her wishing, just by an act of her mind, her will. It was a beautiful place; she must do something here worth remembering, so that the memory would give her a greater possession of it. Isolde, like many other young ladies, kept a memory book. But hers was not an album covered in velvet in which she detailed in beautiful handwriting incidents of no interest to anyone. Isolde never committed her reminiscences to paper; a fortunate thing, although they would have been of interest to many.

She was dressing in a simple navy blue walking dress with a white collar and cuffs when she heard a tap on the door. It was Elizabeth.

"Hurry, I want to show you something before

breakfast," said Lizzie. "I was up early and found a wonderful hidden staircase. I don't think it's really a secret staircase, but it seems like it to me." Taking Isolde by the hand, she led her down the long corridor, up a narrow, rounded flight of stairs, and up to a little window that looked out over the park. Standing at the window, the two girls could see for miles. The beautiful English countryside stretched out before them.

"What do you think of the place?" asked Isolde.

"The place?" said Elizabeth. "I'm wild about the place. I've never seen anything like it. It's almost edible."

Isolde shivered. The image was too vivid; she could imagine licking the greenery and nibbling pieces off the long low stone walls that lined the narrow road. "How strange! And yet I do love London, in its untidy, bustling way. It seems odd, too, the way they talk to each other, but perhaps that comes of them all being related. I don't believe I have ever been to a place where so many people are cousins. They seem to be insulting each other all the time, but I suppose it is all just family joking."

"I don't know," said Elizabeth. "It sounds to me as if these people, and especially Mr. Thornbrough, are related to everyone in England. His aunt was reciting his pedigree to me last night, and the number of titles who form branches of his particular twig is perfectly astounding. How do you like Mr. Thornbrough?"

Isolde reflected. "Mr. Thornbrough has possibilities. He has definite possibilities."

"Possibilities for what?" asked Elizabeth.

"For providing me with amusement, of course," said Isolde. "Shall we go down to breakfast?"

"What do you think of the earl?"

"Odd but nice. Very nice. Shall we go?"

Mr. Thornbrough, Lord Albert, Cathleen, and Edwin were there before them. Mr. Thornbrough and Lord Albert seemed to have disagreed about something, while Cathleen and Edwin glowered quietly. It was not a cheerful party, but Isolde and Elizabeth were full of good humor, and the mood of the room soon changed upon their entry.

"What would you like to do today?" asked Lord Albert. "I am your host, you know, and I must see to it that you do whatever you like best."

"Does that include me?" asked Georgie, entering at that moment with her husband. "Have you eaten all the kippers? I know what I should like best."

"No, it doesn't include you," said Bert. "I'm not a fool."

"What I should really like," said Isolde, "is to go for a long walk alone. Perhaps with a picnic lunch. Is that a rude request?"

"Let's let her do it," said Fweddie. "And then let's shut the house down, take all her clothes and money, and all go back to London. When she comes back, no one will be here. Wouldn't that be funny?"

"Neither you nor your wife is a proper person," said Mr. Thornbrough firmly. "I can't think how you were ever invited here."

Elizabeth looked up and caught Bertie's eye. Very quickly, almost secretly, she winked at him, crinkling up the left side of her face. Just as quickly, her blue eyes widened again, assuming an angelic ignorance once more. Bert choked and was rendered speechless. Beautiful women in London seldom looked at him and never winked in his direction.

"I believe I have been promised a few lessons on the bicycle today," said Elizabeth. "I have been so used to horseback riding that I have completely ignored its invention. I must change my dress, though."

"Perhaps the party could divide into two," said Mr.

Thornbrough. "You and Bert and Cathleen and Edwin may stay here and practice on the machines; we will leave the brougham so that the doctor can be fetched when the inevitable occurs."

"*I* never broke anything on a bicycle," said Bertie indignantly. "Really, when I think of how many people I know who have broken their necks on fences, or can never have babies again or awful things like that, I think it's appalling that you should criticize the bicycle."

"True, Bert," said Mr. Thornbrough. "But you must remember that even your bicycles cannot jump over fences."

"Mr. Thornbrough," said Miss Pendleton, "is the other party by any chance to include you and me?"

"And the Brookes," said Mr. Thornbrough. "We really cannot have you wandering off alone, Miss Pendleton. You don't even know the countryside, and we promise not to annoy you too greatly."

"Now, now," said the major. "Let's not go making pwomises we can't keep."

"Be silent, Babylon," said Mr. Thornbrough. "Think, Miss Pendleton! A guide to point out the names of the trees and flowers and recount local legends will not be too great a burden."

"We must all do as Martin orders us," said Bertie with gay courage. "I expect he has his orders from Aunt Honora. Think how terrified you would be, Miss Pendleton, if Aunt Honora discovered you had disobeyed her lieutenant!"

"That is not wespectful," complained Frederick. "Weally, I don't know when I heard someone talk about his aunts the way you do, Bert. I would be tewwified to be one of your aunts. My weputation could never withstand it."

"Well, *I* do not wish to ride bicycles," said Edwin, "and I do not believe that my aunt would wish me to either, since she considers them to be a dangerous invention."

"Then you may join us on our walk, of course," said Mr. Thornbrough. "Or you may devise some entertainment here by yourself. I am afraid I cannot mount you today."

"And I won't have you going out and shooting things," said Bert. "You can shoot at wafers if you wish, but unless you brought your own gun, you won't even be able to do that. I don't have any here."

Edwin, faced with a long tramp through the countryside on foot, decided he had better stay at home in case the foot he injured playing Rugby last season should start to bother him again. Cathleen was wiser; she intended to slip away quietly to the kitchens as soon as everyone was gone. No one would notice her defection, and the cook had taken a liking to her when he found out she was the daughter of a lord. He had promised to let her help with the vegetables today.

After breakfast the gentlemen lounged about while the ladies went to put on their walking shoes. Aunt Honora was still attempting to offset a cold, suffered from the bitter May drafts whistling through Toye which had somehow avoided all the others. This was fortunate, since she would not have cared at all for the gray tweed knickerbockers Miss Wilcox wore. They created something of a sensation even in the little party that gathered at the bottom of the stairs, since knickerbockers were seldom worn in England, although they were often worn in France by women of style. It was difficult to arrange these semi-manly garments properly, with their short full bags caught in just below the knees, but Elizabeth wore them fearlessly, slightly pleated at the knee, and then caught in with a black band. She wore a broad belt with them, and a little black bolero coat that gave her quite a dashing appearance and set off her small waist to admiration. Isolde was still dressed in her plain navy blue dress, but she had added a simple sailor hat with a buckle to it.

"Upon my word," said Georgie, as she saw them come down the stairs. "It really is too bad to have all that money and a figure like that too! I am going to begin to smoke cigars, Fweddie, it's the only thing left, and become very rude. Then at least I will be distinguished."

The parties divided. Mr. Thornbrough, Miss Pendleton, and the Brookes set off for a walk around the park, and Bert and Miss Wilcox headed for the stables. Cathleen and Edwin were nowhere to be found, and no one looked very hard.

"Hello, Fielding," said Bertie, as he entered the stable door. "We have just come to get the bicycles. I don't think anyone will be wanting horses today, at least not until later this afternoon."

"Very good, sir," said Fielding, and retired to a corner where he could stare more openly at the American lady.

"I feel rather awkward about bringing you into a stable on our first meeting," said Bert. "I hope you like stables. I always did. Of course they do smell a lot."

It was a fine old building, built of elm several centuries old, made to stand for a long time. Most of it was empty, but it was clean, and at one end Bertie had converted stalls into housing for his beloved bicycles. Over a dozen of these were lined up in gleaming order, a wide variety. There were vehicles with dangerously large-looking back wheels and small front wheels, safeties, ordinaries, and extraordinaries all in startling array of spokes and seats and gleaming metal. Against one wall was a long workbench, littered with the debris of dissected machinery and

tools. There was also a pile of old velocipede frames
without their tires, tires without their velocipedes,
and seats and chains that belonged to nothing at the
present moment.

"Thornie says I'm the only person he knows whose
hobby horse *is* a hobby horse," said Bertie, looking
fondly at the display of machinery. "I know not everyone is interested, but the designs of these velocipedes are always changing, always improving. New
patents are being issued almost every month."

"Do you hold any patents?" asked Elizabeth.

"Me? Oh, I take things apart and make a mess, but
that's about all. It's not easy having something patent-
ed, you know. You work at it for months and then
another fellow slips in with it ten minutes before
you."

"Have you ever tried?"

"Just now and again, nothing important, you
know, nothing earth-shaking. I don't go in for sports
much, you see, and my father drank up everything in
the cellar here before he died, so one must have
something to do."

"I really know nothing about velocipedes, except
from songs of course. And at a party once I met the
man who rode around the world."

"Did you? What was he like? I don't consider it
really fair to claim you have ridden a bicycle around
the world when everyone knows that four-fifths of the
world is covered with water."

"Tell me about your bicycles," said Elizabeth.
"What shall you teach me to ride today?"

"Well, here we have a boneshaker, the original
thing. This is what we all learned to ride on. You see,
it has no steering mechanism, so I tie a rope to it and
run with it downhill while you get the hang of sitting
on two wheels."

"I don't like the sound of that," said Elizabeth

firmly. It was a two-wheeled velocipede made of steel with a wooden seat and wooden tires. All the bicycles were in an excellent state of preservation, but the boneshaker looked rather too much like its name for comfort. "Does everyone begin to ride them?"

"Oh, no," said Bert. "Many ladies prefer to stay with the tricycles. I have one here that used to belong to my mother, a Cripper. No danger of falling over, you know, but it's rather heavy, about one hundred pounds, whereas my little safety weighs in at forty-seven."

"I can't be seen on a tricycle," said Elizabeth. "There seems something very cowardly about them, and I am not a cowardly sort of person."

Lord Albert was respectfully silent.

"I will have a safety too, if you have one, but I won't get on that boneshaker. I don't like the name of it. What is the name of the safety? Are there two?"

"There are four," said Bertie proudly. "If I can't have a stable, I should think I could have a few bicycles, and they are such very nice ones. They are the new Rovers, you know, with equal-size wheels and a diamond frame. The best and the newest thing on the market, I promise you! And the road into the village is not macadamized—of course—but it is not at all a bad road. Shall we have a go? Do you think you can manage?"

"Is it possible—I don't like to sound unsportsman-like, Lord Albert, but could we start off somewhere where there is a little hay lying around on the ground?"

"A great enormous pile," promised Lord Albert. "Off we go." The stable was situated at the top of a little hill, so after Fielding laid some hay along either side, they began down it. After a few falls, Miss Wilcox managed to coast down the hill without incident, and after a few more tries she had caught the hang of pedaling. Very pleased with her new skill, she and her host started off for the town. The journey was rather a long one for her, unaccustomed as she was to the exercise, and the road was full of rocks and holes, so they were forced to stop and rest several times.

"I believe we will borrow the grocer's cart to bring us back," said Bertie, fanning Lizzie with his hat. Her color was greatly heightened. Her cheeks were quite pink in the cool spring morning, and her eyes were bright with the exercise.

"Dear Lord Albert, let us rest a little here," she said, gasping a little. "Tell me about Toye Castle. Did you grow up here?"

"Oh, no, I was hardly here at all as a child. I grew up in a house in Leicestershire, near Thornie's Thorn Manor. At least I was there most of the time. My father didn't care for the Castle, and my mother was always busy doing something else."

"It must be wonderful to possess such a large and beautiful estate," said Lizzie. Lord Albert presented the appearance of a very ordinary young man about town, but when she tried to put her finger on certain notes, he became very elusive, an unknown quantity.

"Oh, I don't really possess it at all. It sort of possesses me, you know. At least it haunts me. I don't feel as if it does what I tell it to, and I think a possession should, don't you?"

They were silent for a few moments as Elizabeth looked back over the road they had taken. The narrow lane was lined with walls made of Cotswold stone in the old tradition, the stones, pale pink to gray in color, giving off almost a luminescent sheen. In places the wall had tumbled down and grown over with flowering weeds, looking very picturesque, but somewhat sad.

The village was very small, almost a line of houses down a single street. For the most part, the cottages were very tumbledown. Roofs looked patchy, as if they must leak a great deal. Windows were broken out and fences were falling down. But it was spring and flowers bloomed in odd corners of every yard. Neat gardens were laid out in rows. The plants had obviously not sprouted yet, but soon beans and corn would be growing out of the rich ground. Pigs could be seen in pens. There were quite a lot of children and Bertie seemed to know everyone by name.

"Please don't tell the others," said Bertie, "but I am going to take you into the public house and introduce you to some very old friends of mine, Mrs. Gilbert and her husband. Pay no attention at all to the husband. She is not at all kind to him, and it only annoys her if anyone seems to notice him."

"You were never here as a boy, were you?" asked Elizabeth. "What is your long association?"

"Oh, I come to the inn in the winter, when Toye is too chilly even for my taste. Everyone in the village comes here then. Smell is a little strong, mind you, don't deny that, but we are very cozy. Besides, I like onions. But it won't smell like onions today. I should think you would like a glass of cider, though. Don't have cider in America, do you? Whenever anyone talks about American parties, it's always champagne and lobster, champagne and lobster. Never cider and lobster."

"If I like cider, just for a change, I shall give a cider and lobster party as soon as I return to New York," Elizabeth promised. "I am sure it will be a hit."

Bertie ushered Elizabeth into the Red Drum, a very small and rather dark place. Lizzie blinked as her eyes became accustomed to the dim light of the room, paneled in dark wood. There was no one in the place at all, but Bertie cried out, "Maggie! Maggie, where are you! New trade, Maggie!"

Coming toward them from a door by the tap was a very large woman dressed in an old-fashioned round gown. Lizzie felt herself being inspected very carefully, and then Maggie's eyes turned on Bert.

"And where have you been these months?" she began to scold. "You were going to be down for your birthday, and I baked you a cake. I had to feed it to Samuel."

"How shocking!" said Bertie. "But I must introduce you. This is Miss Wilcox, and she is staying with me at Toye this week. I have just taught her how to ride a bicycle, but we must borrow your gig to carry her home in. Think I've tired her out."

"Miss Wilcox, is it?" said Maggie. "Well, well, I think news has come into town that there are visitors at Toye."

"Dear Maggie, I came as soon as I could, so please don't scold. Miss Wilcox has never had any cider before. From New York, you know, and they only eat lobster patties there and canvasback ducks and drink champagne."

"I'll have Samuel fetch you a glass this instant," Maggie promised. "Now you sit down here, and I'll go get a plate of meat pasties out of the oven that have just been cooking for lunch." Eyeing the knickerbockers again, she took herself back to her kitchens. Presently Samuel, a surprisingly cheery individual, appeared and set down a glass of amber-colored liquid in front of Elizabeth, then drew a tankard for Bertie.

Elizabeth sipped cautiously. "Lord Albert," she said, "I do believe this drink is alcoholic."

"What, all by itself?" asked Bertie, his sandy eyebrows upraised, and his blue eyes widened in the way that made him appear to be slightly popeyed. "I don't see how that can be. I've heard it said that I'm alcoholic—and I know that poor Glowersby is, but you can't blame him, with a wife like that—and I'm also pretty sure that half of the people in my club are and all the men in the Jockey Club. But how can a glass of cider be alcoholic? It doesn't drink itself, you know. You have to drink it."

"Then I shall do that," said Elizabeth. It tasted like sweet wine.

Soon Maggie bustled out with a plate full of meat pasties. "Now, you eat those. It's almost lunchtime anyway, and after that long ride, you'll be needing a bite. I think you've lost a little weight, Lor' Bert. That Tuttle can't cook for you, and neither can Mrs. Eastman, I've always told you that. Another glass?"

"No, no, sit down, Maggie." She pulled out a chair and was about to seat herself when he added, "But you have to promise faithfully that you won't make any personal remarks about my mustache. There it is, right under my nose, and there it's going to stay. Just because you can't have one is no reason to be critical of others."

Maggie grinned and said, "I've gotten used to it."

"Good. There. Now sit down, we need to talk to you."

She sat at the table with them and watched Bertie consume the last remains of the meat pasties; it appeared that she was not used to formality when dealing with his lordship. Elizabeth, for all her flag waving, had never actually sat down and discussed affairs with the staff in her own home or at one of the fashionable restaurants she and her father sometimes patronized. To make this first republican step under the guidance of an earl struck her favorably, especially in her view of the earl.

"My cousin Thornbrough is down with us, you know," said Bertie, "and he has ordained that in honor of our American guests we must hold a treat at Toye this year. Splendid news, isn't it? Tea and cake and bread and butter and games and that sort of thing, and you, dear Maggie, must help preside. It can't be done unless you will take it in hand and help me with invitations and handing things round and organizing it all."

"Who have you got at the castle now?" asked Maggie. She glanced at Elizabeth and added, "But perhaps we should make our arrangements later on, my lord."

"Yes, let's do that," said Bertie. "Miss Wilcox can't want to hear all this."

"Oh, but I do very much," said Elizabeth in her silvery voice. "My parties in New York were famous; and I can't forego an opportunity to see how a village party is done in England. After all, Lord Albert, I am a woman, and I do think I should be allowed to arrange a party."

Maggie, who did not approve of knickerbockers, said shortly, "Several hundred people will come to this, miss, and they won't be the kind of people you're used to rubbing shoulders with."

Elizabeth replied, "Of course, Mrs. Gilbert," and smiled sweetly. Maggie was satisfied. She was not used to nobs coming in and perhaps she wasn't as polite as she ought, especially since she had heard that this was the girl who owned so much money in New York. She certainly was a looker, though, just the thing for poor Bertie, and why shouldn't he have a break after the life he'd led, scraping and saving on nothing.

"There now," she said, "I've gone and lost my tongue, but that you can't blame me for, for I've no one but Samuel to sharpen it on all day. I should be glad of your help, miss. Perhaps you would like to help pick out the prizes? We could all go over in the gig next week."

Elizabeth assented, and she and Bertie left the Red Drum shortly after. He invited her for a turn about the village before they set back and Elizabeth was much charmed. At the end of the little street, secluded behind a short field, was a small but quite perfect old church. It was four hundred years old, and the churchyard was full of old headstones carved with ancient verses in memory of old-fashioned names.

"We should pick some thistles from the churchyard for your friend," said Bertie. "Seemed like the kind of girl who would like thistles from a churchyard."

"Does she indeed?" asked Elizabeth.

"A whole bouquet of them. We must have them in her room when she gets back from her walk. I hope Thornie is being amusing; he can be."

"What makes you think she would like such an absurd thing?"

"Not absurd at all," said Bertie indignantly. "Didn't you know that you can do all kinds of things with them? Cure worts. Clear out ghosts. Just the kind of girl who would really go for a ghost. I wonder if she table taps."

"She doesn't," said Elizabeth definitely. "Am I the kind of girl who would like a bouquet of thistles?"

"Dash it, no. You're a very businesslike young lady, I can see that. Kind of woman my mother always dealt with, even though she was very absentminded herself. No, you would want something sensible like roses. Roses, that's it; not lilies, no, nor orchids either. Lots of roses, red ones."

Taking Lord Albert's arm, Elizabeth replied, "No, the lily should be your flower, Lord Albert. The Easter lily, with a large white head."

"Nothing picturesque about me!" protested Bertie. Elizabeth smiled.

Chapter 11

The trip back was a short one, and they spent the time in the kind of light, evasive talk of which Bertie seemed to be a master. Elizabeth silently reserved an afternoon next week with Maggie. Getting information out of Bertie about Bertie seemed to be quite hopeless, but he was quite willing to talk about society in general and the other members of the party in particular.

Back at the castle, it was quite late, after three o'clock, and Aunt Honora had emerged from her bedroom and was waiting in the courtyard for her guests to arrive for their tea. Elizabeth, who had been very nonchalant after breakfast about Aunt Honora's authority, wanted to be a little more circumspect after her morning ride. She dashed up the stairs and changed into a very demure tea gown of unexceptionable, even quiet style.

Isolde came in as Elizabeth was brushing out her hair; the walk had been a longish one, but they had returned for lunch and afterward she had gone to her room to rest. Her color was much higher than usual, and her pale, perfect features were quite pink; she seemed even more beautiful than when she was enacting the death of Camille by languishing in her bed.

"Well, your walk does seem to have done you good," said Elizabeth. "How do you like the countryside? Isn't it beautiful? We bicycled into the village,

and Bertie picked you some thistles from the churchyard."

"Thistles!" Isolde laughed. "Oh, then he has been
reading the Andersen fairy tales. What an odd person
he is! Did you have a good time?"

"Oh, lovely. I was introduced to Mrs. Maggie Gilbert, who runs the Red Drum in town, and was
treated to a glass of cider, but that is supposed to be a
secret; I suppose the terrible Mr. Thornbrough
would frown at the connection. After being looked
over very carefully, Maggie decided she would allow
me to help her with the treat, and I am going to see
if we can put some fun into it. Just think, they actually go out and buy a toy for all the children in the
village! And although no one is starving there, it is
not at all a very luxurious place, so it will be just like
Christmas. But tell me, how was your walk?"

"Oh, nice enough," said Isolde vaguely. "The trees
and the flowers and birds and things were very
pretty."

"And what do you think of Mr. Thornbrough?"
asked Elizabeth.

After a little pause, Isolde answered casually, "I
suppose he is just what an English gentleman should
be. I don't know. He knows a great deal about the
countryside, so he was very useful. But it was Georgie
who knew all the names of the flowers. They are a
very funny pair, the Brookes. Did Edwin and Cathleen go with you?"

"No, just Lord Albert and I, but I don't think
Aunt Honora is supposed to know that either. Tell
me, did you like Mr. Thornbrough?"

Isolde picked up some of the pins on Elizabeth's
dressing table and began to line them up. "He was
very polite," she said absently.

Elizabeth sighed. It was obvious that she could get
no information out of Isolde. Indeed, it seemed as if

the girl had never even learned how to gossip. If she could, she would have liked overhearing the Brookes's conversation as they changed their muddy boots, but the strength of their marital tie was due in large part to their fondness for each other's gossip.

"What do you think of Thornbrough and Isolde now?" asked Georgie. "I'll start giving you odds after tonight."

"You're always a chump," said her husband. "You said the same thing when Ginger stawted widing his hunters in the pawk! As if Thownbwough would eveh mawwy an actwess. Why are you so anxious to mawwy him off, anyway? He's vewy handy to us as a single man."

"If he married a rich American girl, he would be even handier. I could borrow from her and you could still borrow from him."

Her husband, who was throwing dice, one hand against the other, thought about this for a bit. It seemed reasonable.

"Twue. But what do we know about this girl anyway? I thought there was only one heiwess, and now the house seems full of them. If I'd known this was going to be the case, I would have bwought my little bwother Chahlie with me. But I've heard Amewican fowtunes can melt like the dew."

"How refreshing, Fwed," said his wife. "But truly didn't you think there was something a little bit odd about that girl this afternoon?"

"Vewy odd. I thought she was mad."

"Not precisely mad, but certainly unusual. Making daisy chains, and then wearing them—I don't know anyone who has done that since she was about eight years old. And yet they *suited* her."

"It was the way she muttered poetwy all the time that got me," said her husband.

"Perhaps it might have seemed different to an American, but it all looked like the same old dirt to me. I never have much cared for the country. But she was *breathless*, Fweddie. And you know how men get set off when women are always inhaling rapidly and breathing sighs of contentment and all that."

"Vewy odd girl. Not at all Thownie's style."

"Well, what is Thornie's style?"

"Mawwied women and actwesses."

"Nonsense. Look at how he carried on all last year with that awful Lady Gwladys. She made all her servants wear shades of mauve and purple, and a lot of silly robes made up for her guests to wear, encouraged by that ridiculous Oscar Wilde character. Even her curtains had to match. They were all gray. And I know that he spent more weekends than one with her."

"And who can blame him?" said her practical husband. "Lady Gwladys is one of the most beautiful women in London. A bore, but beautiful."

"Well, there you are!" said his wife triumphantly. "And Isolde is not even a bore. Mad, rich, and beautiful!"

"I omitted a detail," said the major carefully. "Pe'haps I should have said, 'a *mawwied* bore, but beautiful.' "

"It does come down to that, doesn't it?" sighed his wife.

"Thownie is very fond of otheh people's wives," said the major. "Especially when they awen't using them themselves."

Mr. Thornbrough could pick and choose his companions. He was much sought after; his name ranked near the top of the list of eligible bachelors. Several young ladies in London were prepared to fall in love with him with very little encouragement on his part.

He was considered good company in the cigar smoke-filled air of the Pelican Club, and yet he was received by Princess Alexandra.

Isolde, coming from another continent, was an enigma to him. She was ignorant of his exalted status; in fact, she seemed to be ignorant of innumerable things he took for granted. She had exclaimed over the countryside just like a child, and yet her manner was not the gushing one so many young ladies he knew affected. She seemed to have an other-worldly quality that surrounded her like an aura. Mr. Thornbrough did not know quite what to think of Isolde. He had thought he might spend the week enjoying a little imaginative flirtation with her, but she did not seem to know even how to flirt. Mr. Thornbrough did not reflect that she might be even more imaginative than he was.

Tea was served outside. It seemed that Bertie or Tuttle was determined to keep the party outdoors as much as possible. This suited Isolde. She liked to see the shadows lengthen.

The others were all talking about what plays were current in London, and Elizabeth was discussing Oscar Wilde's and Lily Langtry's separate but triumphant tours through the United States; a town in Texas had named itself after her. The others thought that very amusing, sounding out their own names and wondering how they would add to the prestige of a respectable, bustling American community, full of people who spoke English with very strange accents.

Isolde was silent. She withdrew a bit to the edge of the party. Edwin came and sat down beside her very glumly. Feeling pity for him because of her own experience with boredom, she tried to draw him out, but he was no great reader, and since she had no knowledge of current English affairs, especially those of an extremely petty nature, she had to resort to general trivia.

"What have you found to occupy yourself with today, Mr. Battersbottom?" she asked. "Did you bicycle?"

"Bicycle? On one of Bertie's cheap penny-farthings? I should say not. It's all very well for the working classes to amuse themselves in that way, but I am accustomed to a good horse when I go into the country. I have hunted in the shires, you know."

Lost in trying to understand Edwin's ill-used feelings, and failing to realize when he was trying to brag, Isolde struggled on. "Indeed? I have not hunted much, due to my health, but Elizabeth is very fond of riding."

"Tell me this," said Edwin, lowering his voice and glancing around, "are there really great fortunes to be made in Wyoming?"

Politely, Miss Pendleton answered, "I should think there were fortunes to be made anywhere in the world, Mr. Battersbottom, if one only knew how to go about it."

"But in cattle, you know. I've heard it talked about as a sure thing. You buy the beasts and then turn them loose on the range and herd them up and ship them off all fattened up to the cities. Thousands, hundreds of thousands of pounds could be had, perhaps."

"I'm afraid I know nothing about it, but I shouldn't think it would be a wise idea to invest in an industry and a country completely unknown to you. Does Mr. Thornbrough share your interest?"

"Thornbrough! I should think not!" said Mr. Battersbottom. "Why, he's as rich as Midas. He entertains the Prince of Wales, and you know that takes some doing. Prince Tum-Tum—not that *I'm* one of his friends—wants everything to be of the best. Horses, food, drink. He's a great womanizer too."

"The prince or Mr. Thornbrough?" asked Isolde.

"Both. They're friends again now, but once they had a terrific falling out over Carrie Alderson. Beautiful little beauty of the bedroom, you know, and she went with Thornie to Cowes for the Royal Yachting week. After the prince had been eyeing her for months. It was all over London."

"Indeed?"

"Oh, yes. We should feel very grateful to be honored with Thornie's presence. He's used to more exciting parties than this."

"I understand, however," said Isolde coolly, "that he has merely come on this visit to reassure himself that his cousin would woo an American fortune."

Even Edwin felt it unwise to answer this question directly. Miss Pendleton was a female, and females seldom liked their portions to be discussed openly, especially on short acquaintance. They would prefer to go through some mummery about love and all that instead of laying their cards on the table like a man. So Edwin, in an effort to be charming, said, "Why, you can tell for yourself that he is enjoying himself a great deal. I've never seen him make up to a single female the way he did last night to you, and I'm told he spent a good deal of today sitting in your pocket. He never allows himself to be monopolized by single girls, you know. They're too dangerous. He likes his bachelordom."

"How scandalous!" said Isolde lightly.

"Oh, no scandals yet, all between gentlemen."

"And gentleladies as well, it seems."

"He's never been named as divorce correspondent, if that's what you're thinking of. Never any messy business."

"Perhaps your cousin's attentions to me were due merely to an interest he feels in the United States."

"Thornie? Thornie's not interested in anything except London in the season, Europe in the summer, grouse shooting in Scotland, and all that. He thinks Americans are a devilishly underbred lot." Perceiving then, upon a moment's reflection, that he had perhaps spoken a little too openly, he added, "For the most part, that is! Never know when a diamond in the rough will appear."

A cool, quiet rage now being Miss Pendleton's uppermost emotion, she said, "Why does he hold my countrymen in such contempt? You appear so knowledgeable, Mr. Battersbottom. Do we behave very badly here?"

"Oh, Americans are the joke of the town. You should see the fun *Punch* pokes at them. They go visiting all the ruins they can find and saying, 'Oh, say' and carrying their everlasting Baedekers about as if they were Bibles and they were inspecting holy shrines. I had some good fun with one once. He was wearing an awful suit of clothes, just bought out of a department store, I should think, and he walked square up to me in the park and said, 'Oh, say, friend, can you point out the way to the Tower of London?' You can imagine how I felt at having some fellow like that calling me 'friend' in the middle of the park, as if we had been at Eton together. So I winked at Barny, who was with me, and I gave him directions to South Kensington! A good joke, don't you think?"

"No, I do not think it was a good joke," said Isolde. "I think you are an ill-tempered snob. And," she added roundly, "since I, too, am an American, you are remarkably stupid to tell me such a story and expect me to find it amusing. No doubt that young man did work at some honest livelihood in the United States.

You do not appear to know how to do anything at all, and I should be ashamed if I were you." And with that she swept out without glancing at the others.

"Why did Isolde leave so suddenly, Mr. Battersbottom?" asked Elizabeth, before she noticed his florid color. "Was she feeling well? Should I go to her?"

"She just didn't feel like staying," said Edwin weakly.

"Edwin, you try the patience of a saint," said Lady Honora. "Miss Wilcox, is it the custom for American ladies to whisk out of a room like this? I have heard of brisk manners, but this seems to pass the bounds."

"Aunt Honora, I have spent the afternoon with Miss Pendleton," said Thornbrough, brows darkening, "and can assure you of her good manners. Of Edwin's, however, I say nothing."

"That's it," said Fweddie. "You've said something off color, haven't you, you little toad. I don't know why anyone bwought you; you can't be left alone at a tea pawty for five minutes without saying something nasty."

"The toad in question," said Lady Honora, "is a nephew of mine."

"A pity, ma'am, a pity. Still, what can the family do? Twy to hush up the scandal, lock him away somewhehe, or flaunt him in the face of society? Have you thought of sending him to India?"

"Let's send Edwin to Australia," said Bertie. "I've often thought he should be happy there, among the headhunters."

"I didn't say anything nasty," said Edwin. "We were just talking about America, and I told her some jokes, and she got all upset and left. I don't know what's so strange about that. Girls always behave like that, feeling faint or having headaches or having to go to their rooms for something."

"Poor Edwin," said Georgie gently. "You don't

even know, do you? A girl isn't going to say, 'Look here, you are a twirp, not the man of my dreams, and a bore besides. I'm not going to stay for the end of the dance even.' They don't have headaches or any of that nonsense. They just detest you."

"That's just like a woman," said Edwin savagely. "Always dishonest and making excuses. Well, at least this one was different. She came right out and told me and if she could do that, why can't you all?"

"Came out and told you what, dear Edwin?" asked Thornbrough. "Perhaps you could tell us just exactly what you were discussing."

Feeling very uneasy, Edwin began to writhe about a bit until his aunt dismissed the affair regally. "No doubt some inopportune comment was made and the young lady, not being certain of the English code of behavior, felt better in leaving the matter in our hands and removing herself from the scene. It is a relief to see a young person display a little dignity in these days! It was certainly not her place to criticize Edwin."

All were indignant on this point. Bertie went so far as to point out that criticizing Edwin was one of the few sports they could enjoy indoors on a rainy day, since the billiards table was broken down.

Cathleen, as usual, was hideously embarrassed by her brother and felt even worse about her aunt jumping in and taking his side so obviously, but she said nothing, just as she always said nothing. She was Edwin's junior by two years, and when they were growing up, he had been known to make her life quite miserable when she told on him or found fault with him in any way, or when she simply did not fetch and carry for him as he commanded. Of course, now that they were both out of the nursery, things were different. He didn't tease and pinch and poke her as he used to, but it was still a relief to creep away from his company. It was no joy to see her brother made fun of like this. She had thought sometimes how splendid it would be if her brother were another person, someone like Agatha's brother Septimus, who took her for walks in the parks some mornings and occasionally even went to a play or the opera. Septimus was not handsome, being almost as thin and colorless as Agatha, but to possess a brother people did not laugh at must be a great comfort.

And then Cathleen, catching herself up, thought of how wicked a thought like that was, and how awful she would feel if anything happened to Edwin. But the sentiment, pious as it was, was only half felt. The chances of Edwin meeting with a fatal accident were extremely unlikely, since he was very cowardly and never took any dangerous risks, like walking over footbridges in spring when streams were transformed into raging torrents, or riding fearlessly at night on a brute of a horse over dangerous country. Of course, it would be awful if anything like that were to happen, but in the meantime it was awfully tedious having all one's friends say, 'Oh, is he your brother?' and then having them tell you some story their brothers had told them about what a worm he was.

Tuttle tapped Bertie on the shoulder and said in his ear, "I have ordered the gardener to pick a small nosegay for Miss Pendleton at your orders, sir. Perhaps you would like to send up a note as well. The young lady seemed rather put out, as it were."

"Blast that little rotter!" exlaimed Bertie.

"I'll take it up," announced Thornbrough, astonishing his guests. "Where is the young lady?" he asked, following Tuttle into the grand hallway.

"I believe she is presently climbing about on the turrets of the castle, sir."

"The turrets! Good god, no one has been up on them in years! How did she climb up?"

"It would seem she simply climbed up, sir; the lady must be nimble. But as you say, the stone may not be at all firm in places."

Thornbrough found Isolde up several winding flights of stair, each in greater disrepair. She was leaning against a wall looking out at the grounds below, an undeniably impressive sight, since sunset was coming on and the fields were green covered with the leafy heads of ancient trees.

She looked up as he stepped out onto the battlement. There was no conventional greeting, no easy smile in her eyes. She seemed sad, not at all pleased to see him, and after looking at him for a short period, she turned her eyes back to their view of the countryside.

"Excuse me," he said, his wrath with his cousin growing, "I must apologize to you for whatever Mr. Battersbottom may have said to you."

"Not at all," said Isolde, "not at all. I'm certain he was only voicing an opinion you all share."

"Edwin is not capable of sharing an opinion with me; his mind lacks the capacity."

"A prejudice then." Mr. Thornbrough waited. Isolde sighed after a few moments, and said, "I love your country so, Mr. Thornbrough. It's like a beautiful garden, and also like the setting for every fairy tale I've ever read. A wonderful country, full of amazing beauties. I came to see, to understand, to admire. But I can never possess it, because the people here— and you are one of the people—scorn us all. We may spend a few coins, we may put up for the night. But all our actions are noted down, and when we are gone, you laugh at our gaucheness. 'Ill-bred' is the term, I believe." Turning her large, dark blue eyes toward him, she looked up at him and said, "Sometimes it is a little sad, to love, but never to possess."

"I assure you, no one could ever feel anything but

admiration for you, Miss Pendleton," said Mr. Thornbrough, taken aback. The sparkling tears which had been adding brilliance to her eyes began to spill over, running down her ivory cheek. Mr. Thornbrough had been wept at before, by women who were angry with him, needed him or his purse for something, wished to change his mind or habits; women, in short, who had wanted something from him he was unwilling to give. Tears held no charm for him. But he had never seen any given as freely as these, over some anguish he could hardly comprehend. Perhaps she was lonely. She wasn't as self-sufficient as that companion of hers.

"Excuse me," she said stiffly. "My problems are none of your affair." Wiping her cheeks, she added, "Indeed, you must forgive me for bothering you at all. Elizabeth would call it nonsense."

"No, not at all," said Thornbrough. "I do admit that there is a tendency to use the Americans as a butt of our jokes, but nothing serious is meant by it."

Isolde was silent, and the memory of some of his own past remarks upon her fatherland returned vividly to him. He revised none of these, but they disturbed him. He was even more disturbed at thinking over the possibility of what that sneak Edwin might have repeated to her. Always in the worst of bad taste, was Edwin, and nauseatingly fond of reporting to other people the various ways their friends had spoken lightly of them in their absence.

"If I myself have said anything that might have hurt you, please forgive me," he said urgently. Again she gazed at him with wide, unseeing blue eyes, so dark they seemed to hold some mysterious searching quality. Her expression was almost one of mourning; her classic features seemed to grieve for a lost essence, some vital being.

She shivered in the cool air as evening began to

come on. He reached out to touch her bare forearm. She stepped back, but his hands grasped her arms gently. The light down that covered them seemed to stand up, and as he touched her she shivered again, as if from an electrical shock. She stared up at him and he folded her into his arms, holding her body but staring into her face with his eyebrow raised. She did not turn her gaze away. He felt her sensitivity, not a casual readiness but a depth of feeling with no shyness, no shrinking. He lowered his head and kissed her on the mouth, and she returned his kiss, warm and open.

After a few moments, she broke away abruptly. "It is too soon," she said, standing apart from him. And then she was gone, while he stared after her.

Chapter 12

Dinner passed smoothly, served by the admirable Tuttle on very simple china with fine-flowered borders. The Brookes were as amusing as ever, but Bertie and Mr. Thornbrough were a bit silent. Isolde was very quiet, wearing the abstracted face of a daydreaming child. Mr. Thornbrough would have expected her to be either flirtatious or shy, two distasteful outcomes of his hasty action on the castle battlements that afternoon. He had not expected her to be absentminded. She was a curious young woman.

Cathleen was never bubbling over with good spirits, but when Elizabeth commented on the fine flavor of the French beans and the buttered peas, she blushed and looked down at her plate. Aunt Honora talked a great deal. She had just spent the day reading a most shocking book, one which described the heathen lives of the Chinee, and she was determined to spread a little of her knowledge gratis, accompanied by a number of observations about the kinds of lives her own nieces and nephews were leading, especially as compared to what they could be doing. Mr. Thornbrough looked annoyed; Elizabeth was amused. The Brookes obviously did not feel it their duty to incur her wrath by trying to turn the subject. It was left for Isolde, in her hazy, assured way, to say, "Yes, but the abuses you speak of, ma'am, are to be found in every country. Why, even in England, no doubt just a few miles from your home in the city, many paupers crowd together in misery no worse than that of China, and their ignorance of Scripture is just as great."

Everyone held his or her breath. Some felt great admiration for Miss Pendleton; others awaited an explosion.

"It is true that the conditions of the poor people of the great cities are not good, but they have shown again and again that they are a very shiftless lot, unwilling to learn the basic tenets of a religion that would raise them above the mire in which they wallow."

"That's a very interesting point," continued Isolde, unaware that she was stirring up controversy. "I wonder if you have read much Thoreau? I mean, Henry David Thoreau, our American philosopher. He had some very interesting beliefs of what religion should and should not be. At any event, it seems rather foolish to worry about the Chinese when you have plenty of poor people of your own so much handier."

Even Aunt Honora was silenced for the moment. After dinner was over, however, and she had ceremoniously removed the ladies to a salon, she ordered Miss Pendleton to sit beside her for a moment.

"How long do you plan on staying in England, young lady?" asked the grand dame.

"Only for a few weeks. We were supposed to go directly to Italy for the spring, but it seemed a pity to send Elizabeth away by herself, and Lord Albert's kind invitation did seem interesting."

"Indeed? You find yourself interested in the English?"

"Oh, yes," said Isolde, puzzled. "Especially the countryside. It is very beautiful here."

"I notice you have been spending a good deal of your time in my nephew Thornbrough's company."

There was a pause. "I should warn you that Thornbrough is, despite his reputation, quite a high stickler for form. It would never occur to him, for example, to marry below his rank. He is of a very old family, one of the oldest in England, and his income is also one of the greatest. Many a matchmaking mother has attempted to catch him, but I must warn you he is very elusive."

"Indeed?" said Isolde coolly. "Does he frequently require your services to warn off ineligible young ladies?" asked Isolde, her neatly dressed, slender body upright in the antique, straight-backed chair.

"My nephew Thornbrough, unlike so many of his contemporaries, seldom associates with any of inferior rank."

There was nothing more to be said. Isolde's conscience pricked her at times when she thought of poor Gerald Connell hunting lions in Africa as he tried to forget her. She felt a trifle unkind when she thought of handsome, young John McNally in Paris, trying to be a struggling art student simply in the hope that that vivid world of starving artists and their models would drive New York society from his mind. But over Martin Thornbrough she could feel no qualms. He was handsome, he was wealthy, he was well-born. His manners were self-assured and his experience with society and with women in general was wide. On the surface, he could be a pleasant companion. Isolde did not doubt that underneath he was as insufferably proud as his relatives rated him. Isolde, an only child, was accustomed to being much petted and spoiled by her own mother and father, and sought after when she did go into company. She certainly did not need to hunt a husband, but Mr. Thornbrough would be an interesting interlude, a challenge after her succession of simple, sweet, handsome young men.

Feeling Lizzie's suspicious eyes upon her, Isolde moved across the room to sit next to neglected Cathleen. Just about then, the men entered the room. Mr. Thornbrough looked about, and seeing her, he smiled, but she turned her back just as he sighted her. Whether or not she was turning her back on him or merely leaning forward to listen to his cousin was not apparent, but at that moment his watchful aunt demanded his attention. Annoyed, he obeyed her summons and was soon hot into the question of whether or not dear little Missie, her pug dog, an animal which he had been strongly inclined to take out and shoot in his younger days, had mange of the eyes, was going blind, or had some kind of fungus, and what the best treatment could be for the dear little animal.

"What have you been doing here, Miss Battersbottom?" asked Isolde. "I suppose you must have visited here many, many times."

"No, never," said Cathleen, her wide-eyed look of terror softening even Isolde's tumultuous feelings. She was a poor, thin little thing, with sandy hair, sandy eyebrows, and freckled skin that simply did not look well in maidenly white. Her hair was done in a rather awful style, too, but her face seemed nice enough.

"How odd! Aren't you Lord Albert's first cousin? I should have thought you would have visited at the holidays and all that."

"Mama didn't get on well with Bertie's mama," said Cathleen. "Why do you call him Lord Albert? I know it's the polite thing, but no one else in London does and it must be strange for him."

Isolde felt her wrath rising again. "It's very odd, Miss Battersbottom, but I think the English must possess a faculty we Americans lack. They seem to think we can learn all their ways by instinct, as if we remember our past lives spent here, perhaps. I hope you never travel in the United States; you will be surprised that life is not *exactly* what it is here."

"Now you are angry!" Cathleen exclaimed. "I did not mean to offend you. Please forgive me. Ordinarily no one pays any attention to me or what I say at all, so it's difficult for me to know what other people may find offensive." Seeing that Isolde was rather confused, she added, "You see, if no one pays any attention to what you say, it doesn't matter how insulting you are; they never notice."

"Do you insult people often then, unobserved?" asked Isolde, amused.

"Oh, I can say almost anything to Aunt Honora, if I use the proper intonation, and she never notices. One must do something if one is forced to play backgammon with her hour after hour. Most people don't want to hear your answer, so it doesn't matter what the answer is."

"How different you are from your brother," exclaimed Isolde.

"I know," said Cathleen. "I have always hoped that I was the result of an indiscretion on the part of Mama. She certainly treats me like one."

"Do you really? How amusing? And do you imagine that you had a very grand father? A prince, perhaps?"

"Oh, no. Mama is very plain and not at all charming. And we have never been wealthy. I don't think Mama knows any princes. If I do have a secret father, I think he must be a servant, a handsome footman or a butler or someone like that."

"Miss Battersbottom!"

"I do, because all my life I have had a terrific urge to learn how to cook. I have always been the one to make the tea, you know, and now here at Toye they are so kind as to allow me to take lessons from Pierre, Mr. Thornbrough's cook. He is a very great cook, even though he swears so awfully at the kitchen here. But I do love cutting up the vegetables and if we are here long enough, he says he will teach me to make *choux* paste. That's a kind of pastry dough," she explained.

"So you have ambition! And what will you do when you leave?"

"Well, I am very poor, you know, and when Papa and Mama die I will be even poorer, so then I will be able to do what I want and cook everything as I wish. It does seem a shame that I won't be able to cook for parties the way Pierre does. There is so much I'll never be able to learn in the time we're here."

"What fun it sounds. Do you mind if I come down with you tomorrow?"

Cathleen hesitated. "I don't want to seem rude, but Pierre is very fussy. He is French, you know. He might not be willing. But the kitchen is so big—you can practically stand up in the fireplace—that I really don't see how he can mind. I'll come and tap on your door, and we'll go down straight after breakfast and ask politely."

Cathleen was an amusingly forthright person. It seemed odd that her strict upbringing had not cramped her soul, but it had not. Isolde learned Cathleen's life history, and it was an interesting study. She had been sent to boarding schools, and then presented for grim season after grim season. She seemed to spend the greater part of her life trying to escape from petty servitude to domineering adults. She was resigned to discomfort, but not inured.

Isolde felt Mr. Thornbrough's eye upon her several times throughout the evening. There was no denying that he was good-looking. She could see, from the corner of her eye, his dark, slanted eyebrow climb his forehead. But she remained close to Cathleen until she retired early that evening. Only once did she allow herself to meet his gaze, and then she met it head on with a long look from her dark blue eyes and a secret smile, a knowing smile, the kind of smile lovers exchange, full of understanding and openness.

The next morning everyone was up early. Lady Honora, attired in an outmoded gown of startlingly ugly shades of mauve and green, attempted to marshal all the young people into order. She had formed some delightful plans for the day. Miss Pendleton, Edwin, and the Brookes might go for another walk around the park, if they desired, and they might take her dear little Missy with them. Missy, sweet thing, wanted ever so much to go for a walk, but Miss Pendleton must not walk too fast; she was afraid Missy's heart was not strong and could not take violent exercise. Mr. Thornbrough might find entertainment in the study; she was sure he had some business to look into, and she needed Cathleen to attend to a few letters she had to send off. She thought she had heard Miss Wilcox express a desire to be shown over the castle; that would be best done by Albert.

But, refraining from making rude remarks, the young people drifted through her fingers as easily and quickly as the air went out of a puncture in one of Dunlop's new inflatable tires.

Cathleen and Isolde, dressed in their simplest clothes, went down to the kitchens. Cathleen was very timid, but Pierre was surprisingly amenable to having two young ladies in his kitchens instead of one. The American one was very pretty, and Pierre never objected to having pretty girls about. Besides, he was very interested in the Americans. The English one, the plain one, did not understand French very well. It made it difficult to explain things to her, even though she was not unappreciated and seemed to have good hands with a chicken. But the American one, although her accent was, of course, an abomination, spoke fluent French and was able to tell him just how food in America was served. He had heard that the rich Americans were great eaters and wondered if they, unlike the English, were capable of appreciating the more delicate points of cuisine a French genius could offer. Mademoiselle doubted this, but she pointed out that there were snobs in America just as there were in any country who would want others to think they were capable of such appreciation. And there was money to pay for such things. She told of the night her father had dined with Diamond Jim Brady, and although Pierre could but deplore such gourmandizing—was it possible, could any man eat six dozen oysters, lobsters smothered in crabs and steaks smothered in cutlets, several gallons of *orange juice,* a platter of pastry, and one or two boxes of candy to finish off—he did see there were possibilities in such a place.

Miss Pendleton had never possessed a great appetite, and she really did not care to see quite so many ducklings lying about without their heads and parts of cows and baby sheep hanging up on hooks. When she found herself growing a little faint, Pierre was all understanding. Cathleen, who had a very practical nature, admired such delicacy greatly. Pierre fussed over her, and put the offending corpses out of her sight, saying he would attend to them later. They could eat a simple lunch upstairs today, soup and fresh bread and butter and perhaps a salad with his own dressing and of course a few joints of ham and beef. Perhaps the lady would care to see him make one of his special sauces. Curses on such a kitchen as this! He could not make so much as a soufflé or bake proper bread. Isolde stayed and watched him bake bread and a cake, two very interesting processes.

She had never actually seen bread being made and got quite a lot of flour on herself while watching.

Pierre gave her and Cathleen each a piece of dough, just as if they had been little girls playing house, which was how Isolde suspected he thought of them. As she stood at the long wooden table, made of thick beams scored over and over with countless knives in the big, stone-floored kitchen, with all its gleaming copper pots, brought by Pierre, hanging about, she could imagine herself as a kitchen maid working in the kitchen of some Sir Walter Scott hero. While her long fingers kneaded the ball of dough, her mind drifted into the past, merging with other female figures who had stood in this same kitchen in other centuries, kneading bread just as she was now. She became oblivious to everything but her dreams.

"Miss Pendleton?" said a voice in her ear. *"Miss Pendleton?"* the voice repeated, and the present came rushing in on her. She smiled her faint, absent smile and said, with as much modernity as she could muster, "Yes?"

"Are you through kneading? I think you are. There is a danger of kneading too much, you know," and Cathleen wrested the sticky lump of dough from her hands, gave it a few efficient, floury pats, and put it in a little pan. "There. Now we must go wash up, or the others will be suspicious. Lunch will be ready in an hour or so, and although Pierre is being very polite to you—how nice it must be to be rich and pretty, everyone seems so polite—he doesn't like anyone to hang about just before he begins to serve a meal."

She went up to her room, dutifully washed up, and smoothed her hair, even changing her dress for lunch. The others trooped in in a very gay and noisy spirit. They seemed to be busy trying to compare jokes that the two continents had in common. Even Lady Honora was swept up in their mood and deigned to tell a very long, rambling anecdote about some very funny accident that happened to a friend of hers in her youth, but since the tale had no punch line, and went on for well over five minutes, she only managed to cast a silence over the company.

Isolde's silence was so notable that after luncheon Elizabeth followed her upstairs and asked her if she had the headache. Realizing how convenient an excuse this was, Isolde replied in her quiet way, "Only a very small one, dear Elizabeth. I'm sure it will go away if I am quiet for the afternoon." Elizabeth, who had never suffered from a headache in her life, was full of sympathy. She had not had Isolde's mother's training in recognizing Isolde's symptoms. Isolde had had a very sickly childhood, and for many years past her childhood her parents had watched over her carefully, coddled her, and believed her when she excused herself in a faint voice from the dances, calls, brisk walks, and trips to the seaside they had thought would have been so beneficial, so cheering, and so conducive to the kind of vigorous good health they enjoyed. Isolde's mother, however, was the first to notice that these attacks frequently coincided with the purchase of a new novel, and that no matter how tired and drained Isolde seemed one day, she was always well enough the next to visit some artist or writer in whom she was particularly interested. Mrs. Pendleton described her suspicions to her husband, but he was loath to believe that a daughter of his could be such a daydreamer. Besides, she was not at all scholarly; in fact, in his opinion she was painfully ignorant about some matters. They hoped the trip to Europe might alter some of the lazy habits she had acquired during her childhood. They were certain that a visit to the countryside, full of interesting new people and many sights of interest, would be just the thing.

Elizabeth, however, was in ignorance of all this, so she plumped up Isolde's pillows most sympathetically, leaving her with a copy of Tennyson's *Idylls of the*

King, which would have made Mrs. Pendleton suspicious immediately.

"Mr. Thornbrough asked me in particular if you were feeling quite the thing. He said he would feel honored if you would cheer him on to victory." Mr. Thornbrough and Bertie had laid mock wagers on who could beat the other at a bicycle race.

"I really can't, Elizabeth. You know how everyone will be shouting and jumping about. I don't want to throw a damper on it."

"Poor thing. Shall I give him a message for you?"

"Message?" repeated Isolde in tones of blank innocence. "No, no message."

"Do you think you will be ready to take a quiet walk later in the afternoon?"

Isolde opened her book again, leaned back on her pillows, and looked very wan. "I'm so sorry to be this way, Elizabeth, but perhaps if I stay very still all afternoon, I'll be able to get up tonight." Mystified by the nature and gravity of Isolde's illness, Elizabeth left her alone.

Isolde listened to the sound of Elizabeth's retreating footsteps as she went down the hallway and descended the staircase. The castle was silent; the others were all outside, larking about near the stables. Isolde knew Elizabeth well enough to have noticed that she was not one to tire easily, and certainly would be back just in time to change her dress for tea, if that. So when Isolde was certain that all was silent, she took her slim little volume of verse, and creeping out into the corridor, found a pair of stairs and climbed up into the battlements.

A gray fog hung down like a curtain over the horizon, but the grayness only served to make the sky seem more a part of the castle, a paler extension of it, turned to gas and exploded outwards, or castle vapors that had not yet crystallized into solid form. Isolde, standing near the edges of the battlements, could see the yellow daffodils below, and the dots of red campion and hyacinth in the green lawns, edged with stone walls that snaked out of sight. She felt quite happy, quite satisfied, as if she had found a nice bit of England to break off and put in her pocket, something that would be hers forever.

In the distance Major Brooke, who was by the stable, chanced to glance up at Toye and see a figure in white standing on the southeast turrets, her gown blowing gently in the wind. "What an odd gel your fwiend is!" he exclaimed to Elizabeth. "There she is, up on the top of the woof!"

"Isolde!" exclaimed Elizabeth. "She told me she had a headache and could not possibly rise from her bed this afternoon. How strange! I suppose she wanted to be alone for a while. It must be a wonderful view."

Women in whom Mr. Thornbrough had expressed interest did not usually make excuses and go creeping away to their rooms with tales of headaches. She had seemed to like him, and he did not think she was shy of him. Like the others, he paused for a moment or two and watched the figure dressed in white stand serenely against the gray sky.

Chapter 13

Major Brooke decided to alleviate the inevitable boredom of Sunday in the country under the rule of a martinet like Aunt Honora, who would certainly refuse them even the simplest pleasures, like gambling or drinking, by getting extremely intoxicated the night before. Certainly no one would have objected to this scenario, since a headache the next day was his own business, after all, if he had not chosen to allow Edwin to stay up and be his drinking partner.

"Weally, Georgie, it's not my fault," said her spouse indignantly. "And it's vewy bad manners of you to come in and shout at me like that when you must know that I don't feel at all well myself. How was I to know the silly fellow had neveh been dwunk before?"

"Everyone is very irritated with you," said Georgie. "I wouldn't be surprised if Lady Honora asked us to leave."

"I wouldn't be supwised if I did leave too," said her husband. "It wasn't even good wine. And he was weally a little bwat about it."

"Well, so were you, waking up the whole household singing obscene songs."

"They wewen't obscene songs. They were just vewy funny songs, pe'haps a twifle off coloh. And I had to do something to cheeh him up—he was so sick to his stomach. Weally, Georgie, I am supwised with Thownbwough, and Bertie too. First this aunt. Now anyone can have an aunt like that. But a cousin too? And then to invite two people who you call your fwiends and go off and leave them all alone for the night with someone like Edwin. Do you think we *can* stay, in all honoh, Georgie?"

Major Brooke, who was lounging in an armchair in his room dressed in a braided and brocaded jacket and smoking a cheroot supplied to him by Mr. Thornbrough, did not impress Georgie as being extremely uncomfortable.

"It was three o'clock in the morning," she said firmly. "You should have gone to bed yourself. Bertie should have made you."

"He twied," Fweddie admitted. "But you see, if one becomes extwemely well off on Satidday night, there's that much less of Sunday to wowwy about. You see, I finally went to bed at five o'clock in the mowning. That was weally five o'clock *Sunday* mowning. That meant I had gotten wid of five whole hours of the Sabbath before I even went to bed. Then, considewing I have to sleep for an least twelve hours or so, and wake up with a headache, and have to have things bwought up to me, I can get thwough Sunday pwetty well."

"You're a bad man," said his wife, shaking her head. "You may have even given me grounds for divorce. I'll post a letter off to the Queen when we get back to London to ask her for her opinion. Think of the suffering and embarrassment you brought on poor Edwin. He was ill all over the staircase, from top to bottom."

"Well, it's his own fault," said Fweddie. "He's an awful little wotter, and I almost punched him sevewal times last night. Think of poor Tuttle. No, Tuttle's too smart to get saddled with a detail like that. I'll think sadly for someone else. But I'm not sowwy."

It was left to the unfortunate Cathleen to administer to Edwin, who proved extremely ungrateful, poised, as he thought he was, on the brink of a hideous death that none of the others could appreciate. His head throbbed with pain, and he knew he was feverish, but when he sent Cathleen off with a request that the doctor be sent for, his aunt was filled with rage and the others with laughter. Mrs. Brooke ran up to her husband's room again to tell him this good joke, the servants quickly passed the news around in the kitchen, and his Aunt Honora appeared by his bedside like a vengeful spirit.

"These are the wages of sin!" she intoned deeply. "Last night you allowed yourself to become disgustingly inebriated, in a manner which must bring shame to your breast, as it does to mine. Any pain you may feel now is only temporary, alas. I could wish that your head would ache for the rest of your life, so that you would remember forever this lesson in degradation. How your poor mother will bear the news of this scandalous affair I do not know, but she certainly must be told of her only son's fall from innocence."

Blanching under this threat, Edwin was quick to point out that he had been led astray. His drinking companion, as she knew, was far more experienced than he, and had forced him, through what means he could not as a gentleman reveal, to match him drink for drink.

She hesitated. It was a tricky business. Edwin should be sent away, but that would be a pity considering there was still the matter of more than one American heiress to be disposed of, and several more days before the end of the party. Thornbrough seemed to have come to his senses and was displaying his usual aloofness to Miss Pendleton, so Edwin just might have a chance. She had long thought that Ed-

win was clearly unfit for any profession, save perhaps
the ministry, and since the family living had long ago
been sold, it would be difficult to place him even in
this. No, it must be the heiress, so after finishing her
scold, adjuring him to abandon the companionship of
those who were already abandoned (neat phrasing
had long been a pride of hers, although she had
taken the saying from Palmer's *Sermons*), she out-
lined once more for him just what he stood to lose by
such silly, schoolboyish behavior.

The others all enjoyed themselves very well. After
the services, the vicar showed the young ladies over
the church, which was a Norman building with a
single tall, gray tower and inside, the bier of some
long dead ancestor of Bertie's. When they passed
through town, the villagers, wearing their Sunday
clothes, bobbed curtsies and took off their caps. It all
seemed unreal to Isolde, as if she were caught up in a
dream, finally living in something she had made up.

To Elizabeth, the people she was with were very
puzzling. She couldn't quite figure why Bertie was so
poor, or why he was such a bad landlord, as he obviously must be, and yet had so many tenants who were
obviously fond of him. The Brookes were no curiosity; there were Brookes in America as well as England,
although they spoke with different accents. Mr.
Thornbrough was an oddity. He was really extremely
handsome, but must have a very bad temper. He had
galloped his horse over an extremely bad road yesterday as if he were actually angry over something.
Nothing was transparent to Elizabeth—and Elizabeth
liked order.

Chapter 14

Elizabeth had quite decided what to do with her hosts, her hostess, and her fellow guests the next day. It might be for Lady Honora to pass through life thwarted at every step by disobedient servants, recalcitrant offspring, and disappointing relatives, none of whom would ever quite learn to march to the tune she played. She never understood why redoubling her severity did not seem to answer the purpose. Nor was prayer of avail. Only threats seemed to answer, and even these could only be successful on the weak and dependent.

But Elizabeth Wilcox, gifted in life, knew how to set people in motion for their own good as well as hers. She had long ago learned a number of tricks from her papa, and working her magic on all the teachers and maids and the New York society matrons of her papa's acquaintance, she had managed to pull through, pleasing everyone and doing exactly as she liked.

So on this day, when Aunt Honora began to make plans to divide the group into amicable couples of her own choice, everyone was somehow intent on quite different occupations. Everyone wanted to spend such a glorious spring morning outdoors. Elizabeth had discovered in herself quite a mania for bicycle riding and begged Bertie to lend her one of his new safeties. She would be quite careful. No, no, she knew he wanted to stay home and work on his new portable device for inflating tires. She would be off by herself.

In this rush of spirits Isolde found herself outdoors, too, and it was for Mr. Thornbrough, an old hand at the art of manipulation himself, to suggest that they take a walk. He did not suggest that they bring any-one along to chaperon, and Isolde, with her usual acumen, didn't think of it.

"I know you are a great rider, Mr. Thornbrough," said Isolde. "I am sure you would prefer to be exer-cising your horses."

"Not at all," he replied. "You see, I have been at Toye enough times to know a number of things about it that the others haven't discovered yet. I'm afraid Bertie is one for the beaten path. He can't seem to bring himself to go anywhere where one can't take a bicycle, and that eliminates the violet wood."

Isolde did not reply, and to prod the conversation, he said, "I hope you were not too shocked by my cousin Edwin's behavior yesterday?"

"Edwin?" she said, looking up into his face. "Oh, no, but it's clear that he fancies himself and that's a shame because he's such a spotty kind of young man."

"Excuse me?"

"Let's talk of his sister," said Isolde. "Do you fre-quently spend a great deal of time with your cousins at parties such as this?"

"I'm afraid I am not extremely well acquainted with Cathleen," he said. "She is so much younger than I am and never seems to be anywhere about, ei-ther."

"How odd," exclaimed Isolde in soft accents, as she lifted her skirts to climb a sloping hill. "She cannot have inherited this trait from Lady Honora."

Mr. Thornbrough was highly annoyed by this re-mark. He was feeling some emotions of distaste for the temerity of *nouveau riche* when Isolde exclaimed, "Oh, what kind of bird is that? Do you know, I have only seen birds like pigeons and sea gulls before."

It was a moorhen, and Mr. Thornbrough, feeling that she seemed almost naive in the manner of a child and so could not be responsible for outspoken remarks, decided to help her find the nest.

"I've never been bird's-nesting in Warwickshire," he said. "But it's the same wherever you are. Come, let's see." The nest was very difficult for them to locate, hunt as they did. They finally found it in the stump of an old alder tree at the edge of a pond, just out of reach of the bank.

"I've never seen a bird's nest before," she said in soft tones of amazement, holding it in her hand with a quiet strength. She really was beautiful, he reflected, with her classical features and glossy brown hair and lovely eyes. She was so quiet, so still in company, and she never seemed to call any attention to herself, that it was hard to know she could shine forth like this.

Isolde was in a newfound element. Her mother had always taken pride in cultivating Isolde's interest in the conservatory, encouraging her to paint and sketch there and arrange picturesque seats among palms and ferns. England in spring put a rubber plant to shame. The plant's broad, glossy leaves could never impress themselves on her in the startling way that an unkept hedgerow could, with its tumultuous white blossoms and its myriad occupants: bees, nest-building birds, and rabbits.

Isolde's mood became one of her dreamiest, and Mr. Thornbrough, abandoning the attempt to start a coherent conversation between them, led her onward.

After a walk of almost an hour, they came to the violet wood, a place that Isolde secretly thought might exist only in Mr. Thornbrough's imagination.

But there it was, full of firs and sycamores, the sycamores in full leaf of bright new green. The ground was covered with wild arums, all in flower, and the heads of violets covered the lush floor of the wood. A rabbit, seeing the couple approach, disappeared into a burrow near one of the trees, and all was still.

"Mr. Thornbrough," said Isolde, "do let us stop here for a few minutes and rest." And without fussing over her gown or the wetness of the dew, she lay down on the ground, luxuriating in its touch.

Seating himself awkwardly beside her, Thornie began to suspect that she was an aesthete, but she did not talk enough for one, and if this was all posturing, it was very convincing indeed. Mr. Thornbrough, who knew instinctively the inexperienced from the experienced, and usually chose the attentions of the latter, could not even tell if Isolde was actually tired or merely wished to seem picturesque. Actually, she seemed neither. She seemed just to be relaxing into the texture of the earth, but he had never seen any women with their tight corsets, their gigantic sleeves, their carefully ratted and arranged hair and other hindrances of fashion, loll about on the ground in such a manner. She was decidedly an unusual kind of female, very different even from Miss Wilcox; he had the feeling that her innocence was due not merely to her nationality, but to her own uniqueness. However, it was to be hoped that she would not behave in this manner with a number of his acquaintances, his sovereign prince, for example, or even the loathsome Edwin.

He could feel her blue eyes gazing up at him, and he turned to meet them. Her eyes met his and then, smiling a little, she shut them, her delicate, purple-veined lids with their long dark lashes closing. Mr. Thornbrough bent over and kissed her. She kissed him back, her eyes still closed.

A kiss is like a question that cannot be too delicately phrased; but Isolde was ready with the answers. Martin, who had been prepared at best to act as a guide, to exchange carefully chosen poetic quotes which might border on romantic, and perhaps a solitary and fleeting kiss, found himself lying on the earth with the beautiful young American being kissed slowly and gently over his cheeks and hard jaw. And then she was warmly pressing her mouth on his with the expertise that comes with practice or strong desire.

For some time they kissed, and then Isolde sat up again with a small laugh. "I still have my hat on," she said, smiling. Out came the hatpins and the hairpins, and down came her dark wavy mass of hair, tumbling down around her waist. She shook it out before her, tickling him on the chest with the tips of her curls as he watched her in silence.

Her stockings and shoes followed the hat, as they too were discarded on the bank of the creek. Her feet were long and slender; she dipped them into the water as she watched Martin out of the corner of her eye. She watched his strong figure stretched out on the riverbank, and an excitement uninspired by revenge or perversity rushed through her.

"It is so beautiful here," she said, her tones soft, persuading. "No one has ever chatted here. No one has ever made small talk. One could become immortal here. Like the gods."

Calmly, easily, she began to unbutton the row of pearl buttons that fastened her dress in the front. Standing, she stepped out of the gown, prolonging the pleasure of undressing before him. She wore several fine, thin, white cambric petticoats under her dress and she pulled these off over her head one at a time, pausing for a moment each time as she let him watch the picture she was creating, standing half-naked, her hair down her back, one foot in the pool of water, the other on the bank, and the violets behind her.

The last petticoat was pulled off over her head. Since she had always had a wispy figure, she never wore the corsets affected by her more thickly waisted, buxom friends. She stood by the brook for a moment naked, her small breasts white and her waist flat, her long legs stretching down to the ground, smiling at Martin as he lay, brows darkened, on the ground.

"There should be a time for dreams," she said softly. "There should be magic places and magic times. Let this be it. Let us create a perfect moment here in the violet wood. When we rejoin the others, let us pretend that none of this ever happened. I will go back to the United States, and you will go back to London. When someone mentions your name to me, I'll smile to myself; I chanced to meet you one weekend in a castle. Only I will know that near the castle was a violet wood. Come, Martin," she said, kneeling beside him now and beginning to unbutton his vest. "Let us create our perfect moment. Let us pretend we are gods."

Thornie had made love to women hurriedly, a bundle of skirts and stays, while their husbands obligingly stayed at their clubs so that he might come "for tea." He had enjoyed more relaxing rendezvous in houses he rented in St. John's Wood, temporary but sufficiently satisfying relationships. And he had taken his pot luck at a variety of establishments that ranged from highly decorous to rompishly disgusting.

But never had a young girl seduced him in a violet wood. His conscience warned him against it; he tried to quickly, pessimistically, think of some purpose, some worldly motive Isolde might have.

But none occurred to him. He reached out shaking fingers to touch her hair, her shoulders, her breasts.

When he felt her fingers gently stroking him,
reaching between the layers of cloth to touch his
flesh, he needed no more encouragement. She had
been all eagerness; but his fingers were skilled, too,
and his mouth, and that which he plunged into her
soft, ready body.

All thought of triumph and manipulation had left
Isolde's head. She gave herself up to an ecstasy no vir-
ginal young man had ever elicited from her. And the
rhythm of their two bodies working together for one
end was like a rock dropped into a still lake; neither
could see where the waves would stop lapping. But
they gave no thought to that now.

Chapter 15

Lizzie, in the meantime, had found plenty of occupation for herself that morning. She rode into town on one of Bertie's bicycles, and by the time she reached the village, she had a number of regrets and several bruises to show for her pains. It was not as easy as it had seemed when Bertie was with her. He had ridden the road many times and knew just when the wagon wheel tracks would become so deep that they must get out and walk, and when the gravel at curves was so thickly strewn that they must slow down or tip over.

Elizabeth, unfortunately, did not know these things. Nor did she know how to repair tires that exploded on any little rock in the road. It was with deep relief that she hailed a wagon passing on the road after she had waited at least half an hour.

The wagoner, without showing too much scorn or derision for the machine, loaded it up onto his cart and carried it and her into the village "I know they're cheap to run, miss. They don't eat oats the way my horse does, but reliable they'll never be. Take my advice. Buy yourself an old mare with a few good years left in her, and you won't regret it."

"I think you must be right," she said. "Let me assure you that the thing is not mine at all, but Lord Albert Taunton's. It was he who let me go off on this ill-mannered creature."

The wagoner nodded. "Aye, that would explain it. A very odd one, Lord Albert is, from all accounts. It's not proper for lords to be messing about with these things, not to my mind. I like a lord with a stable myself."

The castle at Toye was a noble edifice, but it was not much larger in size than the stable housing the various horses owned by Miss Elizabeth Wilcox and her father. Horses were something of a hobby with them, and at their country place they allowed themselves the pleasure of breeding dozens of the animals. Miss Wilcox had left behind her a string of hunters, a number of good mounts, and three teams of carriage horses, to say nothing of the beasts belonging to her father and those that they kept about for the use of their guests. Sitting in the old, rather muddy wagon, bumping over the bad roads with the silent wagoner, Miss Wilcox could not but agree. Horses had their uses.

It was now about luncheon time, and she went into the Red Drum to order tea. When the hulking Samuel saw her enter, he winked at her, turned his back to her and, without speaking, headed for the kitchen door. Miss Wilcox could hear him shouting, "Maggie, Maggie. It's that girl who was here with . . ." and then his voice trailed off. In a few instants, Maggie appeared, wiping her hands on her apron and smiling mightily.

"Eh, and it's Miss Wilcox here. Welcome, miss, I'm sure. Is there anything I can do for you?"

"I should like tea, if you please," said Miss Wilcox.

"Tea you shall have, but in the private parlor, miss, not in this common taproom." The parlor was a small room on the second floor of the building in the rear, looking over a neatly plotted kitchen garden. It was very quiet in the village this morning. Elizabeth, tired from the morning's exercise, was glad to sink into an old armchair.

"What a beautiful room this is," she said to Maggie. "Your inn is very lovely. We have nothing so fine in New York."

"It's stood for quite a few years and it'll stand for some more," said Maggie. "You put your feet up there, and I'll be back with your tea in an instant."

Tea was served with a fresh loaf of bread, a small pat of butter, and watercress. Maggie was inclined to fuss over Lizzie and insist on making the tea for her, and Lizzie, lounging back in her armchair, was disposed to let her. She had not come for the tea, after all, but to see Maggie.

"I am growing very fond of England already," she said lightly. "I am so glad to have been invited to visit in the country. This is a very different England from the crowded streets of London."

"Perhaps it is a nice enough country," said Maggie unwillingly.

"And it all seems to be farmland, too," continued Elizabeth. "I don't know anything about farming, but in America I know farmers are a very well off lot."

"Well, they aren't here," said Maggie shortly. "Oh, I can remember a time when the countryside was all small farms worked by proud men, but those times are over. They've all had to give up and go to the cities and try to squeeze out whatever they could there."

"Why?" asked Elizabeth.

"Because of your American wheat and because of this New Zealand lamb and mutton that comes in on these new refrigerated ships. It's ruined English farming forever. It seems it has to be the Corn Laws and starvation for the poor people, or all this cheap wheat and mutton and ruination for us country folk. Nothing's what it used to be, and I can only hold a roof over my head and be glad that my landlord won't sell my inn out from under me."

"Then you don't own this inn? Oh, I thought you did."

"Lordie no, it's his lordship's, Lor' Bertie, who owns the whole village, and most of the land about, too."

"I must say I don't think he's much of a landlord then," said Elizabeth. "Some of the houses in the village seem to be in sad order."

"He's as good as he can be, with never a penny to put back into land that has been cleaned out. He could turn us all out, or sell us to someone who would. Or he could just sell us out to some rich factory owner with a mind to become a lord of a manor; I've heard of them. They buy up estates and the villages too, breed a lot of birds and have shooting parties, and interfere with all the local customs."

"But Lord Albert has enough money to live comfortably in London or here in the country."

"Beg pardon, miss," said Maggie, grinning a little grimly. "Three servants at Toye is not living comfortably and Lor' Bertie stays there when most of the nobs are off with their boats or visiting Paris."

"It does seem to me, though," said Elizabeth, "that with all this land he could think of some productive way to use it."

Maggie shrugged. "No coal mines in these parts, miss. It's the lords with mines and factories on their lands that have the incomes to spend these days, miss. Nothing like that around Toye. His lordship wouldn't have the income to start anything like that if he wanted to."

"I see. And Mr. Thornbrough's income? It is derived from—?"

"Coal mines, I believe, miss."

"How interesting," said Elizabeth. "This is really delightful tea. Is it Darjeeling? I'm afraid I know very little about teas; in America we drink so much coffee."

Maggie knew a cue when she heard one, and she was also determined to find out as much as she could about America from this young lady. Her favorite aunt had gone there ten years ago and sent letters back from a place called Dakota Territory; had Elizabeth ever been there? Elizabeth had to shake her head, but she was able to tell Maggie that the Dakotas were a fearfully cold place to winter in, that they were renowned for their gophers and Indians, and that the crops raised on the prairie soil were supposed to be good. Elizabeth was able to give Maggie glimpses of New York street life, and what life among a set of swells would be like there.

Maggie, like most of the villagers, had been greatly surprised at the news that Lor' Bertie was soon to be entertaining at Toye, and to be entertaining nobs, too. It had been more years than anyone could remember since a proper party had been held there, a real nob party with servants and lords and ladies.

When they had found out the identity of the members of the party, the hopes of the locality began to rise. It would be a great thing if this American girl were to marry Bertie. He would have money to live like a proper lord then. Wealth would come into the countryside again. Men would be hired to work on the estate, in the gardens, and in the house. Girls would be trained as maids. Trading would be done at local shops. Even if none of these long-term dreams materialized, the Americans were known to be a strange breed, throwing their money away as if they had it made to order in their own country. Wild stories were told of waiters who had been tipped so generously they had been set for life. Some had heard of one American merchant who didn't bother to change his currency back to American dollars and had simply bestrewn his path with bills and coins, leaving thousands of pounds in his wake for whoever could scramble quickly enough to pick them up.

It was with these sentiments at heart that Maggie said, "Not knowing any other nobs—Mr. Thornbrough has never stepped into my place here—I would be hard put to find anyone else more understanding and helpful than Lor' Bertie."

Maggie went on to describe Bertie's excellent qualities, his fondness for children, his kindnesses that verged on eccentricity, such as letting the villagers take a few birds from his land for the pot now and then. She described some of his less desirable habits, such as his everlasting tinkering with those silly velocipedes. That was clearly childish nonsense; just a fad for a boy. He would outgrow it. He was full of whims and fancies, as Maggie was sure Miss had noticed, always cutting a joke and playing the dunce.

Elizabeth was glad that they were drinking tea and not something more alcoholic, for by the end of this eulogy Maggie was waxing almost tearful. Not everyone understood Bertie, but how could anyone complain about a lord who was as thoughtful and pleasant as he? And he hadn't had a proper upbringing. His father had never taught him anything but how to gamble, she'd wager on that, and his mother was one of these modern women, always being thrown into jail and having to be bailed out and needing money for pamphlets and what was Bertie to do? It seemed the women in his family always needed money, and for bail tickets, of all things. And Vicar might complain that he set a bad example to the people by not being at service regular, but he was as Christian a man as you could find.

Elizabeth, who had heard young men eulogized before by hopeful relatives, was obliged to cut this flow of speech short and gently guide Maggie back to the subject of the treat which was being planned for the end of the week. She was fearfully ignorant of such matters, but she rather thought there weren't many teacups at Toye, and certainly not hundreds and hundreds. Could such things be hired? And Pierre, Mr. Thornbrough's cook, balked at the suggestion that he be required to supply cakes and bread for a large quantity of peasants and their children. Elizabeth was not even certain about the tea; where should it be ordered? Everyone at Toye seemed rather confused, and the housekeeper was so enthralled with the prospect of cleaning and preparing the castle for the invasion that she had urged Elizabeth to seek out Mrs. Gilbert and leave the matter in her hands.

Maggie was pleased with the housekeeper's good sense, and although she was intelligent enough to know that she had been put off the track of her subject, her hopes were still high. The American Miss had added—in that accent of hers which did *not* sound the way American accents were nasally imitated in music halls yet did not have quite the tones of an English girl's—that she hoped this treat would be a very special one. She said that she felt she owed a great deal to this part of England for showing her its beauty, and that she would like to be sure that the party would be a very special one to show her gratitude. Very nicely put, but perhaps there was something behind that fancy talk.

"You haven't met my friend Isolde, Mrs. Gilbert," said Elizabeth. "I'm sure she'll want to go to Chillingsworth with us to help pick out the toys. We may make up a party of it. Would tomorrow be convenient?" Maggie agreed, and the conversation being over, ordered Samuel to drive Miss Wilcox home. She certainly couldn't ride that bicycle back at this time of the day, she'd burn in the sun, and if Maggie didn't have all these cakes to see to, she had a mind

to go along too and tell Lor' Bertie what she
thought of his hospitable ways, letting a young girl
ride off alone on a road like that with one of those
contraptions, and a peculiar new one, too, that
seemed to be no better than a seat between two bal-
loons.

Samuel was sphinxlike on the way home, so Elizabeth had plenty of time to gather her thoughts. Maggie obviously had schemes, and one couldn't blame
her, but how much of it had been precipitated by
Bertie himself? He hadn't seemed like the kind of
man who would go into the local tavern and begin to
brag over a conquest that he hadn't yet made. In fact,
nor did the Red Drum seem like the ordinary tavern,
or Maggie the ordinary innkeeper. Of course, she
knew nothing of such things in England, but in
America she had never encountered a hostelry that
seemed so much like a family home. Rosa Hurst, as
she reflected, ran her hotel along grander but equally
intimate lines. Lady Battersbottom might condemn
Bertie's moral tone and his lack of social responsibility, but Maggie and Rosa gave him the highest
recommendations. Their judgment might be tinged
slightly by greed, but Lady Battersbottom's was
brightly colored with that avaricious quality that she
thought her due to exercise. It was difficult to like
Lady Battersbottom. Elizabeth was glad that no one
else made any effort to do so.

No, if anyone had bragged of conquests, it would
have been Edwin. No doubt, reflected Elizabeth with
amusement, he had already half convinced himself
that she was in love with him. He had that insufferable air at breakfast this morning that he could do no
wrong in her eyes. Perhaps he wasn't aware of just
how ridiculous he was. It was the spots. But that
mustache of his was absurd, too. So was Bertie's, for
that matter, but at least his was dapper.

The wagon pulled up before what had once been the Toye drawbridge, which after a short wait was opened for her by Tuttle.

"Drive the velocipede around and unload it at the stables, Mr. Gilbert," said Elizabeth, handing him a coin. "I don't feel fond enough of the thing to want to safely stow it there myself, and no doubt his lordship is anxiously awaiting its return to the fold."

"His lordship is in the courtyard, miss," said Tuttle. "Perhaps you would like to join the party there. Mr. Geoffrey Smythe is here."

"Then I do think I should change my dress first, don't you, Tuttle?"

"Indeed, miss. One might almost think you had been riding on one of his lordship's latest. I will send a maid up with some hot water."

She started up the staircase, but turned back after the first few steps. "Tuttle," she asked, "how long have you known Bertie?"

"Seven years, miss," said Tuttle.

"Have you ever thought of hiring out to anyone else? My father has written me asking him to find an English manservant."

Tuttle's heart swelled. America, and in the service of a millionaire. But his eyes remained fixed.

"I am deeply honored, miss, and would be happy to make inquiries for Mr. Wilcox. But I have been too satisfied in the employ of Lord Albert to consider a change."

"Ah, well," said Elizabeth. "I'm sure Bertie deserves you." And she continued up the stairs.

It was a little early for tea gowns, but she couldn't be bothered with changing again. She had noticed that none of the others seemed to dress quite so lacily as she did. Her father had always upheld Diamond Jim Brady's policy of when to wear precious stones: "Those as has 'em, wears 'em," but Elizabeth did not

seriously think either her father or Diamond Jim to
be true authorities on fashionable dress for the English countryside. So she refrained from fastening a
diamond dog collar around her white throat and
wore one of her simpler gowns, from Doucet, and not
Worth. It was cut just as superbly as the others, however, the bodice fitting her admirable figure to perfection. Perhaps a pink parasol, since it was still so
sunny out, and pink parasols were so becoming. She
left out her gown to be brushed off, if it was not ruined forever, and hurried downstairs wondering just
what a Geoffrey Smythe might be.

Everyone was sitting out in the garden. Isolde,
whose complexion was usually interestingly pale,
must have gone on one of those invigorating walks
with Mr. Thornbrough again; her cheeks were
flushed a bright pink, and her spirits must be high
since she was talking in the most provocative way
with a young unknown, who was quite good-looking.
How amusing! And Mr. Thornbrough seemed so
bored and irritated, too! What an interesting time
they must have had of it.

All the gentlemen rose as she entered, and Lady
Honora announced in her sonorous voice, "Miss Wilcox, let me introduce to you Mr. Geoffrey Smythe.
His land, or I should say, his father's land, borders
my nephew's on the south."

Elizabeth shook hands all around, and Mr. Smythe,
who had light brown hair and a very nice mustache
that curled just a bit at the ends, said with a twinkle
in his eye, "I can't think why my dear friend Bertie
has neglected to invite me over for dinner this week.
It is really too shabby of him. I never knew you were
so selfish, Bert."

"Not selfish at all," said Bertie. "Ask anyone. Ask
Thornie. Now Thornie's selfish. Ask Georgie. Ask

Tuttle. *He'll* tell you. Ask anyone you meet. *I'm* not selfish. I'm intelligent, but I'm not selfish."

"Then why haven't you invited me to meet these two beautiful young ladies, oh, generous neighbor?"

"Because I'm so intelligent. *I* know what you are, Geoffrey. You are *not* coming to dinner. If you are still here when tea is served, you shan't have any."

"Oh, not a crumb?"

"Not unless you agree to stay under the table and eat out of my hand like all the other dogs-in-the-manger around here."

"This is too bad of you," said Mr. Smythe lightly. "I feel quite insulted. Let me appeal to the ladies. Lady Honora, think how long my family has known yours. I believe we were tentmates during the Crusades. Why this ugliness now?"

Mr. Thornbrough's voice, containing a quality of annoyance which adults sometimes express toward distracting and noisy children, cut through, saying. "Of course you will stay if you wish, Geoffrey." He glanced warily at Isolde, but she was gazing dreamily at the sky.

"How too kind of you," replied that young man. "Do you know, Miss Wilcox, as I was just telling Miss Pendleton here, your face is quite familiar to me. I have already seen it in every shop window in London. You and Miss Wilcox seem to have already begun your careers as professional beauties. You will be quite swamped when you return to London."

"Good heavens," said Elizabeth. "How odd! I felt no differently when I woke this morning."

"Soon you will be setting all the fashions. Your dresses will be copied, your hairstyles will be copied and people will stand on chairs to see you drive through the park. All society will ache to meet you, and you will turn down invitations by the score. Ah, I wish I were a beautiful young lady. How pleasant life must be."

"It isn't at all," said Isolde. "We have to wear these dreadful skirts and our saddles are most inconvenient."

"True, I hadn't thought of that."

"And ladies awen't supposed to smoke, either," said Fweddie.

"Neither are *gentlemen*," Lady Honora said scathingly.

"How can you say that, ma'am?" asked Major Brooke helplessly. "Why, evwyone does. HRH does, you know."

"His Royal Highness is a Coburg," said Lady Honora. "Hardly of ancient English lineage. If you wish to smoke, Frederick, please remove yourself from this garden."

"Perhaps we'd all like to take a little stroll?" asked Mr. Smythe opportunely.

Elizabeth was anxious to reconnoiter with Isolde, who seemed to be in rather emotionally charged spirits this afternoon. She had discovered a view she was anxious to point out to Isolde. Mr. Thornbrough expressed his eagerness to share the view; perhaps it was one with which he was familiar and could describe in greater detail. But Isolde turned toward him and said in her quiet, polite voice, "Oh, no! Please don't let us disturb you. And someone must bear Lady Honora company." Cathleen was already doing so, but Thornie, after lifting his dark brow once or twice—perhaps it went by itself—left them.

Edwin tagged along with Bertie, Fwed, and Geoffrey, where he was very much unwelcome, especially since cigar smoke made him queasy.

"What casts our friend Thornbrough into such a gloom?" asked Smythe, as they strolled down a gravel path. "I say, Bertie, I'm not going to get my new trousers dirty, am I?"

"No, you're not," said Fweddie. "The wildehness doesn't begin for anotheh hundwed yards or so. I wonder if anyone has eveh told you how pwetty you look in white flannel with a stwaw boateh?"

"Why no, they haven't. How sweet of you to say so."

"Not at all. I'm mewely telling you the twuth."

"Bertie has come on to a good thing here, hasn't he?" said Geoffrey. "The good offices of his gruff but kindly cousin Thornie, I presume."

"Oh, be quiet, you cads," said Bertie. "I think it's disgusting the way you all talk like mamas with a daughter ready for the market."

"Not us, dear boy, not us," said Geoffrey. "I'm a rival, remember. Perhaps Fweddie here, having won the hand of the matchless Georgie, feels solicitous of your chances. I'm betting on myself for this one."

"You're disgusting," said Bertie.

"Isn't it sweet?" said Fweddie in a loud whisper. "He actually fell in love with her. Isn't Bertie wonderful? I hope when I die it is in Bertie's awms. He's so understanding. So sympathetic."

"Pathetic," asserted Geoffrey. "Perhaps you're right. Which one? The dark one or the fair one? They're both quite pretty. What a honeyfall they are! Together they seem too good to be true."

"Awen't they?" said Fweddie. "And the best of it is, they awe both wich."

"I think I'll leave," said Bert. "I wouldn't have invited you if I'd known what you were really like. I didn't invite you," he said to Geoffrey. "I *know* what you're like."

Fweddie and Geoffrey both shook their heads.

"And what's more," said Fweddie, lowering his voice, "the dark one, Isolde—I think she is aesthetic

or something like that, pe'haps she wites poetwy—
went for a long walk with Thownie this morning. A
vewy long walk indeed. And when they weturned,
Thownie was not himself."

"Who was he?"

"He was absentminded. Can you imagine Thownie
absentminded? Not at all like Thownie."

"And she?"

"She is *always* absentminded. But this afternoon
she was vewy cheehful. You were speaking with her
just now. Owdinawily, she hawdly says a word, but
just looks all about her like a disembodied soul who
isn't sure what star she's landed on."

"No!" said Geoffrey. "And what does Georgie think
of this?"

"Georgie was the one who told *me,* of course," said
Fweddie. "You don't think I'd notice something like
that? But when she pointed it out, it did hit me as
vewy odd."

"Thornie with a new flirt! A young new flirt, too!"
exclaimed Geoffrey. "What will Lady Daisy say? She's
been keeping him on a tight rein for over a year now,
and I thought for a few months when she made him
get rid of poor Dora of music hall fame that she was
going to leave Alistair for him. What a stir this will
make! It's not at all like him."

"So why don't you just leave then, dear boy," said
Bertie. "Allow us these few days in peace."

"My dear fellow, aren't you going to introduce the
young ladies to the county? What odd notions of hos-
pitality you have. And I hear you are going to invite
all the villagers in to wear their smocks and eat cake
and be quaint for you. Doesn't a full dress party, with
half the county present, come with it all? I'm sure
that was always part of the Toye treat. It's what we
do over at Holden, but of course we're not so grand
there in our tastes as you are. Really, Bert, I don't

like to mention such an indelicate subject to you, but does either young lady know in what condition the family fortunes stand? Or did you hope it would be love at first sight? Or do they like titles? You do have a title, don't you? It's been so long since I've heard anyone call you anything but Bertie, but I'm sure I've heard you mentioned somewhere as being a viscount or an earl or a marquis or something like that."

"Oh, don't be so absurd," said Bertie. "Elizabeth Wilcox is no fool; she just had to look around the village once or twice to know how things stand."

"Oh, so you've been letting her wander around without blinders on? That was foolish, wasn't it? Does she know about your past?"

"What about my past?" asked Bertie indignantly. "I'm the only person I know who hasn't got one."

"I think he wefers, in a vewy tactless way, to your deah mama, Bertie," explained Fweddie.

"Elizabeth Wilcox believes very strongly in the rights of women to vote. Mattie met her in New York and told her to look us up. Not everyone thinks only of their gloves and buttonholes the way you do, Geoffrey. Miss Wilcox is a very serious, strong-minded woman."

"Dearie me!" exclaimed Geoffrey. "I suppose a strong-minded woman is above all temptations of the flesh, and that is about all I have to offer. And Miss Pendleton—the poetic one—is she also a strong-minded woman?"

"I haven't figured her out yet," said Bertie. "I don't know much about females, compared to someone like you who spends all his time going to tea parties and flirting with other men's sisters and fiancées and aunts and cousins. Why don't you leave? It's not too late for you to get back to Holden in time for tea. I'm sure it will be a very jolly one, much nicer than tea we have here."

"I thought Georgie told me Thornbrough brought his cook with him? Bertie, you do not realize! London is buzzing with news of them. Where are they? Where did the beautiful unknowns disappear to? All the county will be down on you in no time. Besides, I promised Harry that I would send him a wire to come down for the weekend if they were here and to bring a few friends. Yes, and the Desboroughs wanted news, too, and the Linters. I hope you have a number of spare bedrooms."

"Don't make him cwy," said Fweddie. "That is weally too mean of you. Let us wejoin the others, and we will all be polite to you and not happen to mention a word about that chawming lady of the town I see on your chestnut hack in the pawk evewy aftehnoon. That is, as long as you mind your manners and keep your mouth shut."

Elizabeth, in the meantime, had had a very frustrating session with Isolde. She would give much to have some sort of explanation besides, "Oh, we talked . . . about this and that," for a summary of Isolde's jaunt with Mr. Thornbrough. Isolde seemed to be on the best of terms with him. He was certainly quiet. He spoke less than Edwin, and yet when he did comment, his views were clearly derived from a well-informed mind. He did not seem to possess a bad temper; on the contrary, this afternoon in particular his underlying spirits seemed more akin to a cheerfulness, almost a quiet joy, then anything like ill humor.

Chapter 16

Mr. Smythe stayed to tea and to dinner as well. He and Fweddie introduced a new element to the dinner, and almost managed to monopolize the conversation, gossiping back and forth. Everyone was very amused, and the party did not break up till rather late.

After Bertie's guests had all left, going up to bed one by one, each casting a shadowy circle illuminated by one old-fashioned but romantic candle in a single candleholder, Bertie and Thornbrough remained alone by the fire, drinking glasses of brandy from a decanter on the sideboard.

"We tried," sighed Bertie. "I knew it was too good to be true."

Mr. Thornbrough was silent, staring into the flames.

"They're both such serious young ladies," said Bertie. "And yet they aren't the sort of bores that talk about flannel petticoats and giving speeches in slums."

"They are two completely different females," said Martin impatiently. "Isolde is nothing like Miss Wilcox."

"No?" asked Bertie, running his finger around the rim of his glass experimentally. "I haven't seen much of her. She seems deadly serious to me."

"Miss Wilcox is the social reformer," said Martin. "Isolde is very different."

"Just as you say," said Bertie.

"Miss Wilcox's mind has a very serious tone, it would seem, Bertie," said Mr. Thornbrough. "I know you have a liking for her. And your chances of success with Miss Pendleton are nil," he added, his tones strangely ferocious.

"I haven't spoken two words with her yet, dear boy! You're the one who goes off on these long jaunts with her. Very pretty girl, very pleasant, too, nothing to say against her. Thing is, doesn't glance in my direction. No reason why she should."

"Well, you know your own business best," said Mr. Thornbrough and with these astonishing words he left Bertie to himself to wonder whether Thornie were ill, in love, or whether or not he, Bertie, had actually, finally grown up, as they had promised him he would all those years.

That night Isolde received the expected note from Mr. Thornbrough. That is, she had expected the note; he had not at all expected himself to write it until the very moment that he found himself setting pen to paper. It asked her to meet him on the roof of the castle at dawn the next morning, and she folded it up and tucked it away. Like Sarah Bernhardt, she saved love letters, although she did not lie in a coffin filled with them when she felt the need for a little cheering up.

With a delicate smile illuminating her innocent features, and an enjoyment of her lover's sense of the romantic, coupled with a desire to keep some excitement in the affair, she refrained from answering him. He could wait through the night and see his answer in the flesh. They could watch the sunrise together. But no more perfect moments . . . not for a while, at least.

It was with an anticipation of pleasure that Isolde

ascended the stone staircase the next morning, flitting up in a thin white dress.

Martin was already there, pacing the battlements. She had meant to be cool, to be aloof, but when he turned and saw her, his face lighted up and he came forward and gathered her up in his arms, holding her for a few moments while the sky behind them dressed itself in morning colors. He was so thick and strong it was easy to lose herself in his arms and forget her quiet plotting, and when he bent over to kiss her she was eager for the touch of his mouth.

"Isolde," he said, after kissing her, "I want to ask you to marry me."

With a shudder, she came back to reality. A pity she could not relish this moment the way a girl of Thornie's own race and order might. But what sensation of triumph could she, the daughter of more millions of pounds than he had ever possessed, feel about ensnaring this unwilling victim. A small part of her, very deep and unapproachable, wished to cling tighter; the rest of her turned loose his coat sleeve immediately.

"You are sweet," she said, standing on tiptoe and kissing him on his beautiful, high forehead. "And now you've asked. Please don't ask again. Thank you so much."

"But no?" He asked, his brow shooting up.

"I'm afraid, no."

"Can you tell me, after what occurred yesterday, whether or not you find me repulsive?"

"Of course I don't find you repulsive," she said soothingly. "But you aren't being fair. Remember the terms of our stolen moment? Now wouldn't you be outraged if I were the one who changed my mind and told you I decided I wanted you to marry me after all? Believe me, I'm honored by your proposal, but I have no desire to accept."

"If you have no desire for me, then why did you share that—that moment with me at all?"

Remembering Dora and her flourishing pistol, remembering the tales of hopeful young maidens left with broken hearts, remembering all these things and giving way to anger, Isolde smiled very sweetly and said, "There was no one else available. And I know how much you loathe Americans, Mr. Thornbrough, so perhaps you had best think this matter over a little more before you renew your offer. You may wish you had never made it. I will reassure you; I do not intend to marry you, now or ever. Does that make you feel better?"

"No!" he said wrathfully. "Damn it, Isolde, I came up here to ask you to marry me. Why should I feel better when you say you won't consider it?"

"Recollect your hatred for low-born Americans," she said kindly.

"I have never, *never* discussed you with any of my relatives."

"How odd. Because I assure you, they have discussed you with me at length. They repeated very faithfully to me every animadversion you have made against my compatriots, and I take them at their word, and you at yours. First Bertie told me to be careful not to fall in love with you because you were cold at the thought of Americans. That was at a party to which I had not been invited, and Bertie didn't know who I was—I believe you recollect the occasion?—so it really wasn't his fault. Then Edwin told me the same thing, but his phrases were a little more nastily chosen. Your Aunt Honora gave me the same advice, in such terms that persuaded me it would be a terrible mistake to ever become a member of your family."

Mr. Thornbrough, his eloquence deserting him, said after a pause, "But none of these accusations was made by me. I criticized you to no one. And if you felt such animosity toward me, why did you yield yourself so generously yesterday in the violet woods? What do you really feel, Isolde? Do you know?"

"I am terribly sorry, Mr. Thornbrough, but we are not discussing the matter any further." She kissed him kindly on the cheek, turned, and left him. The red flush of the sunrise had faded out of the sky, leaving it uniformly blue. He stood looking out, and then went down to breakfast.

Isolde, alone again in her room, was unable to think the matter over with any clarity of perception. She had expected little self-gratificaton from her seduction of him, little more than a perverse thrill at making love to a man with whom she shared nothing but mutual dislike and some odd fascination.

But Mr. Thornbrough, far older than her New York young men, who would have been ornamental but useless in a violet wood, had succeeded in bringing her to a peak of sensuality that made her secretly ironic speech, made while she undressed before him, about 'reaching for godhood' and 'seizing the moment' almost a reality. It seemed almost cruel of him to propose marriage now, to try to force her into surrendering herself up completely, body and soul, in all legality. He already held more sway over her than she cared to admit or could understand. The very colors of the room did not seem quite right, the air too heavy. She could not marry. She did not wish to even think of it; it was all wrong. It was a door that must be shut. She wanted no part of his world in which he figured with such strength. And if he had any genuine knowledge of hers, of her inner moods, her secret deeds, even of her very birth, he would surely want no part of her either.

Chapter 17

That day at breakfast Bertie announced that he was driving to Chillingsworth with Maggie to pick out the gifts for the treat, and he invited anyone to come along who was interested.

"Go to Chillingsworth on a day like this?" asked Fweddie. "You must be cwazy."

"Let Tuttle and Maggie go," agreed Georgie. "I should think it would be very dull."

"They don't know what to get," said Bertie, taking a piece of paper out of his pocket, unfolding it, and reading it over.

"And you do? How impwessive!" said Fweddie. "I had not known you to be so philanthwopic. How do you manage it?"

"There, you see, that's another reason why bicycles are so much better than horses," said Bertie. "Every child in the village has come out and gaped at me whenever I ride through and asked questions and talked about the machine as if it were an infernal invention. You can't say that about a horse. You just ride by in the clouds and no one ever speaks to you."

This argument met with a great deal of criticism. Mr. Thornbrough pointed out that he had been taught his first words by stable boys and grooms and for many years thought that the Derby was some sort of vastly important religious event or like the opening of Parliament. Fweddie suggested that the children were merely hoping to see him fall on his nose in the dust—not an unlikely occurrence, eh? Georgie added that no matter what good could be said about them, it was hard to look beautiful while peddling uphill on one of the things, and certainly never very dashing. Bertie shook his head; they were all old-fashioned. It was a pity that they were so set in their ways. Lady Honora pointed out that until one acquired steady habits of application to devotions, study, and business, one could not hope to achieve anything. The conversation, thus chilled, was ended.

"I should like very much to come with you," said Elizabeth in the silence that always seemed to follow one of Lady Honora's admonitions.

"You would?" asked Bert, his eyebrows beginning to rise. "Really?"

"Yes, of course. I promised Maggie I would. I rode into town yesterday and took tea with her, you know."

"Well, there's nothing to do here," said Edwin fretfully. "There isn't any tennis or even a croquet set. I may as well come with you."

"Oh, Edwin, how too civil of you," said Georgie. "What a little sunbeam you are. Let's all go. I shall wear my new hat."

There was not enough cattle in the stables for all to go at once, and Mr. Thornbrough and Cathleen claimed they had other occupations planned for the morning. It was agreed that Fweddie, an excellent whipster, unlike poor Bertie, should take the brougham and drive one of the ladies. Everyone else would ride. Maggie could take her gig, which would be needed for the purchases on the return trip.

"Well!" said Georgie in her room as she put on her riding habit, "very civil of Martin to lend you his team! Unusual, too, isn't it?"

"Unheard of," said Fweddie. "If I could wire this

stowy to London tomowwow, it would be considered
headline news. Something must be going on. But with
which one?"

The Brookes would have been in no doubt had
they been able to follow surreptitiously Mr. Thornbrough's footsteps to the boudoir of his intended.

Propriety and Aunt Honora would have demanded
that he send a courteous message via a footman, who
would deliver a written note via Isolde's maid into her
fair white hand. In the private seclusion of her bedroom, she would have been able to pen an answer, after reflecting for some time in a maidenly flutter. Mr.
Thornbrough dispensed with these amenities. He
knocked on the door himself. A quick, demanding
knock, nothing like the rhythmic taps of her maid.
Isolde looked up in surprise, but by that time Mr.
Thornbrough had let himself into her bedroom.

She was sitting at her dressing table, her long hair
in two braids. She was supposed to be dressing for the
expedition, but she was writing a few lines of poetry
that had struck her in the morning. She was expect-
ing Elizabeth to enter, demanding explanations and
trying to dress her for an outing like a disobedient
child. But never had a single gentleman, or even her
own papa, stormed into her room in this manner. At
her parents' houses it was impossible; they would
have had to run a gamut of too many butlers, footmen, housemaids, and personal maids. Even when she
traveled, it was always on her parent's personal railroad car, always waited upon by one of her parents'
staff members, attired in the Pendleton livery.
Besides, none of her handsome young men would
ever have dared to make so unconventional and illicit
an entrance. They had been obedient, biddable.
Isolde could see now that Thornbrough was not.

He was angry. His jaw was set and his body tensed
as if for a fight. He was older, more muscular than

her other lovers; she knew a touch of fear when she
saw how rigidly he held himself. But that touch inflamed an anger within her; disheveled as the castle
was, dissolute the owner, she did not believe that
Thornbrough had or could have any power over her.
In a cold voice, she said, "I believe you have mistakenly entered the wrong room, sir."

"It was not a mistake," returned Thornbrough savagely.

"Then it is an intrusion."

She could see his shoulders, held taut, make an effort to relax, and in a lower voice he said, "Isolde,
what did we share yesterday? Was that not an intrusion into your body?"

"Of course not," she said simply. "I had invited
you." She turned back to her desk, taking up her pen
again. Some part of him still felt fury; but as he
studied her profile, a greater part was amazed by her
lack of concern, shyness, or the knowledge of her own
wrongdoing.

"I will not be one of my cousin's party. So you may
join the others in their outing with no fear of being
forced into my company."

"You underestimate yourself," Isolde replied
lightly. "Your company is always enjoyable. However,
I find my brain fevered by a poem I wish to set down
today, and I could not leave while it stirred my soul."

Diverted, Mr. Thornbrough could not feel anger.
Isolde floated gracefully too far above the earth to encourage such a passion for long. One had only to look
up to see her and be amused. The Americans were a
curious lot; far more curious than the *Times* or *Punch*
had led him to believe. Perhaps he had underesti-
mated the race, attributed to it the characteristics of
the English middle-class shopkeeper, eager to hobnob
with a lord, rather than that of a child finding itself

in possession of a vast abundance of new, gaudy toys, and no rules of how to use them.

"Come, let us part friends, Isolde," he said.

"It is hard enough to be lovers, Mr. Thornbrough," she said quietly. "Let us not try to strain ourselves in attempts at friendship."

"It is no strain."

"You don't belong here, Mr. Thornbrough, in my room or in my life, nor do I in yours. I am a foreigner to you."

"Why are you so angry?"

"I am not angry. I am merely not stupid. Everyone has warned me, Mr. Thornbrough, that you are concerned chiefly with your own pleasure. Perhaps you should have been warned that I too am fond of my own ways. Now please go, before someone finds you here."

Mr. Thornbrough was lingering by the foot of the stairs when Elizabeth came down, attired in her snugly fitted riding habit and a jaunty veiled hat.

"Please step into the library for a moment, Miss Wilcox," said Mr. Thornbrough seriously. He was so solemn, in fact, that for a moment she wondered if perhaps some cable had been received about her papa and some terrible accident. He drew her into the room and, closing the door behind him, said to her, "You must be aware by now that this house party was manufactured to bring you and Lord Albert together."

"Yes, I had become aware of that, Mr. Thornbrough. No one seemed to make a great secret of it." Her wide blue eyes were fixed on his face. No expression of emotion disturbed the tranquillity of her countenance.

Mr. Thornbrough paced the room, his expression set. "I hope that nothing I or anyone else has said appears to denigrate your nationality. I have always had a great deal of respect for your nation, and in the past few days, I have developed a respect for you and your friend as well. Indeed, you and she impress Lord Albert and me as very serious, very worthy young ladies. I hope nothing we have said or done makes you think that we regard you in a frivolous light."

"A frivolous light, Mr. Thornbrough? Just how serious a mind do you think I possess?"

"I am aware of your interest in the enfranchisement of women, as well as your concern for even deeper problems of poverty and education, which should be the first concern of every citizen of every nation. In addition, in the past few days Lord Albert and I have observed the behavior of you and your friend and found you to hold yourselves with a decorum that would be admirable in any society. I wish in some way to apologize if I have seemed to scheme upon lesser notions of an interest you might have in acquiring dignities and titles which I know now someone with your depth of mind would find hollow."

With difficulty Elizabeth refrained from smiling. This was indeed the speech of a man who had been thrown from his high horse. Poor fellow! But to call her all those names! She had thought the story of the last ball she had given in New York, which had cost some twenty thousand dollars, would surely have reached this side of the Atlantic. She had ordered her guests to come dressed in rags and some, entering fully into the spirit of the occasion, had blackened their faces. It had been a riotous evening, and before it was over several people had had to be fished out of the ornamental pool. Some of her uncle's Western acquaintances, whose fortunes had begun deep in the earth in the form of silver and gold metal, had grown so sentimental about their youths that they had begun to shoot things. Quite a lot of singing was done; some of it had been arranged carefully beforehand, staged by the finest performers in New York and enjoyed in a prim circle of ladies, including Mrs. Vanderbilt and Mrs. Astor, who were no longer feuding. More spontaneous exhibitions had been given in the basement, the library, the backroom, and various nooks and crannies where her father's older cronies had gone in search of a place where a man could smoke a cigar in peace. Champagne had flowed by the caseload, and Elizabeth had had a marvelous time.

"So you and Bertie consider me to be a very serious young woman?" asked Elizabeth. "Something like one of the Pankhurst sisters?"

Mr. Thornbrough smiled, rather painfully. "I am sure that, however strong your views are, you would stop short of calling attention to youself in public and destroying property to gain your end. But come, you will wish to be on your way."

Mr. Thornbrough remained in the library while Elizabeth passed out into the hallway, looking for the others. She saw instead Tuttle, lingering about with various coats, hats, Thermoses of lemonade, and flasks of brandy that might be required on the arduous journey. "Ah, Tuttle," she said. "Just the fellow I wanted to see." And she took him off into one of the little salons to confer.

The ride up to Chillingsworth was a pleasant one, as was the visit to the toy store there. Bertie was very definite in his ideas of what he wanted and what he didn't want. He did not approve of cheap crackers and had obviously given a great deal of thought about what each child should receive. He and Maggie had long arguments about this, as well as where to buy the sweets and what kind. He preferred peppermints and rock candy, whereas she thought hoarhound drops were much more sensible and healthful.

They had a long disagreement about this, and in the
end everyone had to sample the wares and cast a vote.
Bertie won; the hoarhound was horribly nasty.
Fweddie spit his out.

While they were in town, Bertie also picked up a
croquet set. "It's absurd that we don't have one," he
said.

"I don't know how to play," said Isolde.

"What a pity," Georgie remarked in a smooth,
Cheshire-cat sort of voice. "We'll have to get Thornie
to teach you. He's quite the expert."

The next few days everyone was in festive spirits.
Vast quantities of buns, cakes, and loaves of bread
were baked, butter was purchased, mugs were obtained, and tables and tents were assembled. Mr.
Geoffrey Smythe turned up, and finding Elizabeth
already busy bustling about with Bert, giving orders
and organizing their party, he managed to locate
Isolde and extricate her from Thornie's frail grasp. It
was easy for her to go off with Mr. Smythe and be
given a lesson in croquet and listen to his amusing
nonsense. Thornie's presence was beginning to make
Isolde feel uncomfortable; but at the same time she
was drawn to him by some emotion she mistrusted.
Thornbrough was left with little to do but watch the
two slender figures idling about, playing halfhearted
croquet and flirting on Bertie's newly mown green. It
was not a sight he enjoyed.

About this time Lady Honora noticed that Cathleen was never about when she was needed, but since
Edwin was always gone, too, she attributed this to the
fact that they were both sad disappointments. Her
poor brother, she said, had much to contend with in
this lifetime. She was afraid his wife, in addition to
being a shockingly poor manager, had reared some of
the most unattractive children in England. What they
would do with the girl she could not say, but she had

too many dependents of her own to be able to let her make a home with her. She was afraid neither had made good use of the opportunities she had given them. They both had a shocking disposition toward ingratitude.

That was on Wednesday morning. Mr. Thornbrough, who had to listen to these complaints, tried to point out that both were young, and that there was plenty of time for both to make advantageous marriages. Even he, however, was hard put to explain to Lady Honora the note that was found left on Cathleen's bed that night:

Dear Aunt,
    I am very sorry to cause you displeasure, but I am marrying Pierre de Jardin and since I know you will be angry, we are running away together. He is a great chef and I love him very much. The cakes and things for the treat are in the bread safe in the kitchen. I will write a letter to Mummy. Do not think we are going to disgrace the family, because we are going to go to either Brazil or the United States to open a French restaurant.

Your very obedient,
CATHLEEN

"The deuce!" exclaimed Mr. Thornbrough. "My cook! She's run away with my cook! It took me three years to lure him away from the Café de Paris."

"A good man is hard to find," said Georgie. "Is it true? How delicious! And for her, too! One would never have suspected."

"I am too shocked for discussion," said Lady Honora. "That a niece of mine could have married a tradesman! The family is ruined. And we are giving a dinner party tomorrow, too!"

"We are ruined," said Bertie. "Tuttle makes wonderful poached eggs, but we can't serve that up to half the county. Why did we have to invite all those people anyway?"

"It seemed the polite thing to do to honor your guests," said Thornbrough stiffly. "Never mind. Windmore will have to do his best in the kitchen; he was undercook before he decided he preferred to keep his hands clean. No doubt he is still somewhere about, very well rested, I hope. I haven't seen him in the last week, but I hope he will be able to serve us a plain dinner."

Elizabeth, who seemed disturbed, excused herself and stepped out of the room. Tuttle was lingering handily outside the door, so she did not have far to go.

"Tuttle, you did not arrange this, I hope?" she asked. "I had no intentions of altering the course of human destiny just for one night of amusement."

"The situation belowstairs was somewhat touch and go, miss," said Tuttle. "If I lent aid to either side, it was because I felt the best interest of both parties would be served in doing so. Frivolity is all very well in its place, but I did not like to see the young lady, who does not seem to be appreciated by her own peers or family, go through life in what could only be described as a servile position."

"Ah, Tuttle, you are a breath of fresh air. I wish I had known; I would have lent Cathleen a bridegrown. I hope she looked orange blossomy as she left."

"Even her mother would have wept," Tuttle assured her.

"I'm certain of that."

Windmore was found and dried out, but the complaints were many at dinner that night. Windmore had attempted to roast a leg of lamb on the spit and cook some vegetables and sauces on the nob, but the results were very disappointing. His heart was not in the task, and the equipment in no way resembed that on which he had been trained so many years ago. So while the servants dined pleasantly enough on stew and fresh bread, the gentlefolk upstairs gagged their way through burnt and half-raw sheep flesh.

"A lesson to us all," said Fweddie, pushing his plate away. "How pleasant some nuts and bewwies would be wight now. Is there enough perfume in Awaby to wash away the dweadful smell of this dinner?"

"I'm disappointed in you," said Mr. Thornbrough. "I had looked to you for more conviviality, more merriment over short rations, like de Bergerac at the siege, pulling his belt in while joking. And here you are the first to crumble. You don't hear the ladies complain."

"Tuttle, why don't you fetch us all some of those nice fresh buns for the treat tomorrow and a pitcher of milk to go around?" asked Bertie. "And tomorrow, we can give our dinners away, or just let all of my tenants come through my mansion and taste a few dishes to see how the other half lives. Should keep grumbling and unrest down for the next twenty years."

The next day was the feast day, and since everyone had spent most of the day either avoiding work or doing it, the night had a kind of Christmas Eve quality to it, and everyone drifted off to bed early.

Elizabeth, tired with the day's activities and full of plans, was wishing everyone good night in the grand hallway, and picking up her skirts to ascend the centuries-old staircase. Isolde had preceded her, more silent and sad at dinner than usual. She was often reserved and quiet for days on end, but tonight her thin shoulders drooped and her songs had been slow and sad. Elizabeth watched her go up, and she noticed that Thornie, standing at the foot of the stairs, watched, too, his eyes following the back of her head. At the top of the stairs Isolde turned and for a moment glanced down. She looked directly at Thornie; Elizabeth could feel their eyes lock, and without changing her expression, Isolde withdrew down a corridor to her room.

Elizabeth, in the hopes of sharing some confidences with Isolde, who seemed so troubled, knocked on her door and entered. Isolde was preparing for bed, disrobing and brushing out her long hair. After some hesitation Elizabeth said, "At all events we have stayed in a castle."

"Very true," said Isolde. "It is a castle."

"And we've become acquainted with lords and ladies."

"Yes, Bert is quite wonderful, isn't he?"

"Mr. Thornbrough is not such a bad man."

"No," said Isolde with quiet finality.

"You enjoy his company, do you not?" attempted Elizabeth.

Isolde shrugged.

They stood together for a few more minutes, Isolde looking out a window and Elizabeth looking at Isolde. The shadows of their two candles were long and dim. Everyone had been so full of speech in the party that now the air around them, unbroken for once by waves of sound, was as restful as a soft, enveloping bed. Elizabeth wished Isolde good night and left.

Isolde got into bed and blew out her candle. She was alone again in the great fortress; the others had all gone to bed. But she felt small. The castle was no longer a smooth round river rock she could pick up and hold. It had grown, or she had shrunk. Instead of possessing it, she felt like a small pea or a pebble rattling around in it. And she was alone. The others were asleep, absorbed, soft and comfortable. Only she was left to be shaken; no one could hear her.

Isolde sighed. Of all her imaginary illnesses, the strange misery that sometimes crept over her, depriving her of sleep no matter how exhausted her body was, was too real. Her mother did not understand it and tried to take her out for more exercise. She had even taken her to see doctors, but they could find nothing wrong with her either. Sometimes she drank laudanum, which gave her strange dreams. Then she would awaken late the next morning, her head aching, and her mind full of strange half-forgotten nightmares and imaginings, as if she had passed through another world.

She wished she had not blown out her candle. She got out of bed and went over to the window. Just as she had thought, the moon had risen and was full; its yellow light streamed onto the castle. Perhaps a walk outdoors in the moonlight would tire her. It would be better than lying in bed here. The weather was warm, and the grounds must be beautiful at night. She had not been beyond the courtyard at night yet. She caught up a shawl and went out, still dressed in her thin white nightgown.

She wandered down the corridor, past Elizabeth's door, and down yet another corridor, drawn by a feeling she did not acknowledge to herself. She went past Thornie's door; and there was a light under it. He must be awake. She paused in the hallway, shivering, unsure. As this thing nibbled away at her, it gnawed away her pride and certainty of worth. She no longer felt beautiful or even attractive; she could only remember that he had once called her a French whore. In another mood she might tease and lead him on; tonight she was afraid of his disapproval, of his contempt.

She turned the knob of the door and opened it as quietly as she could. Perhaps, if he were asleep, she would not disturb him. But as it chanced, he was seated in an armchair directly opposite the door and looked up immediately. She wanted to withdraw into the shadows, but instead she just stood as he stared at her, an eyebrow raised. He had not yet undressed, but had simply taken off his coat, replacing it with a light smoking jacket. He was reading some papers in the light from a lamp on the table next to him.

"Really, Isolde," he said, his tones light and mocking, "I thought Elizabeth was the suffragist. If you mean to behave like a man, I must urge you to be a little more gentlemanly toward your prey."

"I am sorry," she said. "I couldn't sleep and I saw your light."

"I like that one. It's a shame the weather is so good, though, or you might have used the 'I'm afraid of the thunder' one. Do you women teach each other these things? Although I must admit, Isolde, you are unique among the predatory females I have met. You are single. What an accomplishment! However, I really do advise you to acquire a partner if you mean to keep this up. I'm sure Geoffrey Smythe will be happy to oblige. And of course in London plenty of chaps will line up for your millions."

Anger welled up in her, giving her strength like new blood. She longed to puncture the silence of the sleeping castle by slamming shut the big beamed door, but she closed it gently without words, stealing down the stairs and out the door.

She had gone beyond the courtyard, across the

moat, and into the forest nearest the castle, her steps hurried, pushed by her own rage, by the time Thornie caught up with her.

"Where are you going?" he asked, catching her elbow and whirling her around.

"Go back to your room," she ordered, spitting the words at him. "I did not give you permission to follow me."

"Are you mad? Bertie encourages poachers in these woods." He looked down at her and saw that she was wearing a nightdress. "My God, you look like a ghost."

She gazed at him, her eyes smoldering. Then something seemed to click off in her head, as if some switch had turned. "What awful things you can say. Now I shall never be able to sleep."

"Is it true? Does the moon bother you?" he asked, as it hung over her shoulder, like a third person eavesdropping.

"Sometimes. Not always."

"I'm sorry then. But it's true what I said, Isolde. You are unique."

"It seems you can use that phrase as a compliment, an insult, and a threat, depending on your mood. No doubt we are all unique."

"No. I know hordes of young ladies—and gentlemen, too, if you will—and I find them all depressingly alike."

"As you pointed out with such crushing astuteness, possessing several million dollars is an aid."

"Perhaps," he said, leaning down to kiss her, her lips and tongue meeting his with ready sensuality. He pressed his lips to her long white neck, admiring the short tendril that curled there. "And tomorrow? Will you flirt with Geoffrey all day again?"

"Very likely," murmured Isolde. "Bertie is too much in love with Elizabeth."

"Poor Bertie. How painful love is."

"I wouldn't know."

He paused and stood for a moment watching her face. "How many men have you had before me, Isolde?"

"Not as many as I hope to have afterward."

"You are a whore," he said, pulling her down into the grass, and pushing up the skirts of her nightgown. "A rich whore." He kissed her breasts, her navel, her sex. "I will never again ask you to marry me."

"Please don't."

"I will not acknowledge you in London."

"I think I can exist."

"And you may come and admire the light under my door anytime."

"Be quiet," she said, kissing him. She had forgotten her dislike of him, forgotten her mistrust, forgotten that she had once thought his looks didn't suit her, that his body was too heavily masculine, too athletic. Thought and feeling were suspended as she felt him near her, touching her flesh with the fury he brought into lovemaking. In the violet wood, she had held back even in her arousal, distrusting him, distrusting her own body, certain she must hang back to take the edge off the bitterness she always felt afterward. But there had been no bitterness then, no frustration, no feeling of a trap door opening underneath her. Only pleasure, exquisite, overwhelming pleasure. Tonight she reached for Thornie with unfeigned desire, with a fervor that surprised him, with a desperate need to feel him within her once again. Under the wide-trunked trees in the moonlight he entered her, entered and found her, thrusting again and again, touching her with gentle fierceness in a rhythm that finally left them both lying exhausted in a satisfied ecstasy, side by side on the grass.

Afterward, they walked in silence back to the castle, holding hands. Isolde slipped into bed and went to sleep, a deep sleep without nightmares. But Thornie lay awake for a long time.

Chapter 18

The next day was the day of the treat and the last day of the house party. Streamers had been hung, and the tables were decorated with bunches of spring flowers picked by Isolde and Georgie. The women hired to help make the tea and cut the bread began to arrive very early, and Tuttle seemed to be everywhere at once. Very early in the day Fweddie, Georgie and Lady Honora established themselves in wicker chairs on the lawn.

Bertie and Elizabeth entered wholeheartedly into the arrangements. Elizabeth offered a prize to the best jump roper, and even took a few turns herself, lifting her skirts up to her ankles and hoping that her hair would not fall down her back. She and Isolde taught an American jumping rhyme and a few songs to the little girls who gathered around them. They thought Elizabeth an odd lady. She looked like a nob, but seemed very practical in a way that ordinary ladies were not. Ladies often had a way of telling you to do something and then standing by and waiting for you to think up how the thing was to be done. Miss Wilcox was not of this ilk; she entered into the spirit of the festivities with as much enthusiasm as his lordship. And they were all used to Lor' Bertie poking about and suggesting a better way of doing things. Sometimes his ideas were absurd, and sometimes they were just impractical, but occasionally he had a very good one, and they always had a good laugh over the outcome.

Elizabeth found, indeed, that Lor' Bertie seemed to occupy an unusual place in everyone's heart. He was not accorded a great deal of reverence, and they all knew his weaknesses—his fondness for machines and his occasional glass or so too many—but he seemed to be every child's favorite uncle, every woman's beau, and every man's drinking companion.

In a break from the rural observances, he found an empty chair by the rest of the house party and sat down for a breather.

"I've never seen anyone enter into one of these things the way you do," said Georgie. "My father used to give these once a year, and they were all managed in the most decorous way possible. Tables arranged side by side for miles, it seemed, and he got up at the head and gave an inspirational speech. Then everyone filed away after supper in the most respectful way possible. I think they all shook hands with him once."

"That is the proper way to handle an affair such as this," said Lady Honora. "I'm afraid Lord Albert was taught some lessons by his mother that are not at all in keeping with the preservation of a high tone of behavior."

"At all events, it has made me very hungry for my dinner," said Bertie. "I hope Windmore does a little better today than he did last night. I shall really loathe serving General Crankeshaft burnt mutton with curdled sauce. I don't think he would appreciate the humor of the situation."

"*General Crankeshaft?*" repeated Lady Honora in a fluttery manner. "I did not know he lived in this county."

"Yes, to the southwest. He's a good old fellow, too, but stiff, very stiff."

"I knew General Crankeshaft in India," said Lady Honora. "I assume that your reference to him as being 'stiff' means that he is a gentleman of the old school. I shall be happy to entertain him again."

Bertie and Georgie exchanged glances. "Did you see him often, then, in India?"

Lady Honora, her long fingers looped over her jet fringe, said casually, "In India a countryman was always welcome."

Presently Geoffrey, Thornie, and Isolde appeared, the latter flushed from the exercise of croquet. Bertie ran his eye reflectively over Miss Pendleton. He had certainly never before seen his cousin behave in such a strange manner. Whatever quarrel they may have had last night at dinner was resolved today; they treated each other with easy courtesy. Lady Daisy, whom all London rumored was his paramour, would tear her locks if she could see them together, Isolde slightly breathless and very demure, and Thornie, very skillfully jostling Geoffrey out of place, seating her in a wicker chair and ordering her tea. Martin looked pleased with himself; perhaps Isolde was being kinder. Martin did usually get his way in the end.

"You have allowed Martin to tire you out," said Georgie solicitously to Isolde. "I don't believe you are very strong."

"Oh, I'm much tougher than people think me," said Isolde in her soft voice.

"Are you indeed?" asked Geoffrey lightly. "One wouldn't have thought you were a tough young lady, Miss Pendleton. One thinks of tough young ladies as wearing sensible boots and very ugly dresses and reading only improving sorts of books. Do you read only improving sorts of books?"

"Yes," said Isolde. "In fact, I never read anything except the Bible and the Book of Common Prayer."

"Indeed?" said Geoffrey. "What an odd name you have for a Puritan."

"Don't I?" said Isolde sweetly. "And you, Mr. Smythe, what sorts of things do you read? Books of love, I suppose. French novels."

"I wouldn't mix them up," said Geoffrey. "They're not at all the same sort of thing. Don't you believe in love? Georgie, you're a married woman. Tell us about love."

"Geoffrey, how too absurd you are! Like asking an old deaf man to tell you what the little birds he listened to in his youth sounded like."

"I don't think that's vewy nice of you at all," pouted Fweddie.

"I'm just teasing, dear," said Georgie, patting his hand.

"You will end up dwiving me fwom your side, Georgie," said Fweddie. "Don't think there awen't plenty of women in London who awe intewested in me. There awe."

"And men, too, I daresay," said Georgie. "There, there, not another word. You know how I prize you, dearest, and don't stick out your lower lip like that. You look too ridiculous."

"So this is married love!" exclaimed Geoffrey in mock astonishment. "It would seem the female casts the male aside after she has extracted from him all the promises and legal contracts she requires. Lady Honora, give us your views on this subject."

"A woman is not in a position to love at all until after she is married," said Lady Honora regally. "A young unmarried girl must maintain an innocent, open disposition toward these matters, and let those around her determine whom she will love."

Martin raised a thin, black eyebrow and glanced at Isolde. Her eyes were turned demurely upon a group of children gathering in front of one of the

tents, her expression vacant. "Give us your views on
this subject, Miss Pendleton," he said to her in a
voice whose tone was meant to exclude all others
present.

"I cannot agree," she said simply. "An unmarried
girl is no different than a married one; they are the
same being, although one may be more innocent. But
to marry without love—that would be absurd, like
drinking without thirst."

"I knew it!" exclaimed Geoffrey triumphantly. "So
you have a romantic disposition, Miss Pendleton."

"I don't know that it is so romantic," she disclaimed.

"But own that if someone fell on his knees before
you and offered up his life to you—one of those fellows from books, you know, who never, never care
how dirty they get the knees of their trousers—own
that you would be a little overcome, perhaps swept
off your feet?"

Isolde, blushing a little, said, "No, no, not at all. I
couldn't marry someone because he claimed to love
me, but because I loved him. How selfish that would
be of me, don't you see? I have met many men I respect, even many men I could perhaps live happily
with throughout life. But I feel that a woman should
enter marriage with the attitude of a female spider."
As the rest of the company stared at her, she explained. "After the female is done with the male, she
eats him up. And I have never met anyone who I
have felt that way about. That feeling of wanting to
devour someone whole. Spiritually, of course."

There was a short silence. Georgie glanced curiously at Martin and was surprised to see an expression in his eyes of deep, fiery purposefulness. The
eyebrow was still raised, but his eyes were fixed upon
Isolde as if he were seeing her in a new light. Feeling
his gaze upon her, she glanced up at him. Her heart

beat faster, suffusing blood in a pounding rhythm to her cheeks and throat, turning her white skin a rosy pink, too warm to her touch. She glanced away again immediately; but Thornie had always had a good eye for color and detail.

Chapter 19

Dinner that night was to be a very formal affair. Elizabeth had arranged for the maid to attend to Isolde first, and then to come next door to Elizabeth's room. Fortunately, Isolde had left off the tight lacing that had been so much in vogue a few years before and which was still employed by many of their contemporaries to achieve a fashionable hourglass figure. Isolde, naturally slender, did not have to hold onto the poster of her bed and try with as much fortitude as she could muster not to shriek out in pain as the strings were tightened around her waist. Her father had forbidden all that at the doctor's recommendation, and Isolde, never fond of discomfort, was happy to comply.

In addition, she had chosen a simple gown for the evening, one that did not have to be lowered over her head by poles held by stout maidservants. Her sleeves were more extravagantly cut than her dress itself, billowing out in folds of pink until they were caught in by wide bands that buttoned halfway up her arm. The maid buttoned her up and helped her with the catch of her necklace. Isolde sent her next door; she liked to do her own hair, and she knew Elizabeth's preparations were far more elaborate.

By the time she had knotted her hair, Elizabeth was dressed somewhat more magnificently in white festooned with rows and rows of blue gores cut jauntily crossways across her dress. Her fingers had dipped into a crammed jewelry box and picked out a few sapphire and diamond trinkets to wear, including one very fine star sapphire she was rather proud of. She was having a little difficulty with her rows of short, fair curls over her forehead, trying to make them obey her and lie down. Indeed, these curls were possibly the only things in Elizabeth's life that stubbornly held out against her willpower, and her daily struggle with them quite silenced her as Isolde entered the room, her attention all on the wayward hairs.

"Are you ready?" asked Isolde. "Can I help you with anything?"

"No, no," said Elizabeth. "Let me meditate on the evils of hairdressers for a few moments, and I will be down. But stop, what are you wearing? Pink? Shall we go down together? I have this blue all over the trim of my dress, and don't you think pink, particularly that shade of pink, and blue are just a trifle insipid?"

"I could change my dress," said Isolde absently. "You look nice enough. I don't think anyone cares."

"Ah, Isolde, that is not the right attitude," said Elizabeth, applying a last touch or two to her fringe. "You must pay more attention. I really don't think you are noticing anything at all."

"Of course I am," said Isolde indignantly.

"Are you going down just like that? You look so plain. Can I lend you something, perhaps a rope of pearls or so? My, but that is a quaint way of doing your hair, but I suppose you tall women can wear any fashion you wish. How nice that must be. A little powder?"

Isolde was refusing all offers when their maid knocked on Elizabeth's door.

"Excuse me, miss," she said, "but not knowing where the other miss was, I thought I'd ask you before I looked elsewhere. But there you are," she said to Isolde. She handed her a small nosegay of wildflowers, red campion, and wild hyacinth, saying, "These are from Mr. Thornbrough, miss, with his compliments."

"My, my," said Elizabeth with a laugh in her voice, as the door closed behind the girl. "The garden is full of rose bushes and he sends you these tender little blossoms."

Isolde gently fingered the petals of the tiny flowers. With dignity, she said, "Please don't make a game of it, Elizabeth. Mr. Thornbrough happened to know that I have a fondness for these flowers. I hope you aren't going to make jokes about it all through supper."

"No, indeed, not I," said Elizabeth, a bubble of humor still in her tone. "There will be plenty of other things to laugh at during dinner. Shall you wear them in your hair?"

"Of course not," said Isolde. "This is simply a private matter. No doubt Mr. Thornbrough noticed them while out for a walk and thought of sending them up."

"No doubt," said Elizabeth. "Still, I think it would only be civil of you to wear at least one of the poor little things, perhaps here in your hair. No, you are right, they would wilt sadly, poor things. Come, let us go down."

They were rather late entering the drawing room. They found Lady Honora, wearing her blackest gown, profuse with jet ornaments, Edwin, a dark scowl adorning his pimply features, and the others broken up into small groups throughout the room, talking to newcomers the American heiresses had not yet met. Geoffrey was there with his mother and fa-

ther, two gruff, weather-beaten individuals who spoke
a great deal about huntin' and fishin'. General
Crankeshaft was also present, a large, straight-backed
old man who was engaged in a discussion with Lady
Honora. The Desboroughs had arrived with all three
of their plain daughters. Bertie was attempting to be
convivial with them, but as Elizabeth entered the
room, he allowed himself to meet her eyes for one
long, speaking moment. It was not a cry for help as
much as an exchange of information, and Isolde, who
watched the two curiously, wondered if the impossible was going to occur; that the girl who had been
hunted down by half the men in New York would
end up choosing an indigent English peer.

Her brow furrowed at the thought and, perfectly
unconscious of the fact that she, too, was considered
an interesting topic of conversation, she entered the
room with a completely absentminded air, went over
to a window seat away from all the others, and sat
down. It was a bit too high for her, and sitting back
in it, she let her feet swing back and forth.

"Here comes the lady you hope someday will make
a meal of you," said Geoffrey, nudging Mr. Thornbrough. "I wouldn't object to being consumed by
her."

"Alas, poor Geoffrey, it can never be your fate. Do
your best to cut out my cousin."

"I don't think I will," said Geoffrey, watching
Isolde appreciatively. "She looks as if she is fishing.
She is probably the kind of child who never could
keep her face clean when she was playing. A
charming woman. My kind of woman."

"Dear Geoffrey, you are so generous with your favors and so indiscriminate with your taste, that I am
afraid we can say they are all your kind of woman. I
believe your mother is beckoning you." Geoffrey
sighed and obeyed the maternal call. Thornie joined

Isolde on the window seat, and soon he too was swinging his legs.

He remained there long enough for Georgie to nudge Fweddie and point them out. "I've cabled Woss to lay money on Bertie being mawwied by the end of the season," said her spouse confidentially. "I got odds at a hundwed to one, but the way things awe going, I'm tempted to switch it to Thownbwough."

"Don't forget that Daisy is waiting like a predatory feline in London."

"I'm not. I'll keep my money on Bertie. I don't think poor Miss Pendleton can hold on to Thornie in the big city."

"How much did you put down?"

"A hundwed pounds, all the money Thornie loaned me. We'll be wich!"

"But how will we pay that tradesman?"

Georgie sighed.

Elizabeth was at her most captivating that night. Bertie watched her glumly as she progressed throughout the room, always with the same delightful bubble of good humor that Isolde had noticed in her earlier. The Smythes thought her chaming and invited her to their hunting box in Scotland for the grouse, if she was still in England then. "Carries herself well," said the elder Mr. Smythe. "Wonder if she has a good seat."

"I wonder about her seat myself," said his son.

"Plenty of good bottom, though, that's certain. Tells me she hunts in the States; never heard of such a thing. Regular pack, she says."

"Oh, I don't doubt it," said his son, watching her move across the room where the Desborough girls, like three slender volumes of the same dull novel, sat aligned on a sofa. Soon she had charmed laughter out of them. The Arum-Blythes were a little too difficult for her; such odd people, Mrs. Smythe thought. They were always invited, and they always went, and they never said a word to anyone, and they always left, seemingly perfectly contented. But how could anyone be content who dressed like that? Perhaps they went everywhere to show people what might happen to you if you were to begin to buy clothes ready-made in department stores.

Geoffrey's taste for gossip was inherited from his mother, and it was not long before she noticed Mr. Thornbrough and Isolde secluded in their corner.

"What is this, Geoffrey?" she demanded of her son. "It is unlike Thornbrough to carry on a flirtation with such a young girl, but I suppose he has been very bored here in the country. Still, it is unusual behavior for him."

"She's a very unusual girl, Mama," responded her son. "Quite a primitive, or rather, primeval, like Longfellow's forest."

"Don't you think she's quite pretty, Geoffrey?"

"Yes, Mama, I do, but as you can see, another man is before me."

"Thornbrough! He won't see her twice when they return to London." Her son looked wise and shook his head.

Tuttle announced dinner and they went in in pairs. It was a little difficult, because Lady Honora had been very short on gentlemen, but finally they were all seated. If there was a degree of informality she could not approve of, she smiled serenely at General Crankeshaft and assured him that this rude country living was entirely due to the disgraceful way in which her nephew Bertie managed his affairs.

On this pleasant note, Tuttle reentered the room and said in his master's ear, but loudly enough for all to hear, "Certain urgent duties in the kitchen require my direct supervision, my lord, so dinner will be served by this young man, whom I have carefully chosen for the responsibility. If you will excuse me . . ." The door opened, and Tuttle slipped out, while a man, rather stout and not at all young, entered. His nose was red and he had none of the solemn gait that Tuttle cultivated so admirably.

"I hope you likes your dinner tonight," he said in friendly tones. "They tell me it's been cooked special just for all you ladies and gentlemen, so just sit down and pay attention to what's coming." He left again. There was a pause in the conversation, but smooth as the water in a lukewarm bath, the voices began again, commenting on the extreme warmth of the season, on the extreme coolness of the season, and on the good views to be had in this part of the county. Only Bert looked a little puzzled, and Mr. Thornbrough irritated. Elizabeth's expression was as absently pleasant as Isolde's.

The man reentered. "P'raps Tuttle didn't tell you who I am," he said. "The name's 'Arry Sheps. I suppose if I were going to be a footman, you'd all be calling me 'Arry, like we were old friends, but I've come to buttle today, so Sheps it is. We have some very nice soup here. That Windmore fellow has been sweating into it all day." And he proceeded to go around the table, pouring soup into everyone's flat, wide soup bowl from a coffee pot. He spilled a little when he got to Edwin's place, and said, "Whoops, there, fellow, hold still now." Licking his fingers, he finished and was gone.

The pause was somewhat longer. Then, at last, conversation began again. Mr. Thornbrough glanced across the table at Bert, who shook his shoulders helplessly. The soup, however, was quite flavorful, and although Edwin seemed a little annoyed at having to eat his in a little pool, the others did the best they could and continued their polite discussions.

After some time, however, even the slowest guest had finished his portion and the man still did not return. Finally they heard a pounding on the butler's door. It grew louder until Bertie finally sprang from his seat and opened it.

"G'blimey, lord, I been knockin' for five minutes on that door!" said Sheps, his nose red with indignation. He set a large silver tray down on the sideboard. "And you all set about in here like a lot of walkers in Haymarket. Well, never mind, you're the gentry, I suppose. Now, I'm to take away these bowls. I can't make all those trips back and forth, lady, it must be a mile to those kitchens. Just stack them up there for me, would you. Now set down you, you're the head lord, ain't you? Set down, and I'll give you a nice big chop with plenty of good fat on it."

"I don't believe I am hungry," announced Lady Honora.

" 'Course you're hungry," said Sheps. "You've got a lot to keep up, you have. Another one never hurts, that's what my mum always said. There you go. Now how about some of these nice taters? Good taters? That's right, miss, you eat these up, they'll put some flesh on you. Irish strawberries, that's what we call them. Did you hear the one about three Irishmen, they'd all died and gone to the pearly gates? They were all three named Paddy—"

"That will do, Sheps," said Lady Honora.

"I do love to hear the way you nobs talk!" said Sheps convivially. He had served everyone the entree, and evidently feeling his job was for the most part at an end, he poured himself a glass of wine from a decanter on the sideboard and stood at the head of the table behind Bert, ready for talk. "That will do, says the lady," he said in mimicking tones. "Now when I go into a store and say, 'That will do,' I mean, that will do, I like it, I'll buy it, just that, it will do. But when you nobs say—" He puckered up his face and mimicked again, " 'That will do.' It means, 'g'wan, get outa here.' Yet, could my lady say, 'Get outa here, Sheps!' when she was through with me? Oh, no, she has to say it gently, politely, nicely."

Elizabeth bit her lip and continued eating, her appetite unspoiled by the scene being enacted around her. The others, for the most part, were spellbound.

"It is time for the ladies to withdraw," said Lady Honora emphatically, not attempting to subtly draw the eyes of the other women at the table and wait for the perfectly orchestrated moment to exit. The others had not quite finished, perhaps, but it was time this dreadful scene was finished.

"Oh, don't leave now," said Sheps, putting his glass down hurriedly. "After they've worked all afternoon making meringues, and I don't know what kinds of ladies' food there for you. I'll be right back, when you've finished eating, throw your bones to the dogs and stack your plates, if you don't mind." And he rushed out of the room.

"Albert," said Lady Honora intensely, as the door shut, "this is too much!"

Bertie was about to agree when Sheps came rushing back from the kitchen, dropping macaroons as he ran. Isolde and the Desborough girls had already risen, and he shouted across the room at them, "Here, catch, take these along with you!" He began pitching tarts and pastries at them. The Desborough girls had never had brothers and so had not learned the rudiments of catch, or even how to dodge, so they stood shrieking with their hands covering their faces.

"I say, this is too much," shouted the elder Mr.

Smythe, seizing Sheps by the collar. "Get out now, you beggar."

"It's me job, and I've been paid for it," said Sheps, wriggling free. He jumped up onto a chair and shouted, "I won't leave until you've all had a decent feed. Call yourselves a bunch of lords! You ain't even drunk yet!"

Mr. Smythe grabbed for his legs, but he jumped onto the table, running carefully amidst the china and silver, smashing up only a few things here and there.

"Father, Father, please," said Geoffrey, who was collapsing in helpless laughter on the floor. "This is 'Arry James, the music hall personality. I don't know why he's serving us our dinner, but he isn't a blackguard. He's a comedian."

'Arry began to execute a hornpipe on the dining room table, singing in a terrible falsetto, *"Ta-ra-ra-BOOM-de-ay, ta-ra-ra-BOOM-de-ay."* He doffed an imaginary hat and said, bowing on all sides, "That's right, ladies and gentlemen, 'Arry James is my true moniker, and I'm glad to find someone's who's caught me act out in these wilds. I saw a cow today for the first time. I know it was a cow because it had hooves and a ring through its nose. I thought I would take a little ride on it, always wanted to drive a 'ansom when I was a boy, so I . . ." And as he continued with his patter, Tuttle and two other footmen entered the room, placing small tables near the chairs of the diners who had removed further back from 'Arry's stage/dining room table. These tables Tuttle proceeded to cover with fresh white cloths, placing a small vase full of spring flowers on each, and he brought in plates full of delicate sandwiches, caviar puffs, lobster patties, and olives all in silence while 'Arry entertained the company.

'Arry gave them some twenty minutes of patter,

sang several songs a cappella, either in a ridiculous falsetto or in a rather pleasant baritone, which seemed more tinged with a Scots accent than cockney.

"Now my curtain must go down," he said finally, "even though this establishment hasn't got one. And so, dear ladies and gentlemen, adieu. Please forgive me if the dinner weren't couth; I'm not used to these rarefied heights. No doubt having such high-born folks as you about threw me off. So long, and if you have a chance, come in and look me up at the Variety—you don't even have to leave a card. A half crown will do."

And he jumped down and was gone.

By this time everyone had dined very pleasantly, if lightly, from the small, elegant tables placed by Tuttle. Except for cups of coffee and a few petite fours sitting about unmauled, the viands had been consumed, and a common feeling of amusement bonded the group. There was a pause as everyone digested the last of 'Arry.

Finally, Lady Desborough said pleasantly, "What a splendid idea, dear Bertie! And how unique! I must confess, I was quite taken in, and I'm afraid my silly girls completely lost their heads."

"It was a good idea, wasn't it," Bert agreed. "I wonder who thought of it."

"Am I to understand that the entertainment, if such we must call it, was not chosen by you, Albert?" asked his aunt, her tones leaving no doubt what her opinion of such a display was.

"Splendid thing, splendid thing," said General Crankeshaft. "Thought this would be another boring dinner party. Glad it wasn't. Grateful to you, Bertie, grateful. You may look me up anytime, dear boy. I haven't been surprised many times in my life."

"I'm so glad everyone enjoyed himself," said Bertie. "However, in all honesty I must confess that I, too, was hoaxed. Don't know anything about this. Nothing to do with it."

There was a longer silence. Everyone watched everyone else's face, but Elizabeth's eyes remained firmly fixed to the floor, and Isolde's deep violet gaze was as mysterious as ever. Mr. Thornbrough had his eyebrow up, but he was also smiling a little.

"It must have been Tuttle," said Bertie, in his pleasant, vague manner. "Always one for kidding is Tuttle. It was you, wasn't it, Tuttle?"

"I had some knowledge of the arrangements, my lord," said Tuttle.

"It is of no import," said Lady Honora grandly. "Ladies, shall we withdraw?"

"It was the Americans," said Mrs. Arum-Blythe unexpectedly, in a high, squeaky voice. "And I believe something has been splashed on my new gown, too."

This was a little too petit bourgeois for Lady Honora's taste, but before she could think of a sufficiently withering remark, Elizabeth said with a smile, "I must confess, if damage has been done. I hope the fellow has not broken too many of your glasses, Lord Albert, but the joke was irresistible. And I had my reputation to think of, too, because it has recently come to my ears that I am considered a deadly serious modern young woman, and I'm sure nothing could be more deadly than such an unjust imputation. Just because one rides a velocipede and wears knickerbockers and throws bricks through windows—are these such serious things? I wanted to make certain that before my visit was ended, I would have impressed myself on the company as being truly frivolous and light-minded. And also this is the last evening of the party; it has been such a splendid one that I thought I must do something out of the way to commemorate it, and fireworks were so hard to get at the last minute."

There was a low moan across the room, and before all those gathered, Lord Albert laid his head in his hands in simple grief.

"Let us leave the gentlemen to their wine," said Lady Honora quickly, and the ladies all withdrew. Soon the pleasant sounds of Isolde's guitar and the singing of the Desborough women were heard filtering into the dining room, but Bertie, still in obvious anguish, refused to lift his head. Tuttle hovered over him anxiously, saying "A little brandy, sir, some of Mr. Thornbrough's. A good year, always known to lighten the spirits."

Bertie lifted his head and stared with a wild, dazed expression all around the room. The others watched him curiously. Mr. Thornbrough finally said, "Why don't you propose to her, Bertie?"

"Ha!" said Bertie, throwing back the glass of brandy. "Don't be funny." He added bitterly, "I'm not handsome. I'm not rich. I'm not anything at all. I'm not even an aesthete."

"There is the title," said Geoffrey.

"Hundreds of titles will be waiting in London to claim Elizabeth," said Bertie gloomily. "She'll probably be a duchess. Oh!" he said in an agonized voice. "She'll meet someone when she goes to London, have a splendid season, marry at the end of it, have a wonderful establishment, and very likely invite me to dinner parties at her London town house." He buried his head in his hands once more, saying, "Oh, how am I to stand it!"

"Better to have loved and lost," said Edwin.

"Have some more brandy, my boy," said General Crankeshaft. "These little affairs are soon over. But you always have your mind, my boy."

"I think I was cheated there, too," said Bertie gloomily. "Tomorrow they'll be gone. Tomorrow!"

The gentlemen went to join the ladies quickly after they had finished their cigars and brandy. Mr. Thornbrough stayed with Bertie for a few minutes, lingering over a last glass. Thornie was accustomed to maintaining a wall of privacy around all his emotions. He would never think of sharing his confidences with Bert. Still, he would have liked to have been able to tell someone just how unusual a girl Isolde was. Unusual, enjoyable, and eminently unsuitable. No doubt she would marry one of the titled fortune hunters who would surround her upon her return to London, pushed by her underbred, social-climbing parents. She could not remain an unmarried girl for very long. But the thought of Isolde and her slender, naked body filled with a promiscuous passion for someone else struck in his mind, planting a seed of anger against her, a feeling that his emotions had been brutalized, ill-used by her outrageous behavior. He thrust the sensation away; it was childish.

Bertie's business was very sad, of course, but there was nothing to be done about it. The girl was very attractive and Bertie was right. She would have every advantage in London. But who knew? She had seemed to enjoy his company during the visit. Perhaps she had found out some of his lovable qualities while she was here. He was no picture book hero, but she looked and behaved like a girl with sense, unlike Isolde, and Mr. Thornbrough suspected she had left plenty of picture book heroes behind her in New York. Perhaps she had been able to detect in Bertie what Thornie had found and been drawn to even as a youth; that Bertie was full of kindness. More than one high stickler of English society forgave him his erring ways, his vagaries, and his brandy fumes, just as they had forgiven his mother for pamphleting and petitioning the House of Commons. Perhaps they were both a little odd, but they possessed such essentially hospitable manners that whoever they entertained came away feeling that at least he had one good friend in the world.

Mr. Thornbrough did not monopolize Isolde that night, but his eyes followed her throughout the evening. General Crankeshaft, abandoning Lady Honora, sought her out and begged her for a song, so she spent most of the evening playing on her guitar and singing some of her odd American songs. She did not perform in the manner most young ladies were taught. Her governess had heard it said that music was elevating, but she herself was almost tone deaf, and could neither teach her pupil nor evaluate or encourage any attempts Isolde made. A music teacher was engaged, but Isolde could never be persuaded to sit at the piano at a certain hour on a certain day of the week to gain the proficiency the teacher thought essential. Her attention wandered, and she was ill too often to get up and practice as much as she ought. She had a good ear, however, so the music teacher recommended that she be given a simpler instrument, and selected a guitar and a flute for her. On these she practiced when the mood struck, learning uncomplicated tunes she heard. Her technique was not formal by any means, and her repertoire contained nothing more complex than Scottish ballads, American Negro spirituals, and songs she had picked up from immigrant Irish. Her voice was not as pure as the elder Miss Desborough's, but the tone with which she half sang, half chanted a spiritual—her dark head bent over the gleaming wood of the guitar as her throaty voice mourned for the promised land—was far more effective than the arias currently in vogue.

The spirits of the company were so high that the absence of the host did not throw a pall. Bertie was

missing, and Edwin as well. Lady Honora considered
the first inexcusable, but Edwin's escape she had
come to accept as inevitable and even, during the
long hours she had been forced to spend with him in
the last week, desirable. The party was quite comfortable without them; Elizabeth was in the best of humors and Mr. Thornbrough determined that each
guest should be singled out for some attention, with a
dutifulness, if not a warmth that Bertie could not
have matched in his present state. The Desborough
girls and their mama, who could never have hoped to
receive more than a nod from Mr. Thornbrough in
London, now dreamed of great things in the next season and left the castle with high hopes. General
Crankeshaft managed to elude Lady Honora's attentions by remaining at Isolde's side and flirting with
her. Isolde was interested in the East, and soon stories
of Indian fakirs and tiger hunts filled the air. Geoffrey found plenty of time to impress on Elizabeth just
how amusing a chap he was. Fweddie and Georgie,
meanwhile, wandered about the room, making remarks in the manner of Tweedle Dum and Tweedle
Dee.

When the company had departed, and Georgie and
Fwed were just excusing themselves, Bertie walked in,
his gait only a trifle staggered but obviously a little
bit on the go. Elizabeth rose from her chair and said
sweetly, "I think I should like to stroll in the garden
in this delicious moonlight. How beautiful it is outdoors! Lord Albert, I must mention a few details
about the villagers to you before I leave tomorrow. I
wonder if you could give me your arm outside for a
few moments?"

He looked doubtful, but Elizabeth managed to
spirit him quickly out of the room. The garden really
was wonderful, if a bit chilly, full of May moonlight
and the shadows of overgrown rose trees. Bertie hesi-

tated, but Elizabeth took his arm and they went down a gravel path together.

They stopped, and he turned to face her. "Elizabeth," he said, enunciating his consonants with great caution, "hope you understand. Don't wish to embarrass you. Want you to know, just how—well—dash it, so glad you could come, y'know."

"Oh, really, Bertie," said Elizabeth indignantly, "I really think it is too much for you to be intoxicated just at this moment."

"Not really intoxicated," said Bertie. "But oh! Elizabeth, I shall miss you. And please, whatever you do, don't invite me to any of your damned dinner parties after you marry that duke. I won't come. I can't come."

"There, there," said Elizabeth soothingly. "I'm not going to marry a duke, dear Bertie. I'm going to marry you."

Bertie stared at her.

"And I think it is too bad of you to be in this state when I want to be proposing to you," she added.

"You must be crackers," said Bertie in complete disbelief. "Think of what you're saying!"

"Shocking, isn't it?" said Elizabeth. "But one of us must say it, and I can see that if I leave it to you, you won't get around to it for years and years, no matter how many opportunities I give you or how many hints."

"Elizabeth!" Bertie wailed. "You can't have thought! You know what kind of shambles my home is in! This is all I have to offer you! It's wrong, Elizabeth, all wrong!"

"Bertie, dear, you are wounding me terribly," said Elizabeth gently.

"Dear Elizabeth," he said solemnly, taking her hands in his, "you must go to London. There you will have a wonderful time. You will meet hundreds of people. You will fall in love. You don't want to be stuck with the first castle you see."

"Now I am angry. Dear Bertie, dear *sweet* Bertie, has no one ever told you what a darling you are?"

"Oh, Elizabeth, I love you so much. You must have a perfect life. Perfect everything. Perfect, everything perfect, don't you understand? Don't you see that, Elizabeth?"

"Yes, I do," said Elizabeth indignantly. "That's why I have chosen you to be my perfect husband. What kind of man do you think is the perfect husband? Choose him for me. Tell me what he looks like, so that I'll be able to recognize him."

"All I know is that it won't be me, Elizabeth. I bumble. I always have. Used to bother me, but now I'm used to it. No one else I know seems to like the same sorts of things I do. I bore girls to death. You'll *dazzle* society. I can't help you dazzle anything. I'm not dazzling."

"You're impossible," said Elizabeth. "All right, we can't be engaged now, I suppose. How about a trial courtship, just to begin with? Give me your solemn pledge that you will call on us in London."

"Elizabeth, oh, Elizabeth, I do love you." He took her in his arms and kissed her once, lightly, then released her and strode toward the house, his face expressionless.

Elizabeth watched him go. Dressed in his black frock coat, he seemed like a shadow in the moonlit garden. She picked up her skirts as she hurried after him, catching up to him just as he was entering the doors to the drawing room.

Knowing that the eyes of all were upon them, she turned to him and said, "Dear Lord Albert, it was a lovely visit. I hope to see you again many times in London. I do not know when I have enjoyed such beautiful scenery as this country possesses, or found the company more entertaining. I depend upon you and your cousin to visit me *often*," and her eyes found Mr. Thornbrough's, directing a glance of definite purposefulness toward him.

Bertie mumbled something inarticulate and fled the room.

Chapter 20

Mr. and Mrs. Pendleton were very glad to receive
their daughter and Elizabeth back into their midst.
Rosa had done her best to make their visit a lively
one, but Mrs. Pendleton could not feel wholly comfortable about having her only daughter swept away
for a week in the country before they had even settled
into their hotel rooms. During the absence of the
young ladies, she and her husband had become better
acquainted with Rosa and the peculiar personalities
who inhabited her hotel, such as the doorman,
Freddy, and his dog, Scott, the ever gloomy butler,
several gentlemen who seemed to live always in the
Swanhome's bright, cheery rooms, and those who
merely came to visit three or four times a day. Mrs.
Pendleton, who was unaccustomed to hotels, felt almost as if she were visiting someone's home instead of
merely putting up in an establishment. The rooms
were filled with freshly cut flowers, broad, comfortable couches, and wing armchairs. There was a great
deal of informality, so much so, in fact, that Mrs.
Pendleton was at first not certain that they had
landed in a truly respectable hostelry. But after
seeing Rosa sweep off one night to go to the theater
with Lord Ribblesdale, dressed in sables and white
velvet and speaking broad cockney, she decided that
perhaps after all if the place were not particularly respectable, it was certainly fashionable. The food, as

Mr. Pendleton pointed out, was almost worth crossing an ocean for.

The young women from America arrived late Saturday afternoon, bringing with them in their train, in addition to four trunks and a variety of hand baggage, Mr. Martin Thornbrough. He had come down with them on the train from Toye and, having had the forethought to wire his carriage to meet them, was able to convey the young ladies safely back to their parents.

He treated Elizabeth and Isolde both with the same easy good manners; but Elizabeth sensed some special understanding he and Isolde shared, some unexpressed agreement.

"So!" said Rosa, emerging from her office as Freddy and Scott ushered the party into her lobby. "And you all have been off on a party just at the beginning of the season. Anyone born? Anyone dead?"

"Alas, no," said Mr. Thornbrough. "Just a family affair down at Toye with Bertie Taunton."

Mr. and Mrs. Pendleton came down and were introduced; they invited Mr. Thornbrough up to their sitting room, but Rosa insisted on having the party come into her office and she opened a magnum of champagne for the occasion. The American party was quiet, but Mr. Thornbrough and Rosa were chattering away cheerfully about the latest gossip of the week when in strolled Georgie and Fweddie Brooke.

"Hallo, Wosa," said Fweddie. "Got any extwa wooms? We've just come up fwom the countwy, dwopped by our lodgings, and found the woof had fallen in."

"How disappointing for you," said Mr. Thornbrough dryly.

"Not at all, not at all," said Georgie. "We haven't paid our rent in about three years anyway, so they can have the place. They've been very rude about it, too, following us around everywhere and sending us the most dreary letters. It is too tiresome, and Fweddie and I really need a change of scenery."

"Haven't you just had one?" asked Rosa, a little puzzled by the invasion. It was quite unlike the Brookes, who were not noted for their extravagance, to cast discretion to the winds and come for a stay at one of London's more expensive hotels. Although they knew the best people, the entertainments they gave were small and informal, albeit very amusing. They had been to the Swanhome more than once for supper at someone else's suite, and Rosa liked them both very well. Never mind that she would probably never see a penny of their money. She would figure out a way to put them on someone's tab, and in the meantime they would be very good company and liven the place up a little.

"Can you tell us if Bertie will be coming up to town soon?" asked Elizabeth.

"On the twain with us," said Fweddie cheerfully. "Vewy cozy party; Tuttle was there and we had a few hands of bwidge."

"How nice," said Elizabeth. "I hope we shall be seeing a lot of him this season."

"I'm sure you will," said Fweddie.

Shortly after, in walked Tuttle. He did not actually hold Bertie by the hand, but judging from the extremely reluctant expression writ large on his face, Tuttle had had to exercise a great deal of tact and persuasion to bring him to Rosa's establishment. Bertie stood on the threshold of her office and looked around gloomily at the company.

"I know, I know," he said helplessly to the company at large, "but there was nothing I could do about it."

"Well!" exclaimed Rosa. "What's the matter with you? Has your roof fallen in too?"

"Something like that, madame," said Tuttle smoothly. "Upon inspection of Lord Albert's lodgings, I discovered that some repairs were urgently required, and so we must seek accommodation here in the meantime."

"Are you Lord Albert?" asked Mrs. Pendleton, her curiosity greatly aroused by this parade of people.

"Yes," said Bertie shortly. "I daresay all this seems odd to you. It seems damned odd to me too."

Mrs. Pendleton, to whom the situation seemed to be an interesting but not unreasonable coincidence, protested and drew his lordship off into conversation. Elizabeth, Isolde, Mr. Pendleton, and Mr. Thornbrough joined in, leaving Rosa to loudly whisper a few questions at the Brookes.

"Now what is all this 'ere?" she demanded. "A lot of roofs to fall in all at once with no rain."

"Dwy wot," said Fweddie.

"And that's just what all this is," said Rosa indignantly. "I don't mind carrying on in my 'otel—that's what it's for—but there's no need to be so 'ush 'ush about it. And I'd like to know who's going to foot the bill for all this. You and Bertie don't 'ave 'alfpence of yer own, not as far as I know."

"If I may explain, madame?" asked Tuttle.

Rosa eyed Tuttle from head to toe. "If you are this Tuttle I've heard so much about, go ahead. I've been wanting to meet you this age."

"The situation is a delicate romantic affair," said Tuttle. "It must be handled with great care if all is to reach a happy conclusion."

"Which means marrying Bertie off to one of those young ladies, I suppose? Well, I've heard that snowballs can't melt in hell, but I'm not inclined to put my money on it."

"No, madame, as you say. However, there has been some indication that one of the young ladies already

looks upon his lordship in a very favorable light. And
as one who has served Lord Albert for many years,"
he added righteously, "I'm glad that there is someone
at last who can appreciate some of the more excellent
qualities he possesses in such abundance."

"My, my," laughed Rosa, "but will all this pay the
bill? And yer bill?"

"You don't undewstand," said Fweddie. "She *pwoposed* to him. As God is my witness. That's wight, the
blond one. She took him out in the gawden and
pwoposed to him. Now who is going to believe such a
stowy? Would I have believed it, if I hadn't vewy
pwovidentially happened to be out on a neawby path
in the gawden smoking a cigawette? Cewtainly no one
at the clubs is going to believe it. I can get odds of at
least twenty, maybe fifty to one. A few pounds put
down now, and when the announcement is in the
paper, Georgie and I will be wich—well, solvent—
again. And if you want to know another sure thing,"
he added, lowering his voice even more, "Thownbwough is after Miss Pendleton, the dweamy
bwunette. Ah, Wosa, the supwises we had at Toye!
Why, Cathy Battewsbottom—you know, that pig Edwin's sister—eloped with the cook while we wewe
there. It was an exciting week."

Rosa was inclined to take an interest in the whole
affair and suggested that they all dine at the Swanhome that night, when the handle of the door turned
and Geoffrey Smythe strolled in. Always noted for his
neat and even dandified appearance, the arrangement
of his white linen suit and fresh buttonhole was quite
perfect, his creases were all beautifully starched, and
his mustache turned up neatly at the edges.

"Hello, all," he said breezily, taking off a hat
scented with hair oil. "Drove by my lodgings and to
my dismay, found the whole ceiling of my sitting
room lying on the rug. What a shock. So I thought,

might as well hop in a hansom and come around to Rosa's and see if she can put me up. Eh, Rosa? You do seem to have a crowd tonight."

"Ha!" snorted Rosa. "I suppose you're here now, you might as well stay. Do you know these people? Want an introduction?"

"As a matter of fact, m'father's land borders Toye, and we spent our last evening at a too wonderful dinner party Bertie gave there."

"My, my, how nice," said Rosa. "Well, you're always a welcome face around here, Geoffrey. We were just wondering who was going to buy the next bottle."

Chapter 21

As Isolde lay in bed, resting before dinner, she reflected over the events of the past week and resolved to be done with Mr. Thornbrough. He had too many insufferable qualities and was unmanageable besides. She needed someone. At times, especially at night when everyone else slept, or during pleasant afternoons when everyone else seemed to be able to go about such business as making calls and changing for dinner, Isolde sometimes felt the walls shutting her in, pressing on her, the routine of her dull maidenly life oppressing her. A lover could set her free for a few moments; but meetings were difficult to arrange and infrequent. Her scribbled poetry sometimes moved the walls back; but sometimes it only inflamed her further, leaving her to pace her room with a strange anxiety until she took a dose of laudanum. Sometimes she thought she would soon go mad. The young men were a harmless little amusement she allowed herself by way of contrast.

Perhaps all she needed was someone who would be there when she beckoned, ready to love and comfort her, not a strong and demanding man who attempted to overpower her with his judgments.

But as she lay in bed, emptying her mind of thoughts, lazily allowing herself to drift off to sleep, she felt a mouth on hers, a ghost mouth, the impression of a body holding hers, an impression but not the substance. She did not think she missed Thornie, but it was ghostly to feel him against her again, making love to her. The memory of the pleasure he had given her in the violet woods and in a moonlit forest came back to her, haunting her.

If Thornbrough possessed memories as happy as Isolde's, he did not dwell on them. He could not quite comprehend the whole business, and this rankled. There was nothing to explain to him why Isolde acted the way she did, and he could find no factor in her family, her social background, or even her American nationality to help him understand. She seemed to be unique. Her mother was a typical woman in every way, enjoying the prestige of meeting people of rank, going shopping, and attending operas.

Thornie would not have been surprised to return to London after a week's absence to discover that Mr. Pendleton had indulged his uncultivated *nouveau riche* tastes in all that London could offer. But no rumors were winging around the clubs that a rich new mark had come to stay at Rosa's, so, remembering an open invitation to dinner, he decided to appear there at night after all. Bertie was there, of course. Tuttle was really quite wonderful. And the Brookes would not overlook a chance at free food; it seemed quite like the old party. Elizabeth still sparkled; but when Thornie glanced at Isolde, she did not return his gaze; her eyes unfocused and were very, very far away.

The Pendletons would have been secretly pleased to see their daughter courted by an earl, however indigent he was rumored to be, but he behaved in a very odd manner. He said almost nothing during dinner and kept his eyes on his plate, except for an occasional glance at Elizabeth. Such a taking girl! It was a pity that Isolde did not have her knack of expressiveness. Isolde looked like a silvery shadow in her white dress, hardly there at all.

"And now that you are safely back in London," Geoffrey addressed her, "what is the first thing you wish to do? The city is yours. You can command anything you wish."

"This is story time then," Isolde answered laughingly. "I can't command very much, I know that. For one thing, I don't know where anything is, and for another, I don't know any people here. Mama tells me she has already gone to see the Tower, so what else *is* there for me to do? I suppose I ought to go buy an umbrella."

"Whatever for?" laughed Geoffrey. "An umbrella! And what will you do, Miss Wilcox?"

"Oh, Bertie has promised to take me to see the nearest bicycle factory," said Elizabeth smoothly. Thornie glanced at his cousin in surprise, and seeing his expression, his lips twitched noticeably. Elizabeth was undoubtably redoubtable. Bertie had sat up straight in his chair and looked up from his plate. His eyes traveled all around the table, like those of an animal seeking a means of escape. Not finding one in the faces of his erstwhile friends, they settled helplessly on Elizabeth, his brows fluttering up and down on his forehead

"A bicycle factory!" exclaimed Mr. Pendleton. "Are you interested in such things, your lordship?"

"Yes," said Bertie, his eyes fastening on his host. "Would you like to come with us? We'd desperately love to have you. Do say yes."

"Upon my word, I think I won't. I've been waiting this week for Isolde to come back so that we could go and call upon Whistler."

"You could do that another day," suggested his wife.

"But I don't want to see a bicycle factory. Elizabeth

will discover the details if they are important, won't you, Elizabeth?" To the company at large, he turned and said, "What a head this girl has for business. No doubt she'll sell them a contract for steel while she is touring their facility."

"Please, Mr. Pendleton, spare my blushes," said Elizabeth, amused.

"Who is it you wish to see?" asked Mr. Thornbrough, not quite trusting his ears.

"Whistler. The painter, you know."

"But he's not a very good painter," said Thornbrough, visibly appalled.

"Oh, I know he isn't fashionable, like Burne-Jones or William Singer Sargent. But I've seen a few things he's done, and I'd like to purchase some of his nocturnes. And have him paint Isolde's portrait."

Thornbrough glanced at Isolde; she glowed. Had Thornbrough discovered in Mr. Pendleton the bourgeois tastes typical of his class and country, he would not have been disturbed. Had Pendleton begun to collect a retinue of impoverished peers, monocled counts, and various bogus grandees in search of someone to prey upon, he would have known no surprise. Had he begun to look for a suitable castle of his own to purchase, disassemble, and ship back to the States, Thornie would have shrugged in resignation. Had he gone through the city tossing thousand-pound notes about and demanding that art treasures, fine carpets, or cellars full of vintage champagne or a particularly pleasing cognac be delivered up to him, Thornie would not have been impressed, although the enigma of Isolde's nature would have continued to tantalize him.

But Mr. Pendleton had done none of these things. Mr. Pendleton, it seemed, in addition to being the inventor of a process of refining copper that had made him and his business associate happily wealthy, found the absurdities of spending vast sums of money too troublesome to be bothered with. Silver desk sets at twelve thousand dollars each—why should he waste his time? Marble bathtubs in a private Pullman car looked very well, but the splashing was horribly inconvenient. Becoming remarkably intoxicated on even the finest of champagne night after night annoyed his spouse and became stale.

No, Mr. Pendleton entertained a secret ambition that would disturb Thornie more than any of these things. He wanted to be a painter. Not an ordinary painter, not one of these scenery and flower painters. A real, true artist, a good one. Behind his wife's back he had acquired a copy of Du Maurier's book about struggling young artists in Paris, and he yearned, if not to become one of their number, at least to make an attempt at learning the art himself. Being rich was a hindrance; but he did not have to waste all his time at the opera or the clubs or at parties or out driving or shopping. Some of that time he could spend being a struggling artist. Rumor had it that Whistler was one of the characters in the book, fictionalized, of course; perhaps if he met the painter, he could learn some of his secrets.

"He is accounted to be a rather strange kind of person, you know," hinted Georgie delicately.

"Wather abwupt," Fwed added helpfully.

"Actually insulting, in fact," said Georgie. "And he requires dozens and dozens of sittings, too, so tedious, and even then you might not come away with a painting. Why, haven't you heard what he did to Sir William Eden?"

"No, tell us," said Elizabeth cordially.

"Sir William Eden is one of Rosa's particular favorites," said Georgie. "I don't know why, but he always has been, has known her forever, too, it seems. At any rate, he asked Whistler to do a portrait of his wife, and on the date set, which happened to be February 14, he handed Whistler an envelope containing the payment and took away the portrait; it was quite a small one, just of her head. When he handed him the envelope, he said, 'Here is a little Valentine's Day present for you,' which Whistler seemed to find insulting, and when the Edens left and he opened the envelope, he found that it was a very little present, indeed. According to Whistler, less payment was made than was promised. And so after a few weeks, he called upon the Edens and asked that he might have the portrait back again so that he could clean it properly for the last time and attend to any small, overlooked details. They agreed, and he took the painting away. Then he refused to ever give it back! They had to take him to court for it, and even then he fought a long battle for it. He absolutely loathes giving up a picture, I'm told, even though he is quite willing to receive payment in advance. You must be careful, and have it shipped off to the States immediately, or it might disappear in the dead of night. And don't bring him here; Rosa dislikes him because he was so rude to her precious Sir William."

"Sad," said Mr. Pendleton. "Sad, but understandable."

"Do you find such behavior understandable?" said Thornie. "I don't. It is certainly not good business."

"But Whistler is no businessman. He is an artist, a genius. Sad, isn't it, that an artist must give up his work? He must labor to produce the most perfect picture he can, and then sell it and never see it again. At least a writer can always read a copy of his book. But a painter loses his creation forever."

Thornie tried again. "One can, perhaps, feel some sympathy for a struggling artist. But Whistler's first reception in London, many years ago, was very promising, very rewarding for a painter of his strange technique. He provided his own publicity; he has always had a quick tongue. But his temper is bad, his contempt for his patrons enormous, and his certainty in his own powers unlimited. Look what he did to the Leytons. They asked him to add a few touches to their dining room while they were out of town, and he painted peacocks in gold leaf all over the walls, which were covered, I believe, with hand-painted leather brought to England by Catherine of Aragon."

"Perhaps you had better commission Sargent," said Mrs. Pendleton.

"Well, my dear, we could have both. But I do want to meet Whistler."

"I must admit I do too," said his wife.

Thornbrough would have liked to have taken Mr. Pendleton aside and told him that Whistler lived with a mistress in his house, a state forbidden to any other man but permitted to an artist because, of course, he needed a model and because artists were not expected to possess the same morals needed in other circles. But he could not. He did not know or understand Mr. Pendleton well enough. He did not wish Isolde to spend day after day in an artist's studio, surrounded by people who often did not marry properly, as they should. This was permitted them, because they were artists. The actress Ellen Terry had two children born out of wedlock, but she was still accounted the finest actress in London. Perhaps, however, Isolde would not understand why her life must run through a different channel than theirs. He glanced at her. She was like a lighter-than-air balloon; if one let go the ropes, she would fly up, unweighted. She was quite capable of taking on some artistic lover, having a baby illegitimately, and going to Paris to set up a little salon on the fringes of artistic society, always sure of visitors when she fed them good dinners. It was hard to know what she wanted.

But he could not tell this to Pendleton. He could not give such friendly advice when the memories of their acts together remained so vividly in his mind.

"I should love to go to a bicycle factory," said Geoffrey brightly. "What a good idea! I wonder we have never thought of it before."

"By all means, come," said Bertie with cordial desperation. "In the morning then? Is that all right, Miss Wilcox?"

"If Mrs. Pendleton does not need us tomorrow," said Elizabeth.

"No, go ahead, dear. I hope I shall like this Whistler," she said absently. She was highly suspicious of all those roofs falling in at once, but she was not English and could not be sure of the facts. It was possible that here in England roofs were put up in such a shoddy manner that they collapsed periodically. Such a thought was unlikely, but one had heard of thatching, and thatching did not sound particularly sturdy. Then, it was possible that the everlasting fog and damp in this city ruined the plaster, forcing the people to be continually building up their houses again over their heads. Perhaps that accounted for the stories one heard of so many living in squalor; all their houses had fallen down. But it was quite possible, and even likely, that this set of people had come to the hotel just because Elizabeth and Isolde were here. She was quite pleased, on the whole. If only Isolde would behave, and if only her father would not encourage her to behave so eccentrically.

Thornbrough was silent. He had no wish to visit Whistler or a bicycle factory.

"Perhaps I may drive Miss Pendleton in the park tomorrow afternoon," he said. "I must exercise my teams; they have not been driven this week." Georgie exchanged a meaningful glance with Fweddie. It was imperative that any bets should be laid before this event occurred. Mr. Thornbrough was not known to drive young ladies, and if Isolde was seen occupying a seat by his side at the fashionable hour of the promenade, the odds would drop rapidly.

"Perhaps we will have returned from visiting Mr. Whistler in time to meet you," said Isolde softly. The Pendletons, who as yet had not been informed of his position in London society, appeared unconcerned. Only the others were aghast, and Bertie thought it a good joke, despite the fact that he was too dismayed at what he must bear up under the next day to laugh. Thornbrough was annoyed, and some part of him wished they were all comfortably back in the castle. There was no way he could think of to arrange a meeting in the city, except in a place too public for what he would like to do to Isolde. He snapped his mind back; he would not think of such a thing again, he promised himself.

Chapter 22

Elizabeth, Bertie, and Mr. Pendleton departed in the morning, immediately after breakfast, accompanied by the essential Tuttle. Bertie and Tuttle had had a few words the night before as Tuttle was putting him to bed, but since Bertie was rather incoherent, and Tuttle in full possession of his faculties, Tuttle won the argument. Bertie tried to remember in the morning just why he was wrong to try to leave Elizabeth alone so that she could find a man worthier than he. Tea didn't help; it was all very muddled. He tried to follow Tuttle's line of reasoning, but he wasn't good at that sort of thing, not the way Tuttle was. Tuttle should have been a solicitor or an inspector or something like that. Tuttle should have been Bertie, he thought gloomily. "Only I would not have been as good as he is at ironing, and being adroit and managing." He paused to envision himself in formal dress, pouring wine into his master's lap, and never remembering anyone's name. He would probably be dismissed immediately.

He tried again to find the path Tuttle had laid out so clearly for him last night. If Elizabeth was fond of him—and he would like to know how they had found out about the proposal so quickly, he thought suspiciously, even that damned doorkeeper Fred and his dog seemed to know—and he wished to spare her feelings, then the proper thing to do was not to turn aside from her in public, but to spend a great deal of time with her, so much that she would weary of him and drop him quickly. Well that was what Tuttle had said, but it didn't sound quite right this morning. What if she did not weary of him? And if she spent so much time with him, how could she meet another man who would be perfect for her? Tuttle hadn't thought this all out properly. If Tuttle knew so much, Bertie thought stubbornly, then just let him run the show. As far as Bert was concerned, from now on he wouldn't worry about being Bert. He would be Tuttle, and let Tuttle worry about being Bert. He was a better man for the job anyway. He looked and acted a lot more the way an earl should; people probably were always getting them mixed up.

The factory was four miles away from London, not much of a journey by train. Tuttle's services were required more than once, however, and not merely to guide the party to the proper train and assure them comfortable seats. Geoffrey showed a predilection for gossip and flirtation that could not amuse either Tuttle or his master. Bert was helpless, but Tuttle was able to interject informative tidbits into the conversation in such a way that it remained general and not simply a conversation between Elizabeth and Geoffrey.

During one of these short speeches, Bertie leaned back in his seat and said quietly to Elizabeth, "It won't do. This wasn't fair, Elizabeth, and you know it."

She smiled at him and replied, "You're not giving me half a chance, Bertie."

"M'mother always took me here and took me there when I was a little boy," said Bertie. "Now Tuttle does it. But I know what's right and what's wrong, and I'm not going to be pushed into a situation like this again, even by you. You know I love you and that's enough. Now go out and meet other people, look around you. You won't be breaking my heart when you find someone else. I've known all along that you would."

Elizabeth tried to keep her composure but her voice trembled as she said, "In New York men used to come after me."

"And they will here too," Bert promised. "In droves. In flocks and in gaggles. All kinds. No need to worry, love. Just look around. Promise?" Elizabeth nodded, and Bert reached out for her hand. Taking it, he held it for a moment, squeezed it lightly, then drew away from her, and said, "Miss Wilcox, you should be sitting here, next to the window."

The journey was completed with little more discussion. They disembarked at the next station and, thanks to Tuttle's management, found the carriage belonging to the foreman of Dierding Velocipedes waiting to take them on inspection. The earl of Taunton was a prize, rather an unusual sight in a bicycle factory. Tuttle had also hinted that the daughter of a famous inventor and tycoon, Mr. R.R. Wilcox, would be making the journey, acting as an agent seeking promising new business ventures. It was this tantalizing information that brought out the company carriage and the foreman to the gate, ready to show the visitors any of the machinery or working arrangements that might interest them. Even in England they had heard of mills changing hands overnight at the whim of acquisitive American millionaires—for exorbitant prices.

He was a trifle surprised that the young lady was so young and so pretty too. It seemed unlikely that she could be a business agent for anyone, but the questions she asked were articulate and showed that she understood the workings and methods of manufacture. Very odd, especially since he had never been able to interest his own wife or any of his five daughters in the business that kept him from his home fourteen hours a day, six days a week.

After a very few minutes, however, he began to realize that Miss Wilcox was interested in the factory in only the most general way, and that it was his lordship who was seized with the fever of bicycling innovations. His questions were technical and showed that he had a wide knowledge of the most up-to-date developments in the field by Dierding Velocipedes and their competitors. He even had a few patents himself, he said modestly, although he had never thought them commercially worth an investment. Soon the foreman and Bertie were enjoying themselves greatly. Bertie felt a momentary twinge of guilt, as he always did when he snuck away from society to spend time with his velocipedes.

Geoffrey and Elizabeth tramped around the factory for longer than they cared to when Tuttle finally stepped forward and, tapping the foreman on the shoulder, mentioned that the lady looked rather tired and perhaps could wait in a quiet place— (the machinery made a great deal of noise) —until his lordship finished the tour. The foreman apologized for having overlooked their comfort and ordered one of the workers to escort Mr. Smythe, Miss Wilcox, and Tuttle to his office, and to have tea served to them.

Geoffrey and Elizabeth were served tea while Geoffrey amicably related to her any number of anecdotes and gossip about Rosa Hurst, her colorful career and the histories of some of the people they had met, as well as current stories about some of the city's more flamboyant characters, such as poet Oscar Wilde, a fellow, he said, who resembled a large, white caterpillar. Wilde was feuding with the Mr. Whistler her friends were visiting at the moment, in the columns of the *Times* too—so handy for all to judge the force of their arguments and the style of their wit.

They hardly noticed that some three quarters of an hour had passed before the foreman returned.

"Well, well, I hope you have not thought we were chewed up in the machines," he said cheerily. He was a plump, pleasant-looking man, the very sort of person who has a pink, round face. "His lordship certainly has a head for the works! Some of his ideas may be a little extreme, but he showed me a few things today I had never thought of, and I've been in this business since I first found my father's old manvelociter in the barn when I was a boy."

There was a pause, which Tuttle broke with the question, "Where *is* his lordship?"

"I couldn't tear him away from the shop," said the foreman, pouring himself a cup of tea and selecting a jam sandwich. "Told me to ask you to please forgive him, but he couldn't leave quite yet and knew you would be wanting to go back to the city. I wish you could see him; he is like a duck in water. Most people come through here—and I've had a lot: a couple of aldermen last week, sometimes the shareholders drop in, all kinds—and from the questions they ask you'd think that we were still living in the days of Good Queen Bess. Why, just last week one of them said to me, 'It seems like a lot of trouble to go to just to make a toy,' and of course I always get hot when I hear something like that. Precision manufacturing, that's what we guarantee here at Dierding's. And of course I never finish a tour but one person at least sniffs and says, 'Well, you can go to all this trouble if you wish, spending all this money and manpower, but it'll never replace the horse.' And why should I wish to replace the horse? The horse is one of God's creatures, I'm sure. The horse wouldn't complain. So it's a treat, indeed, a real treat to meet someone who takes to it all like his lordship. And a sense of humor, too. He asked me if I would give him a job."

"And did you?" asked Elizabeth.

"He's an earl."

"That may be so," said Elizabeth, amused but sad, rising to her feet. She picked up her gloves and her shawl and said, in parting, "But you will find, I'm afraid, that you are going to have a difficult time getting rid of his lordship. If he leaves the premises before midnight, I shall be surprised. Do look after him, won't you? If it gets very late at night, will you find him lodgings? I'm afraid that if he gets a very important idea in his head he may wander around in a rather absentminded way."

The foreman replied that he would be deeply honored if Bertie would eat his mutton with him and meet his family. They would be in a flurry at meeting a real earl. With a safe mind, Elizabeth, accompanied by Geoffrey and Tuttle, departed. They had had quite enough of factories for one day.

Bertie, unconscious of luncheon and teatime, was seized in the grip of the beautiful black-and-chrome machines that worked so miraculously around him and could not watch the hand tooling processes enough. Elizabeth had receded to a dull throb in his heart; his brain was filled with the machines, his mind's eye saw bicycles of a new and more beautiful, more ingenious design being manufactured by bigger and even more wonderful machines. The gloom had dissipated, and he felt his mind expand, filling the walls of the bleak factory building with a wave of new ideas. He must take them out of the air and produce them, make them tangible, give them life, and he would do it in this splendid place. Bertie was filled with optimism.

Chapter 23

The Pendletons went to Whistler's house in Chelsea in a group. None of the others seemed to wish to go at all. In fact, Fweddie and Georgie were a little nervous when Whistler's name was mentioned. Mr. Pendleton went prepared to be fascinated; Mrs. Pendleton went with curiosity, and with some hopes that Whistler would become more fashionable in the future, an artist they could boast of patronizing; and Isolde went with no expectations at all. She could sketch a little and had been taught to use watercolors and chalks, but painting made her nervous; she was not comfortable with a medium that only seemed to render the world two dimensional. The young ladies she knew all painted very nice birds and flowers; the painters she had met in America did scenes of sailing ships, storm clouds over a valley, and sentimental pieces such as "The Proposal" or "The Farewell." Her mother exclaimed joyfully over each one, to be sure and praise the proper one. Isolde found it all very dull.

They found the address and dismissed their hack. It was a small, narrow house on Tite Street in Chelsea. The entrance door was painted blue-green and had a brass knocker. A servant answered their knock and ushered them down a few stairs to a landing and then to a reception room painted blue and white, the floor carpeted in blue matting. The room was furnished with a few Queen Anne chairs, a couch, a grand piano, and a table littered with newspapers. On a wall were three nocturnes. Mr. Pendleton exclaimed, "Now there's the thing!" and gazed rapturously at them. Mrs. Pendleton privately thought them unfinished, dreary paintings, since they were of twilight in a foggy London. Isolde puzzled over them. Their colors were drab—gray, dark gray, and light gray, relieved with a little black—and if they were meant to depict a scene, it was a strangely unreal scene, like a dream, or a nightmare without substance. They were more like moods, feelings, than renderings of a landscape. She was wrinkling her brow over them when the Master entered.

He was a small, wiry, angry individual. His hair and mustache were flecked with gray, but very precisely arranged; one white lock of hair was brushed up over his forehead. He was foppishly dressed and wore a monocle, squinting at them all in a rather disturbing manner. In drawling tones, he said, "Good morning to you. Admiring my nocturnes, I see." The next twenty minutes were spent with Whistler pointing out the various beauties of his paintings. He searched his vocabulary mightily but seemed to find it insufficient in number and range of superlatives necessary to praise their excellence. Mrs. Pendleton was greatly relieved to hear that they were such good pictures.

She was more impressed by the odd manner in which he had decorated his house and wondered if she could carry off such a style in New York. Everything seemed to be very fresh and bright; even Isolde commented on that, and yet it was all quite simple. The dining room was done in blue, as the reception room had been. Brightly colored flowers stood in porcelain bowls on the table, and a Japanese bird cage housed a white parrot in a corner. Whistler's blue-

and-white china collection was displayed there, the Japanese style that had now become so fashionable. Mrs. Pendleton asked him how he had obtained such a splendid collection, and he replied that it had not been easy at all, not at all.

"When I first purchased the set," he said, "I invited a friend and fellow collector to dine; I knew he would admire the china and envy me horribly, and of course I could then enjoy my little acquisition so much more. At dinner he was overcome with the beauty of the dish, and partly from artistic curiosity and partly, I suppose, from a lack of hunger, he immediately turned the dish over to look at the markings on the bottom. Unfortunately, the dish was still full of soup.

"We tidied up and continued our little repast, talking into the early hours of the next morning. I saw him off and went to bed. The next day, when I got up and went to fondle my little bowls once more, I found they were gone. I knew where they had gone to. I had to wait for the dead of the next morning, when the sunshine glows so hysterically as it reaches high noon and all decent artists are in bed, to break into the fellow's house. I went through his entire china cupboard. I discovered secrets there that even I was not ready to learn; the fellow actually possessed a complete set of Wedgwood! There, in the very back of the beastly set, wrapped in newspapers, were my beautiful bowls.

"Naturally, I later confronted him with his wrongdoings. He claimed the Wedgwood set had been left to him by an aunt. I glared at him. He stammered and then claimed he had purchased it for almost nothing for his servants' use. We no longer speak."

They were all amused and banished the Brookes' warnings from their minds; after all, they were all Americans together. Perhaps these English, who were an odd breed, after all, with their traditions and incessant tea drinking and strange rituals, simply couldn't understand the painter the way another American could. And if his house was a bit odd, it was only because there wasn't quite as much furniture as there was in most people's houses. They had heard rumors that Mr. Whistler had gone bankrupt more than once; perhaps that was where all his family portraits, lithographs, fret-work, memorabilia, hat stands, umbrella stands, footstools, carpets, and mirrors had gone. Mrs. Pendleton thought privately that, being a man, he simply couldn't be bothered with such things. Only her daughter and her husband sensed that Whistler had created a place in which he could be comfortable and probably had thrown out all the other things.

"Yes, we are all Americans here together," said Mr. Pendleton. "I'm sure we'll be able to reach a better understanding than you might dealing with an Englishman."

Whistler, thinking fondly of the American sea captain who had sought him out when he was a student in Paris, to pay him for copies of masterpieces from the Louvre, thereby allowing him to live quite well for a student and produce his first work, agreed. "Exactly where are you from?"

"New York City."

"A state in itself, I assume. Naturally, I hail from Dixie."

Mr. Pendleton did not know whether to sympathize or offer his apologies, but Whistler went on without them.

"Mrs. Pendleton, can you come for sittings sometime next week, shall we say? How about every afternoon at two?"

"Oh, no, Mr. Whistler, the portrait was to be of my daughter, Isolde," fluttered Mrs. Pendleton.

Whistler glanced at Isolde and said, "No, I think the first portrait will be of you. A very nice-looking girl, of course, and perhaps I shall do her later on. We will see. But first I should like to start on you. I think an Arrangement in Gray and White, don't you? You will be a No. 1, as I don't have any other Gray and Whites. Unless you prefer to be an Arrangement in Gray and Black; I've had luck with those. My mother was one and Thomas Carlyle was another. But no, I think I should prefer you in more delicate shades." Privately, he was posing her in his mind; she would be a good subject for an Arrangement in Gray and White, with a well-lit background. He liked the way she bulged.

"But Mr. Whistler," protested Mrs. Pendleton, not knowing whether to feel flattered or annoyed, "I thought my husband spoke with you about this. The portrait was to be of my daughter, Isolde."

"Nonsense," said her husband. "I'm glad to meet a man who can appreciate beauty. They make too much over these young girls. Isolde has plenty of time." Isolde, entranced by the force of Whistler's personality, agreed, and Mrs. Pendleton yielded to the persuasions of her husband and daughter. Mr. Whistler was full of instructions. He wanted Mrs. Pendleton to procure a dress cut very simply out of a light gray fabric. There was to be a ruffle of white lace around the throat, but the rest of the dress was to be untrimmed. He sat down and made a sketch of it quickly and gave her a card with the address of a shop where she could find such material.

"Shall we say two o'clock Monday a week from to-day?" he asked.

"Could we possibly come sometime in the morning?"

"Certainly. Would two in the morning be convenient?"

Mrs. Pendleton laughed. "I'm afraid not at all, and then the light would surely be too bad. In the afternoon then." Ready to depart, she then had to search for the next ten minutes to find Isolde and her father, who had wandered into another room, following the trail of framed Whistlers on the wall.

"They are for sale," hinted Whistler delicately, sadly. It would be a pity to lose any of his beautiful nocturnes, but he thought of his beloved Trixie upstairs, and how much the bills worried her poor head. Mr. Pendleton lit up and began examining them all carefully.

"May I have one too, Papa?" asked Isolde.

"Certainly," said her father. "If that is all right with Mr. Whistler."

"No, no, please go ahead," said Whistler, his sadness departing slowly. He had recently brought suit against a critic who had called one of his most favorite paintings a pot of paint thrown in the eye of the public. Naturally he had won, but the philistine of a judge had only awarded him a farthing for damages and ordered him to pay his own court costs. He had been bankrupted by the expense, and the appearance of an American millionaire, ready to buy and commission, was quite a pleasant sight, if only his just dessert for being the greatest artist living in England today. The wife, of course, was rather ordinary; but her husband reminded him of the Bostonian sea captain of early days. The daughter was not unbearable either; she didn't gush, and she had chosen one of his very favorite nocturnes.

"May we take them away with us?" asked Mr. Pendleton. Reluctantly, Whistler took them off the wall and wrapped them up in newspapers for them; they were small paintings, and Mr. Pendleton had the intention of carrying them off under his arm.

"Now let us talk about price," said Mr. Pendleton.

This was something Whistler liked to do. He had five bill collectors living in his house at the very moment. One had been the servant who opened the door. "Let us say 2,000 guineas each. I shall send you over a bank draft this afternoon. And for my wife's portrait, upon completion, 10,000 guineas."

Whistler hated to sell his paintings, but this was too much at too necessary a time; it was obvious that Trixie's God had intervened and had sent this messenger to him to make him rich. How pleasant were the ways of God, even if one did have to part with several of one's most particularly favorite possessions.

With a sigh, he agreed, and the Pendletons departed, Mr. Pendleton carrying the nocturnes under his arm. Four thousand guineas was more money than Whistler had seen in many years. He went upstairs to tell Trixie, who was still asleep.

Mr. Whistler had not particularly noticed Isolde; he was seldom interested in young ladies, who were usually dull and often gauche. But she had noticed him. It might be for Elizabeth and for her mother to manage people and events smoothly, politely, so that their lives flowed easily down decorous, carefully chosen channels of propriety. But they never seemed to feel the walls closing in; they had never mentioned to her that silly little things saddened them, that sleep eluded them, that the world oppressed them. Here was Mr. Whistler, and if he ever did experience such feelings, and she somehow felt he did, he would respond not with tears and doses of opium, but with anger and outrageous behavior. Perhaps that was not her own style; no, certainly it wasn't. But she could admire the strength that underlay his anger and wish to possess it. If another mood came up, she would be like Mr. Whistler and fight it, not yield to self-accusations and depression.

Chapter 24

The fashionable hour of the promenade in the park was four o'clock. Mr. Thornbrough, immaculately attired, drove his four-in-hand to the Swanhome, arriving at a quarter past two, certain that his quarry would have been properly brushed and bonneted by an anxiously waiting mama. If Mr. Thornbrough did not, like the Prince of Wales, employ four full-time valets to attend to his personal needs and the care of his wardrobe, he always presented an appearance of good taste, his figure of strong angles unmarred by the bulge his gourmand prince sported. His clothes fit his well-built frame admirably, and his careful good taste was revealed in the arrangements of his ties, the excellence of his tailor, Henry Poole, and the restraint with which he selected his jewels. A single stone such as an emerald, perhaps, or a signet ring. Diamond studs on occasion. But nothing of a flaunting nature.

He yielded his team with some reluctance to Rosa's doorman; he had not brought his groom. Into the plush, comfortable lobby of the Swanhome he went to find Isolde.

She did not seem to be about, but Rosa was there, talking in low tones to Mrs. Pendleton. Upon seeing him, she winked and shouted at him. "And don't you look pretty! Did you and Miss Pendleton have a good time?"

"Excuse me?" asked Mr. Thornbrough, removing

his homburg. "Isn't the young lady here?" It was too much if her mama had gone off and left her in the clutches of some damned painter, like a common model.

"Oh, dear," said Mrs. Pendleton, as she saw him enter. "I knew it. She's gone out to buy another umbrella, and without telling a soul except Freddie before she left."

"She told me she was leaving," said Mr. Pendleton mildly. "She's gone to look at someone's house. Pepys's, or Nell Gwynn's or someone like that."

"How could you let her?"

"I thought it was a good idea. I wished I could have gone, too, instead of having to call on that silly woman we have to see this afternoon."

Under Thornie's fascinated gaze, they continued their discussion. "I never thought she would behave this way in Europe," said Mrs. Pendleton. "It isn't fair having a daughter like that."

"Nonsense," her husband replied. "Much better to see Pepys's house than this duchess you want to visit."

"She wasn't to see the duchess. She was to go for a drive with Mr. Thornbrough. She is never where I want her. Look at poor Mr. Thornbrough. She has no sense of social obligation."

"She takes after her Aunt Tida," said Mr. Pendleton with resignation. "The women on my side of the family even have their babies late. I should have warned you. But you must remember, Isolde has a poetic nature. Genius cannot be pushed."

"Genius! How can you speak so! She does nothing but read books and scribble poetry all day."

"But my dear, what else could a genius do? You don't think they come out neatly printed and set in type, do you? One must have inspirations. One must suffer. One must live. And then one must apply a spark of godhood and create."

"Oh, really, George," said his wife indignantly. "I don't *want* Isolde to find inspiration. Mothers are supposed to shield their daughters from inspiration."

"There are many kinds of inspiration," said her husband firmly. "We should not protect our young, smother them in our affection. Isolde should be encouraged to go out and look at the world."

Mr. Thornbrough, who agreed with Mrs. Pendleton that Isolde received far too much inspiration for a girl of her years and marital status, said, "Has Miss Pendleton always been given to . . . absentmindedness?"

"Well, at first we thought it was that Miss Axelrod, her governess," explained Mrs. Pendleton. "Miss Axelrod's family must have a streak, too. Perhaps that is why she and Isolde became such very good friends. If I sent a little note up to the schoolroom in the morning reminding Miss Axelrod that I would like to have Isolde on hand in the afternoon at teatime, so that she could meet guests and pass tea, invariably at the hour mentioned it would turn out that she and Miss Axelrod had gone sketching, or for an invigorating walk, or some such thing. And I always suspected that Isolde did not truly appreciate her godmother, a very respectable woman, of course, but perhaps a little too talkative and well, wordy, you know. As Isolde grew older and older, she would have more and more frequent attacks of influenza, or asthma, or mysterious coughs whenever it was necessary to pay her godmother a call. It was most annoying. I thought Miss Axelrod was merely encouraging her in her own ways, but now either the damage is done, or Isolde was responsible all along."

Although Mr. Thornbrough did not relish being lumped together with tedious callers or boring godparents, he could readily appreciate Isolde's tricks. Just the sort of thing he had always wanted to do.

"And how long has the young lady been gone?" he asked. "Is she familiar with this area? Perhaps she is lost."

"All she has to do is tell any cabby that she's putting up at the Swanhome," said Rosa. "They all know the place. Could she remember that much?"

Mrs. Pendleton seemed uncertain, and no one felt very comfortable. "Perhaps you had better advise your daughter," said Mr. Thornbrough, "that it is not customary for young ladies to go out alone in London. The streets are safe enough, I suppose, but one does not like to depend upon luck, and it is the convention here for single women to be chaperoned, if only by a maid."

Mrs. Pendleton exchanged glances with her husband. If only matters were as simple as Mr. Thornbrough made them sound. But short of chaining Isolde to her bed, they possessed no magical control over her; she walked out when she pleased, scold and beg though they might.

Mr. Thornbrough, worried about Isolde, also felt a deep concern for his perfectly matched team in the hands of Rosa's doorman, so he was forced to leave them, promising that he would return at teatime to hear the news. Outside, he found that the day had turned pleasant and sunny. His team was safe and quiet under the slack rein of Fred, the doorman, and Fred himself was being well entertained by Isolde. A feeling of indignation rose up in Mr. Thornbrough's breast, but it was quenched by a stronger sensation of pleasure at the sight of her. She was dressed very simply in some mute tone between a blue and a gray, and wore a nondescript little hat which resembled a belt buckle tied on with a piece of ribbon.

"Hello, Mr. Thornbrough," she said to him casually. "So this is your carriage? Fred tells me that they are very fine things, but I know so little about horses, and even less about sure things."

"You cannot know less about a sure thing than Fred."

"Tell me this much," she said. "In all sincerity, is every male in England named either Freddie or Bert?"

"Not at all. Some of us are named William."

"William. I'm not sure I like that name."

"I don't believe I care for it either. As you know, my name is Martin. I give you the use of it."

"Martin! How well that suits you! You are so like a martinet, you know. I wonder if *martinet* was originally the diminutive of Martin, which would mean you are defined as a very *grand* and important martinet?"

"Isolde," said Martin, helping her into his vehicle, "despite the fact that you resemble a shadow, which I'm sure was your intention, and despite the fact that you are trying to provoke me into displaying my temper, I am now going to take you for a drive in the park. You will enjoy yourself very much and not be bored. I am accounted to be a most amusing companion, I shall introduce you to anyone you like."

"*Dear* Martin," said Isolde lazily, "how do you know I am going to go anywhere with you?"

"Because you are bored." She laughed, and they set off.

"It is too kind of you to take me out like this," she said. "I hope you know how deeply honored I am by your attentions. Rosa and Fred informed me this morning just how rarely bestowed your favors are, which brings the total to five, I believe. Bertie, *dear* Edwin, your aunt Honora, and now Rosa and Fred. How wonderful it must be to know that one is appreciated on all sides. How precious you are in the eyes of the world. Like some rare gem."

"Do you take the opposite point of view, just to prove them wrong, or are you going to rise above such nonsense?"

"I wish I had brought a parasol," complained Isolde, "or at least a picture hat. It is bliss to know that I am soon to be pointed out to all the notables as 'that new American girl next to Thornbrough.' I want to look my best."

Mr. Thornbrough glanced at her appreciatively; he wanted to do more, but he would be taking their lives in his hands if he tried to kiss her in the middle of the whirling traffic, beggars, and street shows of Piccadilly Circus. "You look lovely, as I am sure you are aware."

"Please! Mr. Thornbrough! Remember where we are!"

"May I point out, Miss Pendleton, that this is one of the most public places in the country? Certainly no girl could ask for a more respectable location to be informed of her enticing nature."

"And where is your groom? Surely we should have one about here somewhere."

"The poor fellow was taken ill with a cold this morning. Perhaps it was a toothache."

"And the undergroom? And the underneath groom? And the lowliest stable boy? Surely you could have found one of them to lend us a little chaperonage."

"I concede the hand and the game. Shall I point out interesting landmarks, or have you been here in a former life?"

Isolde disclaimed any knowledge of London streets, due perhaps, she said, to the fact that she had a very bad memory and could not remember more than a few centuries ago, and when one had been dead for a period of time in the meantime, it all became muddled. So as they drove along Mr. Thornbrough pointed out the more memorable sights, as Isolde took in the masses of red and yellow azaleas in full bloom and other profusions of flowers and shrubs which Hyde Park in spring held forth. Their way was crowded with a smartly dressed crowd that seemed to be completely without order; they passed other four-in-hands, Mr. Thornbrough greeting in passing some drivers, who flowed forth in pony carriages, barouches bearing dowagers, driven by coachmen in full powder and livery, passersby, and occasional riders.

As they approached the statue of Achilles, a famous trysting place, Mr. Thornbrough told stories of some of the couples who had sought each other out there. He related the tale of the time Lily Langtry forgot her appointments and made arrangements to meet two rival suitors at the same time under the statue. She was late, and as each waited, he noticed the other. Becoming suspicious, accusations were launched and they began to fight it out right there under the statue until someone came along and separated them. Everyone was rather put out with Lily, who had the good sense to stay home when she remembered her mistake.

Mr. Thornbrough interrupted this tale a number of times to bow and nod to various people. He seemed to be very well known, Isolde reflected resignedly. At last, after they had been driving for about ten minutes, a young Englishwoman on horseback, wearing a very tightly fitted, mannish habit, with a tall silk hat and a snow white Ascot tie, cantered up to them.

"Hello, Martin!" exclaimed this equestrienne. "How long have you been back?"

"Not so long," said Thornie. "Lady Alistair, may I present to you Miss Pendleton?"

"Oh, please call me Daisy," said the young woman. "Everyone does. I think I know you. You're staying at

Rosa's, aren't you? I thought you were Stubblefield's niece, but he says he hasn't one."

"Rosa has told everyone in London that story," said Isolde. "I live in terror that one day Stubblefield—whomever he may be—will appear at the hotel with a sword and behead me for trying to spread it all over town that I am his niece."

"I am sure he would be deeply complimented if he were to actually see you," said Lady Alistair in smooth, sweet tones. "Of course he is of the old school, and it might be difficult to convince him that not all Americans talk through their noses. Such an odd habit! I wonder why they cultivate it so."

"Perhaps it is because we are all so fearfully ignorant," said Isolde. "Left all alone on that great continent to try to teach each other English as best we can."

"Oh, I am sure that cannot be so! I have heard of so many Americans who have done great things. There are Whistler and Sargent—of course, they left as soon as they were old enough—and I am sure you have many other great men as well."

"And women too," said Isolde.

"What I was actually thinking about was my fund-raising bazaar. It is really a too tedious affair, but I was wondering if you knew something about Indians so that we might have a savage Indian booth. We have plenty of East Indians in London, but none of the Western variety, and we hear so many quaint stories about their behavior that I was wondering if you knew any in America. It must be wonderful to have the blood of savages in one's veins."

Miss Pendleton blithely replied, "Oh, it is, completely delightful, I assure you. As it happens, my grandmother was a full-blooded Leeuanhoeck. May I know what the purpose of this fund-raising bazaar is?"

"It is the Christian Women's Bazaar, designed to buy and send Bibles in foreign tongues to needy countries."

"Well, I don't like to drag my heels or appear negative in any way, my lady, but I think I should point out that Indians are very seldom practicing Christians. They are animists, you know. They have a very fascinating set of beliefs, but I don't think they would be impressed with the need to send Bibles to foreign countries. So perhaps the presence of an Indian booth may appear a little odd, unless, of course, you can find an Indian who has been converted to Christianity, and that would be acceptable. Here in London, too. Quite a task you have chosen for yourself. I admire your energy. And your habit. It is lovely. You must let me know if I can furnish you with any other details of American domestic life—we have such fun in the States." Miss Pendleton ended on this light note. Mr. Thornbrough, glad to have been extricated from the situation without further bloodshed, motioned with his whip in salute to Lady Alistair and drove on.

"Leeuanhoeck sounds like a Dutch name," he said.

"It does, doesn't it? Is Lady Alistair a very good friend of yours?"

Since the knowledge was widespread that Daisy Alistair had been Thornie's paramour for almost two years, prevarication seemed to be not the best method of dealing with the question. He was not so concerned with the throbbings of his own conscience but with the certainty that Rosa, Fred, or even Cousin Edwin would not hesitate to blab the truth to her.

"Oh, yes," he said casually. "Daisy and I have known each other for years. She and her husband have often been to Thorn Manor for a weekend. She can be quite rude, but she is never tedious."

"She seems to be quite the mistress of London society, is she not?" said Isolde, turning her dark, blue eyes on him with an innocent gaze.

"Quite," he replied shortly.

Isolde smiled pleasantly and the drive continued in peace. They talked of art on the way back to the Swanhome, Mr. Thornbrough offering to escort her and the rest of her party to Grosvenor Gallery one day where, he hoped privately, Mr. Pendleton might be weaned from Whistler's grasp by visions of true art.

"May I call upon you tomorrow?" asked Mr. Thornbrough as he pulled his equipage before the entry of Swanhome. She assented, and refusing to let him keep his horses waiting, descended with the aid of Fred and Scottie.

Slightly dazed by all she had seen that afternoon, Isolde wandered into the lobby of the Swanhome and up to her room. She was removing her hat when her mother knocked lightly on her door and let herself in.

"Ah, you are back then, dear," said her mother, looking slightly flushed. "Did you have a nice ride in the park? Rosa tells me it is quite the thing to drive there at this time of the day, especially with Mr. Thornbrough."

"You are the sixth person to tell me that," groaned her daughter. "I believe I will see if I can hire a lot of peers to chase around after Mr. Thornbrough and tell him in an undertone, quite off the cuff, you know, that to be seen with the *dashing* Miss Pendleton will make his career."

Her mother smiled, but warily. She had learned never to trust her daughter's jokes. "Perhaps in a few weeks, my dear, that will be the case. Invitations have almost rained in on us today! There is a card from Lady Honora bidding us to a small family dinner at her home tomorrow." Her daughter groaned again, but her mother went on. "Then there is a card, with apologies for the lateness, but they understand that we are just newly arrived for an evening of music at Lady Daisy Alistair's tonight. Do you know her?"

"I met her this afternoon. Not at all a nice woman. I don't think you or Papa would care for her."

"There you are," complained her mother, "you're always finding fault with people. Her letter is perfectly civil, and I think it is extraordinarily kind of her to seek you out after having only met you once."

Isolde was not about to enlighten her mother. At that moment, Elizabeth tapped on Isolde's front door and breezed in.

"Isolde! It is too much, really, it is too much. Yes, I have returned, but very unsuccessfully. Bertie will not leave that wretched bicycle factory! To think it was my idea in the first place. What a fool I was! He and that foreman spent all their time wandering around the place *staggered* with glee at all the lovely big machines they have. Bertie is staying the night with the foreman's family, and I don't think he intends to ever come back! He is the most elusive person I have ever met."

"There, there," said Isolde, grinning. "We will think of something. You contract consumption, or perhaps find Another. I will be the messenger; I must remember to buy a spotted black veil tomorrow."

Mrs. Pendleton broke in on all this. "Elizabeth, tell Isolde she must come with me tonight to Lady Alistair's musical evening. I am sure she would enjoy it, as musical as she is, and you will not be lonely."

Elizabeth turned to Isolde and said in mock-serious tones, "You must go with your mama to Lady Alistair's musical evening, Isolde, as musical as you are. And be very good and don't make yourself sick by eating so many cakes and ices."

"I believe I have a headache coming on," said

Isolde in a faint voice. "I am so sorry to spoil everyone's pleasure, but I feel rather dizzy. Do I have a fever, Mama?"

"No, you don't," said her mother crossly. "You are just a very badly behaved child."

"Here, I'll call Georgie," said Elizabeth. "She'll have been to one of these things." And while Isolde protested, Elizabeth stuck her head out the door and shouted down the carpeted corridor, "Georgie! Georgie, are you there! Come and make Isolde behave."

Fweddie's head appeared in the doorway, neatly framed against the dark woodwork, his blond mustache pointing upward. "I'd like to come and make Isolde behave," he offered. An invisible hand pulled him backward and Georgie emerged.

"Really, this is not the way young ladies should behave," she fussed. "Yelling back and forth in hotels. Now what is Isolde doing? I don't know why you're complaining, Elizabeth. You've been known to take unsuspecting, innocent peers on long rides down lonely paths while wearing knickerbockers. No doubt you will be smoking cigarillos next." Elizabeth, who had tried many years ago to cultivate a taste for her father's cigars, hotly disclaimed this. Mrs. Pendleton, diverted, exclaimed, "Have you a pair of knickerbockers, Elizabeth? I should like to see them, if you don't mind. I have considered buying them for Isolde—perhaps she would take more exercise if her limbs were unhampered—but I have never seen a design that was not grossly unflattering." They were about to fall into a conversation of fashion when Isolde called them back.

"Dearies, dearies," she said. "The question at hand is should I, poor, sick Isolde, who has been in and out all day and really does not feel the thing, leave my bed to attend a musical evening at Lady Alistair's?"

There was a silence, broken by Georgie's voice. "You have been invited to *Daisy Alistair's?* Do you know her?"

"I met her in the park today when I was driving with Mr. Thornbrough," said Isolde. "They seemed to be very good friends."

Georgie was quite put out. She had an interest in Mr. Thornbrough's forthcoming nuptials and had no intention of allowing the vixenish Lady Alistair to spoil her chances of recouping her fortunes. There was no chance that Lady Alistair would ever divorce the nitwit to whom she was married, despite the rumors. She would lose too much, and Thornbrough would probably never offer her marriage. But for someone as bored as she, it must be an amusing game to try to keep Thornie on lead for a while. Georgie, thinking of her own cuddly Fweddie, shuddered; it was not a game she would enjoy. But if Daisy meant to make trouble, would Isolde enter the ring?

"Miss Pendleton," said Georgie delicately, "perhaps we could discuss this in my room. You must tell me what Daisy told you in the park." They left the room, leaving a bemused Elizabeth to try to make explanations to a bewildered Mrs. Pendleton. In Georgie's room, the two women settled down to talk.

"I don't think you are stupid," said Georgie summarily, "so I will not hesitate to tell you that, although Daisy is a married woman, her attention wanders to other men."

"And theirs to her, I'm sure," said Isolde.

"Daisy is a rather spoiled girl. She's always had whatever she wanted, and the result is that she rather likes to play with people. Before you and Miss Wilcox arrived, she and Mr. Thornbrough were frequently seen together. When it is understood that Mr. Thornbrough has an interest—forgive me!—in you,

Daisy will naturally feel that a new player has entered the game and will try to win, as she always does."

"And she will be trying some of those tricks, as you would call them, tonight?"

"That's right."

"Then I shouldn't go, should I?" said Isolde softly.

Frustrated, Georgie urged, "The music will be quite splendid. She has wonderful taste."

"Ah, the music, the music," Isolde repeated dreamily. "How fond I am of music!"

"Then go to Lady Alistair's tonight. It will be good, I promise you!"

"And the lights, the sparkling lights, the people whirling about, talking, laughing. Georgie, are you going to be in tonight?"

"No, not I. I never stay home at night in this season!"

"I suppose everyone will be out?"

"Yes, everyone. Do go!"

"Perhaps I will," promised Isolde. "You see, I am really very fond of music." And, leaving a puzzled Georgie behind, she swept out of the room.

"Well?" asked her mama, as Isolde entered her bedroom.

"I cannot go to a party in London and leave my poor friend Elizabeth all alone," Isolde stated. "This is only her second night in the city. How could you think of such a thing."

"I have already written a note to Lady Alistair, telling her we had a companion we could not in conscience leave. She has sent back a very polite note saying we can bring any guests we choose."

"Good! Can we take Whistler?"

"Certainly not," said her mother firmly. "If she wants Whistler there, I am sure she can invite him herself. Now I have decided you are coming to this party, young lady, so I will ring for your maid and you may begin to dress now."

"Yes, Mama," said her daughter dutifully, smiling.

Chapter 25

Lady Alistair was everything Mrs. Pendleton expected in a peeress; magnificently dressed and jeweled; beautiful, with fine patrician features, and rude.

"Are you actually in business," she said gaily to Mr. Pendleton. "How amusing! I think you must be the only businessman in this room."

"Nonsense," he said gruffly. "Everyone is involved in some kind of business, even if it is the business of lying in the gutter. Perhaps your husband earns his living by receiving revenues from farmland. That is his business. Mine is metal refinery."

"Ah, but I'm afraid my husband is not very good even at receiving revenues. Let me introduce you. Perhaps you can tell him some of the particulars of your work." She swept the party over in the direction of her spouse.

Lord Alistair was famous in London for being married to Lady Alistair. It was not a profession in which he sparkled. Indeed, he could not be described as sparkling at all; he was a thickset, plump man several years older than his wife. Daisy summarily introduced the elder Pendletons to him and left them together with the knowledge that her husband was incapable of entering into conversations in words longer than one syllable, and that he and the Pendletons shared no common interest, acquaintance, ideas, or even public schools. They were well suited for Lady Alistair's purposes.

She left Elizabeth with a dull young man who gave speeches on the East End to the poor. For Isolde she reserved a dowager with a countenance more foreboding than Lady Honora's, and safe in the knowledge that her guests were properly disposed of, she went off in search of her own circle of friends.

"My dear," said Lady Alistair to Thornie, "how wonderful your American friends are. And what an excellent provider you are. Let me see, there is one for Bertie and one for Edwin. But have you heard about our Princess Alexandra? They tell me she has decided to stay with her parents in Denmark."

"I heard that before I left," said Thornie abruptly. "You've invited my Americans then? Where are they?"

Lady Alistair glanced around the room and found, to her irritation, that a small crowd had gathered around Elizabeth and that Isolde was nowhere to be seen.

"I'm not sure. There is Miss Wilcox, encircled by some of our more indigent satellites, like a heavenly body surrounded by moons. You had better be quick if you want to keep it in the family. I can't see Miss Pendleton."

"She must have donned her invisible cloak."

"Excuse me?"

"Nothing. How wonderful you are, Daisy, to invite these people here into your home on their first visit to London, doing all that you can to make them comfortable. I see the Pendletons were left to your husband. Will you excuse me?"

"He has to have something to do. I thought they would be a good influence."

"Oh, I agree, I agree. He cannot be alone all the time, can he? Poor fellow."

And, with a small bow, he turned and was gone.

He found Isolde in the other room, sipping a glass of champagne.

"Good evening," he said.

"Don't tell. Mama says I am not to have champagne, but I think I will need it if I am to stay here for hours and hours."

"Perfectly right," said Thornie, helping himself to a glass. "I always get drunk before I come to one of these events."

"You are not drunk now."

"I sobered up the instant I saw you."

She glanced up appreciatively. He was watching her, his tall figure upright. Their eyes met and held for a moment, then turned away; hers, to admire his broad shoulders, his waist, the strength of his thighs and the proportions of his limbs all encased in perfectly tailored clothes. His eyes traveled from her brown ringlets to her white neck, encircled with pearls, to the neckline of her dress, cut high to show hardly a hint of the breasts he had touched. A pang went through them both, and they were silent, too aware of each other's thoughts and bodies.

Music began in the ballroom, a woman's soprano, singing an Italian aria. Isolde glanced around the room; she knew no one. The people looked exactly like the people she had left in New York, neither uglier nor more beautiful, neither more interesting nor more dull, not more lordly, more royal, or better bred. Worth dressed them all, or Worth imitators; all wore jewels, or suitably sober formal coats and hats. She had heard the aria a hundred times, sung badly by several of her friends and sung well by Melba. The room held nothing for her; the party was all dullness. Only Thornie stood silently by her side. Flirtation was pleasant, but she wanted something more.

"Let's go out onto the terrace," she said brightly. "I

thought I saw lanterns and a few people outside. To hear music in moonlight might make the tones sweeter."

Thornie, still thinking of her in the moonlight at Toye Castle, was suspicious. It was very like Isolde to want to go off somewhere, and take him along too; perhaps they could find a dark enough corner to kiss in. But Thornie was not at all sure he wanted to participate. He was not afraid of Daisy's wrath, although she undoubtedly would find some reason to seek him out, and the likelihood was that she would discover them at the least opportune moment. Isolde was a good companion, her humor light and witty, her understanding easy. But lovemaking in the moonlight must inevitably lead one further down a path he was not sure he wanted to tread. He was a villain if he continued without seriously considering marriage. And, despite his earlier proposal to Isolde, marriage was a state of affairs, in his estimation, that no sane man could ever seriously consider. If one did not need the money or immediate heirs, it was mere madness, like throwing oneself in jail voluntarily.

"Please?" asked Isolde, looking up at him with begging eyes. "It is such a beautiful night out."

"My dear Isolde, for you I think the moonlight always shines."

She chuckled and stood up. He gave her his arm and they went out onto the small terrace. There were a few couples there, and they had been standing under the night sky for a few minutes when Lady Alistair appeared with a glittering smile.

"So! Miss Pendleton! But aren't you a little chilly out here? You mustn't take cold. Your mother tells me she is having her portrait done by Whistler. She should have come to me; I could have introduced her to a painter of more note. I'm afraid Whistler is very much out of fashion."

" 'This is our chief bane,' " quoted Isolde in distant tones, " 'that we live not according to the light of reason, but after the fashion of others.' "

"Cicero?" asked Mr. Thornbrough, startled.

"I'm not sure. I have such a terrible memory. I think it was Seneca."

"So you are not having your portrait done?"

"Not immediately. I was so humiliated! Whistler thought my mother would make a wonderful arrangement and would not look at me. But Papa and I are going to watch him work, and Papa wants to take lessons."

"Papa, the businessman? How unusual!" said Lady Alistair.

"Oh, Papa is very unusual," Isolde agreed quietly. "Do you know, Mr. Thornbrough, I believe I am a little chilly in this night air. Shall we go back in?"

He offered both ladies an arm, both of them placing gloved hands lightly upon this support. The terrace was a few steps below the French windows that opened into Lady Alistair's drawing room; they were stepping up these shallow stairs when Isolde, with a little cry, stumbled, clutching tighter to Thornie's arm.

"Oh, these shoes!" she moaned. "Italian heels, how I hate them!"

"Have you injured yourself?" asked Lady Alistair, shaken loose from her arm and stepping around to help Isolde up the last few stairs to a chair.

"I don't think I've broken it," she said of her ankle. "It's just a little strained. I pulled it once when I was young, and this is what it always feels like when it has been strained; I will have to rest it for a few days."

"Are you in pain?" asked Mr. Thornbrough. Her cheeks were flushed, not white, but she bit her lip as if she were trying to bear pain.

"A little," she admitted. "If one of your servants

could call me a hansom, I could go quietly home. I hate to disturb my parents; my mother has so looked forward to coming to meet you, and Elizabeth would have to come away too. I'll leave a message for her, and just leave quietly."

"Nonsense!" said Thornbrough. "Lady Alistair, tell them to bring round my carriage. I shall escort Miss Pendleton to Rosa's and be back in an hour." Lady Alistair could find no objection to raise, so in a few moments she had the pleasure of seeing her lover leave her party in the company of the beautiful young American girl. An annoying spectacle, but there was no hope for it. She was an odd girl, at any rate. She would surely bore Thornie. Young girls always did.

Fred and Scott were alone in the lobby of the Swanhome; even Rosa had departed, escorted by one of her guests to a party that she had catered. The hotel was quieter than usual; on this night, too early for late-night parties to have begun, it seemed abandoned. Already tense with the desire he did not wish to feel, Thornie helped Isolde up the stairs.

"Are you in much pain?" he asked.

"No, it is not so bad. I'll be better when I lie down."

"Shall I carry you?"

She glanced at him. "Yes, if you like."

"Because of your foot."

"Yes, because of my foot."

"Then I shall," and he swept her up, feeling her body light against his as he slowly, carefully, ascended the carpeted stairs. She turned the handle of her bedroom door, and he pushed it open, laying her on the big bed.

"Can I get you anything?" he asked. "Shall I ring for your maid?"

She shook her head. "She has gone out. And all the

others are gone. I wonder if you could take that wretched shoe off before my ankle starts to swell?"

She held up a narrow, slippered foot to him, and he bent over. The shoe slipped off in his hand, and he held her foot for a moment, its toes moving just a little, as if tickled by his breath. There was no swelling, no redness, no puffiness whatsoever. Her ankle was as fine and narrow as ever, the skin smooth and white, undisturbed, uninjured.

"Damn you, Isolde, damn you," he muttered, turning toward her. "How could you?" She lay on the same bed he had placed her on once before, when they had first met so inauspiciously. Then she had lain like a ghost, muffled in a white nightgown, her hair streaming. Tonight she wore an evening gown, its lines simple but tight around her slender figure. He could see the bosom of her dress lightly rise and fall as her breath quickened.

"I am not a French whore, Mr. Thornbrough," she mocked. "Look around you. This is a young lady's bedchamber. Open my drawers. Go through my underthings. They are all white, virgin white, unstained. No black lace here. I read books at night, and dream dreams, not entertain men. But every now and then I want to see a dream, to touch a dream, and you are the dream I am going to have tonight."

"No, you will not."

"And why not?"

"Because I don't choose to allow you."

She sat up and stared at him.

"Did all your young men make love so obligingly for you?" he asked. "Like trained pets?"

"Of course. Why shouldn't they?"

"You'll have to muddle through that alone, my dear," he said, picking up his hat. "Good-bye. I have to go back to Daisy's."

"Please don't. Please stay."

"No."

"Just to talk."

"We could have talked at Daisy's."

"No, we couldn't!" she said, her voice high with emotion. "I can't go to places like that."

"Why not?"

"Because . . . I'm afraid."

"Of what?"

"Of being bored . . . Of people looking at me . . . Of not being able to get out."

He watched her, remembering her mood when she had sought him out at night at Toye.

"Don't you ever feel like that?" She asked, no longer teasing but strangely serious. "As if the room would crush you, as if the walls would come together and flatten you?"

"Isolde. my dearest," he said more gently, "do you feel like this only in London?"

"All my life. All my life. And Mama never understood. I think Papa does, a little. He is a man; he can go anywhere he wants. How I wish I were a man!"

"Mankind is glad you are a woman," he said with gentle humor.

"I hate being a woman! I hate it!" Tears started in her eyes, trickling down her cheeks in fast-flowing streams.

"Isolde, Isolde," he said, trying to calm her. He sat on the bed beside her, and turned her head upwards, a hand under her chin, to look into her eyes. They were full of distrust.

"There is something wrong with me, isn't there?" she said with fear so old it had grown calm.

"You are unhappy."

"Yes. So I take medicine. You were to be my medicine tonight, Mr. Thornbrough, but you will not oblige." She got off the bed and went over to her dresser, rummaged through a drawer, and got out a little bottle.

"What is that?"

"Laudanum. At least I can sleep." She glanced at him and added in light, bitter tones, "Perhaps we can continue our acquaintance later, when I have acquired a husband. Thank you for your escort home."

"Don't take laudanum. Do you take it often?"

"If you drink all the bottle, you will die. Death in a bottle. I love laudanum. I drink a little death each day."

"Isolde!"

"Did you know that I write poetry? Sometimes I like it better than making love." She set the bottle down and walked back to the bed, sitting beside him casually. "You could have been a fine set of verses, Thornie. I would have made a sonnet around you, and set you in it like a candied violet in aspic. You would have liked that, wouldn't you?" She bit her lip and glanced away.

He grasped her shoulders and she turned around slowly, watching him carefully, her eyes bright with held tears. A few curls had tumbled loose, and in her demure dress, with her hair untidy, she looked like a very young girl indeed, troubled over some childish upset. As he held her, she seemed all innocence, all vulnerability, her body light and delicate. But deep within her he could sense her anger, her needs, her desire, and sensuality coupled with some strange fury he could not comprehend.

He wanted to seize her, to possess her. At the same time, he knew in this moment that he had been seized upon, possessed by her, his senses aroused in a way he could never quiet again, and that he was not making the decisions, led on as he was by the bright glow of beauty which Isolde was for him now. He reached out and kissed her, searchingly, demandingly.

She broke it off. "Don't try to be polite."

"Making love to an unmarried girl in her bedroom while her parents are out of the way is not polite," he said savagely, kissing her again. She was cold, removed. He pulled away and looked at her. "What is it?"

"I don't want you to be a performing pet."

"It's worse than that," he said, partly to her and partly to himself. "Far, far worse than that." He pushed her gently down onto the bed; she stared up at him, waiting. "Isolde, you are beautiful, and you are going to be mine." He ran a forefinger up and down the soft skin of her upper arm, tickling it, making her shiver. "If I am to be your medicine, tonight I will drug you into addiction."

"You can't," she said simply.

"Take your clothes off."

"No, I won't."

"And brush out your hair."

"I'm not a thing you can play with."

"DO IT!"

"NO!" she shrieked back at him. She was lithe and quick, jumping away from him. A few steps and she was in his arms again, pinned against him. The tears began again, but the throbbing in his groin was too strong, too painful for him to ignore.

"Don't cry, my love, don't cry," he said gently to her, stroking her hair with one hand while he undid her dress with the other. "I love you."

"I don't want you to love me."

"You will," he promised. "Tonight with your body and later with your mind. You will, Isolde. You do now."

He undressed her, tearing her petticoat in his eagerness, and carried her back to the bed, laying her on it easily, her legs hanging over the edges, parted. She stared up at him with the eyes of a child.

"You are so beautiful, Isolde."

"No, no."

"Everything will be all right," he murmured in her ear, as his lips kissed it. "If your father doesn't come home early and shoot me."

"Papa only has a swordstick."

"I suppose I can dodge that," he said, kissing her again. Her mouth opened, and her lips were no longer passive. She kissed him back, with anger, with need and desire. Her hands wandered over the strength of his body; his were possessive, each touch declaring the territory his fingers claimed. She was full of anger, but she needed the touch of his hands, the skill of his hands, and his naked body pressing down upon her.

When they were finished, lying together exhausted by sensation, he picked up her hand and brought her fingertips to his lips, brushing them with a kiss of complete intimacy. "From tonight, you are mine," he told her.

She stared at him, her eyes now mocking.

Chapter 26

Mr. and Mrs. Pendleton and Elizabeth returned in a burst of glory later that evening, very pleased with themselves. Daisy Alistair was not so foolish as to be jealous of every pretty woman in London, so she had allowed Elizabeth to enjoy her popularity in peace and was satisfactorily civil to her all evening. Mr. and Mrs. Pendleton, dazzled by so much nobility, might not have objected if she had ordered them to make up the fire, but she did not, and they spent a pleasant evening extracting more coherent information and amusement from the long neglected Lord Alistair then anyone else in London had garnered in many years.

Lady Alistair's initial aloofness to the Pendletons' arrival had been more of an attitude of contemptuousness for a rival than a genuine feeling of outrage at being confronted with a member of the merchant class. Mr. Pendleton and his ilk were considered the aristocrats of America. If they were not much better bred than a Serbian king, they were certainly wealthier; and breeding was easier to assume than nonexistent wealth. The Prince of Wales himself depended on his friend, Sir Ernest Cassels, for companionship in his yachting adventures, and Sir Ernest had not yet even retired from his banking empire.

Mrs. Pendleton was too full of chatter to do more than cluck over her daughter's pallor and promise her a physician in the morning if she was in no pain tonight, before she began to recite the details of a party that had bored Isolde almost to madness.

"Isidore de Lara was there," said Mrs. Pendleton, "and Leonard Jerome's daughter, Jenny Churchill, as they call her here, performed as well. She plays the piano so beautifully. You must keep up with your practicing. Everyone was so kind. What a pity you hurt your ankle, but really, dear, you should have told me before you left. Think of how I would have felt if I could not have found you."

"Did Mr. Thornbrough go back to the party?"

"Why, yes dear, of course he did, and he told us he thought you were not badly injured, so kind of him. He is going to come tomorrow and take you out driving."

Isolde turned her face into her pillow.

Just as promised, Mr. Thornbrough appeared the next day to take Isolde out, bearing up nobly under Rosa's chaff. "'Ere, this isn't like you at all! Well, I just want you to know that my money's on you, and I 'ope you pull it off for all of us." Disregarding this nonsense, he asked if Miss Pendleton was in. Rosa frowned and went in search herself, returning with Miss Wilcox.

"I'm so sorry," said Elizabeth sweetly, "but was she engaged to go with you? She didn't mention anything about it to me, and I'm afraid she's gone out. Sketching, I think."

"Then perhaps you will be kind enough to ride with me in the park." He seemed a little gloomy, in need of a little cheering up, so Elizabeth ran upstairs to put on her hat.

She admired his horses, which were, indeed, a team of chestnuts as beautiful as any she had ever seen, and they began on the subject of horses. Since Mr. Thornbrough had thought, due to her somewhat pre-

tended interest in Bertie's velocipedes, that she was
not a horsewoman, they had never hit upon this subject before. Elizabeth told him of her stable in New
York in such yearning tones that he was touched and
offered to mount her during her stay in London.

"I should be glad to furnish you or Isolde with a
mount at any time."

Elizabeth, who did not like to tell him that Isolde
admired omnibuses immensely, said sympathetically,
"I am sure that Isolde would enjoy going for a quiet
ride with you now and then. She did not grow up in
the stables, as I did, because of her early illnesses."
His countenance did not alter much, but the brows
seemed to lower themselves by a few ridges on his
forehead.

"Tell me, how long have you known Miss Pendleton?"

Upon hearing the more formal use of Isolde's
name, Elizabeth noticed that he had referred to her
earlier, and more naturally, as Isolde. It was odd;
Mr. Thornbrough seemed to be a very formal person,
not like Bert or Fwed.

"Well, you see her father is my father's business
partner, so of course we have known each other for
years. But not well. I don't think anyone knows her
well."

"Do you like her?" With this question, Elizabeth
knew that Mr. Thornbrough was merely prompting
her. He wanted her to talk about Isolde. Her eyes
narrowed reflectively, and she glanced at him. He was
very handsome, but not at all in the same way
Isolde's other young men, her rumored fiancés, had
been. Those had all been young men, slender and
boyish, growing their first mustaches and learning
how to go about in society. Thornbrough was quite
different. He was a man, not a boy, and he possessed
a man's strength and, it seemed, a man's will and as-

surance. There had been no one else at Toye for Isolde to flirt with, but here in London, it was a very curious development that at the first party they attended together, Isolde should injure her ankle—so slightly too!—when he was there to offer his escort home. A very pretty little romantic tableau Isolde planned for herself. Perhaps she had even allowed him to kiss her.

"Of course I like her," Elizabeth replied immediately. "But likability is not her strongest asset, don't you think? It is her touch of eccentricity that most amuses me, and anyone who is capable of amusing is always going to be an important person in one's life."

"Hence your fondness for Bert."

She smiled. "Ah, yes, dearest Bert! But his eccentricity comes to him more naturally than Isolde's, don't you agree? Sometimes I think Isolde assumes it merely as a style, or to annoy her parents."

"I cannot agree with you. I find Isolde's madness to be of equal or greater proportions than Bertie's. Of course, I have known Bertie all his life, and you Isolde. So neither of us can judge the other's arguments."

"We can enter them in a contest. Tell me something Bertie has done that you find a bit unusual, and I will tell you something about Isolde."

"Just tell me something about Isolde."

"How unsportsmanlike of you!"

"Tell me this much. Is Isolde considered to be quite an ordinary young lady back in your New York society?"

"Isolde!" exclaimed Elizabeth with a chuckle. "I understand your fears now, Mr. Thornbrough. Our continent is not filled with any number of Miss Pendletons about to deluge these shores with their new methods of madness. Isolde is quite unique. I believe everyone in New York, including my papa, who I believe knows at least half of the people in the country, or at least the half that counts, as you say here, all think Isolde is very unusual."

"Miss Wilcox," began Thornbrough, "you are everything a woman should be; I hope Bertie realizes his luck before you give him up."

"I am overwhelmed. Perhaps if I were to drop a few words of praise of you in her ears you would be even more grateful."

"You are correct," he said, half in jest, half in earnest. "My intentions are quite serious. Perhaps you think me a serious person by nature, as Bertie does. I assure you that this is the first time my intentions have even been as determined as my character."

"Poor Isolde!"

"If you will convey to her my regards, Miss Wilcox, and tell her that I shall do myself the honor of calling upon her at the same time tomorrow afternoon, I shall be indebted to you."

Elizabeth, feeling a little uneasy at the idea of having to account for Isolde at any time of the day, nodded her head and thanked him for the ride. It had been enjoyable indeed, and besides had given her a new estimation of Mr. Thornbrough. Whatever tangles Bertie's affairs were in, she was sure that Mr. Thornbrough had not purposely arranged them with a villainous intent.

The Pendletons returned about an hour later, just in time to change for dinner. Elizabeth tried to convey Mr. Thornbrough's message to Isolde, but she was completely uninterested. "You should have been there," she exclaimed.

"Where?" asked Elizabeth. "I thought you were sketching in Hyde Park or some such thing."

"Oh, yes, Papa and I did a little sketching, but then we went to Whistler's. What a tongue he has! He laid Papa and me low for coming also, and when he heard that we wanted to watch him work, he was very annoyed. 'Go ahead, talk to the lady,' he said. 'But don't sit about and stare at me, I don't like it. If you wish to be painters yourselves, go buy a set of paints. I don't give free lessons.' And that's what Papa has done. He went right out and bought a set of paints for himself and one for me and a folding easel and canvas. We are going to begin tomorrow at Whistler's. There is sure to be a fuss, but he can't mind it too much, after all. I am going to do Whistler, I've decided, and Papa wants to do the parrot. The parrot has more character, but Whistler is prettier."

"But Isolde, dear," said Elizabeth, "remember what I was just saying? Mr. Thornbrough is coming tomorrow to see you in the afternoon."

Isolde inexplicably blushed. "Well, he should have said it to me, and then I would have told him I would be quite invisible tomorrow. I wonder what he would do if I sent him a message saying I would call upon him the next afternoon at two."

"He would be overjoyed to see you."

"That's beside the point. If he didn't know me at all, he would be quite stuffy."

"But you do know him, Isolde."

"Oh, well, I don't know him very well, after all."

"Certainly you do. You were just a guest of his for a week. And he is going to send us a horse, too, to ride while we are in London."

"*I* never asked for a horse," said Isolde indignantly. "I don't like them in the least, especially to ride upon. They are terrifying, and either they won't do what you want them to do, and are great, enormous, showy creatures, or they will do what you want and everyone else makes fun of you for riding them. And *I* know the kind of horse your Mr. Thornbrough will send. He'll send one of the great, enormous kind, and I'll have to try to ride it in all this London traffic. No, thank you! Besides, does he think he can buy my affections with a horse?"

"I don't know that you and Mr. Thornbrough are at all well suited," said Elizabeth.

Isolde did not speak for some time; her blue eyes were darker than usual, their pupils dilated as she stared off into space, seeing some vision she did not care to share with Elizabeth.

The mood passed and she continued arranging her hair. "Suited! Of course not. How could we be? We are both essentially very selfish, I think. What are we to do tonight?"

"We have an invitation to Lady Staplemore's ball. We met her last night, after you had left. Mr. Thornbrough said her affairs were usually quite amusing."

"Then I suppose we shall see him there?" Isolde asked in casual tones.

"I suppose we shall," said Elizabeth, mocking Isolde's tones. "Really, Isolde, you are becoming too priggish. Just what are your intentions toward poor Mr. Thornbrough?"

"Too priggish! Really, Elizabeth, you hardly sound like a New Yorker anymore. At any moment I expect you to break into a string of utterly utterlies and too-toos!"

"Don't evade the point, dearest. Now what about poor Mr. Thornbrough? Do you deny that you brought his hopes up only to dash them down again when you had wearied of his charms?"

"Does Mr. Thornbrough possess charms?"

"You are nearsighted," said Elizabeth. "I knew that was why you liked all Whistler's strange paintings."

"Elizabeth, dear," said Isolde, smiling sweetly, "your own behavior toward Bertie has not been exactly maidenly."

"Of course not," said Elizabeth. "I never claimed it was. But honorable, yes. I proposed to Bertie in the most upright way imaginable, and he turned me down flat. I merely wait to make my next move."

Isolde laughed. "I thought you two were acting oddly. And poor Mama and Papa are still in utter ignorance! But I don't blame you a bit; Bertie is terribly sweet. Thornie isn't at all, and besides, he is terribly sure of himself. I don't think I could marry a man who knew his own worth down to the last cent. And then he is such an Englishman! All this business about horses! These English are insane on the subject of horses! And I'm sure that even though he never spoke about it at Bertie's, he is the kind of man who delights in shooting hundreds of birds every day on those awful hunting trips."

"They eat them, Isolde dear. You can't deny that you eat them too. Rosa feeds them to us at practically every meal."

"I know, those strange little pies full of claws and shot that Papa so delights in! Well, I will go to this ball, and I will dance with Mr. Thornbrough, if he deigns to ask me, and I will bear up as best I can under the withering gaze of every London mother and daughter. I can feel their eyes upon me, Elizabeth, like monsters in the night! They are all thinking, why, she isn't even pretty! He doesn't need her money! How clumsy she is! How greedy she is! How stupid and silent she is! I assure you, so much attention does *not* increase my enjoyment of an evening."

"I went out driving with Mr. Thornbrough this afternoon," said Elizabeth. "But they are not all so bad."

"Of course they aren't, because fortunately the species is divided into two sexes, one male and one female. Only the female behaves in the above manner. The male is thinking: he doesn't need her money, but I do! Not a bad dancer! I wonder if she talks through her nose. Is she engaged. Exactly how much per year would she have."

"Isolde, you sound like a child waking from a dream. People behaved the same way in New York."

Grudgingly, Isolde said, "I never went out much in New York. And I can't help it if I expect a duke to behave a little differently than my father's friends' sons might, and be disappointed when I find they are even worse."

"Poor Isolde. I expect you read too many fairy tales when you were a little girl."

"A little girl *cannot* read too many fairy tales," said Isolde loftily. "Of course, some people never learn to dream. I feel pity for those people."

"Let's not be snobbish. Are you really going to wear that dress tonight?"

Isolde, who had absently put on the same evening dress she had worn three days in a row at Toye, glanced down and said, "But Elizabeth, it is my very favorite. And after all, I am not a great heiress like you, so I don't know why I should keep up pretenses."

"You are a great heiress, and everyone keeps up pretenses," said Elizabeth firmly, opening the door of Isolde's stuffed wardrobe and beginning to go through it. "Paupers keep up pretenses. Rosa dresses better than you do."

"Rosa dresses very nicely; I can't help that. This is my favorite dress. I'll wear a different sash with it and no one will recognize it."

"Don't be ridiculous. No one wears sashes and everyone will recognize it. Why, look at this. Your closet is filled with dresses. What is the matter with this blue one?" demanded Elizabeth, pulling out a blue satin evening dress, cut rather low over the shoulders.

"It's too tight. I don't like to wear blue."

"Try it on. It doesn't look a bit too tight to me, and if it is, we'll just have to lace you up a little tighter."

"But Elizabeth, it is dinner time, and I have already done my hair. What a nuisance you are! Anyone would think you didn't want to be seen with me."

"I don't, or at least not if you intend to wear the same dress every night we are here. I wonder your mother permits you."

"Oh, well, there's nothing she can do about it when I am always so late anyway. You know, you are a terribly demanding person, Elizabeth. I'm not sure poor Bertie would be happy with you. Perhaps you should have Thornbrough, and I could have Bertie. At least our temperaments would be better suited."

"You and Thornie are wonderfully suited, you said so yourself. You are both supremely selfish and snobbish, although you both have redeeming charms. Besides," she added, as she helped Isolde into the blue gown and fastened her up, "I have it from Fred—"

"Fwed or Fred?"

"Not Fweddie, also known as Babylon Brooke. Fred and Scot. Fred and Scot inform me that Rosa, Fweddie and Georgie, and Tuttle are all attempting to make their fortunes by betting on our forthcoming marriages."

"No, really, Elizabeth! This is too much! And I suppose the inevitable Mr. Thornbrough is to be my bridegroom?"

"They got good odds for it," said Elizabeth apologetically. "It was a hundred-to-one shot. They stand to make a fortune at those odds. But don't think Thornie has anything to do with it."

"Oh, my, I do hope Fwed and Georgie are at dinner tonight," fumed Isolde, a vengeful gleam in her eye.

That night the American party did not dine in their private dining room but in the large, public one that Rosa had just opened that season. It had become quite a fashionable place, but a large table had been reserved for the Americans, Fwed and Georgie, and Bert. Tuttle arrived a few minutes before dinner, however, and whispered something in Elizabeth's ear. She sighed, but appeared resigned. Fwed and Georgie were not quite disinterested enough to keep from asking, "Nothing wrong, hey, Tuttle?"

"No, sir," said Tuttle. "Lord Albert has merely been detained at the bicycle factory for longer than he thought and has asked me to convey his apologies to Miss Wilcox."

Fwed turned to Georgie and shot her a worried look. She shrugged. She had counted on the Bertie and Elizabeth affair being almost settled, but if Bertie was going to act so absurdly, who could tell what the future might bring? She would perhaps have been even a little more disturbed if she could have heard Elizabeth murmur in Isolde's ear, "Sometimes I think I should marry Tuttle instead."

"Everything was so simple when we were at Toye!" moaned Georgie to Fwed. "Now they are going to this ball at Lady Staplemore's tonight, and who knows who they will meet there. I don't blame you, my pet, but it does seem as if they are being terribly contrary." Turning to her host, who was seated on her right at the head of the table, Georgie said, "I hope you and Mrs. Pendleton are enjoying your stay in London. Do let me know if I can be of any help."

"Tell me, do you know how to paint?" asked Mr. Pendleton.

"I tried when I was a girl and did very poorly too," reflected Georgie. "I had to, you know. My governess, who was very strict, made us all paint and took us on dreary long walks in the dawn to sketch views and flowers and things like that. Then we would do them over in oils, or perhaps design embroidery patterns from them. I was terrible at it. My governess was a very moral, religious woman. She assured us that our chances of going to heaven were so slim that we all gave up the attempt at an early age. I think she used to wake us up for prayers at four in the morning. We had to pray on our knees in the cold for half an hour when it was still dark out. And then go practice the harp or pianoforte."

"I should like to do that," said Isolde in a dreamy voice. All eyes turned toward her, her parents' with skepticism, Elizabeth's with amusement, and the Brookes' with dread. "I think there must be no greater peace in the world than being assured of a welcome in the hereafter. How pleasant would be the quiet routine of a nun, with early morning prayer, simple food and work, singing, charitable work, and more prayer. I think I should exult in it."

"I thought you were going to exult in painting with me this month," said her father indignantly.

"Of course I will, Papa. It is too soon to leave you. But think how much joy there would be in painting simple religious figures, day after day, week after week, year after year."

Elizabeth, biting her lip, looked up at the Brookes and found them both staring at Isolde with horror. "*Dear* Isolde," she said, "consider how much you would miss bonbons."

"Some deprivations, of course, would have to be borne," sighed Isolde.

"I don't know how you can talk like this," scolded Mrs. Pendleton. "We aren't even Catholic. Of course you aren't going to become a nun. You are being just as absurd as you were the time you insisted on going to that terrible school in Boston where you came back at the end of the term almost dead with influenza and more ignorant than you had been when you went. I think if I had continued to send you, you would have ended up knowing nothing at all."

"It is the simple life I yearn for," said her daughter in low tones.

"Well, well, and you can make your life just as simple as you please," said her father. "No one fussing over you, is there? Have you eaten any of this game pie, Isolde? It is really one of Mrs. Hurst's best. You haven't had anything to eat at all that I can see, and remember that you are not to go to the ball and eat a lot of ices and sweets and make yourself sick. I know you have a sweet tooth, but you must think of your health. You don't get enough exercise, you know. I think you must begin to take walks."

Fweddie and Georgie exchanged glances. It was all so confusing. It was hard to believe in Isolde's languishing airs, but her quiet, almost secretive nature did seem to be like that of a nun, and Georgie could all too clearly visualize her in a nun's habit. That clear, milky white complexion that made her seem to be made of opals and moonstones, her deep, questioning blue eyes, and her willowy gracefulness had an ethereal beauty unlike that of the coy, well-built beauties popular in these years. She seemed unearthly to Georgie.

Mr. Thornbrough thought much the same when he saw her arrive at Lady Staplemore's with her parents and companion, the Brookes just behind them. A little smile hovered around her lips, lifting them in the corners angelically, her expression all wide-eyed innocence, almost as if she had never seen a ballroom before. He wanted her, now, this night. He wanted to take her hand and hold her by his side, smiling, greeting all his acquaintances, and then slip off in the night to take her to some room, any room, and make love to her for the rest of the evening while the ball continued and the people danced on. He watched her face across the room. She glanced in his direction and caught his stare and turned away without a smile, as if she had not noticed him, or had never even met him. He frowned.

"Is that one of the new American heiresses?" said one of the gentlemen beside him. "Ah, yes, and I see the other one behind her. Good heavens! Both beauties! How our mamas will tear their locks. Now that I think of it, isn't that the girl I saw you driving with in the park today? Thought there was something damned odd going on, and now I find out that you are already on terms with them. Well, introduce us, man, introduce us."

"It is a great pity, James, that you do not have a little more . . . well, one hates to put a word on it, but style, I'm afraid, is a quality you are a trifle lacking in. I am not your host, you know. So sorry. Perhaps Lady Staplemore will be able to present you sometime in the evening."

"If you're going to be so beggarly about it," said Lord Peterston, "then at least answer a few questions for me. Ah, here is Fwed. Fwed will oblige, won't you, Fweddie?"

"Oblige?" said Fwed, approaching them with a glum aspect. "I don't know why I should oblige such gweat bullies as you. You awe neveh kind to me, cut me at the clubs, wefuse to buy me dwinks, neveh give me a little fwiendly advice for the Derby, and have even been known to leave me with the check. And now you want me to be kind. Well, it's too late. I'm going to go to the States and learn to turn base metal into gold like Moreton Frewen."

"Now, now," clucked Lord Peterston, "remember how much gold not belonging to him old Mortal Ruin turned into base metal. In fact, I think everything he touched turned base. Tell us about these heiresses. From what I hear, you know all about them. What are they like?"

"They awe hopeless. They are vewy, vewy odd.

Even Georgie cannot understand them, and Georgie understands evwything. Only at dinner tonight the pale, dark one, Miss Pendleton, told me she wanted to be a nun." He shook his head in confused sadness.

A smile lightened Mr. Thornbrough's face as he repeated, "A nun? Miss Pendleton? Did she tell you in which century she wished to be a nun?"

"Now what the deuce is that supposed to mean?" demanded Fweddie.

"A Pre-Raphaelite?" asked Lord Peterston, as he watched her across the floor. In fact, she did resemble a painting by Burne-Jones, with her medieval simplicity of style and dark wavy hair. Fashion dictated that woman upholster themselves in thick, brightly colored materials, using layers of whalebone and wires till they felt and looked more like chairs than flesh. Mr. Thornbrough, banishing more unconventional, forbidden desires to an attic in his mind, thought of waltzing with her, putting his hand around her, and feeling delicate, uncorseted skin underneath a thin layer of cloth.

"I don't know whetheh she is a Pwe-Waphaelite," said Fweddie. "She admiwes Whistleh a gweat deal, and people who are Pwe-Waphaelites don't have anything to do with Whistleh, do they? Isn't he the one who goes awound and says such nasty things about theih pictuhes?"

This tidbit of knowledge revealed a depth of understanding of the world of art and culture that Lord Peterston and Mr. Thornbrough had not know their sporting companion possessed. "When was the last time you were at an opening of the Royal Academy?" demanded Lord Peterston. The opening of the Academy generally heralded the beginning of the London season, but Fweddie seldom exposed himself to an atmosphere so rarefied. "And where is Bert? I had heard all sorts of stories about Bert and the

blond heiress." He glanced across the floor; Isolde
was still talking to a group of young men, flanked by
her mother on one side and her father on the other,
but Elizabeth was already whirling across the dance
floor with a dapperly mustachioed partner. "In fact,
I don't know why I stand here talking to you when it
is obvious my destiny lies before me," said Lord Peterston. "Anyone care to introduce me?"

"Perhaps Fwed will," said Mr. Thornbrough. "I'm
a little busy at the moment, James."

Mrs. Pendleton had nudged her daughter, in a very
genteel way, of course, and had directed her eyes in
his direction. It was so odd being at a dance at which
one did not know a single soul. Perhaps this was what
being cosmopolitan meant but, keeping a firm grip
on her daughter, her drawing card, Mrs. Pendleton
hoped that she would meet someone soon besides all
these slippery young men. It was so difficult to understand what they were saying; the words seemed to
come out of their mouths in such a refined jingle. But
Isolde did not seem perturbed at all.

Isolde watched Mr. Thornbrough's progression
across the crowded room, her eyes drawn to his figure,
unable to continue her light banter with the gentlemen around her. She shut her eyes for a moment, and
opened them; he was still before her, but closer. She
wished that everyone would disappear and leave
them alone in the room. She wished he would forget
about her and blank out their shared sensuality. It
was wrong, all wrong, but she could think of no way
to right it again.

His arrival scattered her small court of young men
like chaff before the wind, leaving her to feel curiously irritated.

"Mrs. Pendleton," Thornbrough said, bowing to
her mama. "Miss Pendleton," he said, inclining his

head toward her. "Sir," he uttered in pleasant if somewhat aloof tones to her father, offering his hand. "I see you have all elected to join the party."

Accustomed to being bored but not bewildered at balls, Mr. Pendleton said, "It is good to see you, Mr. Thornbrough. Very odd to come to a place where one knows no one."

"We must remedy that," said Mr. Thornbrough. "Ah, Lord Peterston," he said to that young gentleman, who had just followed Thornie's example and, somewhat ruthlessly, pushed his way across the crowded circle surrounding the dance floor to arrive with Fwed and Georgie hopelessly in tow. "I would like to introduce you to Mr. Pendleton of New York. I must tell you, Mr. Pendleton, that Lord Peterston is quite a traveler, too. Been to India and Africa, and he has even visited your continent. He went West with Moreton Frewen to shoot buffalo wolves, was it not?"

"Had a wonderful time," affirmed Lord Peterston. "Although my wife almost died. Of course," he added hastily to Isolde, "she is dead now."

"Oh, I am so sorry," said Isolde in a silvery voice.

"Died in childbirth, the baby with her," he said sadly. "How she loved horses."

"My daughter is not much in the saddle," said Mr. Pendleton, "but Miss Wilcox has a fine stable in New York. I should like to see some English racing while I am here. We have our tracks in America, but I'm told they are mere imitations of the English thing."

Lord Peterston found himself jumping headlong into a conversation he could not and did not wish to avoid. Out of the corner of his eye he watched Mr. Thornbrough whisk Isolde away and in some part of his mind a curse formed. But the rest of his being was given totally to a description of the Derby, Ascot week, and Goodwood, with Fweddie chiming in with the details of pigeon shooting at Burlingham. Georgie, who had heard too much already, led Mrs. Pendleton off to introduce her to other matrons. She was filled with a charitable fondness for the New York matron, induced by a deep feeling for her loneliness and the knowledge that when she took her shopping the next day at the exclusive modiste she knew of, her own ensemble would be very pleasantly cheap.

"How happy it is that Papa is interested in sports as well as painting," said Isolde, as she waltzed with Mr. Thornbrough.

"Is it not?" said Mr. Thornbrough pleasantly. "I have heard tales, too, that you do not like to ride, but I hope after we have been out tomorrow morning—I promise you I am mounting you on a very gentle mare—you will begin to enjoy the sport too."

"Out?" asked Isolde. "We are not going out, Mr. Thornbrough," she said in calm, sweet tones that denied her growing anger.

"Perhaps Miss Wilcox did not convey my invitation to you?" said Mr. Thornbrough warily. "I hoped you would be able to ride with me in Rotten Row."

"No doubt I shall someday, but not tomorrow."

More than a little annoyed, Mr. Thornbrough asked, "Perhaps in the afternoon?"

"I shall certainly never go anywhere with you if you speak in such an insufferable way."

"My dearest darling, I have not even begun to be insufferable."

They continued to waltz. Mr. Thornbrough danced superbly; Isolde, however, was hopelessly clumsy from lack of practice and felt rather is if she were being tugged part of the time and pushed the rest. This did not increase her good humor. Finally, as she put her foot under Mr. Thornbrough's one more painful time, she gave up and said, "Please! You see what a terrible dancer I am. I would prefer to return to my parents."

"Let us sit down and talk for a few minutes. Your father will still be talking horses and your mother fashion. I am not an unamusing companion. Let me find you a chair." Feeling trapped, as if there were no escape, she allowed him to lead her across the ballroom. It was a trifle overheated. Chairs were scarce, but he managed to find one unoccupied; space was also scarce, so he seated her close to a long French window that had been opened into the night. A pair of ancient dowagers sat nearby, oblivious to the music and dancing, deep in a discussion of the way their constitutions reacted to a variety of foods, patent medicines, teas, barks, roots, and leaves. Mr. Thornbrough, inured to crowded ballrooms, paid them no need. Isolde listened in fascination, her evil humors dispelled for the moment.

"Never eat poppy seed cake," said one. "It is poison. I had a tiny slice at the Fontleys' the other night and was disturbed all evening. I could hardly sleep and," she added, lowering her voice, "the next morning my chamber pot was black."

"How alike refined circles are on both sides of the Atlantic," said Isolde.

"I am amazed that you can bring yourself to comment on such a subject at all."

"Did I comment?"

"Let us bring our attention to more digestible topics. When shall I see you again?"

"You see me now."

"And I like what I see. But I would like to see you more often, and perhaps show you London, take you out for a drive."

"Let us be quite clear with each other, Mr. Thornbrough. Everyone around you has pointed out to me, more than once, that I am unworthy of you, and as I give a little thought to the matter, I am inclined to agree. I wait hourly for a letter, written in dialect, of course, to reach me from your nannie, telling me that you are much too good for me. I suppose when that occurs I will have to go into a decline once and for all, and be taken away to Europe by my parents who, not understanding the true cause of my illness, can only watch me worsen daily."

"You worsen daily without illness," said Mr. Thornbrough.

"Sir!" protested Isolde, laughing. "This is unkind of you. I think we had best never see each other again."

"Shall we say tomorrow afternoon? At three o'clock. The park is full of green grass and sunshine and every kind of flower."

"How dull."

"I thought you liked these things."

"Not in London," said Isolde. "In London, of course, one wants to see a lot of fog and dreary gray buildings and beggars. So you see, I am not the ideal partner for you; I can't dance, don't like horses, and absolutely loathe races and shootings. Have you ever considered marrying an English girl?"

"My dearest," he said, lowering his voice into threatening intimacy. "Never. Just as you have never considered marrying an American man. They are bores, aren't they? And, I assure you, I have never made a proposal of marriage to any of the women I have had dealings with. I don't question your past; don't question mine. I want you now, Isolde, as my wife. Not because I need your money or an heir. You are not required to be proficient in riding, fox hunting, or even tooling a small dog cart about. Nor am I concerned with your abilities to dance or say rude things." But she had turned away from him. Leaning closer to her, he said in low tones, "Isolde, I love you."

She was shaking her head, her eyes distant, not with dreaminess but with some emotion that made her voice ungovernable.

"Perhaps you are sincere in thinking that you love me," she said. "But perhaps you are more moved by pity or simply curiosity. I don't know why you wish to marry me. I don't think I could make you happy."

"That would be my duty."

They were silent for a few moments, held in suspension by their emotions.

"Geoffrey Smythe is bearing down upon us, and before he wings his way past the blockade—I do hope that at least one of the ladies is related to him. We should have an extra five minutes for a great-aunt, no doubt, and perhaps a full ten for a grandmother—I must ask you to be honest with me. What are your feelings toward me?"

"I don't believe I have to answer that."

"On the contrary," he said gently, "you do. Let us remember what has passed between us, Isolde. It was not all done in your own imagination. I was your partner, and you owe me something for that."

She would have liked to have said something casual, perhaps witty, but the ground under her feet was uncertain, trembling, shifting. It was difficult to keep a grip on things, on a conversation, or even a value. She knew girls who would have lived for moments like these, who plotted and planned on which gentleman they would flirt with that evening, which they could induce to propose to them, which they would marry and how much income they would enjoy afterward. Perhaps these girls were sensible girls, able to plan their futures in the way her mama would like to plan hers. But Isolde could not grasp the future; she tried unsuccessfully to keep up with the present and all too often found herself a few moments behind everyone else, floundering in other people's expectations, uncertain of where she was and completely unable to plan where she wanted to be.

"I do have feelings for you," she said, looking at him, looking away from him, feeling his eyes on her. It was the most she could say; and Mr. Thornbrough watched her features struggle unhappily to say that much. He did not understand her distress; his own understanding, newly touched by a woman he had never expected to meet, was almost callous in ignorance of her struggle.

One of the ladies, if not a great-aunt, seemed to know Mr. Smythe from childhood, and he lingered to answer their catechism. Before he could finish, Isolde had slipped away in search of a nice corner.

As a child, Isolde had discovered the knack of slipping away from garden parties, formal calls, and little-boy and -girl dances. She had put this trick to good use during her seasons in New York, during much of which she had been completely concealed from almost everyone's eyes, sometimes with a companion, but more often alone. If she could find no place else, the cellar was useful. But there were almost always a few drawing rooms, too shabby or too much used by the family every day, that were shut up during a party. She knew the location of these in most of the mansions in New York; she began her search here, following the corridor with a sure step, if a somewhat blurred vision.

Cautiously trying the first door which, from its battered appearance and shiny doorknob, appeared to be well used, she stuck her head in. The room was already lit, which saved her a search for candles, and sitting in one of the dark red velvet chairs, drinking a glass of some clear amber liquid, sat Lord Albert, earl of Toye. He looked depressed.

"Oh, hello," he said as she came through the door. "Shut it behind you. Don't stay if you're squeamish."

"Well, how rude," said Isolde. "I'm never squeamish, and what are you doing here?"

"Can I ask the same of you? I'm getting drunk, of course," he said, motioning to a bottle, half filled, that stood on a table by his elbow.

"I can see you've already begun."

"Now don't start at me," he begged. "Don't start saying, 'Why aren't you dancing with Elizabeth? Why are you in here alone? Why aren't you out having a good time?' " He sniffed.

"I wasn't going to ask any of those questions," said Isolde, sinking into the companion armchair opposite his. "I already know all the answers. You aren't dancing because you are miserable, you are alone because you are miserable, and you're having a miserable time because you are miserable."

"Ah, these American women," sighed Bertie. "Are you born knowing so much? Elizabeth should have been me, you see, and I should have been Elizabeth. Only she does it so well! I couldn't do it half so well."

"I want your advice," said Isolde.

"You must be mad."

"If I am, you are too, so you should be able to give me good advice. I know Elizabeth proposed to you, and you refused her. I know that Rosa and Fwed and who knows who else, Scot, the dog at the Swanhome, have all laid bets on us, you for Elizabeth and me for Mr. Thornbrough."

"Is that right! What beggars they are! You and Thornie. What a notion!"

"That's what I wanted your advice about."

"Well, I'm sorry to have to be so blunt, but you can just forget the whole thing. In fact, if I were you, I'd leave England right now and take Elizabeth too. Go see Europe; I hear the Alps are very nice. Thorn-

brough is very particular, very particular. I can't tell
you how many people have tried for him. I know it
for a fact that Daisy Alistair has been his . . . companion for two years. He will never marry you."

"He has proposed to me," said Isolde stiffly.

"No! Are you sure you understood him right? On
his knees and everything?"

"I think he specifically mentioned something about
my being a wife, or perhaps it was his being a husband."

Bertie was staring at her. "I never would have
thought you were the kind of girl Thornie would
pick for a wife."

"Thank you. I'm sure you must be Mr. Thornbrough's best friend."

"I sometimes think I am," said Bertie seriously.
"Very rich fellow, Martin always was, father strict,
mother like mine, did crazy things all the time. Never
saw either one of them, left him in a big house with
his old nannie, then packed him up and sent him off
to school. Always did well at games and things, had a
lot of friends, but I got the notion that he never
thought much of people, and that's a sad way for
someone to live, don't you think? You can't wonder at
it, with Thornie. A boy will do anything for another
boy at Rugby if he thinks he can get a toffee or a
bull's-eye out of it. It's really revolting. And these
Londoners are not much better."

Sympathy was not an emotion she had yet felt for
Thornbrough, but she felt it tugging at her now in a
way that made her very uncomfortable.

"Perhaps that is why he took a fancy for me. Because I didn't really want to marry him."

"I doubt it," said Bertie. "After all, you are pretty,
you know. I can think of plenty of girls who could ignore him from now until Judgment Day, and he
would never propose to them. Did he really propose

to you? There's something odd about you. I've often thought it."

"So have I," said Isolde. "But I've never been rude enough to say so out loud."

"I've heard you say many rude things out loud. Why don't you sing a song? You do that so nicely. I'd like to hear a song that would remind me of someone I love very much, someone dear to me."

Isolde glanced at the bottle and saw that its contents were dipping quickly. "You mean Elizabeth, I suppose. Why are you becoming intoxicated so quickly? I want you to be sober long enough to give me some advice about Mr. Thornbrough."

"What advice do you need?" asked Bertie, in a fog. "He proposed, didn't he?"

"But I don't want to accept him."

"Why not? *Everyone* accepts Thornie. Clubs accept him. Women accept him. The *Queen* accepts him. Everyone."

"Well, why don't you want to marry Elizabeth? Everyone likes her too."

"That's different. Elizabeth is so righto, you know, and sometimes I feel as if I'm not here at all."

"That's exactly the way I feel," said Isolde.

"Well, you're a female."

"That makes me want to go down on all fours and bark."

Bertie stopped for a moment, trying to puzzle this out. "I don't think I understand."

"Well, tell me why you came here at all if you just meant to stay in this little room and get drunk. You could have done that just as easily at home."

"I'm not going to just stay in this little room and get drunk," said Bertie indignantly. "You don't understand. You see, I'm afraid Elizabeth thinks I'm something I'm not. She can't have realized just what I'm like, or she would never have wanted to see me

again. So I am going to—mind you, this hurts me very
much—get completely smashed and then go out and
embarrass everyone, including myself, all my friends—
and Elizabeth. Then she will finally realize what an
awful bounder I am and have nothing to do with
me again."

"Do you think it will work?" asked Isolde,
impressed.

"I'm certain."

"Then I must try out something like that on Mr.
Thornbrough. Behave very badly to him, you mean."

"Do you drink?" asked Bertie helpfully.

"No, but I can't ride horses."

"It's not the same thing."

"Well, I'll think of something," said Isolde.
"Thank you for your advice. I'll go out and wait for
you to appear on the dance floor, and while everyone
gathers around and murmurs what a terrible problem
you have holding your liquor, I'll say shocking things
about you and blacken your name."

"You are too kind," said Bertie. "I will just finish
off this bottle and be right out."

Isolde tiptoed out of the room, down the hall, and
back into the throng. She saw her mother standing
fairly close to the hallway door, talking to a group of
women and men, so she sidled up to the party and
waited for Bert to make his appearance. She saw Mr.
Thornbrough across the room; their eyes met for a
moment, and she smiled a little. She would have to
think of something shocking to do, but not here and
now. Elizabeth was standing with her back against
one of the long french windows that lined the ballroom, looking very beautiful in her white evening
gown and surrounded by young men.

Isolde continued to wait. Some ten, fifteen, and
then twenty minutes slipped by, and still Bert did not
make his appearance. Finally, tired from having

danced all evening, Elizabeth rejoined the Pendletons in anticipation of being escorted home.

"You look tired, Isolde," said Elizabeth. "Are we leaving soon? How I have missed Bertie tonight. It seems as if every young man I meet is a copy of him, but just lacking the essence of Bertie that makes Bertie so outstanding. I wonder where he is tonight. Have you noticed how they all have the same dapper little mustaches and all talk in that odd way? They are all like trial copies, little discards, created as practice before the real Bertie could be made."

"I can't think how you can say that," said Isolde indignantly. "Mr. Thornbrough is not in the least like any of them."

"Of course not. He is a race himself. I suppose Bert is somewhere tinkering. I wonder if he knew I was to be here tonight. It would be tragic to go back to the Swanhome and find I had missed him."

"No, he knew you were here," said Isolde. "In fact, he is in the family sitting room about one hundred yards from here, drinking some evil liquid."

"No!" said Elizabeth. "Well, my precious jewel, are you going to show me this room? And how did you find it? Sneaking off again, I suppose. Why is Bert doing this to me? He has always been such a social person."

"He wants to embarrass you."

"By sitting in the family drawing room?"

"No, no, he was trying to make himself very drunk so he could come out and be despicable in front of everyone. Then you would realize his true worth and never speak to him again."

"Oh! I do love Bertie! You can understand why now, can't you? Lead me to this room."

The two girls tiptoed down the hall, and Isolde, very gently, opened the door. They both stuck their heads in. Sitting in the big red armchair, the glass and empty bottle at his elbow, was Lord Albert, earl of Toye. He was fast alseep.

"Oh, isn't he sweet!" exclaimed Elizabeth. "Here, let me leave him a note." She took out one of her cards and wrote on the back. "Dearest Bertie, I hope your head is not too bad this morning. You were grand last night. My love for you grows daily. Yours ever, Elizabeth." With a flower from her hair, she pinned it to his sleeve. "I hope that doesn't scratch him in the night," said Elizabeth, and the two young women withdrew to go home to their respective beds.

Chapter 27

It was not until several days after the ball that Mr. Thornbrough was made aware of the two bets entered on the books at the Royalty Club concerning his and his cousin's prospective marriages. Since one of the bets was entered under the name of Fred Allender, of the Swanhome, and the other was under the name of Frederick Brooke, he could have little doubt that every interested inmate of the Swanhome was eagerly awaiting his nuptials.

Except the Pendleton parents. They seemed quite ignorant of the whole matter. Mr. Pendleton seemed to spend his time either at 'Change, discussing international business, or out sketching the city. He came up to Thornbrough and told him, in relieved tones, that he had settled into pastels as his medium and was doing quite well, he thought. Mrs. Pendleton spent every afternoon at Whistler's studio. During that time, Isolde was completely unchaperoned, and during much of the rest of the day no one could find her anywhere.

Rage was uppermost in Mr. Thornbrough's emotions when he discovered the bet in the books, harassed as he was by Isolde's vagaries. He did not relish the prospect of listening to the odds of his marriage to Isolde lengthen and shorten each day, depending on the weather and their aspect toward each other the evening before. If she had danced only once with him the evening before, the odds would go down. If they had gone out on the terrace at a ball and chatted for more than fifteen minutes but less than half an hour, they went down again. If he were seen driving her, the bottom dropped out. The betting had not stayed only in the Royalty Club; it seemed to have spread throughout London. He sometimes wondered what affect on the odds the revelation of some of their more intimate moments together would have.

Fweddie, aware of his betrayed confidence, was somewhat sheepish toward him. Even Rosa, known to openly demand guests to lend a hand and cut a few sandwiches for her or run down to the basement and fetch up a bottle of this or that, was silent on the subject. Only Fred, the doorman, was scabby enough to whisper into his ear that if he put down a wager today on the marriage *not* coming off, he could cover his money and come off safe either way, if Mr. Thornbrough would just nod yes or no. And since he was low on cash, he asked Thornbrough to supply him with a guinea or so. Mr. Thornbrough was not amused.

The courtship of Isolde proved more difficult than he could have believed. For one thing, she was almost impossible to find. He called every afternoon in hopes of seeing her, but she was rarely in. He more often took a sympathetic Elizabeth out for a drive, pouring his complaints into her ears.

He considered pursuing Isolde to Whistler's studio, where Mrs. Pendleton was being painted. It was a difficult course; he did not like the painter at all and had no wish to have any dealings with him, private even less than business. He distrusted Whistler's morals; it was well known that the fellow had never married but had merely taken a series of mistresses. Moreover, he actually lived with them, a thing no gentleman would do. But neither did he trust Isolde's morals, and if Isolde could not be found except there, there he would go.

He entered Whistler's very odd house, furnished in the strangest taste imaginable, as if he had just moved into Chelsea instead of having lived there for three years at least. He was ushered into Whistler's presence, and the Master demanded to know what his business was.

"Decided to add a Whistler to that family collection of Rubens and Velazquez you were boasting about the last time I saw you?" demanded Whistler.

Mr. Thornbrough glanced around the room. It was light, airy, open, and almost empty of all but artist paraphernalia, and the plump Mrs. Pendleton was poised before a window in what looked to be a most uncomfortable stance. If Isolde were on the grounds, she was even more invisible than usual.

"I have come merely to pay a call on you, or rather, on one of your pupils, Miss Pendleton," said Mr. Thornbrough stiffly.

"Were you to meet Isolde here, Mr. Thornbrough? It is too bad of her," said Mrs. Pendleton genially.

"I dismissed Miss Pendleton some days ago," said Whistler, returning to his palette, "just as I dismiss you now. I have no pupils, nor do I want any. She and her father are no doubt out cluttering up the city with their father-and-daughter easels, palettes, brushes, and slop jars."

"Indeed? Did they mention where they would be, Mrs. Pendleton?"

Mrs. Pendleton confessed her ignorance, and Whistler offered, with some acerbity, to see him out. On the way to the door, out of Mrs. Pendleton's earshot, he said to Thornbrough, "I take some interest in Miss Pendleton; it is such a relief to meet a young woman from America, who is not as astoundingly stupid as you raise your British women to be, ignorant of all

art except birds and flowers. Miss Pendleton is not
without sense, a quality that I can seldom find in
other people. I understand that you are her suitor."

"And how did you find that out? Not that all London doesn't know."

"She told me."

"No! In what terms?"

"I have no wish to find myself ankle deep in a
lover's quarrel," said Whistler aloofly. "But keep
these things in mind and reiterate them to the young
lady. I will not hire her to be a model, and she is not
ready for the life of an art student in Paris."

"You do not relieve my mind. I take it she has
broached these possibilities to you?"

"She does have the beginnings of an artist. Not a
true artist of my genius, of course. But she could do
some things that would not be offensive, in a decorative sort of way. Her father comes into this too late.
For him I have no hope. But you may safely encourage her artistic tendencies."

"It is not her artistic tendencies that interest me. I
wish to marry the girl."

"Sir," said Whistler coldly, "I cannot wish you any
degree of success until you become interested in all
the young lady's abilities and until you refer to her as
something more than 'the girl.' "

"Damn you! I suppose you have never wanted a
woman?"

"All between equals, sir, all between equals. My
various companions and I have always lived together
in a most dignified poverty. More I could not wish
you."

"Very well for an artist. It would hardly do in my
set."

"You dishonor yourself. Please do me the pleasure
of uncluttering my beautiful house with your unattractive presence."

"Much can be forgiven of an old man," said Thornbrough, slamming the door behind him.

Mr. Thornbrough had no recourse but to return to his club. Understanding his interest in Miss Pendleton, his friends and acquaintances were quick to bring stories to him of where she had been seen last. She was seen on the top of an omnibus, seated next to two charwomen, talking with the driver. She was seen shopping by herself in Old Bond Street. She went for a walk alone in the park, taking with her a beautifully groomed borzoi, making a picturesque but scarcely proper appearance as she strolled along with a large white hat on her dark mass of hair, leading the tall, long-haired dog. She was seen sketching on the bank of the Thames, a charcoal smudge on her beautiful cheek, with no father in sight.

Isolde had begun in a spirit of disobedience to the conventions, but since she never really understood what the conventions were, and soon became very interested in what she saw and painted and drew in the city, she forgot that she was trying to annoy Mr. Thornbrough and simply became caught up in the enormous, horribly squalid, incredibly beautiful city of London. It was so ancient, so quaint, and at the same time so filled with modern uglinesses and beautiful modern conveniences. No one had ever planned the city, or designed some uniform method of architecture or even of ornamentation. It was all a jangle that drew Isolde's eyes everywhere at once.

She loved riding about the city on top of an omnibus, an enormous red vehicle pulled by a team of workhorses, plastered with advertisements for Pears' Soap and Lipton Tea. She had never seen the Bowery in New York, but she could not think that anything could be worse than the slums of London. And then to go for a stroll in the immaculate flower gardens of the park! It was easy to spend the entire day outdoors and not begin to grow weary, bored, or sad.

She had begun to paint merely to keep her father company and to indulge a new eccentric quirk. Everyone had always thought her things absurd in New York, her mother shaking her head over them sadly. She painted like a child, with too many colors, and often things were not shaped the way they ought to be. But Whistler did not criticize her canvases for these reasons, although he certainly never gave her blanket approval. So she continued to draw and paint. As she looked around the city for inspiration, she saw with new eyes, as if everything were suddenly flattened onto paper and at the same time far more important than it had been before. Her mother might scold when, instead of painting the flowers in the gardens at the park, she had done one at the docks, with the men loading and unloading. She could understand why Whistler was drawn to the Thames, especially at night. Then it was like everything and nothing, too.

As her eyes changed, so did her spirits. While nothing she saw was of real importance to her, everything was of value, if only for the image it presented to her retina. At the dullest of balls she could arrange groups of people in her head and decide how best portraits would be painted. Nothing seemed to weigh on her so much.

Mr. Thornbrough continued to see her at balls and at the opera, and one afternoon he caught her out at Rosa's, just coming in from a day spent outdoors, and glowing with an enthusiasm and health she had seldom experienced in New York.

"Miss Pendleton!" he exclaimed. "What an honor! After calling here at least seven times—or has it been seventeen, Rosa, it seems like it—I find you in. What luck!"

"Isn't it? Do have a seat. I hope you are not in a remarkably awful mood just now, because I am feeling really *healthy*. If it seems as if I have been rude to you these past few weeks, then it is because I am showing you the bad side of my character."

"I don't believe I have seen any side of your character in the last few weeks."

"And weren't you very angry with me?"

"Not at all. I worship you. Well, perhaps a little."

She raised her eyebrows quizzically. "Just a little? Think what it would be like if you had to live with a madwoman like me. I would never be there to pour your tea. I wouldn't know how to start conversations at dinner parties. We would have mad babies together."

"That is a good idea," he said warmly. "Let's have mad babies together."

"I have no plans for this afternoon," she offered boldly. As he sat beside her on one of Rosa's overstuffed sofas, impeccably dressed in conservative white and black, as he always was, he seemed even more desirable than ever, handsome, witty, and amusing.

The thought of him was beginning to haunt her constantly; the thought of his flesh, his bones, his fingers, and his being. In her imagination he came to her almost every night as she lay awake in bed. A part of him joined her between the smooth white sheets, a pressure on her lips, the weight of him moving up and down against her in her dreams. But he only came to her as a phantom, haunting her, teasing her into a frenzy, and never staying to satiate her.

Always she wanted him, always she missed him, with an agony whose very intensity she relished. As she smiled at him, he smiled back. She knew he suffered as she did; but in his eyes she could see kindness and understanding as well as passion. She felt an urge to concede the game, to end the torment, to marry him immediately, capturing that look forever. But it was not Martin she wanted to test; it was herself.

"Mama and Papa are out," she said temptingly.

"No, love," he said, touching her chin with an affectionate pat and shaking his head.

"Stuffy," she teased.

"If you will. Isolde, in all seriousness, there is some reason for the conventions you flout. I know you think London is a lovely playground to wander about in, but some of it is simply not safe."

"Oh, I know. I'm not even safe here in Rosa's. You wouldn't believe the men who call upon me on the most ridiculous pretexts."

"I am not referring to them," he said in irritation. "I know that Elizabeth's and your arrival has aroused every fortune hunter in London. That is beside the point, although if I ever see you flirting with one, I will kill you. I am referring to the East End, and all the other strange places it is rumored you have been to—Spitalfields, Rotherhithe, for God's sake. Even in Mayfair there have been disturbances in the past few years. You are not completely safe anywhere in the city; riots, murders, and worse happen every day here, and in places where you have been. And you, obviously a girl of wealth, could be murdered just for the clothes on your back! Please, Isolde. I do not wish to clip your wings—"

"Then don't try."

"It has not been so long since Jack the Ripper was at large. And he was never apprehended! Surely you heard of him in the States."

"Oh, in detail. But he was not interested in young artists, was he?"

"Be serious. I find you enchanting in every way, and I understand your need for freedom. But I want you to be more careful . . . If you will not accept my escort, then take your father or Fwed or hire a footman."

"A footman!" she exclaimed, assuming her dreamiest expression. "That is a thought. If he were very handsome, of course—it could be a good idea. So convenient, too. I never thought of hiring a footman. It certainly would be less troublesome than an affair."

"One day you will die, but it will not be at the hands of Jack the Ripper."

She laughed. "Thornie, I think perhaps you are just as sweet as your cousin Bertie."

"Will you do as I ask you?"

"No, but I think it is terribly nice of you to mention it. Shall you go to the Wallingshams?"

Elizabeth came in at that moment and, seeing them on the couch, exclaimed, "Mr. Thornbrough! You must really do something about Bert. He is becoming too much! I traveled all the way out to his factory and he hardly looked up from his work to speak to me. He is very excited. He says he has invented some new way to make cushioned tires for bicycles, and if he does, you must provide him with a great deal of money to get the patent and start production. He will go into partnership with Dierding's. But in the meantime, I do wish he would wash himself off now and then and at least look up at me."

"I have no authority over my cousin," said Mr. Thornbrough shortly. "It seems I have no authority over anyone. I hope to see you later this evening. Good-bye." And he left abruptly.

"Well! I don't see why you have to say nasty things to poor Mr. Thornbrough all the time, Isolde. It is not his fault he is so overpoweringly . . . rich and handsome. He is used to people behaving for him. You should be easy on him at first."

"First might go on forever, though," said Isolde. "He thinks I should not go out without a footman."

"Does your mother know you go to the East End alone?"

"Mother knows nothing but what Whistler tells her, and Whistler's mind is filled with very strange furniture indeed."

"Perhaps you should be more careful."

"Perhaps I should. But I won't."

The next day Isolde decided she would like to make a small sketch of Piccadilly to mail home to some of her friends, a humorous sketch, since Piccadilly was almost entirely concealed by posters and billboards shouting out the names of their grotesque products in the most inartistic way. It was a nice way to spend the afternoon, especially since she had half-promised Mr. Thornbrough that she would go out riding with him if she could find the time. She would thus miss him entirely, a pity. It was a small revenge on him, and petty, but all she could manage. He occupied her thoughts to an uncomfortable extent anyway, as if his nonmaterial presence hung over her. She missed him, always missed him in some way, it seemed, even when her thoughts of him had receded to a barely conscious awareness. She heard his voice and saw his face. She knew when he would be scolding her, and what she could most annoy him by doing. Sometimes she lay in bed and felt him around her. The sheets beside her seemed to grow almost warmer with the weight of his body. Then the nonmaterial presence did not scold, did not annoy her; it lay upon her, a warm pressure. She was lonely, she missed him, but at the same time she relished her loneliness and looked for the depth of her suffering. No, she could not shrug him off, not easily. And wherever he was, alone or sharing a bed with some hired woman, she knew he was missing her, that it was her body he wanted, that it was her body he would make love to.

She listened to the sounds her shoes made on the sidewalk as she walked down one of the little streets of Mayfair that led into Piccadilly, a hushed *clip clop*, and she liked the briskness of the sound, the rate at which she could propel herself down a city sidewalk. A crowd passed along the large street before her. She was glad to be alone.

The people in the street seemed to be a strange, tumultuous throng. If she could get them all to pose at once, what a painting they would be, in their plain, torn clothes and with hatred standing so vividly out in their faces. Something to set in the Gallery for the critics to throw eggs at.

She could still only see the group of people at the end of her little street. It never occurred to her that they were a mob. When she did notice that there seemed to be an awfully lot of them about, she thought it was one of the numerous processions that always seemed to be going on in London. No doubt one of Queen Victoria's new grandchildren was being born, or christened. There were so many of them.

She stopped, waiting about forty feet off until the thickest part of the crowd had gone by, and then calmly pursued her way, entering Piccadilly and turning eastward to go to the Strand.

The cabs and carriages that usually crowded Piccadilly were gone, and then she noticed that she was surrounded by workmen, all going in the opposite direction. They were in groups of eight and ten together and had a sort of larking, hilarious aspect. Looking about her, she realized she was the only woman in sight, and as she went further eastward, she came to the shops and saw the damage left by the mob. All the shutters were up, or half up, and over the tops of some of them peered the white faces of the shop people, looking like terrified white rats. The pavement was covered with broken glass, and frag-

ments of all sorts of things that had been thrown—
stones and old, rotten vegetables and a dead rat, stiff
and stinking. She began to understand the gravity of
the situation, but still she could feel no fear. At last
something had happened to her, something not arranged by her parents or secretly by herself, something real, if awful. She was standing on strange
ground now, but to her it was finally familiar, as if
she had found the world and the time where she
properly belonged. She calmly watched them, staring
at them as they stared at her, standing by a street-
light, feeling the danger in the air but unconcerned,
certain of her own immunity.

But the smaller groups, seeing a young, well-dressed
woman standing in the street staring at them, stopped
and turned back to look at her. Their numbers
joined together into a crowd; Isolde began to feel a
little less brave. The white faces had disappeared
from the windows as if the people within had scur-
ried back into the walls for safety. Ordinarily, of
course, she would never have been afraid, but now
there was a menacing force in the air. There were so
many more of them. But she would not move.
Indeed, there was nowhere to go. The doors of the
stores were locked against intruders, and she knew
that if she turned her back on them, she would be in
even greater danger.

It was all done with a quick motion; she could
hardly see it. A figure, just one of the crowd, moved
by some greater hatred or some greater love of pain,
bent over, picked up a rock, and flung it at her, his
arm moving gracefully, easily, with a practiced motion. Her own body moved in response to his, almost
of its own accord, pulling her head to one side with a
jerk so that the rock just grazed her cheek. But this
gesture acted as a signal for the others; they too
found missiles to throw at her back as she ran away

from them—rotten vegetables and an occasional stone.

A few seconds had gone by, no more, when one of the men shouted, "Look at that nob riding about! Let's see if we can pick 'im off!" Then she could hear it, too, the sound of hoofbeats. She did not think they would stop, although she turned her head slightly toward them.

Almost before she had seen him, she knew. She would almost prefer to stay here in the street and be murdered by a mob of rioting workmen than be taken up in Mr. Thornbrough's carriage. He was already a monster of self-assurance; this would signal the end.

The crowd had scattered again, up and down the sidewalk, arraying itself like a gamut he would have to run. A workman stood next to her, so close she could smell his clothing, see the grease in his hair, watch him as he took aim with a large rock for Mr. Thornbrough, who was sitting up in his four-in-hand looking for her. She brought her hand down with all her strength on the workman's arm, throwing his aim off, and ran out into the street to climb up as quickly as she could into the seat beside Thornbrough before any of the others could aim more accurately. She had torn her skirt, and her face was bleeding. He glanced at her once, full of fury and horror at her bruises, and raised his horses.

After a few minutes, she said breathlessly, "Isn't this a fortunate day? You are finally able to take me out driving, and at the same time you may gallop your horses in Piccadilly, something you will probably never be able to do again!"

"Don't expect me to regard this in a frivolous light," he said rigidly. "With rioting in the city, you can imagine my feelings when I discovered that you decided to go out sketching."

"I admit my expedition was a little ill timed, but

my information was not so good as yours. I assure you, Rosa herself saw me out the door."

"I should like to strangle Rosa."

"She has a number of friends."

"I should like to strangle you."

"I have a number of friends, too. Perhaps not as many as Rosa, and my cooking cannot equal hers, but I think I would be missed."

All the streets were strangely clear of traffic, but Isolde did not notice. They were already back at the Swanhome. Thornbrough stopped his equipage, and taking Isolde by the shoulders, shook her. "You're bleeding! You might have been murdered! Don't you ever do that again! I forbid you to walk in the city alone."

Just as white as Mr. Thornbrough, Isolde replied. "And if I had not been there, Mr. Thornbrough, your head would have been fragmented. I do not depend on you, now or ever, to make these decisions for me. I have tried to discourage you; I have refused you outright; and I have evaded you. Now I say again, this time as clearly as I can: Leave me alone. You have nothing to do with me. I wish to have nothing to do with you. Am I making myself clear?"

"You are," said Mr. Thornbrough savagely. "Fred, help the lady down."

A sad but very interested doorman handed Isolde down from the four-in-hand. Mr. Thornbrough drove off, and Isolde went into the hotel, glancing back over her shoulder only once.

Chapter 28

Rosa was always the most understanding of hostesses. On the day after Isolde's quarrel with Mr. Thornbrough, which very shortly became common knowledge to almost everyone but the young lady's parents, she invited everyone from the original Toye party into her office to open a jeroboam of champagne. "No particular reason," she said cheerily. "It's the middle of the season, and I think everyone is worn out with all the goings-on that have gone on."

Mr. and Mrs. Pendleton agreed. For reasons they could not understand, they had seen their daughter go through extremes of cheerful, dreamy, and troubled moods, and she seemed now to have landed squarely in deep depression.

"What is wrong with her?" asked her papa.

His wife simply shook her head. "She says she has a headache," she said and sighed.

Isolde's headaches were so difficult to treat. There was no telling when they were actually caused by a party she didn't wish to go to or a poem she couldn't get quite right. However, as preoccupied as the Pendletons might be with their clubs, paintings, and calls, even they had noticed that Mr. Thornbrough had pursued their daughter with a vigor and determination they could not but think commendable. Now it had been two days since they had seen or heard from the fellow, and since Isolde's headaches seemed to coincide with this time period, it did seem possible that their daughter was not telling them everything.

"I don't understand these girls at all," said Mr. Pendleton, shaking his head. "I should have said that Mr. Thornbrough was nutty about her. And then here is Elizabeth. All these gentlemen keep calling on her, but is she serious about any of them?"

Rosa's words to Fweddie and Georgie were more explicit. "You stand to lose—I don't care to remind you—how many pounds if this doesn't go through," she said. "And my wager is somewhere in the neighborhood of three hundred, not counting all the pounds and pence I will be out on your shot, since we all know you'll never be able to pay."

"Of course we'll pay," said Georgie soothingly.

"She knows we won't," said Fweddie.

"Put your back into it a little!" said Rosa urgently. "That was a lover's quarrel Fred saw and no doubt about it. Have you ever heard of that stuck-up Thornbrough quarreling in public? And now she mopes around with a headache! And then this Elizabeth. There is nothing wrong with Elizabeth. She's a good enough girl. It's all Bert. Why is he behaving so strangely, going off to fuss over bicycles and toy trains. If he marries Elizabeth, she would buy him all the bicycles and toy trains he could ever want."

"No, no," said Georgie. "You're missing the point. He's being noble."

"He's being stupid," said Rosa. "We must get hold of him and find some way to stop him from being so noble. How did all this go wrong, anyway?"

"I don't know," said Georgie glumly. "It was all going splendidly at Toye."

"Then that's it! We'll get them together at Toye again."

Georgie and Fweddie glanced at the innocent

Americans, whose futures were being so easily disposed of by their landlady, and said anxiously, "But how?"

"But how! We'll invite them, of course! How else can you ever get anyone to go anywhere?"

"But Rosa, dear, Toye isn't the Swanhome. You have to be invited by someone. It isn't noted for its cuisine, you know. People don't just glide in."

"I'll handle the cuisine," said Rosa decidedly. "It would be worth my while just to see old Thornie finally married off. Let's see. Thornie will invite Bertie, Bertie will invite Thornie, and Bertie will invite the Americans. That's proper enough, ain't it?"

"But how will you get them to do it?"

"I'll just send a telegram and sign their names," said Rosa cheerfully. "Lord, there's no mystery in that." And Fweddie, pleased that someone so capable and energetic was at the helm, proposed a toast to England. Everyone drank, and the Americans, although still a little droopy, filed off to bed looking a little more cheerful.

The next morning the Americans received a telegram from Lord Albert. "Hmm, what's this," said Rosa, sorting the letters. "One for you, Mrs. Pendleton. From Bertie it is."

"What is it, Mama?" asked Isolde.

"A telegram from his lordship. HAVING HOUSE PARTY AT TOYE STOP ABSOLUTELY MUST HAVE YOU STOP PLEASE COME ON 3:15 TRAIN STOP WILL MEET YOU."

"How odd," said Elizabeth, fluttering in to the room in a morning dress. "He never said anything about it to me, and I saw him only the day before yesterday."

"Well, I suppose we should go," said Mr. Pendleton. "Been very decent to us; sorry I haven't seen more of him in London. I'd like to get out of the city now anyway." His daughter, who shared these feelings, silently acquiesced.

Mr. Ruggles, the foreman of Dierding's, was handing out the mail at his family breakfast table, at which Bert had long since become a very familiar face indeed. "A telegram for your lordship," he said.

"BERT URGENT BUSINESS AT TOYE STOP PLEASE COME IMMEDIATELY STOP WILL MEET YOU AT THE 3:15 TRAIN TOMORROW THORNBROUGH."

"Well, will you be leaving us, your lordship?" asked Mr. Ruggles.

"Only for the weekend," said Bertie.

"I can't believe we almost have the demonstration model done," said Ruggles. "You've worked and no mistake. We stand to make a nice profit out of this; it's just what the market wants, and we'll have it ready in time for next spring. And that Mr. Tuttle is a wonder; no more snarls in our bookwork now. He has the whole factory running like a watch."

"That's my Tuttle," said Bertie, pleased. "I tell you, Ruggles, it's all I ever want to do. It would be nice to have money—always been short on that in my family, and the roof at Toye is two square miles—but this business is all I'll ever want. Except Elizabeth," he added glumly.

"Well, maybe that Elizabeth of yours will have you, if things turn out all right."

"No, Elizabeth is made of finer stuff than I am. Her father has millions to my thousands."

Mr. Ruggles had met the lady and enjoyed a private tête-à-tête with her. She had asked him to please encourage Bert to begin to think of her as mortal clay, as an easily attainable goal. He tried to think of something tactful to say. "You are an awfully good-looking chap," he said. "Any girl would think so."

"They never looked twice at me till Elizabeth came

along," said Bertie gloomily. "No, I'm afraid I'll never marry."

Mr. Thornbrough's telegram was delivered to him on a silver tray as he ate breakfast. His secretary knew which letters he liked to look over while he was breakfasting, alone at his big table, on the abundance of eggs, ham, steak, and coffee that he considered necessary in the beginning of the day. His secretary had removed the bills; he would make out the checks for these, and duly enter them in the proper places, requiring only Mr. Thornbrough's signature at the appropriate moment. Mr. Thornbrough had been through enough London seasons to find most invitations boring; he went through these himself, but later, in his study. At breakfast he looked over personal letters and perhaps an unusual invitation, something out of the ordinary, to keep him and his eggs company.

Bertie's invitation fell into the category of unusual. Mr. Melkinthorpe, Mr. Thornbrough's admirable secretary, knew, as did every member of his household, that their master had finally fallen in love, and that the lady, an American beauty by all accounts, was proving strangely intractable. There were those who rejoiced that at last Old Thornie was getting his own back again, but such old employees as Mr. Melkinthorpe could not but wish him luck on his thorny trail of love.

THORNIE URGENT BUSINESS AT TOYE STOP PLEASE COME IMMEDIATELY STOP WILL MEET YOU AT THE 3:15 TRAIN BERTIE said the telegram. Mr. Thornbrough turned it over suspiciously. Bertie never wrote him letters addressing him as Thornie. When he was a boy, they had painstakingly begun "Cousin Martin," and now that he was older, every one of the semiannual missives he had received from his semiliterate cousin began, "Dear Martin," Still, Bertie had never sent him a telegram. Perhaps he would change his habits for a telegram. It would be a good idea to telegraph him back, but for once Mr. Thornbrough was at a loss. He could not recall the name of the bicycle factory where Bertie was working. Perhaps that was what the business was about. He had better go down to Toye. It would be good to get out of the city, anyway.

As the Pendletons were guilelessly packing their things for a weekend in the country, Elizabeth was also packing her trunk and at the same time trying to remember what Bert had said to her the last time she had seen him. Toye had not even been mentioned. In fact, he had been more annoying than usual. He had demanded to know whether or not it was true that she was now in love with Thornbrough. He did not blame her, he said, but he knew that she went out driving with him every afternoon. He wanted her to know that he would never stand in her way, that he wanted her to be happy, and that Thornbrough was a tip-top fellow. At the same time, without use of the English language, he managed to convey to her the feeling that his heart was crushed, his trust in her betrayed, and that he thought her brutally cruel to keep him hanging in suspense. When she had offered to commission Whistler or the artist of his choice to paint a nude of her for Bert to hang over his bed at night, in the manner of Lady Estleby's gift to Mr. Vavafar, he pretended to be quite shocked and even more irritated. "You must not speak like that, Elizabeth. You know that you are merely dabbing in the mud with me."

"How delicious mud feels when one squishes it between one's toes," she said. But he merely lectured to her and put her on the afternoon train home.

Then a recollection of the evening before, with Rosa's jeroboam of champagne cheering them all up, returned to her. Surely Rosa and Georgie and Fwed had conferred in their corner for some time. She had been quite caught up in listening to Mrs. Pendleton's amused complaints about Whistler—he was still scraping her face out—and had not heard what the others discussed. Perhaps she had better visit Rosa. Rosa was very forthright and had told her only the day before yesterday, when she returned from the station alone, that her money was on her.

She tripped down the stairs to the lobby, but no one was about, so she tapped on Rosa's door. Inside, Rosa shouted, "Not now, I'm doin' me blasted books!"

"Rosa, dear, only one question," said Elizabeth.

The door opened. "Oh, it's you," said Rosa. "I might have known you would come down. Come in and let's have a talk." She shut the door behind them, and they had a very pleasant little discussion. Afterward, finding themselves very much in agreement, and pleased at dealing with someone with so much ready understanding and ingenuity, Rosa returned to her books and Elizabeth to her packing.

"She's quite right," said Rosa to Edith, her plump, loyal lieutenant, as she gave her last-minute instructions for running the hotel in her absence. "I hadn't thought of that, and it will work in nicely. You do as she asks and we'll have bells ringing."

Perhaps Tuttle was the only truly appreciative member to witness the 3:15 train disgorge its passengers. They were taken aback to see each other, and astonishment was universal, with some merely appalled and others horrified. Only one enormous, lumbering carriage had been sent for them, but Bertie and Thornie elected to walk the six miles.

"If this is meant as a surprise," said Thornbrough in a savage undertone to Bert, "it is in extremely bad taste."

"Isn't it?" agreed Bertie. "I've never known you to make such a slip."

"What are you talking about? How could you invite me like this?"

"But Thornie, you invited me! Didn't you?"

"I invite you to Toye? Why? If you think you can create some kind of reconciliation between me and Miss Pendleton, your methods are disgustingly clumsy."

"Have you and Isolde fallen out?" asked Bertie, diverted. "She got the better of you, then. I keep trying, but Elizabeth just won't let go. What did Isolde do?"

"She was attacked by a mob of workmen during a riot. She could have been killed. She was injured."

Bertie looked taken aback. "Well, I don't think I shall try that. Very sporting of her, though, and now she's done what she wanted and proven to you that you wouldn't suit. But why did you invite me to Toye?"

"Are you mad? Why would I invite you to Toye? I was invited here by you. Here is the telegram." And he handed his telegram of invitation, crumpled, to Bertie. Bertie inspected it and, turning it over, looked at the other side. There was no denying it was a telegram and it did invite Thornie to Toye. "I must have forgotten," he said, shaking his head. "Awfully sorry. Didn't mean to. I've had a lot on my mind lately."

"Don't be a fool. This is some devilish plot devised by your Tuttle or your Elizabeth."

"No, no, don't say that. Tuttle's quite happy now, you know. Ruggles and I are thinking of making him a partner. I don't know why he would want to interfere; he doesn't need any wages I could pay him. We have him on salary. And why would Elizabeth invite you?"

"Doubtless for the sake of her friend, Isolde."

"Why didn't Isolde do it herself? Why blame it all on Elizabeth? I'll tell you who it was. It was Fwed and Georgette. Why else would they have come along? They want to see it all through and collect their bets."

Mr. Thornbrough had to acknowledge the likelihood of this. They were soon passed by a smart carriage bearing Rosa, impeccably dressed in a tailored gown. She was driving to Toye with her fresh vegetables, meats, and the innumerable pots and pans she needed for cooking a weekend of memorable dining. Her dress was spotlessly white, and she wore black gauntlets and was accompanied by an undercook. She waved to them; the dust of her cart settled unpleasantly on their boots, along with their doubts of the masterminding of the plot. It had seemed a bit thick for just Fwed and Georgie to handle. They walked on in silence.

After a time, Bertie said, "You and Isolde not getting along?"

"No," replied Mr. Thornbrough shortly.

"Thought I would ask. It will be a bit embarrassing."

"Undoubtedly."

"Lucky thing Toye is so big. I shall have to spend the better part of my time dodging Elizabeth."

"Look here," said Mr. Thornbrough, "is that girl really making a nuisance of herself around you? It is too much that we are infested with these Americans who do not have the good manners to remove themselves when they become pests."

"Oh, I don't know," said Bertie anxiously. "I'm sure eventually Elizabeth will remove herself, and on that day I'll take out my old trusty pistol, clean it one last time, polish the barrel, load it with one lone bullet, and put it through my head."

"You don't own a pistol."

"I'll buy one."

They trudged on. Neither was accustomed to walking miles at a time. At last Bert said, "Is it true Elizabeth goes out driving with you every day?"

Mr. Thornbrough snorted. "Every day I go to call on Isolde. Every day she is not there. Sometimes, by way of comfort, Elizabeth goes with me to utter a few words of encouragement. But not anymore. I shan't see Isolde again."

"You will see her this weekend," pointed out Bertie. "I always thought her a very odd girl."

"She is driving me insane."

"Indeed?" said Bertie hopefully. He would have enjoyed hearing the details of Thornbrough's newfound insanity. Thornbrough wanted to tell him about Isolde, about their meetings as lovers, about her strange moods, and the way she opened so amazingly, so wonderfully, mind and body, body and being. But he could not. They continued in silence, each with his own thoughts.

The Pendletons, in the meantime, remained in ignorance of the confusion their presence created for their supposed host, fellow guests, and their own daughter. Isolde vanished immediately as soon as they reached the castle. Tuttle, although he had lived the past few months in the more exalted status of head bookkeeper, having risen to that position by obvious brilliance, immediately stepped down again into the role of butler. Rosa moved into her kitchen but was rather disgusted by the way the rest of the house looked; she had expected to be comfortable on her weekend. Elizabeth helped Tuttle with bedroom arrangements and journeyed with him down long halls with many doors in search of such things as sheets and candles. "We should have brought them with us," said Elizabeth. "Mrs. Fielding is no help. Tuttle, I do wish you would talk to Bert. He's being so absurd and stubborn. How do you ever get him to do things?"

"Unfortunately, Miss Wilcox," said Tuttle, "I have never before tried to arrange a marriage for Lord Albert."

"I suppose that's encouraging. Here, we'll have to use these. It's only for the weekend anyway, and if they tear, we can always take more from this stack." Bearing masses of ancient, worn sheets, Elizabeth went off to find the hired girl from the village and instruct her as to which beds should be made up.

The evening could not be described by even the most blithe of spirits as anything but a complete failure. Isolde spent most of the time in a corner, her back turned from most of the company, playing soft, mournful tunes on her guitar, and occasionally singing in a low voice. She comforted herself a little in this way, but threw a gloom over everyone else. And Thornbrough, standing at the other side of the room, could do nothing but stare at her and listen, unable to control memories of a lonely boyhood, a favorite horse gone lame and shot, a time in which no food had taste, no plant a smell, and no sight importance.

Bert quickly became so intoxicated that Tuttle had to lead him off, although Rosa, who had watched his consumption, was suspicious. It looked more like an act to her, and Elizabeth, who shared these feelings, felt rather hopeless about it all. Georgie and Fwed, thinking of their unpaid accounts in London and the fact that they could never, never borrow from Thornie again, did not succeed in adding to the conviviality of the eveing.

Only Rosa managed to find entertainment, her mood still brisk and cheerful. She sat in a corner and talked with the Pendletons about American food. It was one of her specialties. She was the first woman in England to learn how to make waffles, having been taught by the black servant of one of her first English customers. She sold them sometimes at waffle stands in charity bazaars for exorbitant prices, a culinary rarity enjoyed only by the wealthy.

The next morning seemed a bit more promising. Toye's ramshackleness, instead of having a depressing effect on one's spirits, created just the opposite feeling, perhaps because it seemed as if it were a place where nothing mattered at all. The day was a beautiful one, and Rosa suggested that they all go for a picnic lunch. Rosa also saw the way Isolde and Thornie looked up, startled, at the suggestion, each seeking out the other's eyes as if in exchange of some private understanding, and then looking away again quickly as if the understanding were too much.

The elder Pendletons agreed that a walk in the woods before noon would be pleasant. But Bert said, "Not for me, thanks, Rosa. I'm afraid there are some accounts in my library I have to go over. I'm just going to lock myself up in there until lunch. Don't worry about me, though. You all go off and have a good time."

"What accounts do you have in that moldy old library?" demanded Rosa. "I've seen that library. There aren't even any books in that library. The ink's dried up in the well, and there's no paper."

"I see you've been busy," said Bertie loftily.

"A telegram has arrived by messenger from town," said Tuttle, entering the room, bearing the message on a platter. "It is for Mr. Pendleton."

"Well, give him the telegram then," said Rosa. "I don't think you have to stand around and explain. 'E knows what a telegram is."

"Actually, it is a cablegram," said Mr. Pendleton, opening it and spreading it out before him. "And it says . . ." and he stopped, staring down at the paper, his mouth open. His expression was one of shock; he stared down at the paper aghast at what he read.

"What is it?" asked his wife. "Is it bad news? Here, let me see."

"I'm afraid it is bad news," said Mr. Pendleton slowly. "The worst. We are ruined. Miss Wilcox, I wish I did not have to say these words to you. Perhaps you had better read them for yourself."

Turning white, Elizabeth took the paper and read: EVERYTHING GONE AT ONE BLOW STOP TRYING TO SALVAGE SOMETHING FOR PENDLETON STOP MAY NOT HAVE TO SELL THE HOUSE STOP STAY IN EUROPE UNTIL I WIRE STOP LOVE R. R. WILCOX.

"I am so sorry," said Elizabeth to the Pendletons, her gentle voice breaking the hush that followed, her cheek pale. "I'm afraid my father has had some deep dealings while we were away."

"I won't complain," said Mr. Pendleton staunchly. "Perhaps we have nothing now, but I had not much when I met your father. He buys when the market is bearish and sells when it is bullish again. I've seen him lose a hundred thousand dollars in a half hour and make it all back again threefold before closing. I have no complaints. He must have met some bear that just wouldn't change back. Wilcox stock will go up again."

"Well, that's all very well," said Rosa briskly, "but when am I going to be paid? You've been staying on tick at my place for over a month now, and very little of your cash 'ave I seen. And now I find there ain't any! This is a sad surprise for me. We must come into Bertie's library, among all the trappings of his fine business correspondence, and try to plan out some method of payment. Mrs. Pendleton, we'll want you too," she said firmly, ushering them out.

Everyone sat stunned by the ruthlessness of Rosa's rough handling until Elizabeth said, with a sad little laugh, "At last I feel as if I can eat everything on my plate."

Bertie pushed back his chair at the head of the table and went over to Elizabeth's, pulling it out for her in the manner of a footman. He went down on his knees beside her and said, "Elizabeth, it always seemed so silly that I never bothered to mention it. But Ruggles and I are becoming partners in the manufacture of my new tire, and he thinks we shall make a lot of money. Not an awfully lot of money, of course. I don't know how to do that. But enough for us to be married. Would you care to marry me, Elizabeth, dear?"

"How can I marry you now, when I have nothing but debts to bring you?"

Fwed and Georgie, Isolde and Thornbrough all tried to shrink into their seats to look as inconspicuous as possible. But it was of no matter; Elizabeth and Bertie ignored them sublimely.

"Oh, Elizabeth, I love you so," sighed Bertie, holding her hands. Their lips met and, fascinated, Fwed and Georgie, Isolde and Thornbrough watched them kiss. Elizabeth threw her arms around Bertie's neck and hugged him hard. "Here, don't choke me," he protested. Glancing up and seeing all the eyes upon them, he said indignantly, "Well, you might have left the room."

"Not us," said Fwed. "I had a small fohtune widing on that kiss. You and Miss Wilcox have made me a fwee man."

"You're disgusting," said Bertie.

"Let us go for that walk Rosa suggested, Isolde," said Mr. Thornbrough.

"I'll be in my bedroom," she said, abruptly leaving the table and the room. He stared after her; her walk was brisk and assured. Fwed glanced at Georgie, but she only shook her head. It was pleasant being free of debt. It would have been even nicer being rich. But Isolde was a very unpredictable girl.

The Pendletons emerged from their interview with Rosa surprisingly cheerful for two people on the brink of economic disaster. They were greeted with the intelligence that Bertie and Elizabeth were betrothed and by Mr. Thornbrough's formal request to be permitted to marry their daughter, uncooperative though she may be. Mr. Pendleton sat down immediately with Tuttle and broached a bottle of champagne. No one seemed to be suffering unduly; and Bertie offered them a home at Toye for the rest of their lives, if they would care for it.

"It needs someone around all the time," he said seriously. "And until Ruggles and I can get that new mill put up over by the village, I'm afraid it's going to stand empty for a few more years. I would be in your debt."

And so they drank to debts, to engagements, to love, and to waffles.

The day passed by. Elizabeth and Bert wandered around hand in hand, very pleased with themselves, but Isolde was still nowhere to be seen. Mr. Thornbrough thought he could perhaps wait patiently; she must inevitably come down to dinner. In the mid-afternoon, a little before tea, Rosa received a telegram that said: UNEXPECTED COMING YOUR WAY STOP UNPLANNED FOR ARRIVAL STOP NOT MY IDEA EDITH. It was a very enigmatic telegram, and Rosa showed it to Elizabeth. Neither could make out what Edith's meaning may have been. "It could be something nice, though," said Elizabeth hopefully. "Like a carnival. Bert would like that."

As dusk was falling, the long summer shadows promising a warm evening, all the party was gathered out in the courtyard.

"Do you know, Aunt Honora isn't here," said Bertie. "We ought to have invited her."

"Whatever for?"

"Oh, I don't know. I'll have to send her a card for our wedding. I'm sure she'll send us a nice wedding gift. Something we really want, like a bed warmer or a fish slice."

Tuttle entered and said in Bertie's ear, "There is a caller, sir. A gentleman from New York."

"New York!" exclaimed Bert. "You haven't brought a lot of jewelry with you, have you, Elizabeth? They may be trying to collect on it, the beasts. Let me take care of this."

Elizabeth looked blank.

"Here, don't keep me waiting back here," said a deep voice, and a large, portly figure emerged onto the terraced yard. A bristling mustache adorned almost all his face, and he was built on larger-than-life lines. "And what are all these stories I hear? You have been keeping me busy, miss."

"Daddy!" exclaimed Elizabeth, throwing herself at his large frame and receiving a bear hug in return. "When did you arrive?"

"I arrived right now, silly miss. What kind of question is that? Ah, you want to know when I got to London." All eyes were upon him. "Well, don't you all look like you've been to a funeral. I reached London on Friday to find I'd just missed you."

"Mr. Wilcox," said Bert, deep sympathy in his voice, "perhaps these days may seem tragic to you. You have already, possibly, encountered disloyalty among those you have trusted and ingratitude from those to whom you have been most generous. But I want you to know that on this side of the Atlantic you are always welcome here at Toye, welcome as a permanent member of the family, or to come and go just as you like."

"Very kind of you, very kind of you," said R.R. Wilcox, seating himself in a very large, deep-bottomed armchair that squeaked at his weight. "Any of you mind if I smoke?" he asked, as he took a large cigar out of his pocket, produced a small pair of gold scissors and nipped off the end, tossed it into the bushes casually, and lit the cheroot, obviously an expensive brand. "Care for one?" he asked Bertie in his booming voice as he settled back into his chair. "You must be that earl my daughter has been chasing down all these months. And so she finally caught you with one of her fairy tales! Well, well, well, I like a man whose heart is bigger than his head."

Bert was somewhat taken aback by Mr. Wilcox's gruffness, attributing it to embarrassment over being a broken man dependent on charity for the first time in an illustrious career. But Elizabeth said breezily, "Oh, don't be so grizzly bearish, Daddy. He is Lord Albert Taunton, earl of Toye, and this is Toye Castle, but of course everyone calls him Bertie. And you mustn't be rude to him. He manufactures bicycles, you know."

"Taunton! I thought so," said her father. "And he has a cousin named Matilda Taunton whom he has loosed on the continent of North America."

"Stirring up a lot of trouble for the menfolk, is she?" asked Mr. Thornbrough, amused. "But you mustn't blame Bertie. She skipped out on two hundred and fifty pounds bail he had put up for her."

"And who are you, may I ask?" Mr. Wilcox demanded. "Are you another lord?"

"My name is Thornbrough."

"And what are you doing here?"

Feeling more amusement than irritation at such peremptory dealings, Mr. Thornbrough replied, "I am busy becoming engaged to Miss Isolde Pendleton, daughter of your business partner."

"Pendleton! Ha! Are you here!" exclaimed Mr. Wilcox, turning to confront his business partner. Mr. Pendleton had seemed to them all to be the embodiment of an American businessman: stout, mustachioed, wearing a gold watch and several fobs too many on a showy chain. But Bertie, the Brookes, and Mr. Thornbrough all realized that Mr. Pendleton was a mere well-bred shadow before the true embodiment of the principle, Mr. R.R. Wilcox. The Wilcox mustache bristled twice as angrily, the Wilcox bay window extended itself twice as far as Mr. Pendleton's, Mr. Wilcox's suit was far uglier and his complexion much redder, and he wore so much jewelry, so many rings, watch fobs, and stick pins that he almost jingled. And yet, was he not an impoverished, broken man? He did not resemble an impoverished, broken man.

"Pendleton!" he said again, in tones of command. "What are you doing, letting them send these silly telegrams all over England! We shall be held for fraud at the rate you conduct business."

"None of it was my idea in the least," his business partner assured him. "Has any report gotten out? Is our standing much injured?"

"Standing! Ha! That is a joke. These silly Britishers picked up on the Wilcox scare, and some ninny cabled the news to New York, where those boobs all took it as gospel. The market on us became howlingly bearish, and I have just spent all morning long cabling across the ocean. I figure I've earned about a quarter of a million today so far. I should leave town more often."

There was silence. The Pendletons and the Brookes looked warily at Bert and Thornbrough, as if awaiting an explosion, while Mr. Wilcox sat back in his chair and puffed.

"So!" exclaimed Bertie to Elizabeth in a voice of outrage. "This is the way we begin, is it? With trickery and fraud! And how long did you expect to keep up this charade, Elizabeth? For a week, a month?"

"I'm sure I don't know. Let's ask ourselves the same question in fifty years."

"Are you actually going to marry this young man, Elizabeth?" asked her father casually.

"He has been very difficult, Papa. He says I have too much money. It is all very complicated."

"Well, work it out between yourselves. When is dinner being served? Personally, I didn't know it was possible for a person to have too much money. You can always find something to spend it on. And Elizabeth is a very expensive girl."

"That's true," said Bert thoughtfully. "I suppose I could let you buy your own dresses with your own money."

Elizabeth, who felt this was a hopeful, if impractical, start, agreed immediately.

"Isolde and I always go for a walk in the shrubbery when we are trying to resolve a difference," said Mr. Thornbrough helpfully. Wilcox examined his face carefully, while Bert and Elizabeth agreed that it was, after all, a beautiful day out, a pity to waste. They left the group.

"Let's you and I go for a walk in the shrubbery," said Mr. Wilcox to Mr. Thornbrough, as he lit another cigar.

"I don't believe I have a difference with you, sir," said Mr. Thornbrough.

"No, but I have some advice for you."

When they were well out of earshot, R.R. began. "I take it you're the fellow who has been interested in Isolde. Elizabeth has written me all about it."

"I am grateful for your interest in this matter," said Thornbrough coolly.

"Don't be so stiff. You need me. Her parents never know the first thing of what she's up to. I've often noticed it. She needs to get married, settle her down a little."

"I agree completely."

"So why is she going up to London alone?"

"She isn't."

Mr. Wilcox stared at Thornbrough, then laughed shortly. "Ah, there you're off my boy, because I saw her buying a ticket as I was coming in. I didn't stop her, none of my business, but it seemed odd, very odd."

"A ticket *to* London?! But she's been in her room all day!"

"I see you don't know her as well as I thought you did."

"Good God! Then she's in the city alone now! With the notion in her head that she is a pauper!"

"And nowhere to turn?"

"No, this is the chance she's been waiting for. I believe she's always wanted to be penniless. Now she can go ahead and become a barmaid just as she pleases."

"I don't think the girl is quite cut out to be a barmaid."

"Neither do I," said Thornbrough abruptly. "If you'll excuse me?"

"By all means," R.R. returned pleasantly, as he watched Thornie lope off toward the castle. He was glad he did not have to literally run after his women anymore. He lit another cigar.

Isolde had left everything, or almost everything, in her room and no notes for anyone. Thornbrough swore violently as he turned her things topsy-turvy to no avail. Rosa drove him to the station and advised him to check the Swanhome first.

But no one there had seen anything of the young lady. Riding in on the train, watching the city, first a collection of houses, then houses closer packed, and then the city itself, packed and brawling, spread as far as he could see, reminded Thornie of how much trouble Isolde could find in a very short time. Worry erased the capacity for logic from his brain for a few moments, but upon reflection he remembered some of Isolde's more annoying fascinations. If she was not on a street corner playing native American ballads for pennies, she was probably at Whistler's. He headed toward the little house in Chelsea with all haste.

There he was informed that the Master was indeed in but could not be disturbed. He was painting.

"I don't think he'll mind if I drop into his studio," said Thornbrough impatiently.

The butler, who was quite certain that the Master would be very much disturbed indeed, could not be persuaded to alter his mind, even by the offer of largesse.

"Look here," said Thornbrough in a low, furious voice, "if I have to knock you down, I will. Now get out of my way."

Whistler's studio was up a flight of stairs; Thornbrough quickly found the large, bright room. He entered without knocking, glancing around the room hurriedly to see if Isolde was about. She wasn't.

"Trixie!" roared Whistler. "This is the last time! Pack your things, we're moving to Paris." He flung his paintbrush down and turned to face Thornbrough, his hair almost bristling up off his head as his small dark eyes lit with fury. "You, sir, do not hesitate to see my finest canvases thrown in the gutter by your damned Academy. You laugh at my genius. And yet when you have some miserable little personal prob-

lem, you have the temerity to barge into my room
without a tap on the door. Be gone! Trixie, stick
your head out the window and begin to scream for
the police. Blast you!" and he threw a paint pot at
Thornbrough's head. He dodged it easily, and it hit
the wall behind him, a ragged circle of red beginning
to drip.

"I do not hesitate to tell you that I find your style
in painting not at all to my taste." Thornbrough said
furiously. "Your style of life I find even more deplorable. I assume that Isolde has come to you today, so
that you know why I am here. If you have encouraged her to lead some unprincipled existence, I will
have you prosecuted criminally."

"Now, now," said Trixie. She was an older woman,
but she had the kind of face that grows more beautiful with age and the kind of body that seems to become more comfortable, in odd contrast to Whistler's
wire brush straightness of backbone. "Let's have tea."

"I will *not* have tea," said Whistler more pettishly.
"We had it with that wretched girl."

"And she needed a cup very badly. I think Mr.
Thornbrough needs one too. Or a glass of brandy?"

"Give him some of Ruskin's brandy. He'd like that.
Ruskin makes money off every bottle sold in England.
It's like drinking my blood."

Trixie clucked gently. "It's not like drinking your
blood at all, Jimmy. It's like drinking rainwater. It
fell from the sky, remember? We didn't pay any
money for it."

"Oh, all right," said Whistler, and he trotted after
Trixie into one of the salons downstairs.

"You see," said Trixie, as they all drank their wine,
"Isolde did come here, and it seemed best to encourage her. We think she'll be happier doing what she
wants to do."

"But that's why I came," said Thornbrough. "She

was grossly misinformed and ran away before explanations were made. I know it was horribly improper—worse than that, even upsetting to her—"

"Worse than improper?" murmured Whistler. "Ah, the English spirit!"

"—but a trick was played on her and me. We were invited to the country after we had had a disagreement and were not speaking. Our friends wished us to meet amicably, and in order to overcome our differences, they told us that Isolde's parents were bankrupt. Isolde left the room immediately, and before she came down again, an unexpected visitor—the father of her friend, Elizabeth Wilcox—came and informed us of the truth. Isolde's rooms were searched, but she had already left by then, with the mistaken belief that she and her parents were penniless."

There was a pause. Whistler said, "Don't we have anything else to drink but this miserable stuff, Trixie?"

"Oh, be quiet, Jimmy," she said. "He really doesn't understand."

"This is really all more raw emotion than I can deal with," said Whistler. "As our Oscar would say, it is too too. It is utterly utterly."

"Don't be cruel, Jimmy."

"My dear English gentleman, first of all you tell me that Isolde, informed of her *and her parents*' sudden poverty, immediately abandons them at the moment of their greatest anguish, and indeed adds to their suffering with her own self-serving action."

"She didn't want to be a burden. It was understandable."

"Was it? I do have some acquaintance with Mrs. Pendleton, you know. I've spent the last month in her company. I should think that the desertion of her only daughter would be a greater burden than poverty."

"She wasn't thinking. She was too upset."

"Ah, the female mind. Would you say the young lady was unintelligent? Or merely flighty?"

"Don't torture him, Jimmy."

Whistler sighed. "In actuality, of course, Isolde was the first and only victim who was not at all taken in."

"She knew!"

"Immediately. Evidently these 'concerned' friends of yours had some little financial business that hung upon your romantic success? Tangled, isn't it, having your friends bet on your wooing."

"It is the very devil," admitted Thornbrough. "So she knew. Of course. I should have too, but I was thinking of her."

"Of course. The hungry spider."

"Spider?" Thornbrough smiled. "Is that what she called me? Not lion or dog?"

"No, she seems to relegate you to the insect kingdom."

Thornbrough smiled to himself. "It's true. My first thoughts were greedy. Where is Isolde now?"

"That I cannot say. I lent her twenty pounds, which you may pay me back right now, and gave her the name of some artist friends in France."

"I'll kill you!" exclaimed Thornbrough, starting from his chair.

"So this is fine English reasoning at last," mocked Whistler from behind Trixie. "Poor girl, I was glad to see her go."

"But why? Why? Does she hate me so?"

"Of course she doesn't," said Trixie soothingly.

"How could she go alone? What will she do? I could at least have escorted her and made appropriate arrangements."

"You go on, Trixie," said Whistler. "I don't like this part."

"I think Isolde really does love you. She isn't leaving because she wants to leave you. She was just afraid of being married too early. And when her parents and all her English friends went to such trouble to create such an elaborate trap for her, well, she thought of it as a cage being made for her with everyone trying to push her into the matrimonial state."

"But all girls are married! I would have married her and then let her go to France. I set no restrictions on her!"

"Perhaps you didn't, and perhaps you would have tried not to. But it is something of a chore to arrange any marriage at all in your circles, is it not? And Isolde so particularly dislikes the kind of people she would have to meet. I think she is a little frightened still, like a child."

"So you have sent her to a foreign country where she knows no one. Clever."

"No, you still don't understand. She is not really afraid of people in society. She just is not at ease. I know everyone talks about how dull society is, but I don't think you realize how asphyxiating it can be to someone of her artistic talents."

"And has she artistic talents?"

Whistler snorted.

"Jimmy thinks she might.

"She can certainly paint pretty pictures," he said. "She may learn to paint beautiful pictures. It is possible that she may even attain some smattering of my own genius, although her style is nothing like mine."

"I see," said Thornbrough. Whistler and Trixie sat comfortably together while he paced the floor.

After a bit, he said, "But other girls paint and still marry."

Trixie sighed. Whistler cursed.

"Let me explain it," said Trixie gently. "You see, she could marry you and be quite happy. But she would be expected to become a part of your life, would she not? If you were invited to dinner, wouldn't she be invited as well?"

"Not necessarily. I know many husbands who are hideously bored when they chance to meet every few weeks at a party."

"But seriously. Suppose you and she were at a dinner party. And she looked outside and noticed that the color of the sky was particularly inviting. So she rushed out of the room to go back to her studio and paint it. Think how irritated you would be with her. And if you tried to allot some small part of the day to her work, or some small part of the year, all the rest of the time the paintings would be growing stronger and angrier inside her until she turned into quite a nasty person."

Thornbrough continued his pacing. He stopped in front of Whistler and said, "Does she let you paint whenever you want?"

"Absolutely."

"Then how do you explain your nastiness?"

"It's temperament. You don't realize you're dealing with artistic temperament."

"I see," said Thornbrough. "And what did Isolde say of me? Anything at all? Some small token, a word?"

"Perhaps she'll write."

"Well, damn you all," he said. "Damn you all. I don't believe I am going to spend the rest of my life waiting for a girl to be cured of her artistic temperament, a disease also known as ill breeding. You may tell her that. Give her the message that the spider is seeking a less poisonous mate."

"Don't be harsh," Trixie said, following him as he headed for the door. "Don't be hurt."

"She might have left a note."

"She said she would send you a talisman." But he was out the door.

Chapter 29

It was an early spring morning, the London flowers reaching their most blooming best as the neatly turned out four-in-hand, driven through the fashionable section of London by Mr. Martin Thornbrough, headed in the direction of the Grosvenor Gallery. All society would be there; its opening was the semiofficial beginning of the season.

"How kind it is of you to escort me to the Grosvenor today," said Elizabeth Wilcox Taunton, countess of Toye. A year in London society had not changed her at all. The jewels she wore, which had been considered gaudy for a young lady, were now commended as appropriate for a wealthy young matron with a position to maintain. She had almost completely regained her figure after the birth of hers and Bertie's child, a fat, pink daughter, remarkably unlike either of her parents, whose very infancy astounded her awestruck father. Elizabeth was now a woman with all the world in her hand. She possessed a generous income and temper and a husband who adored her. As she went out more into society with the status of a married woman, she had begun to appreciate Bertie even more. Perhaps he was uninterested in any of the doings that concerned her. But his own hours were happily occupied with activity that did not involve other women or card playing. When he was out all night, as happened occasionally, he re-

turned home glowing with some new enthusiasm,
some new idea, exhausted but joyful, not swollen-eyed
and reeling.

The Dierding factory at Toye was still going up.
There were those who had voiced disapproval that
such an ancient place, so well timbered and historical, should now be turned into the site of an industrial factory that would ruin the shooting and the
fresh air. But these critics, as Bertie pointed out, had
never actually been invited to spend a cold winter's
night in the comfort the ancient historical site did
not afford. Even Elizabeth sometimes wondered
whether or not they should just put up a cozy little
cottage next to the gatekeeper's and not attempt to
heat the Grand Hallway. After all, they had the baby
to think of, too. But Dierding went up, far enough
away from Toye Castle not to be seen, on the other
side of Toye Village, while the castle itself received a
few much needed improvements.

The socialists declared the new village to be a great
work; all the latest innovations in housing for the
workers and for child care had been built in. Princess
Alexandra herself had invited Elizabeth to come
down to Marlborough House to discuss some of the
villages she and Prince Albert had caused to be erected
at his place. These were followed, to a great degree, with one exception. Bertie insisted that public
houses were a part of English life. A man had to have
his pint at the end of the day, if he wanted one. But
Princess Alexandra was Danish and she couldn't understand. Maybe in Denmark they didn't have pints.
In England, if a working man wanted his pint, he
should have it, and he would stick to them.

Elizabeth was thinking of this as she rode with Mr.
Thornbrough out to the Gallery. "Do you know, Bertie insists in the face of Princess Alexandra's most
heated recommendations—although I'm afraid these

would be considered merely tepid from any other person—that there must be pubs in the new village?"

"I should hope so. And what is it to be named?"

"Oh, probably the Red Lion or something like that."

"No, the village."

"I don't know. I've never heard anyone call it anything but the new village."

"Then it will be the New Village. Perhaps a thousand years from now, when another language replaces this one, the syllables may sound strange and poetic."

There was a pause. "I have a letter from the Pendletons in America."

Mr. Thornbrough made no reply.

"She has never appeared there, it seems. The detectives quite give her up. They thought they could trace her from that letter she wrote when she first left, asking for money, but it turned out to be mailed by a sailor from somewhere in Europe. She could be anywhere."

"I don't expect to ever see her again."

"Do you hate her so?"

Without a twitch of his features, without even a slight clenching of his lips or narrowing of his nostrils, he maintained that heavy weight of silence that must be his. Of all women, Elizabeth would be the only one he could talk to who might understand. But a lifetime of training in silencing his emotions could not allow him to voice these to any person, even a woman with Elizabeth's understanding.

His was a well-ordered life, a regulated life. When Isolde had disappeared last year, the season had gone on without her. There had been talk, of course, especially because of that stupid betting the Brookes had set forth. But the disappearance of an American heiress, with no puffing up of the newspapers and no attendant scandal, was quickly replaced with a meatier domestic disaster supplied by a baron's wife, a noted divorce case dragged out long enough with evidence furnished by the spouse's friends to fill columns of newspapers for weeks.

Parties were given; the yachts turned out all the same; the hunting seasons were celebrated with their annual slaughter; even the seasons did not stop their changes at the loss of Isolde. All was the same, all. Mr. Thornbrough continued with all the routine without even noticing it. At first it was expected that the detectives would find her immediately in some Paris studio. Then came the letter to her parents, bringing up hopes that the new evidence could help trace her down. And then he had received a letter that he had shown no one. Nor had he told anyone; even Elizabeth did not know. It said:

> Dearest Martin,
>
> Do not worry. I am happier than ever before. If you still love me in a year's time, I will come. I know I have treated you badly. If I had married you, I would have treated you worse. I love you.
>
> Isolde.

That had been six months ago. It was now the beginning of the new season, making it almost a year since she had left. On the surface his life seemed unchanged by her abandonment. He had even kept a mistress for a short time, and he had tried to carry on an affair with a woman he had known for years. But it had all come to nothing, leaving him more bored and bitter than before. Greatly against his choice he had begun to see things through Isolde's eyes, as Isolde might have known them, and all his careful routine seemed a barren passing of time, without joy or fruition. He moved when he did not wish to move, went to places where he was bored, and met people he disliked.

But these motions were stilled within him. He knew he was dissatisfied, unhappy, occasionally even furiously miserable. He had accustomed himself to the rules of his life. To meet a girl who refused to do the same was at first rather interesting. The outcome had been, for him, disaster. He was left without one or the other, and without even the understanding that he had been so tricked. All he felt was a permanent, dulled anger toward Isolde and, to a lesser degree, to the world that had made her. What she was now he could not begin to imagine; it was a trap he could not let his mind fall into. The answers were too many and too disturbing.

"Did you hear that Whistler's portrait of his mother has been purchased by the Louvre?" said Elizabeth, trying to catch his thoughts. "Now he is thinking of moving back to France. He says he has never been happy in London."

"Do you think she has become a painter?"

"It is what she said she was going to be. She was a good singer, too, but not professional."

"Not something else?"

Elizabeth patted his hand. "Isolde would not have left you to romp off to Paris to become a grand horizontal. Excuse me! But it is true. She may have thought about it, pretended, but flighty though she was, it would be impossible for a girl like her to suddenly take to something like that. She would need some hardness, some internal steel trap that I don't think she possessed. She would need to be mad, indeed."

"It has been a year now."

"Come, we're almost there. You must buy me an ice after, and we will talk." But they had talked before.

There was nothing new to discuss, just the same emp-
tiness. Soon he would begin to forget. He had told
himself that the first month after she left. Now twelve
had gone by, and he was still telling himself that. If
anything, he had idealized her memory. He hated her
for having left him, for seeing and stealing her
freedom from him. At the same time, if he had once
been appalled by her behavior, now he considered it
the only natural, sane way to behave on the planet.
Forgotten was her moodiness, her depression. Now he
remembered her joyous self-indulgence, and it was for
this he waited.

The Grosvenor was crowded, as it must be on this
its opening afternoon. Everyone crowded in to see
who had been hung and where; out of the corner of
his eye Thornbrough noted that loathsome creature
Oscar Wilde holding forth to a delighted band of
women. Mr. Thornbrough, as he did often now, grim-
aced; if Isolde had fled all this, she was wiser than he
had first thought her.

He glanced down at Elizabeth, who was watching
the scene with amusement instead of looking at the
pictures. Few seemed of note to him.

"Awful, aren't they?" he said to her.

"Horrible."

They proceeded down the rows of pictures. "Does
Whistler have anything up?"

"No, he claims he is too good for the Grosvenor."

"Ah, and what does the Grosvenor say to this?" But
the gallery did not seem to be in need of the American painter's works. Its walls were covered with canvases adorned with ornate, gilded frames, street
scenes, landscapes, still lifes, even a few portraits. The
more fortunate painters were exhibited at eye level.
The less esteemed were hung too high or too low, so
that browsers strolled by them, ignoring them easily.

Elizabeth kept half her attention on the walls of

canvases, but half was turned outwards, toward all the other people, of whom she knew at least three quarters. So it was Mr. Thornbrough who first noticed a small painting, hung far above eye level. He was a tall man. It was not difficult for him to reach up and unhook the painting from the wall, an action quite forbidden and enough to bring Elizabeth's full attention around.

She stood on tiptoe and looked over his shoulder. "Oh, look!" she exclaimed. "Doesn't it look a bit like Toye?"

"It is Toye," he said, looking up at her, his eyes very serious. "Isolde painted it."

Elizabeth's eyes widened. "How can you know?"

"See the two figures in the corner?" Together they carefully examined the painting. It was of a gray castle against a gray sky with a splash of yellow daffodils in glowing free grass. Two figures, one standing and one lying, just two splashes of white, were on the edge of the woods.

They were very much in everyone's way. People stared as they tried to find a path around them, while Thornbrough held the picture out at arm's length, searching it for details, and Elizabeth stared at her friend's work. As Elizabeth noted its skill of execution, Mr. Thornbrough went further, drawn up by the spirit of the picture. The figures were his and Isolde's, as they had been on their first meeting at Toye. He felt himself drawn into the past, pulled into a world where Isolde was again the creator, and he was happy to let himself be pulled out of the drab London town, and out of the crowd of polite, staring people in Grosvenor Gallery.

"Please! Please, sir!" exclaimed a voice in his ear. He looked down, and a short plump man seemed to be pulling at his sleeve. "The paintings must be displayed for the entire period contracted upon. No paintings may be removed before that time. I must ask you, sir, to hand that picture to me."

"Certainly not. This is my painting," said Thornbrough.

"Please, sir!" begged the little man. "I will be glad to discuss this matter with you or your solicitor, but until we have done so and you have shown me the receipts, I can do nothing legally. On the wall, please!"

"I have no receipts. The painting was given to me."

"Perhaps we could discuss this in the gentleman's offices?" suggested Elizabeth.

"We have nothing to discuss. But I must know this. What is the name of this painter? The canvas is unsigned."

"Oh, really, sir. I would have to check my records. Someone quite undistinguished. I believe this is his first work we have accepted. But you say the painter gave you the picture. And yet you do not know the name? May I know *your* name?"

"Certainly," said Thornbrough. The picture was not large. He slipped it under his arm and prepared to depart. "My name is Martin Thornbrough. Here is my card. You may tell the artist that I admired her work so intensely I could not let any eyes but mine touch it. Tell her I fully appreciate it. And tell her that I would love to arrange a private showing both of her works and of her as well. Very private. Now don't forget, will you?"

"It's all right," said Elizabeth quietly in the ear of the confused proprietor. "I'm afraid no explanations can be made right now that would be quite coherent. But this is Mr. Martin Thornbrough. Perhaps you've heard of him? If your painter sues, Mr. Thornbrough is quite sufficiently wealthy to pay him anything he likes, in or out of court. Let me give you my card. Perhaps you have heard of me as well? I am Elizabeth

Taunton, so pleased to see you. I come every year. My subscription will be particularly enjoyable for me to send you this year, I find so many wonderful things displayed here. It is wonderful work you are doing here. What did you say the name of the painter was?"

"I would have to check my records, madame," said the proprietor, cool, but yielding, like pasty pie dough. "Certainly not a female, however, as Mr. Thornbrough seems to think. We do not make it a practice to display the works of females, although of course we can make exceptions in cases of great merit. But the cases are so rare that I cannot cite them."

"Did you ever see the painter?"

"I would have to check my records."

"Come, Elizabeth," said Mr. Thornbrough firmly. "I am leaving without you." He grasped her elbow, and she followed along with him out of the building.

"I might have learned something about Isolde from that terrible man," she complained to him.

"Nonsense," he said briskly. "What a fool! She arranged to have the letter she sent to her parents mailed from Singapore. Mine was posted at a port in South Africa. Do you think she would be so foolish as to bring her picture around herself? When his stated policy is that he would accept nothing from women? Nonsense. She probably hired someone to go and pretend to be an artist for her, and made up some preposterous name and address, hoping that I would find it out."

"I didn't know she sent you a letter!"

"Why should you!" he said, handing her up into his carriage. "I never told you. I spent three months tracing that letter. I know better now."

"But what will you do!"

"I? I will do what Isolde always wants me to do. I will do nothing. I have claimed my talisman. If she had hoped to leave it there for the rest of London to admire, she should not have promised it to me. It is mine now."

There was no joy in his tones, only something somewhat like triumph and something like savagery. Elizabeth glanced at him curiously. "And what will you do with your painting now?"

"Do with it?" He could take a knife, or better, a razor, freshly sharpened. He could shred the canvas, utterly destroy the image painted on it and throw it out onto his doorstep, leaving orders that it was to be kept there until Isolde could see it, mangled and trodden upon.

He might do that, of course. But he wouldn't. "I shall hang it on a wall, my dear," he said. "What else does one do with a painting?"

But he was tired of waiting. He couldn't wait much longer.

Chapter 30

Thornbrough had begun to dislike certain aspects of his life. Riding and driving gave him as much or more pleasure as they always had done, but on some mornings during the last year, and with increasing frequency, he experienced an intense unwillingness to get out of bed. Such an unwillingness could not be indulged, of course. He always rose at a certain hour and consumed his breakfast served to him in the same manner, eating alone, morning after morning.

But the part of his routine he had never enjoyed and now detested was going over the accounts with his secretary after breakfast. These meetings had been growing more dull for years, but of late had become ponderously, poisonously so. Some decisions he had to make, because he was a very conscientious landlord, and his holdings were extensive.

But today as he sat in his secretary's office in a large, comfortable armchair, he found it even harder to keep his mind on the drone of daily business affairs. His secretary, Mr. Melkinthorpe, was a very gentle, mild sort of fellow, quite aware of his employer's boredom. He went through the accounts as politely as he could every day, but today he dispensed with the ordinary business. It was really nothing out of the routine, nothing he could not deal with. Today there was an item of such importance that he was cer-

tain Mr. Thornbrough could not but be propelled
into fascination and horror by it.

"Sir," he announced, "you have received a bomb
threat!"

"How kind," mumbled Thornbrough. "But send it
back; it is really too much. Was there a card?"

"No, no, really sir," said Mr. Melkinthorpe importantly. "You must listen. A bomb threat. An incendi-
ary notice."

"Well, tell the police."

"I believe this is something that requires your attention. You know your property in East Kensington?"

"Certainly not. I've never been in East Kensington
in my life."

"But you know you own them. Please, sir!" said his
secretary, clearly upset.

"Very well, very well," Thornbrough said. "What
of these properties?"

"You have received a most libelous letter about
their upkeep, followed by the grossest sorts of threats.
It states—here, let me find it—it states: 'Sir, we cannot
live in this state any longer. If something is not done
to relieve the condition of these buildings, we must
blow the place up.' And it is signed, 'The tenant in
the top back bedroom.'"

"Oh, is it?" said Thornbrough, snatching the note.
"This is very interesting indeed. I thought only old
ladies and parrots lived in East Kensington. Rather
odd, isn't it?"

"Well, yes, sir, I hadn't thought of it. I suppose one
of these nihilists or some revolutionaries have taken
apartments there, however."

"Have you ever seen this handwriting before?"

"No, sir, I haven't."

"My dear fellow, have you any way of discovering
for me who is the tenant in the top back bedroom?"

"It would be in the books, sir. At least, the name of the person who is responsible for payment of the rent."

"Could you check, dear fellow?"

"Certainly, sir. It will take a moment, however." He stood up and crossed the room, finding and opening a large ledger, turning pages, and going down the lines with a forefinger until he found the building and room he was looking for. "It would be a Mr. I. Pendleton, sir."

"I'll kill her!" shouted Thornbrough. "Tell them to bring my horses around. Never mind! I'll take a hack."

"A hack, sir?" said his secretary, bewildered.

"Good-bye. God bless you. Tell them I haven't been murdered if I don't come back anytime this year." And he was gone.

"I. Pendleton," said the secretary to himself, repeating the name. "I. Pendleton." A light dawned, and he stared after his vanished employer with understanding.

It was a short ride to East Kensington. Thornbrough put enough money in the driver's hand for him to quit for the day and go home and speak well of men in love. It was a quick race up the stairs to the top floor. He hesitated for a moment outside the door, listening. He could hear nothing. His face solemn again, he knocked.

Isolde opened the door for him. They stood for a moment, staring at each other, looking each other up and down. Then they fell into each other's arms, as they had been for the year past in phantom form only, but solid again, finally taking on substance each for the other. They fell against each other, pushed by their hunger, kissing each other's face.

"How I missed you!" she said in his ear as he held her.

"You'll never know."

"Well, we don't need to argue about who missed who the most," she said, laughing, pulling him into the room. Her apartments were just one big room with a few shelves and a small table at one end for a kitchen, a bed in the middle, and the rest a mass of paint pots, canvas stretchers, and canvas. The walls were covered with globules of paint, a confused muddle of colors.

"I've sworn to murder you, Isolde. How could you just run away like that? Do you know how I've worried?"

"But Martin, dearest, if we are to ever spend time together in the future, it must be with the understanding that you are not to worry about me, ever, under any circumstances. See how well I've done! I've made a living as an artist, and that's not an easy thing to do, either. I was lucky, of course; I sent my things to Australia, and they were bought up so readily that I never even had to suffer, not even a little. And now I have one in the Grosvenor."

"Not anymore you don't."

"No, dearest. But you understand, don't you? You're not going to be still pig-headed and selfish after a whole year, are you?"

"Isolde, Isolde," he said, holding her head with both hands, turning it up so he could look into her eyes. "God, how much I missed you, Isolde! But I would sooner strangle you and throw your beautiful body in the Thames than let you dictate to me how I shall order my affairs."

She chuckled. "Darling one, you have not changed a bit, not a bit. And this is fine. I didn't want you to change. But, you see, I am quite different now. This is my affair too, you know."

She stood apart from him, smiling, her hands on her hips. He smiled back. "You look perhaps a little more lovely, a little more rosy. I think you are glowing now. But you still answer to Isolde, do you not?"

"Oh, yes. But you see, I only answer to Isolde now."

"My dearest, I have never known you to obey the slightest wish anyone asked of you."

"You are so stubborn," she said impatiently. "Come see my paintings. Some of the old ones are very bad, of course, but all of them are great."

He didn't look at the canvases, but he watched her head, with its neat pile of hair, a few curls escaping, as she moved up and down her rows of painter's muddle. He would look later. For now he watched Isolde, relishing her, remembering. He remembered her as being beautiful, but with a pallor and a sadness clinging to her. Now the pale white of her cheeks was unashamedly as pink as her lamp shades, and the sadness was gone. She talked, she laughed, she made faces at him. He smiled and watched the new Isolde before him.

She turned over one canvas, and the pink in her cheeks deepened to red as she turned it away again quickly before he could more than glance at it.

"What was that?" he demanded.

"Well, what do you think of them?"

"What was that?"

"Oh, I did that months ago. My style has changed a great deal since." But he had taken it out of her hand, and she stood by, unsure.

It was a painting of him, quite nude. He was lying in the grass with trees behind him, playing with a blade of grass.

"You'd be surprised at how few paintings of nude men there are in museums," she said nervously.

"When did you do this?"

"Oh, months ago. You see, I missed you so much. And I could never see you. Do you know at balls and things there are always enormous crowds of people waiting outside for just a glimpse of the people going in and out, and they crowd and jostle you and you can't even get one good stare."

"My poor love! Did you stand outside doors watching for me?" And he took her in his arms again. But this time the fury of finding her was gone. Now he held her body, stroking her, as her fingers began to run under his clothing along his flesh. He bent over again to kiss her, their lips meeting slowly, her mouth opening under his. They made love, with desperation, but with a fervor that went on and on, easily, slowly, as they relaxed into each other's bodies.

And when it was over, it was she who held his head in her hands, staring down at his black hair on her white pillows, at his body's strong lines on her narrow bed. "I love you," she said with incredulity. "How much I love you!"

He kissed her hand. "And I love you. So this is what it comes to, that we love each other."

She nodded, closing her eyes, her head on his shoulder.

"And what happens next, Isolde? Do you marry me?"

She opened her eyes again and leaned over him, supporting herself with her elbow while she began to play with the dark hairs on his chest.

"We *could* live together like this forever."

"Oh, I hope we won't," he said, seizing her and squeezing her. "We would need a much bigger bed."

She smiled. "Or we could marry."

"Say the word. Just say the word."

"Well, Martin dearest, there really is a lot we have to discuss before we think of marriage."

Uncertain whether or not she was joking, he glanced at her and was surprised at the seriousness of her expression.

"Martin, this may not mean much to you, but I feel as if you should know it."

He raised a hand to stop her words. "I don't want to know any of the details of your five New York lovers. It's none of my affair."

"I know it's none of your affair!" she shouted in surprise. "And how do you know about them? There were only four!"

"I hired detectives. I've been desperate for you this last year, and I left no stone unturned and no lover unshaken. What is your deep, dark secret?"

"I'm a bastard."

"In your case, however, we would say more properly that you are a bitch."

"No!" she shouted, jumping on top of him and hitting him. "I really am! I'm illegitimate."

"Nonsense. I met both your parents, remember?"

"But they were unmarried when I was born."

"Well, dearest, I'm sorry to have to break this news to you, and I'm certainly no barrister, so it is possible my facts are wrong, but when a man and woman marry legally, all their previous offspring are legitimized."

"No!"

"So if you've been going about all this time with a wonderful notion in your mind that you had some birthright to behave beyond the laws of society—and you certainly act that way—I'm afraid you're all wrong. There's nothing at all the matter with you."

"What do you think of my painting?" she went on, after stopping a moment to digest this news.

"Whatever you like. You can keep this place as a studio or have whatever room you want in whatever house you like for a studio."

"But, dearest Martin, darling, what do you think of my *painting*?"

"I love it. I think it's wonderful. But I don't think it has much to do with our marriage."

"Ah, you don't understand yet, do you?"

He glanced at her with distrust.

"You still have no notion what marriage to someone like me would be like, do you? I can't marry you. I'll be your mistress, I'll have your children, but I won't marry someone who never smiles."

"Isolde!"

"I mean it. Martin! Dearest! Do you expect me to marry a man who never smiles? Who is never happy?"

"I smile!"

"You *only* smile *immediately* after we have made love. I have never seen you smile while you were going about town on ordinary affairs, and I followed you for weeks."

"But I was miserable! I missed you!"

"No," she said, shaking her head firmly. "It's not enough. Haven't you ever wanted to go mountain climbing, or see how they cut diamonds, or even do something perfectly humdrum, like look at the Taj Mahal in the moonlight?"

"I haven't thought about it," he said, taken aback.

"I have."

"Let me understand this. Do you want to climb a mountain, or do you think I should climb a mountain—for my own good, of course?"

"We'll go on a honeymoon," she begged. "A year-long honeymoon. We could learn to ride camels or elephants."

"You can't ride a horse."

"Well, I wouldn't mind starting there."

His expression grew complex as he watched her. Finally he said, as if bringing forth a great maxim, "The gypsies."

"The gypsies?"

"A gypsy once healed a horse of mine. Really, it happened. And I've always wondered, can they really have secrets?"

"Martin!" exclaimed Isolde, delighted. "Why don't we just pop around the corner, get married, you can pick up some things at your house, and we'll be off!"

"No need. I told them not to worry if I didn't return."

Danielle Steel

**AMERICA'S
LEADING
LADY OF
ROMANCE
REIGNS
OVER ANOTHER BESTSELLER**

A Perfect Stranger

A flawless mix of glamour and love by
Danielle Steel, the bestselling author of
The Ring, Palomino and *Loving*.

A DELL BOOK $3.50   #17221-7